Born to Triumph

Born to Triumph

By C. Paul Willis

© Copyright 1992 — C. Paul Willis

All rights reserved. This book is protected under the copyright laws of the United States of America. This book may not be copied or reprinted for commercial gain or profit. The use of short quotations or occasional page copying for personal or group study is permitted and encouraged. Permission will be granted upon request. Unless otherwise identified, Scripture quotations are from The King James Version of the Bible.

Take note that the name satan and related names are not capitalized. We choose not to acknowledge him, even to the point of violating grammatical rules.

The Storyteller's Collection

Destiny Image Publishers
P.O. Box 310
Shippensburg, PA 17257-0310

ISBN 1-56043-651-4

For Worldwide Distribution
Printed in the U.S.A.

Dedication

In the morning light of childhood, I knew her. She was the Tinkerbell that could fly. She could climb a tree higher, race a bike faster, catch a fish bigger, than any boy I knew — so I wanted to be her Peter Pan.

In the full light of day, I knew her. As beautiful as Snow White, as elusive as Cinderella, as sultry as a harem girl from the Arabian nights — I wanted to be her prince charming.

In the setting sun of our life, I know her. She still has her girlish charm and her alluring beauty. But now she has the maturity of a fully blossomed rose and a completed symphony. And when I lay my head down to sleep and dream, only one name will I whisper — hers!

My wife — Mary

Acknowledgements

To Keith Carroll, publisher — You gave the right counsel at the right time or this book would not have been published.

To Kathy Miller, editor — You made the rough places smooth and the story flow.

To Hy Lancaster and Lynn Campbell — You ladies can cross my T's and dot my I's any time.

To Stan Robinson — Your art work for the cover portrays the Apostle and the story beautifully.

1

A white stallion impatiently pawed the cobblestone roadway while his handler tried to calm the excited beast. The horse sensed the anticipation of the crowd waiting at the new Forum of Augustus at the foot of the Quirinal Hill. This was the junction of the avenues of Rome called the Triumphal and Flaminian Ways. The high-spirited animal recognized that he was the center of attention. Red and gold banners waved in the breeze. The Cilician Guard, dressed in their finest red tunics, with their breastplates shined to perfection, stood in dress review. The horse and the legionnaires waited for the rider who would be carried beneath the Arch of Augustus in a Parade of Triumph.

Inside the Basilica, the senators of Rome, dressed in white robes and wearing golden garlands, watched with approval from their seats in the raised galleries on each side of the Basilica as Caesar Tiberius placed a wreath of victory on the head of General Markus Paul Gabinius. Several of the senators leaned forward in their chairs to get a better view.

The General was lean in body and as agile as a gladiator. His features were like those of a bronzed statue. To receive the garland from his emperor, Gabinius removed his helmet and placed it under his arm. His head was already crowned with a shock of white hair. He was much older than the man honoring him.

It was not age alone that separated the men. Tiberius Caesar's face was marked and scarred from acne. His skin was yellow from jaundice. He wore his hair with bangs that fell over his forehead to make him appear younger. Of the two men, Gabinius had the more stately bearing of a Caesar, while Tiberius appeared emasculate, intimidated in the presence of the man of lesser rank and stronger demeanor.

"It is my pleasure to present you to Rome, General Gabinius," Tiberius stated, his voice fluttering slightly. "I see you wear the ring of Augustus, and so you should! It is for your service to my predecessor that you are being honored, and I do not require you to wear my signet! I only require that you serve Rome and me as faithfully as you served him!"

"Caesar is Lord," Markus Gabinius muttered. The words seemed to disgorge in his mouth, as if saying them was extremely distasteful.

Tiberius was astonished at the apparent contempt he heard in the General's required declaration. "The Tribune is not excited about receiving his Triumph?" Tiberius queried.

"It is a long trip between Tarsus and Rome," Gabinius retorted.

General Gabinius had declared the divinity of Caesar, and Tiberius could not reprimand and honor the man at the same time. Moreover, the Caesar was somewhat unnerved by even this much clash with a man of the General's bearing. Tiberius completed the ceremony by placing the victor's wreath on the head of the General. Caesar brought his arm across his chest in a salute. The General knew the gesture meant he was being dismissed. He returned Tiberius' salute, wheeled in a military fashion and stepped toward the door. His sword made a sharp slap against his side as he turned. Caesar drew back a little. The Senate rose to its feet to pay homage to the man whom Augustus Caesar had ordered honored. The massive doors between the Basilica Julia and the piazza opened. The still-shaking voice of Caesar Tiberius carried through the Basilica. He proclaimed the required words: "Behold the man!"

The sound of trumpets accompanied the shout of the crowd waiting outside the Basilica for the Triumph to begin. The stallion reared and pulled against his handler. Legionnaires snapped to attention. Red and gold banners unfurled in a passing breeze, almost as if they had received a command.

Gabinius had waited thirty years to receive this promised honor. Augustus had been Caesar when Gabinius had crushed the revolt in Palestine. Augustus had honored the General by placing his ring on the General's finger and by asking the Senate to give Gabinius a hero's Triumph through the streets of Rome. Augustus had also given General Gabinius estates in Tarsus and command over the Roman Cilician Guard quartered in that city. Rome's delay in presenting the General with his rightful Triumph was related to Augustus' gift of the estates.

While waiting for Senate approval, the new Proconsul had sailed to Tarsus to begin construction on his new home. The properties given to him by Augustus were located outside the city itself on the fertile Cilician Plain bordering the Cydnus River. Therefore, Markus Gabinius had to establish temporary residence in the city of Tarsus itself.

The liberalized population of Tarsus was made up of a mixture of Anatolian, Greek, Roman and Jewish peoples. The citizens were so integrated that one could not tell from their names which culture they came from. Philosophers from Anatolian, Roman and even Jewish families had recently been Hellenized and given Greek names. Athenodorus, the Stoic teacher of the great Augustus himself, was a Hellenized citizen of Tarsus.

Markus Gabinius did not know that the young daughter of the innkeeper, with her flashing dark eyes and raven hair, was Jewish. Not that it mattered, for with his first look, Markus Paul Gabinius — officer of Rome, Proconsul of Cilicia, friend of Augustus Caesar — was in love.

Other men with Markus Gabinius' power might just have taken Saraphina as a concubine, with or without her consent. A Jewess was, after all, from a subject race. Who in Tarsus could have opposed him? Did not the Jews themselves tell the story of their King David who, using the power of his office, took a woman called

Bathsheba? But Markus Gabinius was not like other men. It was not that he was religious — he secretly laughed at the Roman pantheon of gods. To Gabinius, worshiping marble statues toward which men projected human passion was ludicrous. Besides, the Roman gods themselves lacked virtue. The unseen God of Saraphina offered him no hope. The God of Israel had deserted even His chosen people. Markus Gabinius could not worship a God who had allowed Rome to subjugate His people. True, he bowed to the gods of Rome at the proper time in the ceremonies and called Caesar "Lord," but that was a public gesture without meaning.

He did not want Saraphina as a concubine or as one forced to submit to a Roman officer. He wanted her to love him of her own free will. He wanted her to come to him without guilt or shame. He wanted to share more than her body. He wanted her respect, her thoughts and her love. And so, Markus Gabinius went to her parents in proper fashion and received permission to visit with their daughter. The Roman legionnaire courted the Jewish girl with all the fervor of his love and all the courtesy of her traditions. In both the law of Israel and the law of Rome he made her his bride.

In the liberal society of Tarsus, the marriage not only was accepted but was looked upon with approval. The marriage of the Roman Proconsul to a Jewish citizen was politically appropriate in Tarsus, but politically frowned upon in Rome. Rome could tolerate calling all kinds of people Roman citizens, but its racial and social prejudices ran deep. The elite of Rome could not suffer a Roman hero to marry one who was little more than a Roman slave. The scandal of Mark Anthony and Cleopatra had shamed Rome badly enough! A Roman and an Egyptian could flaunt their relationship — if the woman was a queen! Augustus defeating Anthony in the Battle of Actium had ended that scandal! But Markus Paul Gabinius was no Anthony, and the women of Rome knew that his Jewess was no Cleopatra. Each time the edict of Augustus to give

Markus the honor of a Roman Triumph came before the Senate, the wives of Rome prevailed to have it delayed. Now, thirty years after the fact, most of the Senators who knew why the Triumph had not been implemented were dead.

Now Tiberius needed a strong relationship with Cilicia. He feared another uprising in Palestine. His alliances could be greatly strengthened by giving Markus Gabinius his long-deserved honor. Furthermore, he had a plan that would increase his and Rome's wealth. The General, though he did not know it, was a central piece in the game Tiberius wanted to play. If a little parade through the city could be used to influence Gabinius and make him a more willing player, why not give it to him?

As Tiberius watched General Gabinius leave the Basilica, he wondered why the Gabinius family had not been present to see the General honored. Gabinius had a son by the name of Paul. By virtue of the Triumph given to his father, the son would receive an empirical commission in the Roman Legion. To Tiberius, it appeared that the son did not respect his father enough to watch him receive the highest honor bestowed on a mere man.

As Markus stepped onto the piazza, his eyes searched the crowd for a single face. She was veiled, except for her eyes, and with their eyes they talked.

Forgive me, his eyes said.

You have done nothing to be forgiven for, her eyes replied.

I am proud of you, and I love you — her thoughts pressed into his mind as he passed her.

Saraphina had chosen not to enter the Forum. She had wanted to see Markus receive the honor that was due him, but she knew that she could not give deference to the statues of the gods within the Forum. She would rather die than pay homage to Caesar as god! A scene in the Basilica would have disgraced Markus and unnecessarily risked their lives.

Paul had also chosen to miss the ceremony. He could have stood with his father and received honor. Instead, he had asked permission from Markus to remain outside as protection for Saraphina. The General was disappointed that his son would not see him acclaimed by Caesar, but he knew Paul was right. He had compelled Paul to wear his new armor, however, telling his son that he would be even more persuasive as a protector by being armed. Markus Gabinius looked with approval at the tall legionnaire, attired in a guard's bright red and gold uniform, towering above the small, veiled, Jewish lady.

Saraphina turned to Paul after Markus had passed. "Take me back to the apartment," she said with a sigh.

"Do you not wish to see the excitement of the Triumph, Mother?" he replied.

"There has been enough excitement for one day," came the answer.

Paul leaned down to take her arm.

"Walk in front of me and do not be a fool," she rebuked him in Hebrew. Paul was startled that she used the language in public. He knew of no other woman who could speak the ancient tongue. It was a special tool of communication they used when they did not want anyone else to understand what they said, or when they studied the ancient writings together.

"You are a Roman officer and I a Jewess! If you strut like a Roman peacock and I meekly follow, we will draw no attention to ourselves. What is another fool peacock in a flock of them?"

Paul smiled at his mother's words as, with relief, he turned to go. Then a new emotion hit him. His body burned with the sensation of humiliation. The pace of his step increased as his face flushed. For the first time in his life, Paul of Tarsus felt shame, and he did not like it — not at all!

2

The young aristocrats of Rome were caught up in the intrigue and gossip that has been precipitated by Paul's brief appearance on the piazza at the Augustus Forum. No one had to speculate about Paul. His frame, movements and gestures, as well as some of his facial features, were those of General Markus Gabinius. The ease with which he wore light armor and carried the short broadsword slung at his waist was that of a professional soldier. Only his raven-black hair and beard separated him from being all Gabinius.

Those standing on the piazza with young Gabinius and his body slave saw the look that passed between father and son. Why had young Gabinius stayed outside the Forum and not stood with his father to receive the honors? Why had he taken an old Jewish slave woman for a body slave when most young Roman men used Greek boys? A body slave was a sign of wealth and taste. One could judge the wealth and culture of Roman nobility both by the perfection found in their horses and chariots, and in the grace, cleanliness and education of their body slaves. A few kept beautiful concubines to perform their personal service, but only the very powerful displayed them in public. Young Gabinius was certainly rich, but he was not politically powerful. Some said the Jewish slave had been his mother's personal servant, that he kept her in memory of his mother. Others spoke of a long-forgotten scandal. They said that Gabinius' mother was a radiant beauty who had rejected the advances of Caesar. Because Augustus had an eye for the woman, he had removed General Gabinius from Rome by giving him command of the garrison of Tarsus. The woman's rejection of Caesar was also said to be the reason the General was not honored with his Triumph until after the death of Augustus.

Why had Gabinius' son not followed him in the Triumph? Was he being sent on some hidden task? He was, no doubt, a highly educated young man. He had been seen reading the inscriptions on the base of the gods, which were written in Latin, and he had been heard speaking to the merchants in Greek. Some reported that they had also heard him give his body slave instructions in a strange, uncivilized tongue. It would not be peculiar for the son of the Proconsul of Cilicia to have a very broad education. Was not Tarsus the center of many fine schools of philosophy? Perhaps that is what the Proconsul's son did in Tarsus — study to find some new thing.

The more the aristocracy speculated about Paul, the more determined they became to get a seat in the Circus Maximus from which they could see the platform seats Caesar Tiberius had arranged for the General and his guests at the evening's games. This would be no easy task since the Circus Maximus could seat a crowd of two hundred thousand people. Should Paul attend the race with his father, the young nobility intended to scrutinize him even more closely than they watched the charioteers.

Most of the ladies of Rome were discreet. They attempted not to show their interest when General Gabinius and his son entered Caesar's porch. Others leaned forward in their seats and examined Paul as if he were a slave ready for the auction block or a piece of fruit they were about to eat. Paul was embarrassed by the display. In Tarsus married women veiled themselves; maidens wore modest clothing and lowered their eyes in the presence of a stranger. In Rome, it seemed, the ladies stared directly at strangers and wore very revealing dresses. This evening everything they displayed was directed toward Paul.

Caesar Tiberius could not help but smile at the young man's discomfort. He had been informed of the talk among the young nobility. He knew that Paul had been seen on the piazza after his father had been given his recognition in the Basilica by Caesar.

Paul watched his father's every move. General Gabinius formed his hand into a fist and brought his right arm across his chest in a salute. Paul quickly did the same.

"This must be your handsome son whom all Rome is talking about, General." Tiberius' eyes never left Paul's face as he spoke.

"My Caesar, I present to you my son, Paul Gabinius, soon to serve in the Emperor's Legions," the General replied.

Tiberius did not look at Marcus but studied Paul intently.

"Caesar!" Paul exclaimed and saluted as his father had done.

Tiberius seemed to avoid looking at the General and examined Paul as if he was challenging the father through the comparative safety of the son. "I did not see you when I honored your father in the Triumph," Tiberius stated, while objectively studying Paul's face.

"I had my father's permission to attend to my mother," Paul replied.

"The lady is ill, no doubt." It was not a question! Tiberius sneered as he said the words.

It was well known in Rome that Tiberius had married Vispania, the woman he loved. Under pressure from Augustus and his mother, however, he had surrendered her to divorce. He then married his second wife, Julia. It was a marriage arranged by his mother for political purposes. Julia loved the wealth and the position the marriage gave her, but she loathed Tiberius. As wife of Caesar, she often professed illness while he was dealing with matters of state so that she could have time with her many lovers. Tiberius believed all women were deceitful and immoral. He considered his mother and his wife to be the most nefarious of all women.

Since no question had been asked, Paul decided not to reply. Tiberius acted as if General Gabinius were not present and the General's training did not allow him to speak to the Emperor unless first addressed.

Paul noticed twelve carceres located in the west end of the Circus Maximus. The chariots would line up there to start the race. From his position on the raised platform, Paul could clearly see each carceres and the handlers preparing the horses.

"My favorite for this race is Julius Laco," stated Tiberius, directing his remarks to Paul. "He is the son of the Praetorian Prefect."

The elder Gabinius explained quietly to Paul that Laco was the Commander of the Praetorian Guard and second in command to Caesar.

"Julius will be in carceres number three," continued Tiberius. His expression indicated his satisfaction with the explanation General Gabinius had given Paul.

"Gabinius" — Tiberius' remarks were directed toward the General — "you of course remember Laco who served under your command until you decided to settle in Tarsus." Tiberius' sarcasm was evident. Fortunately, Tiberius was interrupted with the cry — "Hail Caesar! Hail Caesar! Hail Caesar!"

With the first shout, Paul's father leapt to his feet and saluted. Paul and the two hundred thousand spectators followed suit.

With the salute to Caesar, the procession began. The Senators and the civic authorities of Rome appeared, walking on the sand of the arena. They each wore garlands and robes. The bureaucracy was followed by statues of the gods, which were pulled on highly decorated four-wheeled carriages. Six chariots pulled by teams of four horses, each accompanied by a horseman, entered the arena. Each charioteer was dressed in a short, sleeveless tunic. Each tunic was colored in the household colors of a wealthy Roman host.

"Laco wears the scarlet and gold of my Praetorian Guard to show that I sponsor him in the race," Tiberius said as he fingered the scarlet and gold ribbons that hung from his left wrist. Paul noticed that all of Rome seemed to be wearing a ribbon of some color to indicate their favorite in the race. Scarlet and gold predominated!

Attendants appeared in the arena and placed seven balls on the goal at the west end of the division wall. Then the attendants moved to the goal at the east end of the division and placed seven carved dolphins there.

"What are the balls and the fish for?" Paul inquired.

"To keep the count," Tiberius answered. "At the end of each rounding of a goal you will see a ball and a fish removed. When the last set falls, the race is over."

The parade completed, the horses and charioteers moved to the carceres to await the beginning of the race. A chalked starting line was stretched across the arena. The line's purpose was to equalize the start of the race. When the editor of the race was satisfied with the start, he gave the signal to drop the rope. If the line was hit by a horse before it was dropped to indicate a fair start, both horse and driver could be seriously injured. If the driver was hesitant when he approached the line, he lost the advantage of the position next to the division wall on the inner line of the course. The drivers had to be prepared to stop their teams quickly should the rope not drop. The crossing between the carceres and the starting rope was two hundred and fifty feet, which did not allow for a mistake!

The team of Julius Laco was in the third position from the wall. As the trumpet sounded, Paul watched the beginning of the race intently. He did not concentrate on drivers or horses, but on the ring through which the reins passed. All reins were pulled tight except those in the hands of Laco. Laco recklessly pushed his four forward while the others checked their teams in front of the obstruction. Either Julius Laco was mad or he knew that the rope would fall!

Laco's chariot shot ahead of the other contestants, coming so close to the rope that the horses actually stepped on it as it fell. The four turned into the inner lane and stayed so far ahead of the others that the race seemed to be a very fast parade rather than a contest.

"Ah," sighed Caesar as Laco passed through the gate of triumph. "I have won my wager. I knew Julius would win! Come Gabinius! I want Paul to meet the hero, Julius Laco!"

Laco was not quite as tall as Paul. He had a fair complexion and was beardless. Long, blond tassels fell from a leather band that was tied around his head. His clear, blue eyes danced with mischief and merriment. Julius and Paul were nearly the same age — Paul could not decide who was the older. The charioteer had a broad, muscular chest and knotted arms, but he was thin in the waist and thighs. He moved with grace and the precision of a trained athlete.

"Caesar!" he saluted Tiberius. "I have won your wager for you again!"

"Yes!" answered Tiberius with a large smile. "Neither you nor your father has ever failed Caesar or Rome." Tiberius looked at General Gabinius when he made the remark.

"I want you to meet a hero, General Markus Paul Gabinius, whom you honored in Triumph, and his son Paul! Please keep Paul occupied and show him Rome. I have need of his father's presence with me!"

Julius Laco politely recognized the elder Gabinius; then he threw his arms around Paul in a friendly, sincere embrace. "This is the gallant that has all the ladies of Rome in a fever. Caesar, you do not know how you bless me. With victory in the games this evening and with Paul Gabinius as my companion tonight, we shall break all the hearts in Rome. Come, Paul, let us go and fulfill our destiny!"

Paul did not leave the Circus as much as he was dragged from the Circus. Julius' arm around his shoulders guided him through the corridor and out into the court. It was not that Paul was reluctant to go, for he had an instant liking for this unembellished Roman who was the hero of the Circus. Though he could have courted its politicians and made the most of his victory, Julius seemed not to notice the admiration of the crowd nor the opportunity his victory gave him. His recognition by Caesar gave him the choice of any companion in Rome, but he acted as if Paul were the hero and he the one who was privileged to be in Paul's company.

It was dark by the time they reached the exit of the Circus Maximus. Julius directed Paul to a double chair litter. Paul had traveled by boat, cart and horse, but he had never been carried upon the backs of slaves. Julius explained that to alleviate congestion in Rome's cobblestone streets, an ordinance prohibited the movement of carts and wagons from sunrise to sunset. When anyone had anything to haul in Rome, they moved it at night. Because of the movement of market carts and delivery wagons, shopkeepers remained open at night to serve the workers with food and beverages. The only way to get around in the commercial throng was by litter.

Paul soon discovered what Julius was talking about. Large wagons loaded with stone and wares ground the cobblestones with heavy iron wheels. Peddlers, trying to sell their goods, shouted at those who passed by. Camel trains wound through the cramped streets. Paul had to shout to be heard by Julius.

"Is it always like this?" Paul yelled over the noise of the street.

"No, it is worse!" Julius shouted back. "On bright nights when there is much moonlight, those who cannot sleep join the commercial crowd, making it impossible for one to get through Rome."

As they were carried through and around the throngs of people, Paul was glad for the darkness of night. The obscurity provided by the darkness helped him to avoid the dangers of the bright nights and the prostitutes who kept close to the walls that were illuminated by the light of torches. Paul wanted to see Rome and to enjoy the company of Julius and his companions, but he still had his Jewish side. Coming into contact with the harlots, beggars and riffraff of the city would have embarrassed Paul even more than being carried through the streets on the litter.

Above the walls of the street on the Palatine Hill, Paul could see the lights from the palaces of Augustus and Tiberius. He could distinguish the white marble columns, each with its own torch, of the Temple of Apollo, but the temple itself and its porticoes were hidden by the darkness. The stairway from the Forum to the Palace of Tiberius was well lit. Paul could distinguish a company of men ascending from the Circus. Paul knew his father was among the group on their way to an audience with Caesar. The buildings of Rome seemed massive and foreboding in the light of the torches, even as the streets of Rome were dreadful without them.

"Paul, tonight I am really going to introduce you to Rome," Julius shouted above the racket and the clatter. "But I feel I must warn you of her allure. Rome is a whore!"

Julius' words and the loudness of his declaration mortified Paul. For some reason he feared lest the prostitutes along the wall could hear the remark.

"Like those prostitutes, she demands a price — and it is paid in advance." Julius' voice was clear and strong; Paul was sure the harlots heard him. "My father and I pay her demands. We salute the clown she calls Caesar," Julius shouted.

Paul looked nervously into the dark. Calling Tiberius a buffoon, even on a dark street, could be very dangerous. Before Paul could answer, Julius continued: "I pretend to race the chariots, but we make sure Caesar wins. We pay the price of our pride and our manhood. We celebrate in her blood and passion. Yes, we pay her price!"

Julius paused and his voice got softer. Paul had to listen closely to catch the rest of Julius' remarks. "Rome gives us pomp, pleasure and power. She is quite a woman of passion, this city called Rome. She will give you a good time for the price, but be careful. You never know if the price you have paid will be enough. When you make love to Rome, Paul, never remove your sword. Rome might stab you in the back! Ask Anthony! Ask Augustus! Or ask Livia, Augustus' wife! Rome is a lover, a concubine and a whore. Never trust her! The cold steel of your sword slapping on your buttocks may be uncomfortable, but never take it off to make love to Rome!"

The litter had turned away from the commercial noise and Paul could now hear everything Julius said. Paul did not reply and Julius did not seem to expect one. Neither of them talked again until they approached a large hall filled with the light from many torches. Indeed, Paul thought it ludicrous that Julius shouted when he could not be clearly heard and had nothing to say when the din lessened. Only when they stepped out of the litter did Julius speak again.

"The baths! Paul, now I will introduce you to Rome and all her children. You will observe how much the children are like their mother!"

3

Paul discovered that the baths of Rome were more than a bathing place. The litter carriers circumvented a lake and a garden area before they came to an immense entrance that was central to the eighty-eight rooms of the baths. Julius directed Paul into a vaulted corridor. Paul's military eye estimated the room to be just under three hundred feet long. The sky-blue room was well lit with candelabra. From the vaulted ceiling and the walls protruded images of sea beasts, sphinxes, griffins, centaurs, cupids, gorgons' heads, lions' heads, dolphins, winged horses, and eagles. Shrubs grew from the backs of the statues and garlands of flowers that filled the room with perfume hung around their necks. In recesses within the walls were painted landscapes and seascapes that gave an illusion of being out-of-doors. In front of the paintings were couches and tables covered with all kinds of delicacies.

Gold and silver wine goblets were being filled by swarthy slaves; their exposed bodies glistened in the flickering light. In one end of the room musicians played on flutes, dulcimers, harps, psaltery and viol to the beat of drums and cymbals as women, clothed only in thin veils, and comely boys, rubbed in olive oil and spices, wearing only skirts made from grape leaves, accompanied the musicians with timbrels and dance. In another area of the hall poets recited their latest works to the accompaniment of the lyre, dramatizing their poetry with emotion and gestures. In the recesses, among the paintings of nature, could be seen the shadows and forms of youth caught in all manner of sexual passion. And throughout the baths, on couches, rugs and pillows placed on the marble floor, lay the upper class of Rome in drunken debauchery.

In the liberalized city of Tarsus, Paul had never seen the unrestrained behavior that he was seeing in the baths of Rome. The religion of the Jews affected Palestine and all Roman Asia Minor with a code of morality. Rome had escaped that influence. She had accepted the immorality of the Greek and Roman gods and goddesses, such as the god Dionysus, who was worshiped through prostitution, feasting, merrymaking and orgies.

Rome was not worshiping Dionysus this night, but her aristocracy shared in the veneration of another god in the only way they knew how. The god to whom they were giving acclaim — the god they honored in the same manner they would have worshiped Dionysus — entered the chamber with Paul. Paul had not aligned himself with the statues of the gods, but when he entered the baths he came as the consort of the god of the race — Julius!

"Our Lord," came a drunken attempt at a mock eulogy. The speaker struggled to his feet and poured a drink offering from a large pitcher into his mouth till the wine ran down his beard. Paul also heard a soft, passionate voice exclaim, "Oooh, my Lord!"

He saw a slender girl, her body covered only with a sheer veil, sink to her knees and place her hands above her head. Falling backward she exposed herself before Julius and Paul in a simulated offering to her god. Paul's face flushed both in embarrassment and with unexpected emotion.

Julius, seeing Paul's humiliation, took hold of Paul's hand and lifted his arm in a simulated salute. "Children of Rome, I present Paul Gabinius — son of the Proconsul of Cilicia, friend of Caesar, companion of Julius — as a virgin offering to the gods of pleasure!" His voice echoed in the chamber.

Paul was amazed by Julius' brazenness. Never would the legionnaires have used such expressions in Tarsus — at least not before the son of the Proconsul. Before Paul had time to react to Julius' declaration, he found himself surrounded by revelers. He and Julius were pressed to a table. A cup of wine was place in his hand. Two scantily dressed females began caressing his shoulders and the young girl who had presented herself as an offering to Julius looked wide-eyed into Paul's face. "Are you really a virgin?" she asked in mock wonder. "I have never met a virgin god before!"

Deep in Paul's mind he heard another voice. It was the soft voice of his mother, Saraphina, reading to him in Hebrew. "Keep from the immoral woman. Do not lust in your heart after her beauty or let her captivate you with her eyes, for the prostitute reduces you to a loaf of bread, and the adulteress preys upon your very life. Can a man scoop fire into his lap without his clothes being burned?"

"Taste it," the young girl suggested, holding a golden goblet of spiced wine before him. Paul knew the invitation was not simply for the wine. "It's filled with pleasure!"

Paul turned away from the inner voice.

"Drink it," she encouraged. The tone of her voice was filled with desire.

The wine was strong, the room warm, the environment exciting and the girl enchanting. Paul soon found himself caught up in the frenzy and passion of the victory celebration. It seemed as if some outside force was directing the events of the evening. The wine, the swirl of the dancers, the sensation of warm flesh pressed against him — all seemed orchestrated by some unseen force. Perhaps the Romans were right. Perhaps the evening was filled with the spirit of Dionysus, the god of ecstasy, or with the spirit of Aphrodite, the goddess of passion. Whatever the cause, Paul found himself being consumed with emotion and fervor, a sensation he thoroughly enjoyed.

Paul was so caught up in the effects of the wine and of his emotion that he did not know how he left the revelry of the hall. He found himself in one of the chamber rooms of the baths, on a couch with the girl. The bareness of her flesh pressed upon his chest. The warmth of her kisses sent sensations of desire through him. The effects of the wine and of his desire pulsated in Paul's body as he considered yielding himself to the ecstasy of passion.

Paul looked closely at his companion. She was beautiful, with blond hair, pale blue eyes, a nose like that of a carved Greek goddess, and full lips trembling with desire. He was very aware of her female contours. Her hands slipped to his waist and her eyes gave an unspoken invitation. She began to untie the leather thongs that held his sword belt.

Suddenly, as if a gush of cold water had been thrown on the flame of his desire, Paul heard in his spirit the warning of Julius. *Rome is a whore. If you ever sleep with her, do not remove your sword.*

A whore? Could this beautiful creature be a harlot? She had not asked for anything.

Julius' voice continued in Paul's brain: *If you cannot pay her price, she will stab you in the back.*

As his companion was untieing his sword belt, Paul again heard what Julius had told him: *If you are going to make love to Rome, Paul, be sure you can live with the presence of cold steel on your backside!*

The cold air felt good on his face as he walked through the streets, back to the apartment. *The girl is probably already in the arms of another lover,* he thought. Paul's head began to clear. Within him was a strong desire to return to the orgy and the passion of the girl's embrace. He realized that she was no harlot. She was caught in the same spell and desire that had taken hold of him. With all his being he wanted to turn back and experience that from which he had turned away. The sensation and the warmth of the girl still stirred his senses. He had been caught in the spirit of Rome, but a stronger spirit directed his feet away.

Well, Paul Gabinius, he said to himself. *Perhaps you should call yourself by your Hebrew name, Saul of Benjamin. It seems you have more Jew in you than you have Gentile. Or*, he laughed to himself, *you have more fear than passion!*

That night Paul Gabinius slept with a restless, running spirit of desire. His flesh cried out for the pleasures of the goddess of Rome, but his soul searched for the God of Israel. In the morning he awoke with a new passion — an obsession to find out who he really was, a need to determine if his mother's God was really God.

4

General Gabinius watched as Paul and Julius left the Circus Maximus by litter. He smiled, realizing how uncomfortable Paul would be with such a mode of transportation. The only contention the General and Saraphina had experienced in their marriage was concerning how Paul would be reared and educated. With the Cilician Guard, General Gabinius expected immediate and unquestioned obedience. But Saraphina was a different matter. While she was submissive as a wife, she could be obstinate as a mother. She had insisted that Paul be circumcised as a son of Israel on the eighth day after his birth. Their son was given the Roman name, Paul, but she persisted in calling him by his Hebrew name, Saul. The son of the Proconsul did not need to learn a common trade; nevertheless, Saraphina prevailed until Markus allowed Paul to be taught one. But the trade Markus chose for Paul fit the General's notion of who his son should be. Paul was trained in the trade of tent making.

The felted cloth from which army tents were made was a product of Cilicia and the industry was privately owned by the Gabiniuses. In their spare time, the guards worked on the tents that were sold to Rome for its armies. General Gabinius made sure that Paul learned not only the art of tent making from the soldiers but also the arts of war! His father also made sure that Paul was educated in the language and the customs of Rome. Saraphina equally made sure that her son was learned in the ancient language of her people and the customs of Israel.

General Gabinius knew that his son was comfortable riding a fine stallion, marching with the army, or walking with his mother as a Jew. Being carried on the backs of slaves would be something else. The General knew his son to be humble in spirit. He realized that a litter ride through the streets of Rome and a visit to the baths would intimidate Paul; but he also thought Paul needed a little exposure to the real world and its decadence. The General knew that Paul had to make a choice. He could not be both Jew and Roman. Men from Germania, Gallia, Britannia and Greece had risen in power and had been accepted as Romans. Never had Rome received a Jew or a black as Roman. Paul could be whatever he chose to be. With the General's name and estates, and the ring of Augustus, Paul would be recognized as a Roman aristocrat. But what of his Jewish heritage? While the General applauded Jewish morals and was certainly glad his wife had them, they were just that — Jewish! *Perhaps my son will become a Roman tonight*, the General thought as he ascended the stairs to the Palace of Tiberius with Caesar's other guests.

On the Palatine Hill, General Gabinius recognized the Temple of Jupiter and the Palace of Augustus. The Palace was now being used as a second residence by Tiberius. Below him, to the west of the Circus Maximus, lay the avenue called the Vicus Patricius, paved with Numidian marble. From the cobbled streets below came the sounds Paul too was hearing. It was an aggravating racket, even on the hillside. The night air carried not only the sounds of iron grinding cobblestones but also the screech of dry axles and the report of drivers' whips. General Gabinius thought of the peace of the Cydnus and the sounds of river frogs on the estate in Tarsus. Below were clustered the important buildings of the Empire, but they were not clearly visible in the darkness. They were only massive shapes and shadows. The lights of the Tribune Hall called the baths still seemed suspended just north of the Palatine Hill. Gabinius suspected that Julius Laco and Paul were heading there. As a young man, the General had often enjoyed the revelry of the baths. He chuckled to himself at the thought of what Paul's reaction to a Roman orgy would be.

Markus was ushered into a large banquet room. The dining room of the home of Tiberius was elaborately decorated and furnished. Distinguished guests were seated on velvet cushions next to tables filled with delicacies and wine. Slaves catered to the guests' every wish. Music and dancing girls completed the atmosphere. Although the festivities lacked the lascivious nature Paul was experiencing at the baths, Tiberius and the leaders of Rome were not more righteous than their children. They were restrained because many had brought their wives with them. Tiberius made a mental note that the wife of General Gabinius had chosen not to attend. It was not that her absence displeased Caesar. Indeed, her presence would have been awkward. It was the very idea of a general of Rome marrying a Jewess that irritated Tiberius Caesar. He had never met Saraphina, yet he believed that such a woman should never have had the privilege of living in the home of the Roman Proconsul of Cilicia.

As part of the honor of his Triumph, General Gabinius was seated at Tiberius' table. "Gabinius" — Tiberius intentionally refrained from using the General's title — "I am delighted that your son accepted the invitation to celebrate my victory at the race with Julius Laco. I believe you know that his father is second in command of the Legion." The sarcasm in Tiberius' voice was evident. "It is unfortunate that your wife cannot join the celebrations," Tiberius sarcastically continued.

General Gabinius understood that Tiberius had linked the two statements together on purpose. Tiberius was well aware of the fact that Saraphina was Jewish. The General also knew Tiberius believed that Gabinius would have attained Laco's position had he not married a Jewess. Caesar was cynically letting the General know that he approved of Rome's policy and disapproved of Gabinius' marriage.

"My Caesar, I am honored to be in your presence," Gabinius replied as if the sarcasm was not recognized. "I delight that my friend Laco has served Caesar so well, and I hope his son and mine will become comrades."

Tiberius, seeing that Gabinius had deflected the thrust of his remarks, pressed to another subject. "Gabinius," he began, "it was unfortunate for you that Augustus assigned you to estates in Tarsus. I know of Augustus' appreciation for the city." From his facial expression Markus knew that Caesar did not share Augustus' affinity for Tarsus. "When Cassius marched into Syria, the people of Tarsus supported him. To show them his appreciation, Cassius did not destroy Tarsus but only requisitioned taxes. Because of the victory, Augustus became commander of Italy and of the West, which allowed him to take the throne of Caesar. In gratitude for its loyalty, Augustus granted Tarsus the status of a free city, *libera civitas*." General Gabinius knew that Tiberius was not giving him a history lesson but making a point. He waited for Tiberius to continue. "Thus Tarsus, while continuing to be a part of the Empire, is governed not by Roman law but according to its own law. Neither does Rome receive taxes on her export and import trade." As Tiberius was speaking, Markus noted the look of displeasure on Caesar's face. After drinking from his cup, Tiberius continued: "Because of the *libera civitas*, Anthony resided at Tarsus with his Egyptian tramp, Cleopatra." (Markus was shocked that Tiberius would publicly refer to the queen of Egypt as a tramp.) Without lowering his voice Caesar added, "Just because the Egyptian whore sailed her galley up the River Cydnus and entered Tarsus in the pomp of Oriental luxury does not make her less of a whore."

Tiberius studied the face of Gabinius to make sure his point went home. He wanted to be certain that the General understood what he was going to say next. "The Jews have taken the policies of Augustus to make for themselves a refuge from taxes and a place to gain political power!" Tiberius slammed his wine goblet on the table at the word Jew and his face flushed with indignation. "I, Caesar Tiberius, am helpless before them. I do not have the authority to break the edict of *libera civitas* given by Augustus, whose seal you carry on your finger." (This was the second time in as many days that Tiberius had noted Markus' ring.)

The voice of Caesar softened into a whisper. "But you, Proconsul Gabinius, are the law of Tarsus — appointed so by Augustus. I know the constitution of Tarsus states that both Greeks and Jews must have presence in the government. Because Anthony sold Roman citizenship to Tarsians, who changed their names to Roman names, no one can tell who is Greek and who is Jewish. The Senate of Tarsus has in it Gnaeus Pompeius, Gaius Julius and Markus Antonius. Are they Greeks or Jews? They certainly are not Romans!" Leaning closer to the General, Tiberius ground home his point. "You, Markus Paul Gabinius, are a Roman. You can give Tarsus back to Rome. You have the authority as the Roman Proconsul and the power of the signet of Augustus. Rome needs the tax monies. Rome must control Tarsus. There can be no impediment in Imperial authority. Do it for me, Gabinius; do it for Rome. You will have to divorce your Jewess, of course, but keep her for a mistress if you choose."

At Caesar's whispered words "Jewess" and "mistress," Markus erupted. "By the gods, no!" At the retort of the General, everyone in the room recoiled. Had the General been in uniform and wearing his sword, the history of Rome would have been greatly changed. For Markus Paul Gabinius was quite sure he would have proven that Caesar was no god. It took Markus only a moment to regain his military composure. He stood, saluted and dismissed himself without Caesar's permission.

5

Why had Caesar and Rome chosen to honor Gabinius with a Triumph after all these years? Now the General knew. Rome gave nothing away without a price. Did not Tiberius have enough wealth and power? Were his despotism and greed never satisfied? Tiberius wanted Tarsus as a man lusts after a woman who is not his to possess. Tiberius was worshiped as god from Cappadocia to Britannia, from Egypt to Hispania. Only two cities did not submit to Emperor worship — Jerusalem and Tarsus!

Jerusalem would not worship and adore Tiberius, so he enslaved her. But Tiberius could not force Tarsus to submit to him. The *libera civitas* of Augustus kept him from raping her. True, there was an altar to the Emperor Tiberius in Tarsus, but the people put their faith in the Earth Mother, Cybele. Her Amazon-like priestesses made processions through the streets of Tarsus each day.

In her refusal to worship Caesar and pay her dues to Rome, Tarsus made it clear that she would give herself to no man, and Tiberius was a man! Tarsus elevated the female goddess over Tiberius, and Gabinius represented Tarsus. He too dared to refuse the advances of Tiberius. As General Markus Paul Gabinius thought over the day, he realized that to be honored by Rome could be a very dangerous thing.

Paul knew that something out of the ordinary was happening when he was instructed by a servant that his father wished a private audience with him. "Paul" — the elder Gabinius' greeting was fervent. He threw his arms around his son and hugged him.

The Gabinius family had always been an affectionate family in private. Markus treated Saraphina with a familiarity before his son that was rare for a Roman toward his wife. Paul never had any doubt about his parents' love for each other nor about their love for him.

Paul patted his father on the back. "How proud I was of you before Caesar!" he exclaimed. "I saw you and the dignitaries on your way to dinner with Tiberius."

When the elder Gabinius recounted what had happened at the dinner, Paul was enraged by Tiberius' remarks concerning his mother. "He could learn some manners from Tarsus" — Paul touched the hilt of his sword.

"Caesar has certain advantages!" the General replied. "Had he been a man of lesser position, he would already be with the gods; but I fear I have made an enemy of a very powerful and ominous man."

Gabinius seated Paul on a couch where they could look into each other's eyes. "The section of Cilician Guard that accompanied us to Rome will be sailing for Tarsus in two weeks. I want you to accompany your mother and sail with them."

Paul looked questioningly at his father. "Will you be returning with us?" he inquired.

"I cannot be sure," replied the General. "I do not know if Caesar will be through honoring me." (The elder Gabinius smiled as he said it.) "I want you to carry this to Tarsus for me," General Gabinius said as he placed a leather thong over Paul's head and tucked the ring that hung from it beneath Paul's tunic. Paul's eyes widened as he recognized that his father had just entrusted him with the signet ring of Augustus. "I will not need the ring any more in Rome, and there are many here who would like to have it on their finger. Promise me you will show it to no one unless you have to use it for your mother's benefit or to save your life. Authorities have to honor that ring, anywhere in the Empire, and it will always bring you back to Rome!"

His father's concern over the ring worried Paul, but he shook his head in agreement and started to reply when his father continued: "While you are still in Rome, I want you to wear your military uniform, including your sword. I know it was given to you for the ceremonies and some might think you odd, but wear it anyway!" The General's words were emphatic. "Keep near Julius Laco. He is a good man, like his father. You can trust him should you need him. I do not wish to concern you, my son, and this is probably the consternation of an old man. But I have been a soldier many years and my bones feel danger."

"Surely you do not believe that Tiberius was so offended he would cause us any harm," Paul retorted. "If anyone has been offended, it is the name of Gabinius!"

"No, my son," the General said forcefully. "Tiberius does not have enough manners, culture or intelligence to understand either the offensiveness of his statements or my reaction. I have no fear of his feelings. But his greed — well, that's another matter."

Paul wanted to go with his father when the General left for an audience at the Senate, but the elder Gabinius would not hear of it. "Find Julius Laco and explore Rome with him," the General called to Paul as he left for the Senate. "The two of you can join me after the session is over." Paul noted that his father was wearing a simple tunic. It would be ridiculous to wear a uniform to the Senate, but Paul did wish his father had a sword. After all, what Julius said was true: In Rome the feel of cold steel on your side was reassuring!

Julius was amenable toward the suggestion that he and Paul spend the afternoon together while Paul waited for General Gabinius. He had been concerned after Paul had left the baths early. He had also tried to justify Paul against the jeers of the Roman youth. The girl Paul had left on the lounge was maliciously defending her reputation as a seductress by stating that Paul was no virgin god but a castrated, impotent fool. Julius harbored no doubts about Paul's manhood. He thought perhaps Paul had left without cooling the young lady's appetite because of a vow or a religious commitment. When Paul explained what had happened, both exploded with laughter.

"Paul!" exclaimed Julius. "Don't take me so literally! Rome is a whore, but all whores are not Rome!" Paul flushed with humiliation at the joke, but he laughed with Julius at the thought of that night. "I would have loved to have seen your face when she tried to remove your sword belt," Julius jested.

"What I should have waited for," declared Paul, " was the moment she discovered that her virgin god is a circumcised Jew!"

For just a moment Julius was shocked by Paul's disclosure, then his amusement broke into expanded hilarity. "Really, Paul, you must accept your commission in the Legion. Together we will become Roman generals and I will see that you are proclaimed Caesar! Rome calling a circumcised Jew a god! What a thought!" The two new friends more or less yielded completely to their frivolity, never realizing that one day, because of Paul, Rome would indeed call a circumcised Jew, Lord!

That day Julius Laco showed Rome to Paul and Paul introduced Julius to a new world. With his eyes, Paul saw the gleaming, white-marbled buildings and the cold statues with blank eyes and stone hearts that made Rome. With his spirit, Julius saw what Paul described. He pictured the flowering Cilician Plain and the snowy mountains behind Tarsus. For the first time he truly saw the Roman and Greek gods past whom the true Jew walked with averted eyes. He learned of the God of the Jews who lacks body or form to be contained in a structure, but who was worshiped in the Temple in Jerusalem. Neither Julius nor Paul found meaning in the statues of Rome. Paul, circumcised a Jew, was not sure that the

God of Israel was God. But in the heart of Julius Laco there was born that afternoon a desire to see beyond Rome and its gods.

The two young adventurers arrived at the entrance to the Senate just as Gabinius came out of the chambers. Seeing Paul and Julius, he raised his hand in salute and moved past a portico column to meet them. A small man stepped from the column and ran to intercept Gabinius. With one hand the stranger reached to clasp the General's fingers. With his other hand he pulled out a knife hidden under his tunic.

Julius was the first to respond to the glint of steel. He tried to deflect the knife with his sword, but only succeeded in driving the sword into the chest of the assassin who still clung to the General's hand. The murderer's knife had found its mark. General Markus Paul Gabinius fell, dying, into the arms of his son.

6

With contempt, Paul watched the state funeral given to his father. The procession followed the same streets on which the General had ridden the white horse of Triumph. The General's body would not be buried in Rome but would be carried to his home in Tarsus. Paul believed that the same authorities who had arranged his father's Triumph and funeral were also responsible for his father's death. Within hours after the General had been killed, Roman legionnaires had searched the Gabinius apartments. They did not indicate what they were looking for, but Paul thought he knew. A moment before the assassin's knife had struck, Paul had seen the look of shock on the assassin's face when he grabbed at the General's empty fingers. The ring of Augustus Caesar still hung on the leather thong around Paul's neck. He was convinced that both the killer and the soldiers had been after that powerful little piece of gold.

Paul could not share his secret with anyone. How the ring could be used or when it should be used, Paul did not understand. But that he would keep its whereabouts a secret was the last promise he had given to his father; and Paul Gabinius would keep his word.

"Paul —" Julius' tone of voice was somber — "I regret that my sword was both too slow and too fast. I was not swift enough to save your father, yet I was too quick to kill his assassin."

"Assassin?" Paul questioned the sure way Julius made the pronouncement.

"Assassin!" Julius replied emphatically. "The attack on your father was not simply an attempted robbery on the steps of the Senate! Nor was it a murder by an old enemy!" Julius continued. "That would have been done secretly — privately! No! Whoever that man was, he thought he could get away with it — even if he were caught! My friend" — Julius paused — "if I am correct, I fear that nothing will ever be done about your father's death." Julius did not explain further.

Paul told his good friend about the fears his father had shared with him. But he kept his word and did not tell Julius about the ring.

Tiberius waited a week after the state funeral before Paul was ordered to appear before the Senate. There would be a hearing and a judgement concerning the death of General Gabinius. Julius was also commanded to stand before the Senate. Saraphina was exempt from the procedure. Since she was not a Roman citizen, she did not have rights under Roman law.

As Paul ascended the stairs that led to the Senate building and crossed the portico, he had to pass the very spot where his father had been killed. The marble floors had been scrubbed clean of the blood stains. Paul could not help but wonder how much blood had been spilled on these steps and how much more yet would be spilt. In Rome, even the senators and the Emperor, himself, were not exempt.

Once inside the doors of the Senate, Paul found himself in a large hall. The marble floors of the patio continued through the center of the hall and led to a platform upon which were placed two large seats. Between the columns on each side of the floor in elevated seats were the senators, each dressed in a white robe. Julius had arrived earlier; he was standing at attention before the platform. Paul noted that although Julius wore his uniform, no sword hung at his side. Paul went and stood beside his friend, but they did not greet each other.

A member of the Praetorian Guard, the only armed men in the room, struck the butt end of his spear on the marble floor. With the reverberation of sound, all the members of the Senate stood.

"Hail Caesar!" The guards saluted by lowering their spear points, but they remained on alert. "Hail Caesar! Hail Caesar!" came the familiar salute as Tiberius entered the chamber and took a seat on the platform. Paul wondered why Caesar was always greeted three times. As Tiberius was seated, the sounds of the Senate being seated filled the hall. This was not a trial but a hearing. Paul had already been instructed by General Laco as to the procedure. He knew that he and Julius must stand at attention throughout the process.

Tiberius was dressed in similar fashion to the Senators except that he wore a large, gold neckplate and a golden waistsash over his robe. Paul had expected him to have a crown on his head. Instead, Caesar had a golden scarf, which crossed his head and flowed on to his right shoulder, fashioned into his hair on the left side of his head.

The two seats on the platform still bothered Tiberius. He had shared the rule of the Senate with Augustus before that Caesar's death. He had not been Caesar's choice as successor nor was he the son of Caesar except by adoption. The stepson of Augustus by his third wife, Tiberius had been mistreated by Augustus. The Senate and the Assembly had voted Augustus' powers on Tiberius, but they had retained the other chair in Augustus' memory. Tiberius was Caesar, but he was always under the shadow of Augustus.

"I, Caesar," began Tiberius as he picked at a fresh pimple on his face, "find Julius Laco guilty of no wrong."

How outrageous, Paul thought. *My father is dead, and this boyish clown has to have two thrones to pronounce that the man who killed his murderer is not guilty.*

Tiberius continued speaking, but he looked as if he was not interested in the procedure. "He acted in the highest order of the Praetorian Guard by killing the murderer of the friend of Caesar, Markus Paul Gabinius."

Friend of Caesar! Paul wanted to shout. *Does a friend order a compatriot to betray his countryman and dishonor the fallen man's wife?* Paul remained silent, remembering the title and power of Tiberius.

"That such an act would be committed on the very steps of the Senate is unthinkable. But the death of the murderer by Julius Laco ends the matter," Tiberius was saying.

Ends the matter! Paul wanted to scream, but he remained silent and at attention.

With one brief speech, Tiberius closed the books on the murder of General Gabinius, got rid of the witness and made himself appear as Julius' benefactor. "Dear Paul, son of my dead friend Markus Gabinius," he addressed Paul, leaning forward in his chair as if he was very concerned about the General's son, "I deeply regret the death of your father. I will keep the commitment Rome has to him by offering you a command in the Roman Legion." Tiberius paused, a silly smirk on his face, and nervously picked at his pimple again. "Your father's position as Procurator of Tarsus, however, can only be given to someone of his own status. Since your father's estate in Tarsus was a decree of Caesar to the Procurator, you and your mother, I fear, will have to arrange to vacate those properties." Caesar tried to appear warm and compassionate as he stole Paul's inheritance and made his mother little more than his father's concubine. "Except the personal effects of your father, all his belongings will revert to Rome. As a Roman citizen, you have a right to the personal belongings and holdings of your father. But your mother, being a Jew, lacks rights." At the word "Jew," Tiberius' expression indicated to all at the hearing his total disgust with Jews as a whole.

Julius broke his stance at attention just enough to grip Paul's wrist with force. He was afraid Paul might lose his composure and forget where he was. General Gabinius had verbally threatened this buffoon with the title of Caesar at the dinner, but should Paul even flinch with anger now, it would mean his instant death. Paul held his composure.

With Tiberius' declaration, the hearing was over. The Guard indicated that Paul and Julius were to leave the Senate, but as Paul turned to leave, Tiberius left his chair and stopped him. Caesar placed a hand on Gabinius' son's shoulder and placed his face next to Paul's cheek. The Senate was touched at Caesar's show of personal concern for the grief of General Gabinius' son. What Paul heard was Tiberius' whisper in his ear: "Where is the signet ring of Augustus?"

Paul turned, military style, and prepared to leave with Julius. Since Tiberius had not officially asked the question, Paul felt no need to answer. He left Tiberius standing on the floor of the Senate with the question still on his lips. With each reverberation from his boots on the marble, Paul left Rome.

7

The long sea journey back to Tarsus gave Paul time to grieve and to solidify his anger against Rome. There was little he could do against the power of Tiberius Caesar or Rome. That made Paul feel even more frustration. During the journey, Saraphina remained in her quarters, partly due to her grief and partly to stay away from the eyes of the Cilician Guard. Had General Gabinius been with her, no one would have dared to even look her way. With Markus dead, the veiled Jewess could have been more than a curiosity had it not been for Paul's presence. Now even Paul lacked power beyond his sword.

Yet Saraphina's solitude had given mother and son time to talk as never before. Because of the customs of her people, Saraphina saw Paul in a new role. The boy in the family had become the authority of the family. Saraphina needed to entrust to her son great secrets she and Markus had shared.

"My husband," she said, as if Paul was not familiar with the relationship, "realized even before our marriage the danger I might encounter by marrying a Roman. Therefore, he thought to provide for me and for you, our son, should Rome refuse our status and rights. He arranged with my father to purchase the inn where he met me, great portions of land on which the flax for weaving the tents is grown, several money exchanges, and several ships that transport grain to Rome and Egypt. These properties are in the legal ownership of members of my family. Rome does not know of the connection between their Proconsul and Jewish merchants.

When we arrive in Tarsus, it is best if Saraphina Gabinius disappears and one more veiled widow is added to its population."

The mother looked at her son questioningly. "You must make a choice, and it is a difficult one, my son. If you are to remain Paul Gabinius, you must join Caesar's Legion and support Caesar. Or you must become Saul, a Jew of Tarsus. If you take on your Jewish identity, you will lose your position of honor and any relationship with Gentiles. If you choose Caesar's Legion, you will have to sever all relationships with any Jew, including me. Necessity places this choice before us. For as surely as greed killed your father, it will kill both of us if we remain the wife and the son of the former Proconsul. Whoever paid the price to Caesar for your father's position and estates cannot afford to leave us alive and recognized."

Paul did not take long to make his decision. The overwhelming hatred he felt toward Rome precluded his serving in Caesar's army. If he became Saul, the Jew, he would be a wealthy Jew and therefore have some power.

As Paul stood by the rail of the ship and looked at the rushing waves, a plan began to form in his mind. The secret his mother had shared with him gave him the source and the resources for the scheme. Paul Gabinius, son of the former Proconsul, could never strike back at Rome. But in Jerusalem there were Jews called Zealots. The Zealots were always giving Rome problems with small uprisings, but they lacked real leadership and resources. If Saul of Tarsus could become a Zealot — a Zealot with money, power and knowledge of Roman ways — he could strike back at his enemy. But how could Paul Gabinius become Jewish enough to be accepted by the Zealots?

"Mother," Paul said, as he sat with Saraphina in her quarters. "I have considered all that you have said and I have come to a decision. I cannot join the Legion; neither can I act the role of a Jew living in Tarsus. After I see that you are settled in Tarsus, I will go to Jerusalem. In Jerusalem I will become a student and a pilgrim. One cannot be a Jew without knowing the God of Abraham. I will go to Jerusalem that I might learn of Him!"

Saul's words greatly pleased his mother. Like all mothers, she began to make plans that Saul would consider to be his own. *The house of Gamaliel*, she thought. *Gamaliel is the greatest rabbi in all Judaea. Paul Gabinius, had his father lived, could have been the greatest Roman in the Empire. But now, Saul of Benjamin will become the finest Jew of the Jews.*

8

The wharf where the ship docked in Tarsus was lined with the legions of Rome. Bright red cloaks draped over the left shoulders of the legionnaires indicated that they were of the Cilician Guard. Each guardsman held a long staff before him. Brass signet plates on the tops of the staffs glistened in the morning sun. The two lines of legionnaires made a corridor through which would pass the body of their commander, General Markus Gabinius. At the forefront of the passage, Paul saw a larger staff crested with the golden eagle of Rome. Paul waited respectfully as the bier containing the body of his father was taken by honor guard from the ship. He fully expected that he and his mother would follow immediately behind the bier, as he had observed in so many state funerals. But the captain of the guard placed his staff in front of the family to allow the guardsmen on the ship to disembark behind the General's body. After the funeral procession had left the wharf, the rest of the passengers, including Paul and Saraphina, were allowed to leave the ship. No recognition was given to the family of General Gabinius.

It was evident to Paul that word had reached the garrison at Tarsus not only of the death of General Gabinius but also of Caesar's declaration of the forfeiture of his estates and the pending appointment of a new Procurator. Paul and Saraphina Gabinius were of no consequence to Rome. Only a demonstration to the people of Tarsus mandated a funeral procession for the former Procurator. Saraphina's concern for Markus had deterred her from sharing in his Triumph, and Rome's disdain of the General's

Jewish wife precluded her from attending his formal funeral. Now Rome's insensitivity to Saraphina, a widow, cut her off from her husband's entombment. Rome, the murderer of General Gabinius, carried the evidence of its treachery and called it a tribute.

Rather than walk behind the procession as notable outcasts, Paul and Saraphina decided to let Rome applaud its own shame. Thus, the General's wife and son slipped unnoticed into the crowd of bystanders near the wharf. No one paid attention to another Roman soldier and one more Jewess in the mixed throngs of Tarsus. Saraphina led Paul through the back streets of the city. Although Paul had lived near the city most of his life and had ridden through its streets being recognized and hailed by Romans as the son of the Proconsul, he had never ventured into the section of Tarsus to which Saraphina now led him. His mother unquestionably knew her way. As a veiled Jewish woman she had often walked these streets in complete seclusion. Her veil gave her detachment, even in the midst of crowded streets. Paul, in his shining Roman uniform, lacked such luxury. His hand almost automatically lightly touched the hilt of his sword. Never before had he felt hate or seen menacing eyes in Tarsus. But neither had he walked alone, dressed as a Roman, on these back streets.

Tarsus was a trade center. Goods from all parts of the Empire could be found there. The narrow stone-paved streets were flanked on each side by shops and vendors. Greek, Persian and Jewish traders bargained and haggled over the sale of merchandise, both in the shops and on the street. Some Jewish merchants were dressed in Roman attire, while others wore clothing that, while Jewish in design, marked them as from the Jewish aristocracy of Tarsus.

Saraphina found the building she was looking for. She led Paul into the shop and proceeded past the merchants to the back. There she pushed aside the curtains that separated the market from a private section.

"Saraphina!" The voice came from a tall, angular, slightly graying man who stood in the midst of what looked to be a mountain of cloth. "Saraphina, beloved Saraphina. I was so sorry to hear the tragic news of your Markus' death. The entire community is in shock. We share your grief. This morning at prayers, the Rabbi spoke of General Gabinius, his gifts to the synagogue, and his affection for our people. We have been praying to God for your peace and the safety of you and your son." The man was a complete stranger to Paul. Yet he embraced Saraphina with tenderness and great familiarity.

"And this must be young Gabinius," he said, turning his attention to Paul. Quickly the stranger moved to place both arms around Paul's shoulders. Paul was not prepared for the hug or the strength he felt in the arms that pressed his arms to his side.

"Oh, I see I have alarmed the young Roman. Forgive me, Master Paul. Your father and I were very close, and we would embrace each other passionately — it is the nature of my people. I never really thought of your father as a Roman. I am called Simon. Your father and I were business partners. Now I give you honor as his son. I could not give your father proper homage at the Roman ceremony, for his Jewish friends would not be welcome, nor could we salute the Roman gods. But you are here, and the ceremony is in progress?" Simon's question was addressed to Paul, but his eyes were on Saraphina.

"Yes, Simon," Saraphina answered. "I fear that Paul might be in danger. Those who killed my husband would not hesitate to kill my son. Rome has taken all my husband's Roman properties and Caesar is about to give General Gabinius' position to another. My son has refused a position in the Roman Legion. He has decided to study our ways in Jerusalem."

Had it not been for his breastplate, Paul felt that Simon's response would have broken his ribs. Paul was lifted off his feet and held in the air in Simon's powerful grip. The eyes of the

Jewish tailor shone with glee and a smile covered his face. "We will need a complete wardrobe for a very distinguished and wealthy Jewish scholar. We must turn the head of every virgin, bow the head of every priest and rabbi in respect, and make every merchant in Jerusalem more greedy than he already is! Hadassah! Sarah!"

Simon's helpers came into the chambers, looking at Paul with fear and suspicion. "Get cloth," called Simon, "the finest we have — trimming and sashes, prayer cloaks, white undergarment cloth, robe cloth, and sandals. We have to create a miracle."

Later that evening, a man and a woman came out of the shop of Simon the tailor. As they walked through the streets, merchants greeted them with warmth and respect. Vendors politely offered their goods to be inspected. Dark-eyed girls shamelessly studied the face of the young gallant who walked the street with his elderly veiled female acquaintance. Each person they passed greeted the pair with a courteous "shalom" and nodded their heads in deference. Each was convinced that he had encountered a merchant prince trading in Tarsus or a scholar who taught in one of the finer schools of Tarsus. All assumed that the young man was visiting the shops with his widowed mother.

Back in Simon's shop, the team of tailors worked urgently, preparing a wardrobe suitable for a well-to-do scholar in Jersualem. A Roman uniform was carefully packed away in a leather trunk.

"Saul, my son" — Saraphina spoke discreetly as they passed through the throng — "it will be difficult, but you must remember to make way and lower your eyes for even the most common Roman soldier. No Roman soldier would have dared to lift his hand against Paul Gabinius, but even the most affluent Jew can be treated as a dog by the most ignoble of Romans. You have walked as a conquering hero; now you must learn to behave like a conquered slave."

Paul looked into the face of his mother who walked beside him. He remembered the feeling of shame he had known in Rome when his mother had walked behind him as if she were one of his servants. It was strange. In Rome, Paul Gabinius, the conqueror, had felt shame. In Tarsus, Saul of Benjamin, the conquered Jew, looked at his mother and was filled with pride.

The street circled back into the main thoroughfare that ran from the docks to the inland trade routes. At the intersection of the two roads stood the inn where Markus and Saraphina had first met. Paul struck a bell at the door of the outer wall. In a moment the innkeeper appeared. "Saul of Benjamin," Paul announced, almost saying, "Paul Gabinius of the Proconsul of Rome."

The innkeeper smiled as if he heard the hesitancy with which Paul had identified himself. "Of course, sir. We have been informed by your steward of your arrival. Rooms have been prepared for you and your mother. Your wardrobe and other belongings are even now being transferred to the inn. Your steward begs your forgiveness in not being here upon your arrival, but he will join you for the evening meal. He has procured a special room that is being prepared for your guests. As soon as he sees to the settlement of a caravan bound for Cappadocia, he will join you and give you his report."

"Steward? Guests? Caravan?" Paul looked at Saraphina's veil-covered face. All he saw was shining eyes.

The rooms at the inn were not what Paul had expected. He had never been in a public house before, but he knew from the soldiers that the rooms were expected to be small. Normally, numbers of persons shared not only the same room but the same straw bedding. Paul was ushered into a large, graciously furnished apartment. Light filtered softly into the rooms through sheer curtains that moved slightly in the evening breeze. The arched opening looked down on a garden from which came the sweet fragrance of flowers. A couch draped in soft fabric had been placed in such a manner that one reclining on it would receive the full benefit of the breeze. A large basin of water and towels for bathing had been provided. Expensive perfumed soap and soothing balm had been placed next to the basin.

Since Paul had been assured that his mother had an equal resting place, he enjoyed the pleasure of ridding himself of the stench of the sea. A male servant trimmed his hair and beard and provided him with a robe after his bath. Then Paul, reclining on the couch, pondered the wonder of the day's events. He had expected the life of a fugitive from Rome, but here he was lying in the center of luxury.

His surroundings were not what he was used to as the son of the Roman Procurator. Everything had the feel and look of a different culture. There was a gentler, more peaceful atmosphere in all his surroundings. The sounds of Roman guards moving on hard marble were missing. There was only the rustling of the breeze through the curtains, the smell of perfume and the softness of the couch. For the first time since his father had been murdered, Paul felt safe and peaceful. He quickly fell into a much-needed, deep sleep.

"Master Saul! Master Saul!" The voice of the Jewish boy slowly penetrated Paul's mind, bringing him into consciousness. The sound of the greeting was so strange that it took Paul a moment to respond, though there was no one else in the room. The lad, barely in his teens, had flowing black locks and sparkling black eyes. A large smile filled all his face. "I am Aaron, named after the first priest of Israel, the brother of the Prophet Moses. I have been appointed to help you prepare for this evening's meal. These are the clothes you will wear." Aaron pointed to clothing draped over a chair. "This is your prayer cloth. You must always keep your head covered after you leave the privacy of this room. This shows your respect to God." Aaron's countenance indicated that he was enjoying this new role of tutor to his elder.

Paul did not let on that he knew well the customs of Israel. What if the son of the Roman Proconsul had also been tutored in his Jewish heritage by his mother and those she had employed? To be instructed again would only renew his memory, and Aaron was as delightful as the scented breeze that filled the room. The refreshment of sleep and his awakening to the enthusiasm of this new young brother helped Paul put aside the pain of Paul Gabinius and prepare to truly become Saul of Benjamin.

Aaron followed Paul, instructing him until Paul entered the room. The dining area selected was not so much a room as a secluded chamber on the roof of the inn. Lanterns on the outside walls gave the space a soft, warm radiance. A low table with cushions piled around it had been prepared. It was laden with food and wine. Seated around the table were six men. Paul could tell from their attire that all were wealthy Jews. They rose when Paul entered the room. Paul looked in vain for his mother. The only persons Paul recognized were Simon from the tailor shop and the innkeeper. They sat together, across the table from where Paul stood.

A slightly stooped, graying man, walking with the aid of a stick, approached Paul. "Master Saul, I am Ahad Ben Joseph, steward of the house of Gabinius and Salaman. I say steward of both houses because I am the property of your father, to whom he entrusted the care of both his Roman and Jewish businesses. Master, I fear that the property of the house of Gabinius is lost to Rome forever! Your father, however, very wisely divided his holdings and, through the family of your mother, Saraphina Salaman, preserved enough for you and your mother to live very comfortably."

Ahad Ben Joseph stood with arms slightly open, as if asking permission to embrace Paul — desiring to do so, but questioning at the same time the propriety of such a move. Paul swept the old man into his arms. As they clung to each other, Paul felt and heard the wrenching sob that came from deep within the steward's heart.

Paul also saw the tears in Ahad's eyes as he wept. "I loved Markus as a son," the aged man murmured. "Though I have served your father as his steward since he first arrived in our land, he treated me as his father and I loved him as my son."

After momentarily gaining his composure, Ahad Ben Joseph continued. "Saul of the tribe of Benjamin, son of Saraphina Salaman, may I introduce you to your family?"

"This is your mother's brother, Ismar Salaman. Through your father's finances and influence, Ismar controls great caravans of trade for your family." Ismar, a burly man, was dark of complexion from many days in the hot desert sun. His hair and beard were streaked with gray. His eyes showed a keenness and examination that indicated he would be a hard man to deceive. His embrace of Paul was one of respect, but Paul was surprised to feel tenderness as well as power in his arms. Ismar Salaman would be a hard man to deal with, but he was a man who could be trusted.

The next man to approach Paul was a young copy of Ismar. "Meet the son of Ismar, James Salaman, director of the Salaman fleet," Ahad invited. "What the father cannot get by camel caravan for trade, the son brings by sea; what the father cannot sell in Tarsus or on the caravan routes, the son ships and sells in other markets. It is a good arrangement — no?"

James, whom Paul judged to be his elder cousin by half a dozen years, greeted Paul with the same warmth as his father. Somehow Paul knew that he too was a man who could be trusted. Like his father, James would make the best of any business or trade.

The next of the group to whom Ahad Ben Joseph pointed Paul seemed out of place with James and Ismar. He was thin of stature and pale of color. "Isaac Ben-Ami, husband of Athaliah, sister of Ismar, is the moneylender."

Ismar interrupted Ahad: "Do not concern yourself about Isaac, young Saul. He will keep the treasury of the house of Salaman and make a profit on the money he lends. My sister, Athaliah, looks like me. Fear will keep Isaac honest."

Isaac weakly greeted Paul and smiled at the mirth at his expense. Paul recognized that what Ismar said in jest was probably true.

Simon did not wait for a second introduction. He hugged Paul as fearlessly as he had when they had met earlier at the tailor's shop. "I also am your mother's brother, as is Elkin the innkeeper. Both the tailor shop and the inn are ours because of your father's foresight and Ahab Ben Joseph's stewardship. All that we are and have is at your service." Elkin grasped Paul's arm. His eyes said much more than words could have conveyed.

"Let us feast and drink, for we have much to decide this night," said Ahad. He directed the others as naturally as if he had been speaking for his former lord, Markus Paul Gabinius.

"And my mother?" Paul asked.

It was Ahad who replied: "She will not dine with us tonight. While she was very much a part of your father's business affairs, and he did nothing without discussing it with her, they honored our Jewish customs that do not allow a woman to eat or discuss business with the elders. She is welcome to be here with her family, but she thought it best that we observe Jewish tradition."

Ahad directed Paul to a servant who stood waiting with a basin and a pitcher of water. Since both Romans and Jews washed their hands before eating by having water poured on the hands by a servant, Paul knew what to do. After he had wiped his hands on a clean towel, Paul was directed to the low polygon stool that served as a table and the carpet that served as a chair.

Ahad, sitting to Paul's right, began the meal by removing a piece of bread from a central dish. He broke it into two pieces as he said, "God be praised." When Paul responded in kind, Ahad smiled. He did not have to teach this son of Markus Gabinius as much as he had feared. Each in turn repeated the blessing. Ahad formed his bread into a scoop and dipped it into a plate of mutton and gravy. Paul noted the meat on the table, recognizing that it was a sign of a special occasion.

"See," said Simon, "there is more Jew in Saul than Roman. He will not have to learn much of our customs."

Ahad dipped bread in a dish of lentils and passed the dish to Paul. "Master Saul, your father did not wish to keep his business secret from you. He was a man who lived in two worlds. The Roman Proconsul cannot have relationships with an enslaved people. General Gabinius felt that he would be placing you, his son, in danger and at a disadvantage should he expose you to your Jewish family. Your mother wanted you to know your Jewish heritage so your father arranged for you to be tutored in our culture and the Hebrew language. That fact now may well save your life! I want you to know that your father was not ashamed of his Jewish wife or her family. Markus Gabinius was a good man who gave generously to support our synagogue. He was not a man of prejudice. He was fearful for your mother, should something happen to him. He supported us in business so that we, in turn, could look after her. Now it seems that it is our good fortune to serve you as we served your father."

Isaac spoke softly, hesitantly: "Your mother has informed us of your wish to relocate to Jerusalem. I will give you letters of credit that will establish whatever funds you need. It is not wise to carry large sums of money while traveling. No one will be able to use the letters except you, and we will not be charged for money exchange or interest."

"Isaac will protect your money as if it were his," Ismar good-naturedly chided. Paul, realizing the great love Ismar and Isaac had for each other, knew the jesting was the Jewish way of expressing their feelings for each other.

James joined Ismar in the jest: "Father, I have a ship sailing for Jerusalem next week. Brother Saul can have the best cabin. I believe we could safely ship the gold Isaac would give us."

"No, my son," Ismar replied. "Isaac is correct. It would be better for Saul to carry letters of credit. Letters of credit ensure more business with the merchants of Jerusalem. When I put my bread in the dish, I get more out of it than what I put in. When Isaac puts his fingers in the money-changer's bowl, you can wager that he will not only serve Saul but will come out of the bowl with a profit." Ismar put his bread back into the bowl and hooked a large piece of meat with his thumb. When he picked it up and held it above his mouth, those at the table rocked with laughter.

Paul joined in the levity of the moment, finding himself strangely comfortable in the unfamiliar surroundings. He did not really know these men, but he shared and felt kinship. Although he directed his remarks toward Ahad, he spoke to them all: "I thank you for your hospitality and your acceptance of a Roman, though a relative."

"I see no Roman here!" It was Simon who again spoke in behalf of Paul's Jewishness. "A Roman suit of armor was left in a trunk in my shop. The legionnaire who wore it lacks further use of it, as he is dead. I see only my nephew Saul, of the lineage of Benjamin. Saul Salaman, son of Abraham, Isaac and Jacob, whom God called Israel, who named his twelfth son Benjamin and made his descendants heirs to the royal covenant — I salute you!" Simon and all the family raised their cups to Paul.

The acceptance and warmth coming from the men touched Paul deeply. Though their purpose was serious, Paul enjoyed the joviality of their fellowship. For just a moment, in the midst of their good-natured jesting with each other, Paul remembered the camaraderie he and Julius had shared in Rome. He was saddened at the thought that he had lost his friend forever.

Later that night, as Paul lay on his couch, his restless dreams were filled with Julius, the Roman baths, and the slender, blond-haired girl who had pressed her body against his chest. He played with lust and regret in his mind. His emotions were aroused by the memory of her warmth and kisses. He regretted that he had not tasted all she had offered. He wondered what would have happened had he taken her. Laying aside his Jewish virtue, he could have freely joined Julius to become a legionnaire of Rome. They could have served Rome together, sharing great adventures and conquests, both as soldiers and as men. The girl at the baths would have been only the first of many. Paul's imagination filled his fantasy with triumphs and desire. A momentary flash of consciousness brought the thought of how seemingly little decisions can change the course of life. Had he just taken her, how different things would be! He drifted back to sleep trying to catch the fleeting memory of the dream.

"Saul! Master Saul, wake up!" The voice of Aaron shattered Paul's attempt to recover from fantasy.

"Aaron, is it your God-given calling to wake me so brashly every morning?" Paul retorted, displeased that the delusion of the dream was shattered.

"Master Saul, I am very sorry, but Abad Ben Joseph said that I must get you out of the inn and to one of James Salaman's ships that is in the harbor. The Cilician Guard is searching the city. They are forcing people out into the streets. They say that Paul Gabinius, son of the former Proconsul, has either been murdered or taken captive. They are telling the people that Gabinius' son arrived in Tarsus by ship, but disappeared before his father's interment. Soldiers say that they saw him in the Jewish sector. It is also told that the treasury of the Proconsul has been robbed and that all Markus

Gabinius' wealth and papers are missing. You must dress and leave the inn quickly!"

When Paul and Aaron reached the street, Paul was alarmed by the scene that confronted them. The red tunics of the Cilician Guard seemed everywhere. People were lined against the walls of their houses as the Guard searched. Standing directly in front of the door to the inn was an elderly guardsman whom Paul recognized. He had taught Paul the art of sewing tents when Paul was young. There was no way to escape his gaze, but the soldier looked right through Paul as if he did not exist. The guardsmen were looking for dirty, thieving robbers and assassins or for the Roman, Paul Gabinius. The rich Jewish merchant and his attendant were of no interest to Rome. They passed by without arousing the interest of the Guard.

Saraphina was waiting on the dock. She was not going with Paul, but she came to assure him that she would be well provided for. Paul understood that it was her wish that he go. She held him a long time. It was unusual for a Jewish woman to embrace or show any emotion other than grief in public, but Saraphina felt that it would be a long time before she would see her son again. She had a note for him from Ahad. Ahad wrote: "The items in your stateroom will be transferred by Ismar's caravan from the port of Caesarea to Jerusalem. You do not have to become personally involved as they will be kept for you by agents of Isaac in Jerusalem."

Paul noted two Syrian soldiers standing on the upper deck of the ship. "You need not be concerned," said Saraphina. "They came on board last night. They do not know about the search for Paul Gabinius. Here is the key to your cabin," his mother added as she slipped the key into Paul's hand. "Keep it locked always." Paul again saw the mysterious smile in his mother's eyes.

Paul unlocked the cabin door. He had never been in such a large or luxurious space on a ship. The walls were hung with bright rugs from Persia designed to keep out noise and beautify the space. A curtained sleeping chamber filled one corner of the cabin, a washbasin and stand, the other. Hooks for garments had been placed in the ceiling above the wall near the door. Though the cabin was large, the space was limited. An approach to the sleeping chamber and to the washbasin had been left open, but the rest of the space was filled with trunks and leather cases. Paul unlatched the chest closest to the door. It was a trunk from Simon's tailor shop, filled with the clothing the tailors had made for a rich merchant studying in Jerusalem. A second case was filled with leather portfolios in which Paul discovered his father's legal papers. It took both Aaron and Paul to open a third chest that had leather belts and rope ties. When they removed the lid, Aaron gasped. The chest was filled with jewels and items of gold that Paul recognized as having come from his father's estates in Tarsus.

"I wonder which one of my uncles controls a band of thieves?" Paul muttered. But inwardly Paul knew it was not his Jewish relative who was the thief, but Caesar. Ahad Ben Joseph, steward of the house of Gabinius and Salaman, was indeed a good steward. Even following the death of his master, he was diligent in protecting the trust that had been given to him. Paul did not open the other chests. He knew what was in them. Nothing that belonged to Rome had been taken. Nothing that belonged to the house of Gabinius had been left behind.

Paul did not leave the cabin until the ship was well at sea. As he stepped on to the deck, the wind carried the conversation of the two Syrian soldiers to Paul. He clearly heard them mention the name of Julius Laco.

"Pardon me, sirs," Paul interrupted respectfully as he approached the Syrians. "Did I not hear the name of my friend, Julius Laco?"

"What would a Roman centurion have to do with a Jew?" one of the guards retorted.

Paul had to think quickly. "When I was last with Laco, it was at the Circus in Rome. I was invited to Caesar's box to watch the Centurion race four matched blacks that my house had provided. Laco raced them handsomely and won a bet for Caesar."

The attitude of the Syrian soldier changed immediately. "Then you will be delighted to know that Centurion Laco has been appointed over the garrison in Jerusalem. He will be serving the new Procurator, Pontius Pilate, as we will."

"Tell Laco," Paul responded, "that Saul of Tarsus sends greetings. I hope to see him at the games in Jerusalem. Perhaps he is interested in acquiring another team of horses!"

Paul could scarcely control his elation at hearing that Julius would also be in Jerusalem. He knew that the statement about horses would be confusing, but he also knew that Julius Laco would know that Saul of Tarsus and Paul Gabinius were one and the same. Had he done the right thing? Paul considered Julius his closest friend, but Julius was, after all, Roman. Would Julius even know about him? Might the news from Tarsus about the death or kidnapping of Paul Gabinius have arrived in Jerusalem? Should Paul attempt to see Julius in Jerusalem? If he did not, and Centurion Laco recognized him, would he betray Saul of Tarsus? Each wave passing under the prow of the ship brought Paul closer to the answers to his questions, closer to the place where Paul Gabinius could really die. In Jerusalem, Saul of Tarsus might truly find life.

9

Julius Laco continued his inquiry into the death of Markus Paul Gabinius. Not that it was his duty or his right, he just felt responsible. If only he had not been so quick with his sword, they might have gotten the truth from the assassin. Why he felt so deeply about Paul, Julius did not know. Though popular with his comrades and desired by the women of Rome, Julius lacked close companions. A charioteer of Caesar, he was the center of most crowds. Yet he was alone in the midst of them.

Julius did not respect himself or any of his compatriots. All the men he knew cheated at the games and lived dishonest lives to play the game of Rome. All the women in his life, including his mother, were promiscuous and immoral. Julius accepted that this was the way life was in the Roman Empire. After all, weren't all the gods of Rome lecherous and degenerate? But Paul had been a refreshing breeze in the polluted air of his existence. Paul's utter lack of pretentiousness and his naive innocence were part of his attractiveness to Julius. Paul was like a brother Julius wanted to protect.

Paul, in all his unsophisticated guilelessness, was the kind of man Julius would have liked to be. Now his friend had been hurt by Rome, and Julius wanted an answer more than Paul did. The evil of Rome had touched Paul's goodness and Julius Laco needed an explanation. He wanted evil to pay. The only way he knew to make it pay was to find the truth about Markus Paul Gabinius' death. Julius knew where to look in Rome for gossip, and he knew that in every hearsay there is a kernel of truth.

The last time Julius had visited the baths was the night he had introduced Paul to Roman society. Nothing seemed to have changed. The children of Rome were still engrossed in their endless, senseless orgy. The same wine glasses were filled; the same ladies were offering their bodies for pleasure. Julius quickly scanned the room. He was looking for someone who sat alone, someone who was not enjoying the party, someone who would like to talk.

She was so alone, she was obvious. Sitting by herself on a side couch, she was toying with a wine cup, but not drinking. Even from a distance and in the poor light, Julius could tell that she was a beauty. Her solitude had to be by choice. As he crossed the room and approached the isolated woman, Julius was startled. This was the same beauty Paul had spurned on their last visit.

"May I join you?" Julius' approach was polite and different. Ordinarily he would have simply proceeded to seduce her. These were the Roman baths. Neither male nor female expected anything different.

She started to turn away and then recognized him. "Why, you're his friend!" she said. A slight smile touched her nostalgic expression. "He's gone, you know! He left Rome and returned to Tarsus. I will never see him again. I never had the chance to tell him how sorry I am for the way I behaved that night. Oh, not that I was any different that night than any other night. He refused to take me. They have all taken me!" She pointed around the room. "All of them! And I did not care. I enjoyed it as much as they did! I presented myself to him as a gift to a virgin god. Did you know? He wanted me. I know he wanted me, but he would not take me!"

She began to sob as she tapped her silver wine cup on the table. "Never before had I felt like a tramp. I saw nothing wrong with my behavior. I was just having a good time. Everybody in Rome does it. But, oh Jupiter, I feel so cheap! At first I thought something was wrong with him. We" — she looked around the room — "we laughed about it. I told everyone about it. The fool had turned down the best in Rome. Then I watched him in the crowds. I saw him when Caesar honored his father at the funeral. He looked so handsome in his uniform, so manly, so good! I watched him and I knew. All the others are little boys playing with me as a plaything, trying to be men. Paul Gabinius did not turn me down because he is not a man. He turned me down because he is good. He is the only man to ever respect himself, and me, enough to refuse his passion." Her sobbing had become a torrent of tears. She lowered her head and ran both hands through her long blond tresses. "May the gods help me. I've fallen in love with Paul Gabinius, and he is gone. All he will ever remember is the tart he turned down in Rome." She raised her eyes and looked into Julius' face. Even through the tears and the remorse, she was a beauty.

Roman and Germania breeding, Julius thought. *With her delicate features, tear-filled blue eyes, moist red lips, and cascading golden hair that frames her face, she looks every bit the goddess.* Julius had seen her before, but he had not paid much attention to her. He had always been attracted to the more buxom Roman types. *Venus!* Julius said, mostly to himself. *How could Paul ever have turned away from this one?*

"No, Diana," she replied. She thought Julius was trying to remember her name. "Diana the tramp," she added. "I did not know what I was until I fell in love with him. Rome killed his father," she sobbed. "Now I will never see him again. Had he stayed, it might have been different. Perhaps he could have forgotten. Perhaps we could have found each other. I hate Rome!"

Julius could see, even through her tears, that she was not just prattling in self-pity. She knew something! "Rome killed his father? What do you mean?" Julius asked, finding an opening in the surge of emotion that had poured forth. Perhaps this guilt-ridden, love-sick girl had learned something about Markus Paul

Gabinius' death. She certainly knew more about his son than she had received at their one brief encounter.

"All Rome knows that the man you killed was a mercenary," she answered.

All Rome may have known, but it was news to Julius.

"He was employed as a spy and a mercenary by Caesar's Guard," she said matter-of-factly. Her bottom lip pushed out a little to emphasize that she knew what she was talking about.

Julius had to push back the desire to kiss her. What Paul had spurned, Julius would have liked to pursue. He restrained himself and asked her, "How do you know?"

"Do you think I sleep with all the Imperial Guard?" she replied sarcastically. Her lips pushed out further. Again Julius had to fight the thought of kissing and holding her. She did not wait for a reply. "My father is one of Caesar's personal guards. He said that no mercenary would attempt to kill a Roman general at the Senate unless he was paid handsomely — unless he thought he would not be punished if caught. My father," she continued, "believes that the order had to come from another general — from Dodinius, Commander of the Guard; or from Tiberius himself!"

"By the gods! I believe your father is right!" Julius said, sobered by the thought. His desire to kiss her was momentarily forgotten. "And if he is right, Paul may be in danger even in Tarsus." Her eyes widened with fear for Paul at Julius' words.

Julius thought to himself, *I will never understand women. Here is a self-proclaimed trollop who has become a virtuous little girl because she is in love with a man who spurned her. If Paul had tasted of her favors, she would simply have given them to another man and forgotten him. Paul, I could scourge you! Not only have you made a virtuous woman out of Diana, the temptress of the baths, but you are making an honorable man out of me.*

Julius assured Diana that Paul was safer in Tarsus with his Cilician Guard than he would be anywhere else. Then he patted her on the head in a brotherly gesture and left the baths. He did not notice the scantily clad daughters of Rome who flirted with the hero of the Circus.

"Arpino" — Julius spoke to his head litter bearer — "I will walk this evening. Since the streets are very crowded and the noise is louder than usual, I can get through the city better on foot. Walking will also give me the opportunity to think."

Arpino did not need to know why the master did not wish to be carried. He only knew that he and the other bearers' shoulders and feet would be less sore in the morning for not having had to carry Julius and the litter through the cobblestone streets. Besides, the Centurion risked his life in the games for fun. Maybe it was time he tried a real sport. Let him risk his life by dodging the wagons that, at times, ran their axles all the way into the side walls of the streets.

What Arpino realized from daily experience, Julius soon discovered. The streets of Rome at night were no place to think. Walking the streets required more alertness than driving the team in the Circus and more agility than training with the sword. He had to watch his step to avoid the abundance of animal excrement and the filth of the city. A melon seller called to him from a stall; then, realizing the officer of Rome lacked a servant to carry his melon, turned away. An old, burnt-out prostitute, hoping for a drunken, rich costumer, offered her wares. Julius laughed, thinking of Diana. "My lady," he said in jest, "what you charge drunken soldiers for, the young mistresses and their mothers give freely to the officers." The woman, realizing her mistake, sank into the shadows. The wheel of a passing wagon almost caught Julius' toes. He jumped from the street faster than the streetwalker had moved.

Perhaps I should cross to the Via Nova, he thought. *The marble will be easier to walk on and the avenue around the Forum will be empty*. Julius was right. The crowds thronged the commerical streets. The area around the buildings of the Empire was deserted. The Via Nova was dark, except for the torchlight reflecting on the walls of the buildings. Had it not been for the torchlight, he would not have seen the sinister shadow of a man coming from behind with a raised dagger.

Julius waited till the last moment. Just when the shadow indicated that the man was within distance of his sword, Julius wheeled. His sword made a flash of steel as it caught the flickering light. The point of his sword caught the man at his beard and pinned him against the wall. Even in the dim light, Julius could tell that his intended assassin was a swarthy little man whose black beard was turning shiny with blood. The point of the sword had just nicked his throat, but the wound was bleeding enough to make Julius' attacker drop the knife and reach for his neck. The dagger fell with a clang, useless, to the marble pavement.

"You would risk your life attacking a legionnaire for his purse?" Julius demanded. Something about the man was familiar to him.

"You killed my brother," the man replied, shaking and looking at the sharp edge of the sword and the blood on his hand when he took it away from his beard.

"Killed your brother?" Julius inquired. "I have never killed any man except in battle — not even in the Circus. Except …!" Then Julius knew why he recognized the man. "Except the murderer of the father of my friend Paul Gabinius!"

"My brother," the man murmured.

"I did not kill your brother," Julius responded. "The person who killed your brother is whoever hired him to kill General Markus Gabinius in front of the Senate. There is no way he could have escaped."

"My brother was not hired to kill Gabinius," the intended assassin responded. "He killed the General as a last resort — a desperate hope. When he saw you and another legionnaire with the General, he reacted."

"What was he after?" Julius asked.

"The ring" — came the answer — "the ring of Caesar Augustus!"

"Why would anyone want the ring? Or who?" Julius challenged, pressing the sword deeper into the fresh wound. "Tell me and I might let you live."

"It is the key to power in Tarsus," the bleeding man replied. "It insures that the word of Caesar Augustus will be kept. It binds the hand of Tiberius. The one who wears the ring can revoke even the decrees of the Proconsul in Tarsus. The man who wears the ring has the right to be heard by the Senate against even Caesar himself! Who else but Tiberius Caesar would have the Captain of the Guard hire my brother to get the ring?"

Julius' sword arm involuntarily relaxed, and the little man got free from the point. He ran for his life, but Julius paid little attention. The man was no further threat. He was of little importance. The important thing was that Julius had seen the ring hanging on a thong around Paul's neck.

"By the gods" — Julius spoke to the silent statues lining the Via Nova — "my friend Paul is in greater danger than he knows. And he has more authority and power than he could possibly believe!"

10

"**M**aster Julius! Master Julius!" Arpino's excited voice rang through the hallways, waking the whole household. In the atrium, a group of the household servants began to assemble, wondering what the emergency was and if they would be needed. General Laco appeared in the hall, still rubbing the sleep from his eyes.

"By Jupiter, this better be important, Arpino. If it's not, I'll have you whipped for coming into the house and then boiled alive for waking me!" the General exclaimed.

Through the doorway Julius' mother could be seen tossing aside the woven silk covers of the bed. "Lucia! My robe! Lucia!" she called. "My sandals! What is wrong? Is that Arpino — in the house?"

Arpino had stopped calling. He stood with an anxious expression, his eyes wandering up and down the hall looking for Julius. When Julius appeared, Arpino was so frightened he could hardly speak. The senior Laco's words "boiled in oil" had terrified the slave.

"It's all right, Arpino. All generals are like this when they first wake up." Julius tried to calm the obviously frightened man. "What is the problem? I know you would not come into the house if it were not important."

Arpino's voice was shaky and he kept glancing at General Laco as he addressed Julius.

"Sir! I was grooming your gelding — should you choose to ride him — when they came upon me!"

"Who came into the courtyard, Arpino?" Julius asked, trying to keep his patience while watching his father watch Arpino. In just a moment, unless Arpino said something important, he was going to be boiled in oil!

"A unit of the Praetorian Guard led by a centurion." Arpino's eyes widened even further with fear as he told what he had experienced. "They are waiting in the courtyard even now."

"Waiting for what?" General Laco exploded.

"To take Master Julius, under guard, to the Mamertine Prison!"

"Julius, what have you done?" his father questioned angrily. The General had disciplined himself never to show fear. Outwardly, he replaced fear with anger.

"Nothing, sir!" Julius replied in his best military fashion. "Only last night when I was walking home from the baths, a man tried to murder me. I gave him a little cut on the neck, but he got away with no serious injury."

"Who tried to murder you? Why would anyone want to kill you?" Julius' mother had gotten to the door just in time to hear her son's words.

"It was the brother of the man who assassinated General Markus Paul Gabinius, Mother." The word "assassinated" made things worse for the lady.

"I suppose, in some twisted way, he was trying to revenge your having to kill his brother," the General remarked.

"I told him it was not I who had killed his brother but the man who paid him to kill Gabinius. He said his brother had not been hired to kill the General, only to steal the ring of Augustus. His brother panicked when he saw Paul and me in uniform. I asked him who paid his brother to steal the ring and he said it was Dodinius, Commander of the Praetorian Guard, who did it on orders from Tiberius himself!"

"And now the Praetorian Guard is waiting to take you to Dodinius." The sound of disgust in his father's voice surprised Julius. "I have raised a fool! Of course Tiberius had Markus killed!" the General insisted. "That is no news! Tiberius is looking for a new Proconsul to Tarsus. He wants someone who will levy taxes and put Tarsus back into subjection. I have considered asking for the position myself. One could become very rich." General Laco stroked his beard.

"Father!" Julius said in surprise.

"Markus Gabinius was an imbecile," the senior Laco continued. "He could have been the greatest Tribune in Rome. There is even the possibility that Augustus would have made him Caesar instead of Tiberius. But the fool had to marry a Jew! If he wanted the Jew he could have made her his slave — but to marry one?" General Laco shook his head at the thought. "Then he publicly insulted Caesar — twice a fool! The idiot got *himself* killed. Now my son has to make public the secret that all important men in Rome knew!"

The Praetorian Guard could not be kept waiting long — even by the son of a general.

"Marcellus! Antony! Sextus! Metella!" The four servants and many others came from the atrium where they had heard every word spoken. "Pack all my son's belongings, and do it quickly! Arpino, saddle Julius' horse! I will send you to the palace with a request for an immediate audience with Caesar!" Arpino's fright had begun to subside. But the news that he was to ride Julius' horse and carry a message to Caesar terrified him again.

"Metella!" The General picked Metella because she was a very shapely girl. "Tell the Guard that General Laco orders that they provide escort for the General and his son to the residence of Caesar!"

Turning his attention back to Julius, the father spoke with compassion. It was the first love he had displayed since Arpino had alarmed the household. "Only Tiberius can save you from Dodinius, and he will do it only if I can come up with some way to make him think it will be to his benefit."

Tiberius was bathing alone in a large marble pool, as was his custom each morning, when he received the note from General Laco. Arpino had been only too glad to entrust the note to a servant, after which he vacated the palace of Caesar as quickly as Julius' gelding would carry him. Caesar did not relinquish the pool when General Laco and Julius were ushered into the room.

"Laco!" Tiberius called out, dismissing formality because he did not wish to return a salute while naked.

"Tiberius!" General Laco returned the salutation, following Tiberius' familiarity. "You remember my son Julius?"

"Of course! Julius is my champion at the Circus. You must win another race for me, Julius!" Tiberius moved his hand through the water in a circle, pretending his fingers were a team in the race.

"Tiberius" — General Laco was grateful he could use personal terms — "we have a problem that needs immediate attention. If it did not, I would not presume to disturb your bath."

"We?" Tiberius inquired.

"Yes. It seems that young Julius has somehow crossed General Dodinius of the Praetorian Guard. Now, should the Praetorian Guard decide to harm my son, it would be hard for my legions to accept. Since the army I command is situated just outside the city and the Praetorian Guard is stationed just inside the city, I fear for your safety and the peace of Rome." General Laco put on his most diplomatic face. "I believe I have an answer to our dilemma, if Tiberius would care to give it consideration."

Tiberius ducked his face under the water to refresh and cool it once more before his doctors came to pack it in a compress of spiced vinegar, which they said helped heal the acne. All Tiberius knew was that the fumes nearly suffocated him and his face burned for an hour. He wiped his face with his hand and nodded agreement.

"If Caesar appointed my son, Julius Laco, as Centurion over the garrison in Jerusalem, he could embark on the ships carrying Governor Pontius Pilate, which are even now ready to depart the port at Puteoli. Dodinius would have no opportunity to enrage our respective armies and Caesar, through Julius, would have a strong arm in Judaea to counteract the vacillations of Pilate." General Laco paused to let his next statement sink in. "And I would be in Caesar's debt."

Tiberius swam to the edge of the pool, placed both elbows on the tiled floor of the basin, and stuck out his tongue to catch the water falling from his nose. He shouted some obscenities at the waiting doctor and, in one breath, called for his tunic, his toga, his sandals and his stick. As he was dressing, Caesar dictated the order to accomplish General Laco's suggestion, all the while heaping profane abuse on the names of Dodinius, Laco and Pilate and, most of all, on the memory of Markus Paul Gabinius.

"What a vile, vulgar, unprincipled old man," Julius told his father as they were leaving.

"That immoral old man is Rome!" General Laco responded.

That evening, when the Roman galleys sailed for Judaea, Pontius Pilate, the new governor, Centurion Julius Laco and a company of legionnaires were on board. As Julius watched the hills of his homeland fade over the ship's stern, he thought: *Back there is Diana, hoping Paul, with whom she is in love, might sail back to Rome some day. Here am I, sailing away from Rome and wishing I could be with Diana.*

Julius' thoughts moved on, even as he looked wistfully toward the fading horizon: *I am Roman, but I no longer have any authority or power in Rome. Paul is a half Jew, and he carries around his neck the supreme authority and power of Rome! Paul, the Jew, is living in Tarsus, in the home of the Roman Procurator, while Julius Laco, the Roman, has no home left in Rome and is on his way to Judaea! The gods of Rome must be having a hilarious time! If the God of Israel is God, He must enjoy a good joke!*

Julius understood just how preposterous the situation was. He also knew that there was nothing either he or Paul could do about their respective plights. Both seemed to be driven by a force beyond themselves. Speaking to the breeze that pushed the ship forward, Julius asked: "What do you have for me in Jerusalem?" He waited to see if he could hear the gods laughing, but he heard only the movement of the ship through the sea.

11

The blue of the Mediterranean first turned dark green then light green as the galley approached the shores of Judaea. Fine sand, washed to sea by the pounding of waves, reflected the sunlight, making the difference in the colors of the water. Grasses and debris torn from the bottom and the shore of the sea by the same wave action floated on the surface of the waves. The galleys dropped their sails and the long oars began a steady beat to carry the ships between the stone breakwaters that had been built by slave labor to protect the harbor on its northern and southern extremes. Julius saw white-topped waves as they crashed up through the crevices in the rocks. Attached to the northern breakwater, but running perpendicular to the sea, was a great wall. Built into the wall and, in places, towering above it were the sentry towers of a Roman fort. To Julius' surprise, the city rising on a hill behind the fort appeared to be Roman. Built halfway between the cities of Joppa and Dor, the city of Caesarea had been named for Caesar Augustus by Herod the Great. He had intended it to serve as the center of the Roman provincial government in Judaea.

Although Julius had been assigned to the position of Centurion of the Fortress Antonia in Jerusalem, Procurator Pilate had decided to make his residence in Caesarea. The Centurion would stay in Pilate's command and presence until he and his legion escorted Pilate to Jerusalem.

The departure of Pilate and his household from the galley was impressive. A line of soldiers, their breastplates, shields and spears sparkling in the bright sun and the reflected light from the surging sea, framed both boundaries of the sea wall. The standards of Tiberius waved in shimmering gold and red against the blue-green background of the sea. Except for those disembarking and the legion standing in dress review, no one could be seen on the docks or on the shore.

Julius had not seen the Procurator on the long sea journey. Pilate and his wife had enjoyed the luxury of having their own galley and their own slaves to attend them. Julius and his legion were the first to disembark, but he did not have the good fortune to stretch his legs or explore the city. The legion had to join the garrison already assembled on the wall to welcome Pilate to his new post.

Tiberius had been searching for a man to fill the post vacated by the death of Valerius Gratus. Senator Sejanus had taken advantage of General Gabinius' outbreak at the supper following the General's Triumph to recommend Pilate to the position. Sejanus had mistakenly taken Tiberius' remarks as being simply a denunciation of the Jews. He had not understood the economics involving Tarsus. Sejanus considered the Jews his personal archenemies. Mistaken or not, he could have found no better ally than Pilate. The new Procurator was a man of little stature with a stern and mean disposition. He had ordered the legions to be prepared for a military departure from the galley as a display of force to the Jews — even though no Jews were present. He also had ordered the legions to carry standards on which were depicted the portrait of Tiberius. He knew that any Jew in the vicinity of the docks would consider this an act of idolatry and he wanted the report carried to the priests in Jerusalem.

As the troops were dismissed, an officer of the Caesarean garrison turned to Julius: " Centurion Laco" — the officer was of the rank of a principes, which indicated that he had a great amount of experience and time in the army, but no political power — "we received word of your presence from the first dispatch of the galley. You would have been given formal recognition had it not been for duty to the Procurator."

"Our duty is always to put the Procurator first," replied Julius.

"Yes," responded the Principes, "but if the Procurator marches into Jerusalem with the same presentation of the standards of Tiberius, our duty will be to save his life and restore peace."

"What do you mean?" asked Julius.

The Principes smiled at the Centurion's lack of knowledge. "I mean," he replied, "the Jews will consider the standards a graven image and there will be hell to pay. Their one God is so jealous that He will not allow any other gods in His dominion — not even the human god, Caesar!"

"But I see statues to Caesar from this very spot," Julius rejoined.

"This is Caesarea, not Jerusalem; and I am Popygos, not the centurion in command of the Fortress Antonia. If I were Laco and not Popygos and I wanted to live, I would learn the difference quickly!"

"The Jews cannot be that bad nor that dangerous," Julius said, thinking of Paul's humility and innocence.

"You have one hundred legionnaires to protect Rome's interests in Jerusalem, the capital of a nation of millions of people. There are Jews, and there are Jews! Some Jews called Zealots hate Romans. Some Jews hate other Jews. Some Jews just hate everything. Jews called Pharisees are defiled if a Roman comes through the gate of their house. Jews called Sadducees will invite important Romans to dine with them. Pharisees and Sadducees both worship in the same Temple and have the same High Priest; but once they leave the Temple or the Jewish court, they will not speak to each other. The Zealots will kill a Roman if they can, but they will kill a Sadducee or a tax collector just as quickly. The Jews also have their prophets!" Popygos sneered when he said the word.

"Prophets?" inquired Julius.

"In addition to their historical prophets to which, like Roman gods, they give supernatural power, there are magicians who meander through the country amazing their followers. One they call John the Baptist lives in the south near the Dead Sea. He has a nasty habit of calling King Herod an insidious fox and an adulterer. That one could cause trouble! There is a new prophet from a place called Galilee in the north. This one, it is reported, tells his followers to love their enemies. The Pharisees, who preach righteousness, hate the Baptist, who preaches the same thing. The people who are not righteous love him — because he calls Herod to the righteousness they do not have! The Pharisees hate the Galilean who preaches love because they have none; he reveals their own unrighteousness. The Jews are a bizarre people!"

By the time Popygos had finished his commentary on the Jews, he and Julius had reached the officers' quarters. "I have found only one clever statement made by a living Jewish prophet. The one from Galilee, called Jesus of Nazareth, was asked what to do about Roman taxes. He asked those questioning him whose image was on the coin! They replied, 'The seal of Rome.' Jesus answered them, 'Give to Caesar the things that belong to Caesar.' No one ever got to be Caesar of Rome by being good or virtuous. Tiberius is Caesar because he has power and an army. Give to Caesar the things that belong to Caesar. It is very good advice for a Jew — or for a Roman. This Jesus of Nazareth is one Jewish prophet who tells the truth!"

Julius remembered his last encounter with Tiberius. *Very good counsel indeed*, he agreed, as he laid his head on the first unmoving bed in weeks. He had not "rendered unto Caesar," and it had cost him his chance to enjoy Diana, his future in Rome, and his bed. *Very good counsel indeed*, he sighed, as he collapsed into much-needed sleep.

12

Julius' duties in Caesarea were limited. He would not assume full responsibilities until Pilate moved to Jerusalem. Most of the Procurator's time would be spent in Caesarea where he could enjoy the sea breezes in the hot climate of Judaea and live in a more Roman style. He would take up residence in the Herodian Palace in Jerusalem only when matters of state demanded his attention. Julius, however, would not have the luxury of returning to Caesarea with Pilate. Once Julius went to Jerusalem he would stay in Jerusalem. Therefore, he took every possible moment to enjoy Caesarea.

There was much to enjoy. Caesarea served as a showpiece of Roman culture. In the evenings there were plays in the enormous amphitheater where the audience could hear every word spoken by the actors and still enjoy the evening sea breeze. Herod the Great had built an enormous temple dedicated to Caesar and Rome. The population of the trading village was a mixture of Jews and non-Jews from all over the Mediterranean. Julius enjoyed bargaining for papyrus on which he could write letters to Rome, boxes of Phoenician cedar, perfumes from Egypt and chains of gold. During one of Julius' shopping excursions a merchant ship entered the harbor. In his absence, Popygos interrogated the few arriving passengers, including a young Jewish merchant prince, Saul of Tarsus, who arrested Popygos' curiosity.

"Your papers are in order, Saul Salaman." Popygos studied the face of the rich Jew. This one was too young to have accrued such wealth and status. "You are perhaps related to the Salaman family whose ships carry cargo between Rome and Caesarea?" he inquired.

"The same," Saul answered. "I am a nephew on my way to study religion at the school of Gamaliel in Jerusalem. I am at the same time escorting the trade goods of my uncle, James."

This confirms my belief that all Jews are absurd when it comes to religion, Popygos thought. *A young man of great wealth who ought to be making love to beautiful women is on his way to study a God who condemns such things as sin.* Popygos kept his thoughts to himself. Knowing that inspection of the trade goods might be ill-advised since Rome had given permission for their transportation, Popygos decided to scrutinize some of the personal goods of the young Jew. "I will have to check your personal baggage to see that no contraband is being carried from Tarsus to Jerusalem. The Zealots have used personal pouches to smuggle weapons."

Saul cringed as a trunk was opened. What would this poor soldier think if he discovered the goods from the house of Gabinius? The trunk contained only Saul's Jewish clothing. Popygos passed over the next trunk and chose one covered in leather. When the second trunk was opened, more of Saul's new clothing came to view. *The student of religion will do more than study in Jerusalem,* Popygos observed, smiling. He recognized that much of the attire was designed to be worn at festive occasions. Not to further disturb the clothing, Popygos placed his hand on top of the pile and pushed. Something under his hand was hard and unmoving. He pulled the clothing back to reveal the most beautiful sword he had ever seen. The scabbard was inlaid with silver and ivory. The hilt of gold contained a large ruby fashioned into an image of the Roman eagle and the Roman crest. This was a weapon, but not the kind used by the Zealots. Had any ordinary Jew been in possession of such a sword, Popygos would have arrested him immediately.

"This sword belongs to you?" he questioned, his eyes intently watching the eyes of Saul.

"Yes, a present from a friend in Rome," he lied. Saul knew that the sword of Markus Paul Gabinius in the hands of a Jew would bring suspicion.

"And what would a Jewish merchant need with such a sword?" Popygos continued, probing further.

"Need! No one needs a sword like that one! It would be unholy to place such beauty into the bowels of an enemy! I have no need of it, but I carry it to sell to some officer in the garrison at Jerusalem. I will use the funds as an offering in the Temple!"

"What would you take for such a treasure?" inquired Popygos, wishing he could afford to own the sword. *What would the fine aristocrats think should I wear such a sword?* he thought.

"Ten talents," Saul replied, wanting to make the sword expensive but not beyond reason.

"Ten talents," echoed Popygos. "Why, by Hercules!" he exclaimed, his countenance falling, "you will never sell that sword in Jerusalem. Not even a centurion has that kind of funds."

"It could be yours," whispered Saul.

"Who would I have to kill?" Popygos replied.

"All you would have to do," answered Saul, "is to see that all of my cargo gets safely to Jerusalem."

"That I can do!" exclaimed Popygos. "I will be escorting the Governor to Jerusalem within days. I can see that your goods are carried to Jerusalem with the army goods."

"Good," said Saul. "It is done! You may take your sword now if you wish." He was delighted to get out of the inspection so easily and to get his goods transported so cheaply.

"What if I just keep the sword and do not deliver my end of the bargain?" Popygos asked.

"If you were not an honest man, you would be wearing the rapier now," replied Saul. "What could I, a Jew, do about it? The sword will truly be yours when you deliver my goods to the residence in Jerusalem that my servant indicates."

Saul left Aaron and Popygos standing in the midst of his treasure. He was convinced that Popygos would be so eager to show off his new possession that he would not check the remaining baggage. Saul was right. Because Popygos could not wait to show Centurion Laco his prize, he immediately went to the market to find him.

When Popygos found Julius, he waited for Julius to spot the sword. He did not have to wait long.

"That sword — where did you get it?" Julius demanded.

"From a Jew," Popygos responded quickly, afraid he had done something wrong.

Julius' hand went to his sword as he looked around at the local merchants. He thought Popygos meant one of them.

"Not one of these merchants," replied Popygos. "He was on an incoming merchant ship." Fear gripped him as he saw Julius' response. "I have done nothing wrong! The Jew said I could earn the sword by seeing that his goods got safe passage to Jerusalem. He is a wealthy merchant, the nephew of one of the Jewish shipping families. He can be easily found if you need to verify my statement!"

"What was his name?" demanded Julius.

"Saul — Saul Salaman of Tarsus," replied Popygos, his fear mounting because of Julius' reaction to his explanation. At the name "Saul," Julius' face broke into a large smile. This change in the response of the Centurion confused Popygos.

"Is something wrong, Centurion Laco?" Popygos asked, unsure at that precise moment of his personal relationship with Julius.

"Everything is fine, Popygos," Julius assured him. "In fact, I know this man Saul." Then, playing Paul's deception, Julius added: "I gave him that sword."

"You gave this sword to a Jew?" Popygos' eyes moved back and forth from the sword to Julius' face.

"Yes! I gave him the sword to protect him from the ladies of Rome. He was the guest of Tiberius Caesar at the Circus in Rome."

"Tiberius Caesar?" Popygos swallowed hard.

"He is not all Jew," Julius explained. "His father was a very important Roman general, and he has the personal guarantee of Augustus Caesar. That Jew is a very powerful man!" exclaimed Julius.

"I will offer to return his sword when I get to Jerusalem," responded Popygos. "Because he has the right to Roman protection, I cannot earn the sword."

"No, it is only a toy to him. If he did not want you to have it and you had taken it, you would be in a great deal of trouble. But he gave it to you, so there is no problem. Besides, Popygos, hanging on your belt it looks distinguished. It would look ridiculous hanging from the prayer cloth of a Jew."

Popygos laughed at the silly picture Julius had painted. Then he shifted his new sword so the jewel in the hilt could reflect the evening sun. As he and the Centurion walked toward the garrison, Popygos watched Julius Laco closely. He also decided that when he saw the Jew again he would be careful. *In fact*, he thought, *I need to serve the Centurion very well.* To think that Laco personally knew Tiberius Caesar — as did the Jew — was staggering. *Yes*, he said to himself, *I will serve Laco well. And when I meet the Jew again, I will treat him like a Roman — like a special Jew!*

13

Aaron understood why Saul had to leave him with the baggage and why Saul was in such a hurry to get away from Caesarea. It would be dangerous to trust a Roman, even a friend like Julius Laco. Loyalty to friendship and allegiance to Rome could conflict. Julius of the Circus and Centurion Laco could be quite different. At least one uncertainty of Saul's would soon be put to rest. Now he was certain Julius would know that he was in Judaea. Knowing he was there and finding him in the maze of religious Judaism was another matter. Because he had left Aaron in the position of servant, Saul felt that Aaron was not in any personal danger. Aaron was not so sure.

Saul found his way to the marketplace right behind Popygos. He did not wait to see the meeting between the Principes and the Centurion but stopped at the booth of the Jewish gold merchant where he identified himself as Saul Salaman, nephew of Isaac Salaman of Tarsus. He explained that because he was having trouble with the Roman Centurion in the fort, he needed quick and unnoticed passage to Jerusalem. Had Julius and Popygos not been so engrossed in their conversation about the sword, they might have noticed a man pass them, leading a camel. The camel was headed toward the inland caravan road to Jerusalem. On its back was a pack and a rider dressed in the clothing of a Bedouin. The Bedouin, strangely enough, was holding on for his very life.

The two guards took Aaron into a small sentry room. It was bare except for a small table and a bench. One rectangular-shaped window had been cut high in the circular rock wall. When the

Romans left the room, one guard slammed the thick wooden door shut behind him. Aaron, investigating the room, discovered that the wall was wet from the temperature of the sea that pounded against the other side of the wall. Not knowing what else to do, he sat on the bench and waited.

It was dark when the door opened and a guard holding a torch escorted two Romans into the room. Aaron recognized Popygos and noted that Saul's sword was still hanging from his side.

"You are the slave of Saul Salaman?" the other Roman asked.

"I am his attendant," Aaron explained.

"Stand when a Roman centurion addresses you," commanded Popygos.

"Why is your ear not pierced? Why are you not wearing the earring of a slave?" inquired Laco.

Before Aaron could respond, Popygos answered Julius' question. "Jews do not mark slaves as Romans do, sir!"

"I am not a slave, but I have been assigned by the family of Salaman to attend to Master Saul," Aaron replied.

"Who is the head steward of the house of Salaman?" Popygos asked, hoping to catch Aaron in a lie and thus prove that the sword was not the same one Laco was thinking about.

"Ahad Ben Joseph," Aaron returned.

"He speaks the truth," Popygos assured Julius.

"You need not be afraid, young Aaron" — Julius spoke softly, attempting to calm the frightened boy. "I am a friend of Saul of Tarsus, except when I knew him he was called Paul Gabinius, son of the Proconsul."

"I know no Roman Paul Gabinius," Aaron replied. "But I know who my master is — he is Saul Salaman. He owned that sword" — Aaron pointed to Popygos' side — "and he gave it in good faith that all his goods would be delivered to him at Jerusalem, including me!"

Julius laughed at Aaron's sudden courage and impudence. "I am his friend. Being his friend got me sent to this place forsaken by the gods. This sword is a message to me. By placing this sword on Legionnaire Popygos, Saul knew that I would know he was here. Why did he leave without seeing me?"

"My master is a Pharisee," retorted Aaron. "A Pharisee has no relationship with Gentiles. I know nothing of Paul Gabinius, but I do know that my master can not be in the school of Gamaliel and have anything to do with Romans."

At the word "Pharisee" Popygos cringed. "What is the matter, Popygos?" Julius inquired, noticing his expression.

"You know about Pharisees — the religious fanatics! I told you about them! The Jewish prophet Jesus called them glorified tombs — white-washed on the outside and full of rottenness on the inside. If your friend has become a Pharisee, he is dead to all feeling and relationship."

"You seem to know a great deal about this Jewish prophet, Jesus," Julius rejoined.

"He is the only Jew I know of who tells the truth. I hope Saul Salaman is the second." Popygos patted the scabbard of the sword. "I will take his belongings to him, including his servant." He looked at Aaron. "Then I will tell you if he is your friend Paul Gabinius or a Pharisee."

The journey from Caesarea was excruciating and overly prolonged. Pilate chose to travel north up the Plain of Sharon to Shikmona — crossing the tip of the Carmel Mountain range — east through the Kishon Valley to the Jordan, south along the river to Jericho, then west to Jerusalem. The Procurator wanted to explore the possibility of building an aqueduct to bring mountain waters from Carmel to Caesarea. He also desired to circumvent the mountains of Samaria and get a feeling for the territory he had been sent by Caesar to control. The sea route by way of Joppa would have been more pleasant because of the prevailing breeze, but it would also have been more crowded and more exposed. What Pilate had not counted on was that the deep-rutted river highway teemed with creeping caravans, filling the air with dust.

"We will be able to bathe at Jericho and rest at the inn there," promised Popygos.

"A bath and a real bed will be a blessing," replied Julius.

"A centurion who has never slept on the ground and eaten dust for dinner?" mocked Popygos.

"A centurion who prefers the perfumed waters and the silk sheets of the baths of Rome!" Julius exclaimed.

"Ah!" rejoined Popygos. "After the road and the inn at Jericho, the musty air and the rope beds of the Fortress Antonia in Jerusalem will feel good. I will think about you when I feel the spray of the sea and the swinging of a hammock in the breeze of Caesarea."

The bath at Jericho turned out to be a small bend in the Jordan. Following Popygos' lead, Julius slipped away to the spot. The water was shallow and the bottom was filled with small rocks, but willow branches hid them from the eyes of travelers, and the water was cold and refreshing. It seemed that Popygos knew every inch of Judaea and every custom of the Jews. The rest of the Roman guard bathed outside the camp of the Jericho militia from water pots brought from the river and from wells. Popygos slept in a tent on some straw, while Julius, being a ranking officer, slept inside the militia headquarters. The one inn was reserved for Pilate, his family and his servants. Julius felt sorry for Popygos in the tent, but he soon found that the officers' quarters were filled with filth and rats. Popygos opened a corner of the tent, pulled more straw under his head, looked into the star-filled sky and chuckled at his good fortune in not being an officer.

Early the next morning their caravan broke camp. Julius spotted young Aaron loading Saul's property and trade goods. "Popygos, have you taken care of your promise to my friend, Saul of Tarsus?"

"There's nothing to take care of," Popygos answered. "It all travels with the goods of the Procurator. Who do you think would dare touch anything that belongs to Pilate? Besides, Saul's servant Aaron watches like an eagle."

"I have noticed that fact. Servants are usually not so attentive to serve their masters when they are not around. Do many slaves run away?"

"In Jerusalem they do," replied Popygos. "There is a lack of discipline. While the rich Jewish merchants and the Roman officers enjoy themselves, their slaves run away to Syrian Damascus. No one has been watching this Aaron since his master left him at Caesarea, yet he has faithfully tended to all his master's business. Your friend, Saul of Tarsus, must have remarkable control over his servants — but you said that he is a powerful man!"

"More powerful than even he knows," Julius answered. His expression was thoughtful, as if in his mind he were a long distance away.

The caravan followed a winding road that carried them upward from the river through desolate country. The landscape was one of barren hills and deep ravines. Once in a while a wild goat jumped from the narrow road. The goats were the only sign of life, except for isolated clumps of grass or wilted wildflowers.

"Popygos, why haven't we encountered other caravans?" questioned Julius.

"Perhaps they have been informed that we are on the road," answered Popygos. "Another caravan would not stop them from traveling — but who wants to come face to face on a narrow winding road with the new Procurator and a Roman guard? No matter how large the caravan or how many camels in the train, they would be the ones to turn around. Have you ever tried to turn around even one camel when it does not want to go? It's impossible! They just will not walk backward!"

Whey they arrived at a sizable upgrade, the end of which Julius could not see, the procession came to a halt. "We are one hour from Jerusalem," stated Popygos. "The city is located on the crest of this hill. The animals need to be rested here before they make the climb."

A legionnaire came to order Centurion Laco to report to Procurator Pilate. When Julius returned, he informed the officers, in Popygos' hearing, that Pilate had ordered the legion to be divided into two parts. The leading troop would consist of Julius, as Centurion, and the lancers, half of whom would carry unfurled standards of Tiberius. Pilate would follow the standard bearers in a Roman chariot. Behind Pilate would come the rest of the legion, the supplies and, finally, the militia from Jericho. The supply caravan and the militia would not enter Jerusalem. Pilate would enter the city with the crimson and gold of Rome flowing so that all the city would know that he, Pilate, represented Tiberius Caesar, the ruler of the world!

"By the gods," whispered Popygos, "the man is mad!"

It took a while to form the procession, but eventually it was done. The uniformed company marched up the long hill toward Jerusalem to the caustic command of trumpets. The red and gold banners bearing the image of Tiberius could be seen for miles.

Half an hour into the uphill march, even the trained legionnaires were panting for breath and it was all the standard bearers could do to hold the colors of Tiberius upward. When the road narrowed between two crags of rock, the legion was pressed close together to maintain parade march. Suddenly a standard bearer pitched forward. Julius thought the man had passed out — and no wonder! Thirty minutes forced march in desert heat carrying a standard could lay low the stoutest man. Then a stone stuck Julius in the chest, making a clanging sound on his breastplate. Spears and stones coming from both sides of the rock wall filled the air.

"Centurion!" Popygos shouted at Julius. "Order retreat! We need to get into the open where we can use our lances and our chariots. We must fall back and form a defensive line." Popygos knew that he was taking a significant risk. How could he, a principes, tell a centurion what to do? But Laco had never fought as the commander of a legion, nor had he faced an ambush. Popygos knew that unless Julius gave the command to retreat, the legionnaires would be killed one at a time. Whoever their attackers were, they would attack again and again unless they were forced into the open.

Julius heard Popygos' shout, but he gave his own order: "Trumpeter, sound the retreat! As soon as you clear the rocks, sound assembly! Officers, have your men place their shields as a barrier before the Procurator. We must not let his life be endangered!"

Behind Julius the company was in total disarray. The second section of the legion was trying to get around Pilate, his household and his goods. Women from Pilate's entourage were running and screeching — although they did not know which way to run. A donkey, frightened by the screams, was kicking in every direction, flinging cargo all over the road. The Jericho militia was swept over by camels, asses and supply wagons trying to get away from the sounds of the trumpet.

The legion responded to Julius' orders as if they were one man. The skirmish did not last long. As soon as the protective shields were in place, the legion was outside the range of rocks and lances. The enemy, which Julius had felt and heard but not seen, must have had no weapons to fight at the greater distance, for hostilities ceased. Julius had two dead men — both of them standard bearers!

Popygos walked close to Julius. "Sir!" — he used formal address in case others heard him — "the onslaught seemed to be aimed at the standards. Perhaps the image of Caesar is offensive to their religion."

"What if it is?" asked Julius with great irritation in his voice. "Caesar is the god of Rome. Dare they attack Caesar?"

"Two dead men and a legion behind their shields unable to advance tells me they do dare. We are too far from the Antonia Fortress to get word to Jerusalem to send help. You cannot get aid from the militia in Jericho, for they have a caravan of goods in front of them on this very narrow road. Even so, you must protect the Procurator. Unless you advance to Jerusalem, darkness is going to catch you on this road where our assailants can overrun you in the dark. It seems to me that it is time to do something brave and daring — something like talking to them. They know they cannot win in the long run — it is not their intention to fight all the power of Rome! The question is — how can this be settled now?"

Julius sent a runner back to Pilate, informing the Governor that he personally wanted to confront the offenders. "I do not believe that those who have attacked the Governor's party know who Your Excellency is. I believe the attack came from religious zealots who assaulted the standards of Caesar. They do not understand that the standards are not a god but a symbol of honor to the ruler of Rome. I can best protect Your Excellency and save the lives of my men by informing them that the standards are not gods and that we did not raise them to offend their god. I know Tiberius, and I believe he would want this done! Please assign Legionnaire Popygos as my aide in this matter — and as my assistant in Jerusalem."

When Pilate received Julius' message, he was furious until he read the part about Tiberius. *He was assigned by Caesar, himself!* he thought. *He calls Caesar "Tiberius"! If word gets back to Caesar that there was a riot before I even got to Jerusalem, he might question whether I can handle this post.* Pilate was more frightened by the possibility of Caesar's displeasure than by the attack. Thus he sent a message back to the man between him and the stones: "Tell the Centurion to handle the matter as he chooses. If this Popygos can be of help to him, he may have him!"

Julius and Popygos approached the narrows. "I am Centurion Julius Laco, commander of the Fortress Antonia. I am escorting the new procurator, Pontius Pilate, to Jerusalem," he shouted to the shadows. "You do not wish for Rome to send her armies to Judaea to crucify millions of Jews! Should the Procurator be harmed, that is what would happen. I understand that you are offended by our standards and the image of Caesar. The Procurator guarantees separation of powers. He will not interfere in the rule of your priests, neither will he raise images of Tiberius if it offends your religion. Caesar is not our supreme god. Our supreme god is Jupiter. Jupiter has no interest in Jews!" The only reply Julius received from behind the rocky cliffs was the cry, "Jehovah is Lord!" He and Popygos walked through the narrows unharmed.

When the caravan entered Jerusalem, the turrets and the domes of the city were glowing with the light of sunset. That was the only gold and scarlet to be seen. The trumpets were silent as Pilate and the legion, with banners folded and lances lowered, slipped into the Fortress Antonia.

Only that night in the privacy of his bed did Pilate cry out: "Damn you, Jupiter! Damn you, Mars and Zeus and Apollo! Damn all the gods of Rome! Damn you, Tiberius, for sending me to this godforsaken land! Jehovah, the God of the Hebrews, has humiliated us all; and He did it with sticks and stones!"

14

Saul traveled from Caesarea to Jerusalem by a different route. Without a caravan, he could take the more direct trail through the mountains of Samaria. The camel driver wanted to stay on the Plain of Sharon, following the road through Antipatris and turning east on the road from Joppa to Jerusalem. He explained to Saul that the flat country would be better for his camel. He also advised Saul that no Jew, because of religious purposes, would be caught dead in Samaria. Saul learned that someone had to walk with the camel. He also soon found that walking was more desirable than riding the beast. Yet, if one led the animal, he had to be wary of being bitten; to follow behind was even more intolerable. Saul left beast and handler at the junction of the roads to Antipatris and the city of Samaria. He chose the risk of being assailed by robbers on the trail over the longer journey by the caravan route.

Expecting only the worst after hearing the fears of the camel driver, Saul was pleasantly surprised to find himself traversing a mountain range that was covered with olive gardens, green pastures and small, isolated cottages. The sky was deep blue, the air was clean and cool, and the wind hugging the mountain valleys was filled with the scent of small, brightly-colored wildflowers. The occasional travelers Saul met greeted him warmly, though they wondered at the strange Jew who was walking through Samaria. As Saul came near the city of Samaria, the isolated cottages became estates that reminded him of Rome. He discovered that the area was populated by discharged mercenaries who had been given land by Herod. In spite of his Jewish dress, Saul had no problem acquainting himself with two former mercenaries who were traveling to what they called by the Greek name "Sebaste." Messalla, a man of Greek and Roman descent, had fought for Augustus in the Judaean campaign. He was a large man with a full, black beard that almost covered the scar that ran from his left eye across his cheek. "Everyone asks me how I got the scar, so I tell them before they ask. It is from a sword blow that nearly split my head. But what would a Jew merchant know about warfare?"

"A little," replied Saul, feeling it was safe to be himself in these isolated mountains. "My father was General Markus Paul Gabinius, the late Procurator of Tarsus."

"Gabinius! By Zeus, there was man!" Messalla exclaimed as he struck his companion on the back. His friend smiled. "Forgive my comrade for not sharing in our conversation," Messalla interrupted his exhilaration over General Gabinius. "The Turks cut out his German tongue and made Damon an ideal friend." The second man gave a gesture of greeting.

"You knew my father?" Saul questioned.

"Knew him, young man? No! The likes of me, a mercenary, does not get to know a general. Fought in his army? Yes! That is where I got this" — he pointed to the scar — "and I am proud of it too! Come! You must visit with us in Sebaste. We have a temple to Augustus, a basilica, a forum, a stadium and even an aqueduct. We have shops that a Jew could love — nine hundred yards of colonnaded streets and shops! You will think you are in Rome."

How strange life is, Saul thought. *Who could imagine that I would encounter in such a isolated and hated place as Samaria someone who served my father?*

"Why are you, a Roman, dressed like a Jewish merchant?" Messalla asked.

"I am a Jew," Saul replied. "My mother is Jewish — from the house of Salaman. My father was killed last year in Rome after receiving the Triumph."

"I wondered why the General had not received his due recognition," Messalla replied. "So he married a Jew! That is the only reason Rome would need! I would not have spoken to one dressed as a Jew except for the fact that a Jew, Jesus of Nazareth, passed through Samaria. He stopped at a village near Mount Ebal and encountered a woman of ill repute at the well. This Jew did not throw rocks at her. Instead, she tells that he revealed all of her past. He told her that God was not on Mount Ebal nor was He in the Temple in Jerusalem. He said that God is Spirit, and that men must worship Him in Spirit and in truth. She says that this Jesus of Nazareth is the Son of God! This, I do not know about! I do know I have seen no help in the gods of Greece or Rome, or in the God of the Jews!"

"I believe that the gods of Rome are not gods at all," Saul stated. "They are created by men and thus reflect the lusts and the evil that men have. I am on my way to study in Jerusalem. I want to study about Jehovah, the God of my people."

"If you find Him," Messalla replied, "ask Him why He keeps knocking the Jews down, why He doesn't allow them to enjoy life, why He does not learn to dance and frolic? The gods of Rome cannot be taken seriously and the God of the Jews has no other nature! This Jesus, according to the woman, did not condemn her but forgave her and gave her the joy of freedom from her sins. He did not care if she was Samaritan or Jew, sinner or saint! When I saw you, a Jew, in Samaria, I thought you might be a disciple of this Jesus. But the son of General Gabinius? Perhaps there is a divine guide in life. Who knows?"

"Whether I am being guided by some forecast plan, I do not know; but I have come to Judaea to learn about the God of my people. Why is there such a separation between the Jews and the Samaritans? I started this journey with a camel driver who did not want to bring me through Samaria. Now you, a Greek, tell me you are surprised to find a Jew in Samaria unless he is a disciple of this Jesus."

"The Samaritans are descendants of the tribes of Israel whose kingdom was destroyed by Babylonia," came the reply. "They are the children of the people who were not carried into exile. While their brothers were in captivity, those who had been left in their homeland married people foreign to the Jews and assimilated beliefs from their religions. In order to keep His people pure, Jehovah forbade the returning Jews to have anything to do with the Samaritans. That was eight hundred years ago, and this God of Israel does not change His mind! I would not tell the Pharisees in Jerusalem that I was half Roman if I were you, Saul of Tarsus. The God of the Jews is afraid of anyone who is half anything."

"That's strange," Saul said. "I cannot understand how the one and only God could fear those who are not gods or repress truth from whatever culture it may come."

"This prophet, Jesus of Nazareth," Messalla thought out loud, "will not last long. Jerusalem always kills any prophet who brings new light, new ideas or new relationships. If you become a Pharisee, Saul of Tarsus, be sure not to think!"

Saul spent two days in Sebaste with Messalla and his silent friend. It was what Messalla called "Saul's last two days of freedom before becoming all Jew in Jerusalem." The friendliness and warmth of the people of Samaria, the free Roman culture of Sebaste, the reflective wisdom of Messalla and the silent companionship of the man Messalla called "Damon" gave Saul much to think on as he journeyed on to Shechem, Shiloh, Bethel and, finally, Jerusalem.

15

Saul entered the city by way of the Valley of Jehoshaphat on the Bethesda Road. He had not expected to find anything that reminded him of Rome in the buildings of the city of David, but as he entered the city gate, the Antonia Fortress rose to his left. The fortress had been built by Herod and named in honor of Mark Anthony. It was built foursquare, with four massive one-hundred-foot-high towers on each corner. The fortress guarded the north approach to the Temple. From where he stood, Saul could see the Temple to the south of the fort. The Temple was impressive, but he had seen more magnificent structures in Rome. The massive, cold stones of the fortress gave Saul an uneasy feeling. They reminded him of everything he both feared and hated in Rome. He remembered stones covered with blood at the death of his father and the flash of Julius' sword. The Antonia would be the new home of Centurion Laco. As much as Saul wanted to see his old friend, he was frightened by Julius' position as the centurion of a legion. On the towers of the Antonia stood helmeted Roman soldiers, keeping watch over the Temple courts. The ground to the north of the Antonia inclined upward, so that Saul could see part of the Temple courts as he walked. He recognized from his studies "The House of God" on the Temple's west side. To the east of the Temple, the valley fell quickly so that the ground on which the Temple stood became an unexpected pinnacle. Another valley ran through the middle of the city, dividing Jerusalem into two parts. The main part of the city lay on the western hill.

Saul turned and walked into the narrow streets that comprised the Jewish business district. He blended well with the crowd. In fact, this part of Jerusalem felt so much like the Jewish section of Tarsus that Saul expected to see the tailor shop of Simon around every turn. His ears more than his eyes found what he was looking for. The rhythm of the money-changers' call filtered through the noise of the crowd. Saul stepped sideways around a donkey cart and passed a burly guard who watched the customers intently as the coins of many nations were handled and dickered over.

Some Jewish merchants would not accept the coins of Rome because they bore graven images. Those who wished to trade with them came to the money-changers to sell Roman coins and purchase Jewish funds. The Temple had its own coins, but the money-changers in the Temple charged an exorbitant rate of exchange. The need for a better deal brought many to the money-changers in the marketplace. Some merchants were exchanging letters of credit for monies. Others were banking monies for letters of exchange. Still others attempted to trade jewels and items of gold for Roman coins. There was no set rate of exchange, so each participant tried to make the best deal possible. Insults and curses raised by impassioned voices filled the air. This is what had attracted Saul to the place. After the bargain was struck, each person ridiculed the other for having made such a trade and then placated him with another insult.

"The master wishes to buy, sell, or just feel the money?" a voice asked sarcastically.

"To establish an unlimited credit," Saul answered.

"The master thinks he is King Solomon?" came the reply with quick wit.

A turban pinned with a large sapphire graced the moneylender's head. Black hair was tied in a knot at the back and a full black beard stopped where large chains of gold encircled his neck. A loose robe flowed to wide sleeves that were embroidered in gold. His hands rested on a table filled with coins; on each finger he wore a large ring covered with precious jewels.

"Solomon would need all his wisdom to keep his riches if he brought them here," Saul answered. "I am not foolish enough to bring treasure with me. Even now the Roman guard of the new procurator guards it for me."

"Oh, a Jew with such power that Rome guards his treasure?" — the turbaned head fell backward as the money-changer laughed. "Next you will tell me that your power is so great that Tiberius, himself, seeks your pleasure!" Water filled his eyes at the humor of his taunt.

"It is also true," stated Saul, as he handed the bearded man the letter from Isaac Ben-Ami.

Jeweled fingers stroked the beard as he read. "Isaac Ben-Ami I know. I have broken bread with the brothers of the house of Salaman in Tarsus many times, but you I have not seen before. How did you come by this letter?"

"I am Saul Salaman, son of Saraphina, the sister of Ismar, James, Simon and Elkin Salaman and Athaliah Ben-Ami. I have been in training and will be a student in the school of Gamaliel. Even as I speak, Aaron is on his way to Jerusalem with my personal goods. He travels with a treasure caravan that is guarded by a Roman centurion and the Procurator's guard."

"Close the shop!" the voice of the bearded man boomed. "Clean up the coins — close the shop!" he ordered again, as his jeweled hands swept the table money into a leather pouch. Assistants began to pack the monies, gold and jewels into chests. The guard moved close, his hand on the hilt of his dagger, as a potential customer complained. "What have I to do with you?" the broker asked. "Come back tomorrow. Jacob Bar Kochba has a client who is richer than King Solomon — and as wise!" Jacob added.

"I know the treasure you speak of," he whispered softly to Saul. "Who but Solomon would have it carried and protected by a Roman legion?" He placed an arm around Saul's shoulders. "Shalom, Saul of Tarsus! I am Bar Kochba, the son of the star" — he pointed to the blue star sapphire in his turban. "Welcome to Jerusalem, son of Proconsul Gabinius. Tonight we will feast at my humble home; and when Aaron arrives, we will gaze with delight on your riches."

Bar Kochba's assistants, having packed the chests and loaded them on donkeys, pulled a gate made of iron bars across the entrance of the exchange. "My goods will be taken to my treasure trove. Beggars and thieves will follow with greedy eyes." Bar Kochba smiled as if enjoying a good joke. "And my servants will show them exactly where I have stored it and the exact price they will have to pay if they wish to possess it. I have a cave and a sepulcher located in the Valley of Hinnom, south of the city. The sepulcher where my goods are guarded is located at the very back of a large natural cave. A rock wall has been built across the mouth of the cave and two ferocious lions roam freely behind the wall. In front of the wall, a leper colony have been given shelters that I provide for them. When anyone approaches they call out: 'Unclean, unclean!' Could the treasury of Tiberius be safer?" Bar Kochba roared with laughter. "The lepers are afraid of the lions, but they are grateful for a safe place to sleep. Potential thieves are more afraid of the lepers than they are of the lions or my servants. I have not had the courtesy of finding out if my treasure is safe — the thieves will not accept my challenge." Bar Kochba could hardly contain himself at the thought of the game he played and the stakes should anyone challenge him. "But to have Tiberius' legions keep Tiberius from taking something Tiberius wants — servants of the master of all thieves protecting your treasure from their master — Saul of Tarsus, I bow before you, the wizard of the game!" Bar Kochba made a mock bow of homage before Saul.

The house of Jacob Bar Kochba was a large one. The wall surrounding its courtyard took up half of the side of one street. Saul noted that the top of the wall had been implanted with sharp pieces of brass and pointed pottery shreds. The doorway opened into a tiled court.

As they entered the court, Jacob Bar Kochba turned to Saul. "Peace be on you" — Jacob waited for the proper reply.

"And on you, peace," Saul responded.

Jacob placed his right hand on Saul's left shoulder and kissed his right cheek; then reversing the action, he placed his left hand on Saul's right shoulder and kissed his left cheek. A servant ran forward, carrying a copper basin filled with water. "For the washing of feet," Jacob said, as he loosened his sandals. The servant poured water over Jacob's feet, rubbed them with his hands and wiped them with a napkin. Then the servant turned to Saul. "Please wash your feet!" Jacob instructed. "In the market, I am the son of the star and I trade with men of all nations. When I enter my door, I am Jacob of Judaea and I follow the traditions and laws of my people."

After Saul's feet were washed, they entered the main door of the house. Jacob Bar Kochba removed his turban and handed it to the servant who had washed his feet. He bowed his head before an older servant, who poured oil mixed with spices upon the black hair of Jacob. Jacob indicated that Saul was to receive the anointing oil as well. After Saul had received the anointing, the servant offered Jacob a dipper of water. Jacob drank and then presented the remaining water to Saul. After Saul had drained the remaining water from the dipper, Jacob said, "We will talk of your plans and your mission in Jerusalem; then we will put bread and salt between us."

Jacob led Saul up a stairway to a guest room located in an open area near the end of the court. The room was furnished according to the Roman style, with a table and three couches located on three sides of the square table — servants were already placing dishes on the table. Jacob indicated that Saul was to take the couch on the left. Saul looked for additional guests or family, but there were none. Jacob blessed the food, but did not eat. He first looked at Saul and asked, "Now tell me the truth, Saul Salaman of Tarsus. What are you doing in Jerusalem?"

It was as if a dam had broken and a waterfall poured out. Saul had spoken neither of his grief at the death of his father nor of his pain at being separated from his Roman past. Nor had he expressed his loneliness and the remorse resulting from his separation from his mother. His anger at the way Rome had betrayed him and his father had remained buried inside while he put on a brave, assured front before his uncles of the house of Salaman. He had also hidden from young Aaron his deepest feelings and his fears of being ridiculed or embarrassed by the school of Gamaliel. Even in the market he had covered up his anxiety and the apprehension he felt at meeting Bar Kochba. Now Saul told all to this strange man with the black beard and the penetrating eyes who, in some mysterious way, seemed to know already what was in his heart.

When Saul had finished his tale and exhausted his emotions, Jacob tore off a piece of roasted mutton and handed it to Saul. "There is salt between us," Jacob affirmed, his eyes filled with compassion. "We are bound together by a solemn covenant. In giving you the meat, I pledge you every drop of my blood. While you are in Jerusalem, no evil shall come to you. While you are in Jerusalem, we will be as brothers! Now you will meet the house of Bar Kochba." Jacob clapped his hands and two women appeared from behind a curtain as if they had been listening and waiting all the time. Both were dressed in brightly-colored, embroidered, loosely-flowing dresses made from muslin. The older of the women was unveiled.

"This is my wife, Hannah. Like the mother of Samuel, she prays that we might have a son. If we are to know that blessing, Jehovah will have to visit us, as He did Abraham and Sarah." Jacob smiled at his wife. "This is our only child, our daughter, Esther. I named her Esther after the Jewish wife of Ahasuerus, King of Persia, the richest Jewess who ever lived. She is a virgin! I have had many offers for her hand in marriage, but I have turned them all down. She will marry a fortune as great as my own. If I cannot have a son, I will have the richest Jew in the world for a son-in-law!" Jacob laughed with delight at the prospect. Esther lowered her eyes in embarrassment.

Saul could not see Esther's features — her veil covered her face — but he could tell she had the dark complexion, hair and eyes of her father. As he studied her face, without her looking at him, he had an amusing thought: *What if, behind the veil, she also has a beard?*

Saul's thoughts were interrupted by Jacob. "This is your house. You will do me honor if you choose to stay with us during your studies in Jerusalem. I have no son to keep you company, but it would be pleasant for me to treat you like a son and teach you my ways. I would expect no compensation for your lodging as you will be my guest. Should you choose to do business with me, however, I would expect a twenty percent fee."

"Five percent," Saul rejoined.

"Fifteen percent," Jacob argued.

"Five percent," Saul insisted.

"Ten percent is normal," Jacob stated.

"I then will pay a standard ten percent," Saul stipulated.

Jacob Bar Kochba shrieked with amusement as he lifted a piece of mutton. "He is offered the hospitality of my home and does me the honor of paying only the standard commission. King David had it wrong. He should have said, 'You prepare a table before him and he treats you as an enemy.' But, Saul of Tarsus, you have proven to me that you are who you say you are. The last man who made me enjoy losing money to him was Isaac Ben-Ami."

"You will not be losing money at ten percent, Bar Kochba, for Aaron brings great treasures," Saul replied.

"When a Jewish moneylender plans on making twenty percent and only makes ten, he has taken a ten percent loss," answered Jacob. "I will see how much I have lost when I see the value of the shipment. Now, I will take my leave and allow my wife to console me for my great business failure today. I will think of how much money I could have made at twenty percent from the house of Salaman. Then I will picture Isaac Ben-Ami's wife, Athaliah, and tomorrow I will feel better. It is too bad that Saul of Tarsus is not married! Tonight I will dream that Saul Salaman is married to the twin of Athaliah, and I will have my revenge for losing ten percent to a Jew who has pretended that his father was a Roman! Since this is now your house, may I depart with your permission?" Jacob quipped.

Saul folded his hands as if in prayer and, with his elbows on the table, placed his hands to his lips in a blessing: "Depart in peace," he said, giving the usual salutation of a host.

Esther, as she left the room, looked over her shoulder at Saul in bewilderment. She had never seen her father so taken with another man before. *He is a nice-looking prince of Judaea*, she thought. *But he is not serious or pious enough to be a Pharisee. He made blunders in the correct religious procedure as a guest in our home. Perhaps time in the school of Gamaliel will make him more acceptable — since father likes him.* She blushed at the thought.

Saul, seeing the slight movement of the veil and the flush that came to Esther's face, misinterpreted it as female excitement. *She does not look like Uncle Ismar*, Saul thought, remembering that he had been told that Athaliah did. *But under a veil, who can tell*, he reasoned. *I must remember the surprise another Jacob got when he thought he had married beautiful Rachel but woke up with cross-eyed Leah.* The sound of Jacob Bar Kochba's guffaws followed him through the courtyard.

16

The school of Gamaliel was not so much a school as a gathering twice each day in the courtyard of Gamaliel's home for study and discussion. What the arena was to the Roman, the seminary was to the Jew. It was Gamaliel's theory that a constant reading of the sacred books would encourage good actions and unimpaired thoughts. The constant repetition of meditation and action would produce good habits, and good habits would result in proper character. Virtuous character would make a man pleasing to God. Having seen the results of Rome's affiliation with gods of immoral attributes, Saul longed to be virtuous enough to feel himself acceptable to God.

Each assembly began with the reading of portions of Scripture. After the portions had been repeated many times to promote memory retention, Gamaliel explained them. Finally the students shared in a discussion about the application of the Scriptures to daily life so all could live a virtuous life.

Those attending the school had already been affected by the traditions formed by two contemporaries of King Herod — the teachers Shammai and Hillel. Shammai had been an irate, demanding, aloof man. The Pharisees influenced by his life and teaching were sticklers for the detail of the Law. Hillel had been amiable, optimistic and broad-minded; his followers were the same. Shammai saw a Jewish religion based on numerous regulations. Hillel saw a Jewish religion based on the text of Leviticus 19:18, "Thou shalt love thy fellow as thyself." Although Gamaliel himself was a follower of Hillel, who had become the honored head of the leading court of Judaea, the Sanhedrin, his school included Pharisees of both persuasions. The arguments, at times, were bitter and hostile.

One day, after Gamaliel had lectured on the perfection of the sacred writings, the two factions debated how literally the Law had to be interpreted. Those from the background of Shammai argued that the interpretation had to be literal and exact. The followers of Hillel, letting Gamaliel do their arguing for them, affirmed Gamaliel's teaching that the Law had to be interpreted in the light of the tradition.

"Excuse me, please, sirs!" Saul heard himself exclaim. (He had not expected to be caught up in the debate this early in his training.) "I am Saul of Tarsus, a recent arrival in your city. Does not the Prophet Ezra write that Samaritans are unclean because of their mixed marriages, and are not we Jews taught to remain separated from them? But does not the Prophet Moses also state that Israel is to be a light to the nations? How can we be a light to those on whom we cannot shine? I traveled through Samaria on my way to Jerusalem ..." Saul was not ready for the explosive movement. Fellow students almost fell over each other in an attempt to get away from him.

Gamaliel had to smile in spite of himself. "Saul of Tarsus, shalom! I had heard you were coming, but I was not informed of your arrival. Please excuse our lack of hospitality. Your question is of great interest, but the revelation of your recent journey through Samaria is of greater concern to some of my students. You are correct. The Jewish Law states that all who enter Samaria or touch a Samaritan are made unclean and thus require a cleansing ritual that lasts seven days. Anyone who touches a person who has been to Samaria but has not performed the ritual also becomes unclean. Anyone who touches someone who has touched someone or something touched by someone who is unclean becomes unclean. You have just given the class a great problem in the Law. The Law states that we cannot turn away from one who is a stranger in our midst. The Law also states that we cannot fellowship with one who is unclean. How does one reconcile an irreconcilable truth? Some of my students will now go and perform the prescribed ritual, thus missing seven sessions, losing truth and breaking the law of hospitality. Others will seek the truth and your companionship, but they will lose the right to be considered clean. I am a Pharisee, which means that I am a separatist, but I am also a child of God, which means that I cannot separate myself."

"When I was passing through Samaria," Saul continued, "I met two Gentiles who reported that a Jewish prophet, Jesus of Nazareth, had traveled through Samaria where he brought an immoral woman to righteousness and affected an entire village toward virtue. Is he a true prophet, bringing the light of Jehovah to a sin-darkened world, or a heretic who has broken the law of separation?"

"Saul! Saul of Tarsus! How can one neophyte bring such controversy and dilemma to one simple lecture?" asked the Rabbi. "How can one uninstructed traveler become entangled with Samaritans, Gentiles and Jesus of Nazareth on the short distance from the coast of Judaea to Jerusalem? Saul of Tarsus, you are going to make my school interesting — very interesting indeed! No less than the Sanhedrin itself is divided on the questions you ask concerning Jesus of Nazareth." Gamaliel raised both hands above his head in a gesture of worship. "Let us go to prayer and seek the wisdom of the Almighty, for Saul has raised questions that only Jehovah can answer."

That evening after the supper blessing, Saul shared with Jacob Bar Kochba the discussion that had occurred at the school of Gamaliel. Saul, knowing Jacob's appreciation for the outrageous, felt that his host would enjoy a good chuckle. Jacob, like Gamaliel, raised his hands, but his action was not an expression of worship but desperation. "Saul, do you not know that the power of religion is political and the control of bureaucracy is economics? Should you be treated as unclean by the Pharisees, then I will be unclean because you are living with me. If I am unclean, my exchange will be unclean. The Sadducees, who are the aristocracy — coming from Zadok the High Priest under Solomon — have the nobility and the money, and thus the power. Most of the Pharisees do not have wealth and, by their law, will not pay interest; but they will exchange money and goods. They sell something and take less than what it is worth. Then they turn around and buy an item, with the same coins I have just given them, for more than it is worth. They are fools!" Jacob emphasized his remarks with an appropriate gesture. "They are such fools that they might take seriously this religious uncleanness! We must not let them be totally foolish, for from such schlemiels I make my profit."

Jacob studied the young Pharisee intently. "Good religion can make people rich. Faulty religion keeps everyone poor: The Temple offering fails, the priests exchange no gold, the prophets buy no anointing oil, and the people lose hope and will not bargain. When the Pharisees have the law — coupled with self-interest and corrupt principles — politics are good and money flows! Yes, young Pharisee, you have much to learn both from Gamaliel and from Jacob Bar Kochba!"

The supper and the conversation were interrupted by the arrival of Aaron and the goods. Popygos placed a guard at the entrance of the courtyard, but knowing Jewish religious customs, he remained in the street. "Legionnaire Popygos brings greetings and best wishes from Centurion Julius Laco, commander of the Fortress Antonia, to Saul of Tarsus," Aaron stated on behalf of the Legionnaire. "Legionnaire Popygos regrets that he could not store your goods at the fortress, but that would be against military policy. He will leave a guard until morning. He also wants to know if he has completed the task and the fee he is holding now belongs to him."

Saul started toward the door when Jacob stopped him. "You are a Jewish prince and a student of Gamaliel. It is best that you cause him no further problems by having more contact with Gentiles. Aaron will continue to act as your servant and inform the Legionnaire that his task has been completed satisfactorily."

After the doors were shut, Jacob could hardly contain his desire to look at the goods Saul had brought. "These are trade goods from the house of Salaman?" he asked.

"No," replied Saul, "they are my personal goods. I want you to sell some of them for me so that I might use the funds during my stay at the school of Gamaliel — at our agreed fee of ten percent," he added.

When Jacob's servants unpacked the goods in the morning, they transferred most of the Roman articles to the market to be sold, placed the jewels and the gold in Jacob's storage cave, and carried the Jewish clothing to the guest room where Saul slept. After all had been seen and set in order, Jacob wrote a letter. The document was addressed to Simon, the eldest brother of the house of Salaman, because Saul's father was dead. Jacob Bar Kochba suggested the marriage of Saul Salaman to his daughter Esther. Jacob assured Simon that Esther's dowry would be large. Since Jacob had no heir, any son emanating from the union of Saul and Esther would be very rich. The contract of marriage would depend upon Esther's consent and the size of Saul's dowry. Jacob stated that Esther was a virgin who obeyed the Law implicitly and, thus, would make an ideal wife for a Pharisee.

17

Saul and Esther were betrothed, with Aaron representing Saul and Jacob representing his daughter. As Saul and Esther stood in the presence of the witnesses, Saul placed a ring on her finger saying, "See, by this ring you are set apart for me, according to the laws of Moses and of Israel."

Saul thought it strange to make such a pledge to a woman whose face he had never seen and with whom he had exchanged only casual conversation. Still, he had too much respect for Jacob Bar Kochba to refuse his offer and insult him in his own house. The betrothal would last a year. During that time, Saul would continue his studies with Gamaliel and establish himself in the Jewish community. Saul and Esther could receive one another in the presence of a family member, and Esther would help Saul learn all the particulars of the Law and the traditions.

Esther knew all the Law and the traditions. Upon their betrothal, she immediately presented Saul with an unusual phylactery. Most phylacteries consisted of small metal or leather boxes that were fastened to the hand or the forehead by straps. They contained passages of Scripture referring to the Passover and the redemption of the firstborn from Egypt. Many Pharisees thought themselves especially pious if their phylacteries were large or they were worn on the head.

Saul thought that the wearing of phylacteries in order to appear devout was ludicrous. Esther, however, was a strict Pharisee. She insisted that he wear a phylactery made from pure gold. She also presented him with a mantle woven at the corners with very long blue fringes. It was important to Esther that Saul fulfill the Law of Moses — and in such a manner that his faithfulness would be obvious at the school of Gamaliel. Again Saul felt that the fringes were ostentatious, but he wore them to please Esther. So precise were Esther's instructions as to the proper prayers, expressions, foods, courtesies and rituals that Saul felt their betrothal was more an indoctrination into pharisaical religion than a courtship.

Gamaliel noticed the changes in his student. Saul of Tarsus, who had been so full of life, challenge and questions, was becoming a traditionalist of the nature of Shammai. Like Shammai, Saul was becoming an indignant, exacting, aggravated man who gathered a following of like-minded traditionalists.

Although the Sanhedrin was not in session, members of the court walked in the silence of the Lishkat ha-Gazit, the Hall of Stones, in the wing of the Temple. Their voices, though hushed, were carried by the massive stone walls. "Saul of Tarsus, is he not the young leader of the most devout Pharisees in the school of Gamaliel?" questioned Kezia, the Ab-Bet-Din — Father of the Court — who conducted the meetings of the Sanhedrin in the absence of the High Priest.

"The very one!" replied Judah Jamnai.

Kezia knew that Judah had lost much of the Jamnai fortune to gambling. He wondered if Judah's request to appoint this Saul of Tarsus to the Sanhedrin had anything to do with that fact. "No one that young has ever been appointed to the Sanhedrin of Israel," Kezia protested. "By law only seventy-one members may sit on the court, and there are many, much more experienced elders available. I will admit that adding another Pharisee to overcome the power of the Sadducees has merit, but what about Solomon, son of Gamaliel himself? Surely if we were to add a Pharisee from the school of Gamaliel it would be Solomon?"

"The school of Gamaliel is divided," answered Judah Jamnai. "Solomon, like his father, does not hold strictly to the Law and the traditions. Saul of Tarsus, on the other hand, is a crusader for them. Both the older and the younger Pharisees follow him."

"But," protested the Ab-Bet-Din again, "he is not even married. No single man can be an elder in Israel!" Johanan's voice was rising in irritation.

"He is betrothed and the marriage will soon follow," argued Judah Jamnai.

"Betrothed?" Kezia questioned, his voice intensifying.

"To Esther, the only child of the merchant Jacob Bar Kochba," replied Judah Jamnai, dropping his voice to a whisper and lowering his gaze to the marble floor.

"So Jacob Bar Kochba wishes to buy his future son-in-law a position on the great Sanhedrin of Israel, does he?" Kezia asked. "Judah Jamnai would be greatly rewarded, I suspect."

Judah Jamnai replied quickly, but he was still unable to look into the face of the Ab-Bet-Din. "Only the return of some of my father's goods Bar Kochba holds."

Kezia smiled and Judah Jamnai quickly added, "Saul of Tarsus is Saul Salaman!"

"No wonder Jacob Bar Kochba has given him his daughter," Kezia replied. "Jacob Bar Kochba has never done anything without profit in mind."

"I must also tell you a great secret," Judah Jamnai continued. "Saul of Tarsus is only half Jew. His father was General Markus Paul Gabinius of Rome."

Interesting, thought the Ab-Bet-Din. *If the Sanhedrin does not know this, it is something that will help us deal with Rome. Having a Roman between us and the new procurator would not be a bad idea.*

"I believe I can help you, Judah Jamnai," the Ab-Bet-Din stated. "It would be good to have a new young Pharisee from the house of Gamaliel on the Sanhedrin. I believe your Saul of Tarsus is an ideal choice."

When Judah Jamnai informed Jacob Bar Kochba of the Ab-Bet-Din's decision, Jacob roared. "Jacob Bar Kochba is always right. Religion is nothing more than politics, and money makes it work!"

Esther could not wait for Saul to return from Gamaliel's school to share what her father had accomplished. With a female slave for a companion, she hastened through the residential area of Bezetha, a section of the city of Jerusalem, to the exact location of Gamaliel's school. It was located to the north of the second wall, near the Samaria Road, with access to the Temple grounds through the Middle Gate. She discovered Saul near the second wall, with a group of students in heated debate.

"Esther!" Saul called out. "My betrothed," he stammered to his companions. Saul was unsure what to do. He knew it was not proper to introduce Esther without her father's consent, but he also did not want his fellow students to think that he was familiar with, or consorting with, a loose woman. Though Esther was properly veiled and attended, it was not like her to be out in public. Nor was it her practice to address any man in society, even her betrothed. "Esther, are you alright?"

Esther, realizing where she was and that other men were present, replied: "Yes, my husband, I am fine. I ask your forgiveness if I have shamed you. I have such good news that I wanted to tell you quickly." Then, looking at the other students, she became aware that she had placed herself and Saul in an unconventional position. "We — that is, my father and I — have just received word that you have been accepted to sit on the grand Sanhedrin. Oh, isn't it wonderful news!"

Saul was totally shocked. Esther and Jacob Bar Kochba did not know what they had done. The last thing Saul wanted was recognition. The Sanhedrin was a powerful and recognizable body. Not only did all Israel know the members of the Sanhedrin but so did Rome. Saul instinctively looked around to see who might have heard Esther. As he looked into the eyes of his fellow Pharisees, Saul detected accusations and insinuations. They had accepted Saul of Tarsus as their leader because he was relentless and uncompromising when it came to the details of the Law and the traditions. How Saul could be appointed to the Sanhedrin without having compromised his stance on the Law and his ethics was a puzzling question. Their suspicion was clearly visible on their faces. While some of his companions were delighted with the news, seeing some advantage in knowing a member of the Sanhedrin, others questioned why an obscure Pharisee like Saul had been selected when Solomon Gamaliel, son of the Rabbi, was the logical choice.

The sensation of guilt quickly followed the shock of hearing Esther's news. Saul felt ashamed and reprehensible, though he did not know why. Esther and her many stipulations on his fulfilling of the Law and the traditions made him feel remiss. Inside, Saul was not as much a Pharisee as he was on the outside. Although he wanted to be accepted by Esther, Jacob Bar Kochba and his fellow students, Saul had a desire to forsake it all — the voice of his mother, Esther, pharisaism and the God of Israel, with His hard demands — and return to pleasant moments in the baths of Rome and the remembered voice of a temptress saying, "I have never met a virgin god before."

Saul vaulted back through the gate. Shock and guilt had turned to anger. He would confront the Ab-Bet-Din and reject the post. Saul of Tarsus would be accepted for who he was, not for what they wanted him to be!

Esther, not understanding anything that had taken place, watched him go. She had brought joyful news and had expected a grateful response. She knew that she had acted improperly by addressing a man in the presence of strangers, but she had not expected to be totally rejected before them. Esther was not angry as she turned back toward her father's home, only confused. *Saul did not have to violate common courtesy just because I infringed on the male-female tradition. He would not know how to act at all if I had not instructed him!*

It took Saul some time and effort to persuade the Temple guards that he was a newly appointed member of the Sanhedrin, and that he needed to see the Ab-Bet-Din immediately.

"So you are Saul Salaman of Tarsus," Kezia stated, after the Temple attendant had informed him of Saul's request. The Ab-Bet-Din was not asking a question as much as he was studying the obviously aggravated young man who stood before him.

"Why have you appointed me to the great Sanhedrin?" Saul questioned. "You do not even know me!"

"It is the will of God," stated the Ab-Bet-Din.

"The will of God!" exclaimed Saul. "I am in the school of Gamaliel seeking to know the God of Israel. I am not sanctified; I am not godly. I have not learned all the law of God, much less kept it. How can it be His will to have me sit in judgement of Israel when I do not know Him?"

Ab-Bet-Din Kezia smiled for the first time. The thought passed through his mind: *This Saul of Tarsus is a better choice than Judah Jamnai realized.*

"Moses did not know Him when the bush burned and God called him to deliver Israel from the bondage of Egypt," Kezia replied. "Saul of Tarsus, God has predestined your relationship to Him and to His people. Will you dare presume to tell God that He is wrong?"

"If it is God's will," Saul said, "I will abide in it. But if it is the work of Jacob Bar Kochba and his daughter, Esther, I will have none of it."

The Ab-Bet-Din gave Saul his most sanctimonious look. "I tell you the truth; neither the High Priest, the Ab-Bet-Din nor any member of the Sanhedrin has as much as spoken to Jacob Bar Kochba, the merchant. Since he deals with both Jews and Gentiles, he is religiously unclean and cannot come into the presence of holiness. You will not be allowed to sit in judgement as a member of the Sanhedrin until you marry and establish your own home apart from Jacob Bar Kochba. Between now and then you will perform tasks for the Sanhedrin that require the investigation of and contact with the ceremonially unclean. You will continue in the school of Gamaliel."

The Ab-Bet-Din knew that he had to get Saul involved in something outside of Jerusalem. Should he ask too many questions about his appointment, dissension might erupt among the Pharisees and even within the Sanhedrin.

"Take three of your best and most principled Pharisees from the school of Gamaliel and prepare for a journey to the north. I will send you to Galilee, where you will inquire into the teachings and the reported miracles of the Rabbi, Jesus of Nazareth. When your investigation is complete, you will return and report to me personally." Ab-Bet-Din Kezia stroked his beard thoughtfully. "We have two members of the Sanhedrin, Joseph of Arimathaea and Nicodemus, who are greatly attracted to this Jesus. Annas, the High Priest, will surely demand information on this Galilean!"

In his exhilaration at the thought of journeying to Galilee with his companions and of having a chance to confront this Jesus who had interested him so much in his journey through Samaria, Saul forgot his irritation at Esther. But he remembered the shame he had received that first day in the school of Gamaliel because he had told the story of that journey. *I must not give too favorable a report on this Jesus,* he thought. *The High Priest is not interested in truth, only in tradition.*

18

The Tetrarch of Galilee, Herod Antipas, was celebrating his birthday. Procurator Pontius Pilate was no friend of Herod, but Augustus Caesar had given Herod the position of Tetrarch and Tiberius had honored Augustus' decision. Thus Tiberius was sending Herod a pair of lions and a chest of gold as a birthday present. The problem was that Herod had decided to celebrate his birthday in his palace on the shores of Lake Galilee, in the new city he had named Tiberias, after the Emperor. Pilate had experienced enough travel on the dusty caravan road of the Jordan. He was in no hurry to risk a repeat encounter with the Zealots on the road between Jerusalem and Jericho. But because Herod had invited all the leading men of Galilee to his birthday party, either Pilate had to go or he had to send someone in his place — it would be impolite not to have a high-ranking Roman to represent him. Who better than Centurion Julius Laco, an officer who had been appointed by Tiberius himself?

"I wish we were going all the way to Caesarea," Popygos complained.

Julius smiled and reminded his companion, "When you were in Caesarea, you were only a principes, walking everywhere you went and carrying a large spear. Now you ride a good horse and carry an excellent sword. Yet you complain."

"When I was in Caesarea, I had clean air, breezes and the smell of the sea. Now I have only dust, heat and the smell of lions." Popygos turned to look back at the contingent that followed them. Immediately behind them were eight soldiers who walked wearily through the heat, carrying their shields and spears. A cart pulled by two oxen that kept rolling their eyes as they tried to see the lions in the cage on the cart followed the soldiers. Almost obscured by the dust created by the ox cart were four more soldiers who were carrying the treasure box. Four additional spear men formed the rear guard of the company.

"I suppose being up here is better than walking in the dust," Popygos muttered, turning back to Julius. "I was getting bored with the Fortress Antonia. All those Jews do is pray and sacrifice, pray and sacrifice. Their good-looking women all wear veils — if they have any good-looking women!"

"The weather will be nice on the Lake of Galilee," Julius remarked, "as well as the entertainment. I understand that Herod surrounds himself with sensual women."

"Sensual? Lecherous is more like it," Popygos replied. "Herod's brother Philip had a wife, but she preferred Herod. So Herod said, politely no doubt, 'I want the wench!' to which Philip replied, 'You can have whatever you want, dear brother. Only make her an honest woman by marrying her like I did.' So Herod married Philip's wife! Then Herod said, 'Brother, you have a provocative daughter. She is as sultry as her mother. I want the pair of them — one for each side of my bed.' 'Dear brother,' said Philip. 'You will have to make a virtuous woman out of my daughter, and you can marry only one woman at a time!'"

"Popygos, you have a vivid imagination," chuckled Julius.

"Imagination nothing!" Popygos exclaimed. "Remember what I told you when you first came to Judaea about the Jewish prophet John the Baptist? If that one is around Herod's palace in Tiberias, we will have our work cut out for us. He publicly calls Herod a whoremonger."

"Popygos," Julius remarked, "I did not know that you were so concerned about morals."

"I'm not," Popygos replied. "We Romans have no code of conduct. Our gods have no sense of shame. But Herod claims to be a Jew, and a man who worships Jehovah as God should have morality. That's what I like about your friend Saul of Tarsus. He tells the truth and keeps his word!" Popygos patted his sword.

"What do you think of a man who denies his best friend?" Julius asked. "I would not be in this god-forsaken place if I had not tried to find out who killed his father. I did it because I thought we were best friends!"

"Don't judge him too harshly, Julius. What is permissible in Rome is not allowable in Jerusalem. Here he is a Pharisee. As such, he cannot be your friend."

"That may be true," replied Julius. "But if the situation were reversed, I do not believe that I would deny him."

"Do not be so sure, Centurion Laco. If Saul loses his Jewishness, he loses himself. And if Centurion Laco were threatened with the loss of Rome and his rank because of his friendship with a Jew, he might not do it so willingly."

"I would give my life," Julius started to say, when he was cut off by Popygos.

"Your life? I believe you would! I believe that we would give our lives for each other in battle! But to give our souls would be a different matter. For a Pharisee to become unclean is to give his soul!"

The procession had arrived at the garrison at Jericho. While the rest of their company bathed from the water pots, Julius and Popygos once more enjoyed a bath in the bend of the Jordan River. Popygos, remembering Julius' description of the filth and the rats that he had discovered the last time they were in Jericho, asked Julius if he might forego the privilege of sleeping in the officers' quarters. This visit, however, proved to be different. Because they were not guarding Pilate but had been sent as emissaries of the

Governor, Julius and Popygos were invited to share a room at the inn.

Traveling with the two lions proved to be tedious. In the morning, fresh meat and water had to be provided for the big cats and their cages had to be cleaned. The smell of the lions frightened all the animals around the inn, including the horses ridden by Julius and Popygos. Many of the men had failed to sleep because of the noise created by the animals. Finally, after the sun was well in the sky, the troop was ready to move again.

"There is one thing good about getting a late start," Popygos remarked, turning to Julius. "We don't have to choke on the dust of trade caravans. The Jewish traders will cross the Jordan at Bethabara into Perea in order to avoid Samaria. But we can continue straight up the west bank to the fortress at Mt. Gilboa in Decapolis."

"I suppose Saul would be unclean if he were to touch Samarian soil," Julius stated.

"Saul of Tarsus is certainly on your mind," said Popygos, as he looked inquisitively at Julius. "You spoke of him only yesterday."

"You are right, my friend, and it is not worth the thought. Yet, somehow, I feel as if our destinies are linked together. The entire time I have been on this journey, I have felt as though Saul and I were traveling together. I felt the same thing as I traveled by ship from Rome. And just after I had arrived in Palestine, you met him at Caesarea. Perhaps it is because you carry his sword that I am reminded of him. Yet I had not thought of him until we started this journey. That we could be linked together is ridiculous! A Pharisee would have nothing to do with Herod or the city of Tiberias. Saul of Tarsus is in Jerusalem feeding at the home of his rich, future father-in-law. I have written to a woman in Rome and told her of Saul's pending marriage. What a fool he is to turn down the most beautiful woman in Rome for a Jewish fortune and the life of a Pharisee!"

"You sound like a man who is in love and maybe a little jealous," Popygos commented.

"Perhaps!" Julius silently rode on, thinking about Diana and what both he and Paul had left behind. Maybe Diana had gotten over Paul, but Julius still had not forgotten his feelings for her.

The Sea of Galilee was one of the most beautiful vistas Julius could recollect. Nothing in Rome came close to its natural beauty. The caravan passed through the city of Philoteria on the southern bank of the sea where it emptied into the Jordan River. Here the Jordan flowed deep and crystal clear between the shadows of willows overhanging the banks. Here and there the water swirled around large rocks that blocked its path. A setting sun curved across green meadows and kissed the waves of the sea with a crimson embrace. To the northeast, Julius saw the mountains and the cliffs of Gaulanitis transformed by the direct sunlight into hues of bright orange and shadows of deep purple against the evening sky.

"We will camp here for the night," Julius ordered. The troopers murmured, realizing that they were less than an hour from Tiberias.

"What will we feed the big cats here?" one complained.

"Fish and rabbits you will spend all night catching," another answered.

"They smell bad enough in the daytime, but to sleep next to them all night — phew," another added.

"Enough!" ordered Popygos. "The Centurion says we will camp in the open tonight — and we will camp in the open! Are you legionnaires or girls?"

"The girls are all in Tiberias," one answered.

"Yes," replied Popygos, "and tomorrow night you can try to catch one. Tonight you catch supper for the cats and for me," Popygos laughed. Later, after the animals had been fed and foddered, a supper of fish, cooked on an open fire, filled Popygos' belly. A gentle breeze carried the smell of grass and wildflowers to them, and the smell of the cats away. And Popygos, having laid his head on a pillow made from his cloaks, looked into a sky filled with stars. He remarked, "This was good idea, Julius, but it's not a good military tactics."

"Look!" exclaimed Julius, as he pointed to lights that seemed to float in the darkness above the sea. "The city of Tiberias is built on a hill next to the sea. The mist from the waters below and the dark sky above the city make its lights appear to be suspended in space."

"A city that is set upon a hill cannot be hid," reflected Popygos.

"I did not know that you were a philosopher, Popygos," Julius rejoined.

"They are the words of Jesus, that Jewish prophet I told you about. This is his region. I suspect he was referring to the phenomenon we are seeing."

"What does he mean, 'A city set upon a hill cannot be hid'? That is true, but what does that truth mean?" Julius questioned.

"I don't know," answered Popygos. "These Jews often speak in riddles."

"That is why I camped here for the night instead of going into the city on the hill," Julius stated. "Herod is still a half Jew. What can a Roman expect in the palace of a half Jew who cavorts with Tiberius Caesar and is hated by his own people? Having only this small band of soldiers to protect gold and lions, and representing a fool like Pilate, I would rather find out in morning light!"

"What do I know about military tactics?" Popygos replied as he smiled in the dark. *Centurion Laco is beginning to think like a centurion*, he said to himself.

The morning light swept over the sea. It was if the mountains had held back the sunlight until the sun suddenly jumped into the heavens. Now Julius could see the city that the night before had seemed to float in air. A sea wall lifted it above the southern tip of the huge lake that the Romans called the Lake of Tiberias. (The Jews still called it the Sea of Galilee.) Herod might have been half Jew, but the city was all Roman. Formidable, massive walls surrounded a Roman garrison and the palace of Herod. Just south of the city, Julius could make out the bath houses surrounding the sulphur springs that, in part, encouraged Herod to choose this place for his residence.

Since they arrived in the morning, it did not take long for Julius and Popygos to surrender the presents to Herod's deputy. Having been relieved of their duty, they took their time wandering around the city. A Roman, dressed only in a tunic, chased a barefooted girl down the beach. A vendor sold them hot bread and fish.

"I have not seen a single Jew since last night," Julius remarked.

"Very perceptive," Popygos said, smiling. "Do you suspect trouble?"

"No, I see no cause for alarm; I have simply observed a fact. We are in Israel, but I have not seen a single Jew all day!"

"You will not see one tomorrow either," noted Popygos. "I told you that the Jews are a peculiar lot. When the Romans were building this city, workmen came upon an ancient cemetery from Thema. Therefore the Jews consider the entire city to be unclean."

"Do you mean to tell me that a Jew walking where someone has been buried — no matter when it was — would be made unclean?"

"That's right," Popygos responded.

"By the gods! Don't they know that there is probably not a square inch of this land upon which blood has not been spilt and in which men have not been buried after battle?"

"If they do not know it, the land is clean. If they know about the burial, the land is unclean. They found the cemetery, so Tiberias is unclean!" explained Popygos. "And it's not by the gods," he laughed, "it's by Jehovah!"

That night was the celebration of Herod's birthday. Tiberius' presents had arrived just in time. Julius was not invited to sit at the head table, but he was requested, as Pilate's emissary, to attend the feast with Popygos, his assistant. The festivities were celebrated in a portico that was lined with large stone columns and tiled with a marble floor. At the upper end of the portico, Herod and his private guests sat upon a raised platform with stairs. The lower end of the portico ended at the water's edge, where a light breeze sent waves splashing onto the pavement. Each column contained holders for four torches, the light of which was reflected in the water. Herod's gifts graced the sides of the stairs, including the pair of lions Julius and Popygos had brought from Jerusalem. At the lower level of the stair, musicians played stringed instruments. The melody was amplified by the stone walls, the water and the marble floor. Dancing girls kept time to the music. Julius assured Popygos that the food and the presentation rivalled anything he had seen in Rome, even at the house of the Emperor.

Toward the end of the evening, Herod, who was drunk, was running out of things with which to amuse himself. He was bored at his own birthday party. He had eaten his fill of all the delicacies on the table. He had drunk all the wine he could hold. He had told many lewd jokes, and he had ridiculed the Jews and blasphemed their God. He had even taunted the lions by offering them pieces of lamb that he then pulled away. That pleasure stopped when one of the beasts almost caught his arm — Herod was not drunk enough to be oblivious to the danger of his game!

"Salome, dance for me!" Herod cried, looking at a young girl who sat beside his wife. "Salome, dance for me. It will warm my blood as wine never could." Herod lifted his cup and leaned forward, leering at the girl.

"And what will you give me if I do?" the girl asked coyly.

"By the gods! Your mother was not as hard to get." Herod laughed and made a lewd gesture toward his wife, Herodias.

"Why, I'll give you anything you choose if you can stimulate my desires," Herod replied, laughing as if he had made a great jest.

"Will you promise upon an oath that even you cannot break?" The voice of the daughter of Herodias carried the sound of sarcasm.

Herod flushed, realizing that she had turned the ridicule onto him and there was nothing he could do about it. "Show me that you are half the woman your mother is and I will keep my word to you, even as I kept my word to her. Your father, Philip, is my brother. I made his wife my wife, and I will make his daughter my whore."

"We will see if you can pay the price for my dance before we see if you have enough manhood to pay for more."

Salome began to sway to the sound of the music. The light veils that she wore caught in the sea breezes as she moved. In the light of the torches the curves of her body were silhouetted within the folds of the costume. Drums softly joined the stringed instruments, and the beat of the music increased. With the increased tempo, Salome's movements became more pronounced and her body more exposed. Herod watched her as if transfixed by the movement and the anticipation of what would be revealed. Suddenly she dropped a veil, which was carried away from her by the breeze. Herod responded to the move with elation, staring at the new revelation of Salome. Again the tempo picked up, and the dancer began to spin. With seeming abandon, Salome twirled faster and faster, lifting the veils higher up her thighs until another was thrown to the wind. Herod gasped in sheer delight. Just as the music reached its fastest beat and the dance its most frenzied pace, the girl leapt past the eyes of Herod and grasped her mother's cloak, draping it around her exposed body.

Herod's face was flushed with desire and beads of perspiration had formed on his brow. His breath was coming in short gasps, and he looked as if he was about to topple over.

"One trip to the Roman baths would kill the old boy," Julius whispered to Popygos. "For a princess, she is not half bad; but the slaves in a Roman orgy would not stop and cover themselves."

"Give me the head of the Baptist!" the girl demanded.

"What?" exclaimed Herod.

"You said whatever I wanted! I want the head of the Baptist! Will you go back on your word after you swore you would not?"

The color drained from Herod's face. All desire and passion had been wiped away. All one could see now was stark fear. "Your mother put you up to this," Herod shouted.

"What if she did?" Salome demanded. "You gave your word! You have shamed me and my mother! You have allowed the Baptist to call my mother a whore in the city square! Now your friends will call you a liar and a cheat unless you pay what you have agreed. You wanted my body, but you cannot pay even the price of my dance!"

Both Herod and Salome reclined at the table, exhausted more from the exchange than from the emotions of the dance.

"Well, I'm glad that is over with," Popygos muttered in Julius' direction.

A servant entered carrying a large silver tray.

"Sweetmeats," Popygos remarked. "When they come, you know the party is finally over."

Herod indicated to the servant that Salome was to be served first. Julius thought it was a gesture of reconciliation until the servant took the lid off the platter. There, swimming in fresh blood, was the bearded head of a man.

A gasp went up from the guests. Julius, who had killed one man and stuck his sword into another, thought he was going to regurgitate his dinner. Popygos, the veteran soldier, looked pale. Salome indicated to the servant that the platter should go to her mother. Herodias peered at the dish and snickered, "So I am a whore, John the Baptist. Now what are you?"

Popygos looked at Julius and exclaimed, "I told you these are bizarre people!"

19

As Saul and his company journeyed to Galilee, they learned much about the man they had come to investigate. At every camp site, the Pharisees heard rumors about the Prophet Jesus. Everyone they spoke with added something about the Rabbi's words and deeds.

"Yes, I am Enos of Magdala and I was there," an old man reported. "It was in Cana last spring. There was this nobleman ... oh, he was rich. Of such fabrics his cloak was made!" The old man's eyes sparkled as he recalled the event. "Indeed, gold had been woven into the neck of the garment!" He gestured with his hands encircling his neck to indicate the covering of gold.

"We do not care how rich he was," interrupted Saul. "What did Jesus have to do with this nobleman?"

"Pharisees from Jerusalem are always interested in rich men," Enos replied before continuing his story.

"This rich nobleman" — the old man emphasized the word "rich" — "was visiting Capernaum when his son became sick and was near death."

"How do you know that?" Saul questioned.

"That is what he said, and he had no reason to lie," the old man answered Saul's question. "The nobleman asked Jesus to come to Capernaum to heal his son, and Jesus told him, 'Except you see me perform a miracle, you will not believe me.' "

"What did he say to that?" Johanan, the youngest of the Pharisees, asked, his eyes wide. He expected to be told something miraculous.

"Why, Jesus said, 'Go home, your son is all right!' So the nobleman turned and started back to Capernaum.

"Capernaum is not far, the next village around the sea from Magdala, so I decided to follow him. Others came! They thought as I did: *If the rich man's son is healed, perhaps he will give away some of his riches in gratitude.* Night caught us and we had to delay our journey until morning; but the next morning we were about half way to Capernaum when the nobleman's servants ran toward us crying, 'Your son is living and well.'

" 'When did he start to mend?' the nobleman asked.

" 'Yesterday at the seventh hour, the fever left him,' the servant replied.

"Well," Enos of Magdala said smugly, "that was the precise time at which Jesus had said: 'Your son is well!' "

"You are very susceptible, old man," said Saul. "We Pharisees have been trained to see the facts. Did you see the nobleman's son, or do you believe this miracle happened just because a servant started a rumor? Tell me, did the nobleman give away any of his riches in gratitude for such a great miracle?"

"No," Enos said, with sorrow in his voice.

"I am a member of the Sanhedrin, and I say to you that the days of miracles have passed. Moses was the great performer of miracles. When this Jesus opens again the Dead Sea, then you will have something to believe in!"

Reuben, one of the Pharisees who wished a closer relationship to one on the Sanhedrin, addressed Saul, "Johanan is very naive. He was ready to believe that Jesus had actually performed a miracle."

"How do you know he didn't?" Johanan demanded, breaking into the conversation that was about him.

"Saul is a member of the Sanhedrin. He can explain it to you," Reuben answered.

"Unless it is proven both that an event agrees with the teaching of the Rabbis, the Talmud and the history of Israel and that it has no rational explanation, it cannot be called a miracle," Saul explained. "Even as great an event as one being cured from leprosy has to be verified by a priest, and proper offering has to be made and received."

"How then can we prove if this Jesus has performed any miracles?" Johanan enquired.

"We will have to find tangible evidence to demonstrate before the Sanhedrin," Saul replied.

The fourth man of the group, Hiram, was the eldest student in the school of Gamaliel. His fellow students assumed that he was not very intellectual. As usual, Hiram had been listening to their conversation without comment. "I wonder," he now began, "what we would have to bring to the Sanhedrin to prove that Moses crossed the Red Sea?"

Because he was the one appointed by the Ab-Bet-Din to gather the evidence, Saul was disturbed by Hiram's remark. "Do you know where this Jesus is now?" Saul asked the man who had told them the story.

"Yes," came the reply. "He has returned to Magdala where he met the nobleman."

"Then we will circumvent the city of Tiberias and follow the west bank of the sea to Magdala," Saul told his companions.

Reuben addressed the old man, "We cannot come near Tiberias lest we become unclean."

The old man held out the dirty rags he wore and he smiled with a toothless grin. "It would not do for a Pharisee to become unclean."

Magdala was a small fishing village located on the utmost western shore of the Sea of Galilee. It consisted of two streets running parallel to the water and several dozen small houses built of mud and straw. A grove of olive trees and some fig trees gave shade to the houses. A large sloping hill covered with grasses used for feeding livestock protected the harbor from easterly winds, and the curvature of the sea bank protected the village on the north and the south. Even so, storms that came across the lake from Gaulanitis and its high cliffs and mountains could come directly into the harbor. Thus, Magdala had never become the size of Capernaum — it was not even large enough to boast a synagogue. When a rabbi or prophet passed through the area, the villagers would gather on the front street — along the pebbled shore among the fishing boats and nets — to hear him speak.

This day the shore of Magdala was crowded. Not only had all the villagers gathered but the Prophet had brought a large company with him. The twelve personal disciples of Jesus, a sizable group of followers (both men and women), villagers from Capernaum, and isolated groups of shepherds and farm workers had joined the fishermen from Magdala and their families along the shore of the lake. Although the arrival of the four Pharisees from Jerusalem would have made a stir in the village on any other day, it did not surprise the community that the religious people had come to hear Jesus of Nazareth. The villagers would not have been astonished if the High Priest, himself, had come.

Tonight, before the boats went out to fish the waters of the sea, the whole village would play hosts to their guests. Fish would be cooked over open fires on the beach. Hot meal bread baked in brick fires would be shared with the guests, as would huge bowls of beans and lentils. Cakes of figs would be served as a sweet. The residents would also supply the wine. Some villagers wondered if there would be enough for so many guests. Others said it would give Jesus a chance to turn water into wine — as it was reported he had done at Cana — or to feed them all — as some said he had done the day before on the mountains behind the village. (Those who followed him said he had multiplied seven loaves and two fish to feed four thousand men plus the women and children.)

Several fishermen used the time to mend their nets as they listened to Jesus. Most of the other men, sitting either on the shore or under the trees where they could enjoy the slight breeze and the shade, just listened quietly. Some of the women tried to quiet the children who were playing nearby. Two boys, unmindful of the Prophet, were skipping rocks further down the shore at the water's edge. Several women were preparing meal for the bread they would need for that evening, while others were tending to their sewing. All, however, except for the boys who were skimming rocks, listened intently to the tall, bearded man in the white robe with the blue-tasseled prayer cloth draped over his head. He was not in prayer but spoke reverently about God, Whom he called his Father.

The crowd paid little attention to the four Pharisees until Johanan eagerly interrupted the Teacher. "Do a miracle! We have heard that you perform miracles. Show us a sign from the heavens so we can tell if you are really sent from God!"

Saul was embarrassed by Johanan's impetuous demand and the attention that had suddenly shifted to them. They were there to investigate, not to instigate reaction.

The Galilean prophet looked away from them for a moment and gazed at the sea. "When the evening comes and the sky is red, as it now is, you say it will be fair weather." The fishermen who stood nearby nodded their heads in agreement. Still looking at the sea, Jesus continued: "In the morning if the sky is red and cast down, you say the day will bring foul weather." Again the fisherman turned to one another as if the Prophet had said something of importance and agreed to the truth of his words. Jesus then turned his head from the sea and gazed at the Pharisees. "Hypocrites, these fishermen can understand the face of the sky, but you self-proclaimed religious leaders cannot recognize the forewarning of the age."

Saul was startled at Jesus' use of the designation "hypocrite." Although he was a legitimate investigator for the Sanhedrin, Saul felt uncomfortable spying on the man. But the word "hypocrite" touched a nerve that Saul did not like. He felt himself tremble in humiliation and anger.

"A wicked and adulterous generation seeks after a sign," the Prophet continued.

The words "wicked" and "adulterous" struck like hammer blows. While Jesus had not called Saul an adulterer, and Saul was sure of his physical sexual purity, the word hit home. Thoughts of his dreams of the Roman girl flashed in his mind, making Saul even more mortified.

"No sign shall be given to wicked people except the sign of Jonah," Jesus said forcefully, as he left the shore and started walking north along the path that led to Caesarea Philippi and intersected the Jordan at Lake Semechomitis.

The disciples of Jesus hurriedly put things together and rushed after their master, who was making such a sudden and unexpected departure. The villagers of Magdala looked anxiously after the departing company. The women glanced with distraught faces at the still-cooking pots of lentils and the baking bread. Some of the fishermen started to run after Jesus to beg him to return, but they soon remembered the night of fishing that lay ahead. Their eyes, revealing their perplexed thoughts, fastened on the four Pharisees.

It was Reuben who spoke softly to Saul: "I believe we too should leave." His voice was shuddering with apprehension. "It would be safer for us to turn back toward Tiberias. We cannot get there by nightfall, but we can make the villagers think that is where we are going. They will not follow. I, for one, would rather be unclean than dead!"

Saul smiled, realizing that the danger was more imagined than real. Nevertheless, he turned and walked back up the path toward Tiberias.

"Why didn't he perform a miracle?" Johanan asked.

"Oh, be quiet," replied Hiram.

Saul, walking softly into the shadows thought: *No sign except the sign of Jonah. What did he mean by that? The miracle of Jonah was that he was in the belly of the fish for three days. Will Jesus go into the belly of a fish? If he does, how will anyone know? What kind of a sign would that be? I wish these Jewish prophets would give straight answers!*

The fire ahead looked inviting. They had traveled only a short distance from Magdala, but it got dark quickly once the sun had disappeared behind the hills. Saul made a decision. There were six men around the fire, and the laws of hospitality granted a wanderer the right to join them. If they were thieves, it would be better to confront them in the light of the fire. Besides, thieves, recognizing that Pharisees didn't carry anything of substance anyway, left them alone! The voices coming from the fire indicated that an argument was in progress.

"I think we had better let them alone," Hiram remarked.

Always impetuous, Johanan said, "Nonsense! The fishermen of Magdala could not get here before us." Immediately he was sorry that he had reminded his companions of Magdala.

"Who is there?" a voice from the fire cried out. The man put his hand on the hilt of a short dagger.

"There's nothing to worry about," Saul said as he moved into the light where the men could see him.

"Only a dog of a Pharisee," one of the men remarked.

Another rebuked him, "Do not speak ill of any holy man."

"Romans, tax collectors and Pharisees are all cur dogs and pig slop," the first man retorted in a surly manner.

"Come to the fire," another invited the Pharisees. "My friend is just distraught. We have had a very upsetting day and we have a difficult task before us."

"Upsetting!" the first man replied. "What is upsetting about burying the headless body of the greatest man you have ever known and then having to find his cousin to tell him about it?"

"That dog from hell, Herod, had the Baptist beheaded. We were his disciples," the man closest to the fire groaned.

Saul caught the designation. "John the Baptist and Jesus of Nazareth were relatives?"

"What do you know of Jesus?" one of John's disciples asked.

"We just left him at Magdala," Saul replied. "He left just before sunset for Caesarea Philippi."

"Perhaps if we leave at first light we can catch him," John's disciple remarked. "The press of the crowd will slow his pace, so we can move faster than he can."

"If you do not overtake Jesus tomorrow," Johanan observed, "you will have to wait until after the Sabbath!"

"It would take a Pharisee to remind us of that" — another of John's disciples joined the conversation. "Jesus said that you Pharisees break the Law in order to keep the traditions of men. Did he call you hypocrites?" The man burst into laughter when he saw Saul's reaction. "If you think Jesus has a biting tongue toward you Pharisees and the Scribes, you should have heard John preach. He told the common man to repent and he called Pharisees and Sadducees alike a generation of vipers. He also called Herod a fox and a whoremonger to his face. Jesus preaches that we should love our enemies. Even he was baptized unto repentance by John."

"John once sent us to Jesus to inquire if he was the Messiah or not. Jesus sent word that his miracles were his evidence."

Johanan interrupted when he heard the word miracle, "I asked Jesus to prove who he was by performing a miracle. But he didn't perform one."

"Is that when he called you a hypocrite?" the man asked with a smile. "If you want to see a miracle, follow me back to Jesus.

When I tell him what Herod did to John, he may call down fire from heaven or summon Michael, God's warring angel. And when he does, woe be to Romans, tax collectors and Pharisees!"

"We have nothing to fear from God," Saul replied. "We are born Jews, sanctified by Temple ritual; and I am of the house of Benjamin."

"All Jews are from one of the twelve tribes," Saul's antagonist reminded him. "Jesus is from the house of Judah and of the direct line of King David, but he doesn't make that his righteousness!"

Saul spread his cloak on the ground near the fire and lay down. "I would really like to see a miracle," he said to the air. Then he thought, *To be from the house of Judah and of the lineage of King David, Jesus would have to be from Bethlehem; but he is a Nazarene. How could such a thing be? But here by the Sea of Galilee lies Saul of Tarsus of the house of Benjamin, who is also Paul Gabinius, son of the Roman, General Markus Paul Gabinius. How, indeed, can such a thing be? This disciple of the late John the Baptist hates Romans and Pharisees, yet he shares his fire with a man who is both. Life can certainly be strange. Nothing here makes sense, but anything can be truth. What is the truth about Jesus of Nazareth?*

When the light of the sun woke Saul, the disciples of John had already left to catch Jesus. Saul was still harboring mixed emotions. While he was attracted to Jesus, he was also very angry. The man was either a charlatan or a simpleton who believed he was performing miracles. If he was a fraud, he was diverting attention away from himself through his attacks on the religious establishment. If he was a fool who really believed himself to be the Messiah, he thought he was beyond the law. Either way, this Jesus had to be stopped. If he was a simpleton, he would betray himself; but if he was a charlatan, Saul would have to set a trap to catch him. Saul began to devise a snare that would trick Jesus into revealing his true nature.

20

Julius, Popygos and the Roman soldiers who had come with them from Jerusalem returned by way of the same dusty roads. The same two oxen that had pulled the lion cart to Tiberias, now pulled it, empty, toward Jerusalem. Herod's slaves had cleaned and washed the cart so as to remove the smell, but the oxen were still bothered by a faint odor. The two lions had been placed in a pit next to Herod's private arena in Tiberias. They would provide a spectacle when Herod had some other poor wretch that he wished to mutilate and kill.

Julius and Popygos had not discussed the night of Herod's birthday. Both wanted to forget the picture of John the Baptist's head, floating in blood, on a silver platter. As they rode, Popygos continued to murmur about how fortunate he had been in Caesarea where Julius had found him. "You said we would find sensual women in Tiberias," Popygos reminded Julius.

"You were correct, Popygos," Julius confessed. "They were either old, ugly or, as you said, lewd! I once met a beautiful, virtuous girl in the baths of Rome, but I saw no beautiful women, much less virtuous women, in all of Tiberias."

"I did not have the impression that modesty or virtue were of any value to you," Popygos replied, prompting Julius as much from boredom as from curiosity.

"Virtue is not of the flesh but of the spirit, Popygos! Had Herodias never left her husband, Philip, and if Salome was to live like a vestal virgin, they would both still be whores!" Julius checked to see that no one but Popygos could hear him. "What a hellish price Herod must be paying every night for that relationship. Once I told Paul — I mean Saul of Tarsus — not to take off his sword when he made love to Rome. Rome will stab a man in the back after making love to him, but Judaea will sting him like a spider before he gets the chance."

"Your advice to Paul Gabinius was wise," Popygos remarked, while patting the sword hilt. His smile indicated that he knew more than Julius intended for him to know.

Early in the evening, the caravan came to the city of Scythopolis. Because of the treasure and the lions, Julius had chosen to bypass the city, which was located at the junction between the Valley of Jezreel and the Jordan, on his trip up the river. Now he needed a good bath and some Roman entertainment. A good bed would also be preferred to another night on the road.

The Valley of Jezreel was filled with subtropical plants and fruit trees, some of them bearing fruit that was foreign to Julius. Rising from the lush valley floor was a huge mound that rose several hundred feet and was several miles in circumference. The mound was the result of one city after another being built and destroyed and built again on the same site. A new city was always constructed on the ruins of the old. The mound, called Beth-shan by the Jews, had been occupied by the Egyptians, the Philistines, the Canaanites, the Hasmonaean kingdom, the Scythians, the Greeks and now the Romans. On the north wall of the mound there was a Roman fort. In the valley, the Romans had built an aqueduct to carry water from several springs, a large theater and a hippodrome. Scythopolis, as a city of the Decapolis, was home for a number of Roman generals and war heroes, who were delighted to entertain the Centurion of the Fortress Antonia as their guest. After Julius and Popygos were settled into officers' quarters at the fortress, Julius dismissed Popygos, who wanted to spend the evening tending to some of their personal belongings. Julius decided to take in a Greek tragedy that was playing at the theater.

The theater was a typical, but small, Roman amphitheater with a large marble stage, a wall set with Roman columns, and an open marble floor. Fifteen terraced seats, sweeping in a semicircle, faced the stage. Saul carried a cushion to sit on and a cloak to keep from being chilled in the night air. Although he expected to find a large crowd because events like this were rare in Judaea, he found the theater less than half full. Once the play started, he understood why. The tragedy was poorly written — the work of some amateur at the fort, no doubt — and the actors were worse than the writing.

"Julius, both the writer and the performers should be hung on the theater wall!" The voice was deep, strong and full of authority. But in the darkness of the theater seats, Julius could not see the speaker.

"Do I know you?" Julius replied to the darkness.

"Not that you would remember; but you are greatly like your father, you know. And General Laco is one of my greatest friends. Laco, Gabinius and I were very close. Pardon me for having interrupted the play for you, but I waited until I was sure that you were as uninterested in the play as I am. Let me introduce myself. I am Velleius Paterculus. I was the senior Roman officer during the Illyrian revolt. A detachment of discharged soldiers stationed in a region that was remote from my command were exterminated to the man and I was consigned to this out-of-the-way fort as punishment. Varus, who ordered me here, was killed with three legions in the Teutoburg Forest. Augustus appointed Laco to Rome and Gabinius to Tarsus. He promised to recall me to Rome as your father's aide, but Augustus died at Nola, in Campania, and Tiberius did not keep his word."

"My father is still in Rome, though in some difficulty because of me," Julius reported. "General Gabinius was assassinated on the steps of the Senate. Paul Gabinius returned to his Jewish heritage and is somewhere in Israel. I am now serving as the Centurion of

Fort Antonia under Procurator Pilate. I am returning to Jerusalem after delivering the Procurator's birthday present to Herod."

"You could have worse duty, young Laco," Velleius Paterculus remarked. "Your father, General Gabinius and I almost froze to death in the Teutoburg Forest."

"My father has never mentioned the fact that he was there," Julius replied.

"Well, neither of us was actually in the battle, and that's the hell of it," Velleius continued. "Varus ordered us to remain in the fortress while he commanded three legions to draw Arminius out of the woods. We were to wait a half day's march and then proceed to attack Arminius from his flank. What we did not know was that Varus would actually enter the forest in order to win the victory for himself and receive the acclaim of Augustus."

"What happened?" Julius asked.

"Varus marched his army into the forest, chariots and all. They were ambushed and hemmed in by forest and marshes. Since we were having a great snowstorm, neither your father's legions nor my own could penetrate into the forest — the snowdrifts on the road were too deep. We were completely blinded by the falling snow. Our foot soldiers had frost-bitten feet and fingers, and all were near to freezing when we reached the protection of the forest. Once in the forest, our going was easier. But when we reached the place of battle — I should say slaughter — we realized that the three legions had been exterminated to a man. We found General Varus' body hidden in the snow behind some rocks. He had driven his own sword through his body. I suppose he had more courage to die than to fight."

"No wonder my father has never told me about this." Julius' voice carried his understanding of how the three friends must have felt.

"When Augustus heard of it," Velleius continued, "he succumbed to a nervous breakdown. He would not allow his beard or his hair to be trimmed; and at times, I am told, he would smash his head against a door and cry, 'Quinctilius Varus, give me back my legions.' Your father, Gabinius and I were not held responsible for the massacre, but it was during Augustus' remorse that I was brought before him on charges of failure during the Illyrian revolt. Thus, Scythopolis!" Velleius pointed in the dark toward the lights of Beth-shan.

The old general and the young centurion drank wine and talked late into the night. "Should you ever need my assistance, Julius Laco, just call on me. I owe your father! And I have sworn, after the Teutoburg Forest, never again to be late in assisting a comrade!"

"You were late coming from the theater," Popygos remarked as they continued their journey toward Jerusalem.

"I met an old friend," Julius responded.

"A friend, here, in this god-forsaken place? Julius, you amaze. Do you know everyone in the world?"

"Only the important people," Julius replied with a grin.

"Who could be important and be in this place?" Popygos inquired.

"How about Tribune Velleius Paterculus?" Julius answered.

"Velleius Paterculus, Velleius Paterculus," Popygos muttered. "I have heard the name before. What is he doing here?"

"Political!" exclaimed Julius. Not wishing to carry the conversation with Popygos further, he spurred his horse ahead.

The caravan was entering the area fed by Lake Hule. The road followed the winding course of the Jordan toward the village of Abel-meholah on the border of Samaria and Decapolis. No longer were they plagued by dust but by flies. The area was swampy, and the road was surrounded by reeds, bulrushes and papyrus plants.

Large trees overhanging with vines cut off the sun. The shade felt good in the sweltering heat of the Jordan. Julius cantered ahead, looking to see if they could spot a wild boar. The Jews would not eat one and they would be offended if they saw a Roman doing so, but here at the edge of Samaria it was unlikely that the caravan would encounter any Jews. Popygos stayed with the caravan and watched for jackals and hyenas, though they would usually run from the sounds of the cart.

The spear just missed Popygos' head and stuck into a tree on the opposite side of the road. The foot soldier next to Popygos was not as lucky as a spear caught him in the chest. With the ox cart in front of Popygos — between him and Julius — the soldiers had no opportunity to advance. The small group of bandits that had dared to attack a Roman attachment quickly blocked the road to the rear. Popygos instantly reined his horse to go around the cart, but he found that his horse became bogged in the swamp. When he dismounted to fight on foot, a sordid, wet man, dressed in the clothing of a Jew, but dirty beyond belief, waded into the swamp after him, waving a rusty Roman sword. Popygos' jeweled sword left his attacker's bowels in the mud.

The spear men were not as fortunate as Popygos. Without room to defend themselves, they fell quickly to an assortment of swords and daggers. Popygos, hampered by his Roman uniform, moved through the mud and the water with difficulty. While trying to protect himself, he also attempted to get to more solid ground where he could fight better.

Julius heard the skirmish behind him. Somehow the attackers had not seen him riding ahead. As he came through the trees he looked on a fearful sight. The oxen had turned the cart over, blocking the road. Only one spear man was still on his feet. With his back to the ox cart, the soldier was trying to defend himself. Popygos, waist deep in mud and water, was swinging the jeweled sword over his head. Bleeding and dying Roman soldiers littered the road. Five of the attackers were still trying to get to Popygos.

Julius' charge caught two of the attackers by surprise. The horse was on them before they could react. Julius' sword decapitated one of the assailants, while the other fell like an animal to all fours. After Julius passed him, he started chasing after the horse.

"Popygos!" Julius shouted. "To the cart!"

Popygos understood Julius' intentions, so he ceased his attempts to attack his assailants. Struggling through the mud, he pushed onto the road on Julius' side of the cart. When Julius reached Popygos, he quickly dismounted. Three of the ambush party were temporarily blocked by the ox cart. The fourth — the man who had chased Julius' horse — continued to come, wielding a sword after the two legionnaires. There was only room for one of them to defend against the attacker, while the other tried to prevent his fellows from joining him.

"This one's mine," Julius called to Popygos as he raised his sword to fend off the assault. The man was a powerful assailant. A Jew of dark complexion with a full, black beard and dark, penetrating eyes, he knew full well how to use a sword. Julius had to use all of his skill, learned in the gladiatorial school at Rome, as well as his instincts. First Julius, then the assailant, took the offensive. The clash of swords vibrated in the still air of the swamp. Julius, not having time to think of Popygos, hoped that the cart would give them some measure of protection from the rear. Suddenly loud noises came from Popygos' direction and screams filled the air. Julius glanced toward Popygos long enough to see the Roman banners. When his opponent lowered his sword, Julius quickly disarmed the Jew. Then he turned to see the smiling face of Velleius Paterculus.

"I told you to call me if you needed help," the aging Paterculus said firmly.

"I was too busy," stated Julius, looking at the neatly formed detachment of mounted Roman legion. The bodies of the other assailants were jerking, pinned to the road by Roman lances.

"They had a spy in Scythopolis," Paterculus explained. "When it was reported to me that he had left by horse, and in a hurry, by way of the west bank, I thought perhaps you were their purpose. I was late again," Velleius lamented, pointing to the dead Roman guardsmen.

"If you had been here, they would have waited in the swamp until you were gone to attack," Julius replied. "Thank you for coming and saving our lives."

"I believe the only life I have saved is that of Barabbas."

"Barabbas?" Julius questioned, wondering how Velleius knew the name of his assailant.

"A Zealot and a robber," replied Velleius. "He is one of the most dangerous and wanted men in Israel. Pilate will be delighted when you bring him, bound, into Jerusalem. Pilate will expect a gift from Herod in return for the lions, but I suppose Herod was too greedy, as usual, to offer the courtesy."

"Too busy beheading a Jewish prophet," Popygos supplied.

"Please excuse me, sir; my aide, Principes Popygos!" Julius explained to Velleius.

"An excellent aide who handles a sword I recognize well," the General remarked.

"A present to my aide from Paul Gabinius, sir!"

"You do not have to defend your aide, Laco," Velleius assured him. "Popygos wears the sword of my old friend General Gabinius well. He would be proud to have him carry it and use it as well as he does."

"You said that I was to take this Barabbas to Jerusalem, but he is your prisoner."

"My prisoner?" repeated Velleius. "I am under orders not to leave the Decapolis, and even now we are in Samaria. How can I have a prisoner when I was never here? No, Julius Laco and mighty Popygos have just captured one of the most dangerous men in the land. Barabbas is the man who led the attack on Pilate when he entered Jerusalem. Tell Pilate that you have captured Barabbas and it will soothe his hurt pride. Parade Barabbas through the streets of Jerusalem in your lion cart when you arrive, and it will place some fear into the hearts of the Zealots. If they think two Roman legionnaires defeated Barabbas' band and brought him to Jerusalem by themselves, they will be more respectful. The truth is that you had already captured him when we arrived. I will send men with you as far as the outskirts of Jericho to keep the Zealots from trying to recapture Barabbas, but you must not tell my part in this venture."

The new caravan made time as quickly as the oxen would travel. Julius and Popygos retrieved their horses, washed the mud and blood from their uniforms in the Jordan, and now proceeded with six Roman cavalry toward Jericho. The fast pace made the cart jump and bounce on the road. With every bump, Barabbas cursed the Romans, the oxen and the God of Israel for not sending the Messiah to burn both Romans and oxen to ashes.

When they reached the fortress at Jericho, there was a great stirring in the garrison. How had Barabbas been captured? What had happened to the spear men? Why was the Centurion traveling with such a dangerous prisoner with only the help of his aide? Everyone wanted to ask questions, but none dared. This Centurion Laco was the commander of the Antonia Fortress, personally appointed by Tiberius Caesar. Furthermore, it was reported that he was a hero of the games in Rome and that he had personally killed many men in the arena. If the Centurion did not choose to discuss his victory, no one in Jericho dared question him. His aide was as closemouthed as he was. But a fresh scar on the Centurion's arm and the tears in their tunics testified that they had been in a fight.

Julius would not make the same mistake that Pilate had made. He ordered troops from the garrison to guard the prisoner the entire journey from Jericho to Jerusalem. Half of the troops were placed in front of the lion cage, half behind. He also gave orders that Barabbas was to be kept quiet during the journey. To make sure that Barabbas remained quiet, Julius told the soldiers to place Barabbas' neck in a noose. The rope from the noose was thrown over the top of the lion cage and tied to a mounted legionnaire who had orders to hang Barabbas at the first sign of trouble. There was none!

The shortest way for Julius to enter Jerusalem was to cross the Valley of Jehoshaphat at Gethsemane and continue north to the Bethesda Road, which they would follow to the fortress. Thus, they would not encounter any crowds until they were into the city itself. Acting on the suggestion of Velleius Paterculus, Julius turned south into the Kidron Valley and proceeded to circumvent the city. Entering the lower city by the Pool of Siloam, the company, including the caged Barabbas, passed through the Tyropoeon Valley and pressed through the heavily populated upper city to the Samaria Road. By the time the company of soldiers and their caged prisoner were in sight of the wall of the Temple, the streets were filled with spectators.

"Barabbas!" the crowd cried. Some women wept as they saw the prisoner, tied by the neck, inside of the lion cage. Others taunted the prisoner. "Barabbas, the animal!" "Where is your roar, Barabbas?" "You were going to free us from Rome. Free yourself from your cage!"

Others in the crowd — thieves, beggars and streetwalkers — cried out, "Kill the Romans! Save Barabbas!" "Barabbas is a Zealot. Free him and ourselves from Rome!"

By the time Julius came into the Court of Judgement, a mob was following the legionnaires and the cage. Pilate had received word of what was happening from the time Julius had entered the city. "Hail, Centurion Julius Laco." Pilate saluted Julius.

"Your Excellency," Julius responded. "We had the misfortune of an attempted ambush by the Zealot robber, Barabbas. I am pleased to report to Procurator Pilate that the outlaw band has been put to death and their leader has been captured."

"Liars," the crowd shouted. "Barabbas is no thief!"

"Barabbas and his band are the same thieves who attempted to delay and rob Your Excellency's caravan upon your entrance to Jerusalem," Julius quickly informed Pilate.

"Lying Romans," someone shouted. Guards from the fortress began to assemble.

"Where did the attack take place?" Pilate asked, hoping to settle the mob by passing the responsibility to Herod.

"Near the village of Abel-meholah in Samaria," Julius reported.

A murmur went through the crowd. *Samaria?* they thought. *Barabbas and his men have been hiding in Samaria? No true Jew would pass through Samaria, much less hide there. No true Zealot would be caught dead in Samaria!*

"The Roman is right," someone called out. "Barabbas is nothing but a thief — a common thief and not a very good one at that!" Someone laughed. Barabbas wanted to shout at them, telling them not to judge him because of where he had found safety, but he was very aware of the rope that was still attached to the horse and the rider. He fervently hoped no one would do anything foolish.

Pilate sensed that he had the upper hand. "So you are the one who forced the banners of Rome to be lowered. Well, you will hang where those banners should be waving right now. Be sure to repent for becoming unclean in Samaria," Pilate taunted sarcastically, "because before the next Passover, you will be hanging in the breeze — on a cross!"

21

By the time Saul returned to Jerusalem, Esther and Jacob were well into plans for the wedding. Jacob had arranged to secure a house for Saul on the same street in which he resided. The owner of the house had been deeply in debt, and Jacob had taken advantage of the opportunity. It was a nice home, fitting for the daughter of Jacob Bar Kochba. Jacob had paid for it with Saul's assets. Esther had been busy picking out the fabric that would form her wedding dress and the gold and the pearls that would be braided in her hair. The gold and the pearls were not of much concern to Jacob, but Esther was also looking for a large and precious jewel to wear on her forehead. The jewel would become hers after the wedding. Constantly Esther visited Jacob's exchange to compare what was being offered and the price of the gems. She wanted not only the most lovely jewel her father owned but also the most precious.

Saul's things had already been moved to the new house and servants had been hired. Remembering how distraught he had been prior to his departure, Saul was eager to reestablish their relationship. Jacob assured Saul that everything was fine, but that Esther insisted that the wedding take place quickly so the couple could have the full, prescribed thirty days of marriage before the next religious ceremony, the Feast of Passover. During the feast, Jacob would offer a substantial gift that would ensure him political power with the Sanhedrin and the priesthood. Esther informed Saul that it would be prudent for the bridegroom to also give a substantial gift in order to show his gratitude for receiving his bride.

She in turn would offer a sacrifice of cleansing for losing her virginity. Saul was expected to have no sexual relationship with her for the next thirty days.

Saul knew that Esther was a purist when it came to the Law. She was concerned with law and tradition as much as any Pharisee. As a Pharisee and a future member of the Sanhedrin, Saul should have been pleased with Esther's devotion, but somehow the whole thing seemed contrived. Where was love and passion? The formulated and planned times to make love were foreign to what Saul knew of his mother and father. Markus and Saraphina had fallen in love. True, they had experienced a Jewish wedding, but Saul, for the life of him, could not imagine his mother, Saraphina, being concerned or feeling that she needed to be cleansed after her wedding night. The love he had witnessed between the two of them had always seemed warm and pure. His coming wedding to Esther seemed cold and contrived.

"You will have to write a report and quickly convey your findings to the Ab-Bet-Din," Esther greeted him. She did not even inquire into his health or the success of his mission.

Saul did not feel that he had been very successful. After all, what did he have to report? He had seen the Prophet, who had called him a hypocrite. He had heard rumors concerning miracles. The Prophet Jesus had paid little attention to the traditions, but he was an uneducated carpenter who was probably unaware of religious customs. Saul had word that Herod had executed the Prophet John the Baptist, and that the Baptist and Jesus were relatives. There was nothing in his report by which the Sanhedrin could bring Jesus to charges. Saul was certain that the Ab-Bet-Din had not sent them to gather general information. He wanted to try this Jesus for heresy.

"I am sorry, Esther, that I lost my temper with you that day on the street." Saul knew that an apology was in order. He hoped he could break through the coldness in Esther's voice.

"You should never apologize, Saul; it is unmanly. I was in the wrong for speaking to you on the street like that, and in front of the other Pharisees. I will not forget my place again as your wife. Your rebuke should have been more severe. Your colleagues should know that you will not put up with insolence in a woman."

Saul could not believe this woman he was going to marry. He could not even tell her that he was genuinely sorry without being corrected and reminded of Jewish customs. He supposed she would feel satisfied if he beat her for every infraction of the Law.

"Esther, I do not want you to be in servitude to me. I want you to be my companion, my friend. I want you to be interested in me, and I in you. I want to know when I have hurt your feelings. I am concerned about what you feel and think," Saul explained.

"If you are concerned," Esther replied, "then do not shame me in public."

"That is what I am apologizing about" — Saul tried to express his sincerity.

"Not to put me in place is to shame me," Esther stated. "When we are alone, you may discuss things with me and treat me any way you feel is appropriate. But when you are with other men, you must treat me as if I did not exist or as if I were indeed a servant. To do less is to demean yourself as my husband and as a man; that is shameful to me. I understand that you are not strong in the customs of my people. We may talk like this in private and I will help you, but in our public life, you must be the master."

Saul thought, *How can I be the student at home and the master in public?* But he kept the thought to himself. Esther was adamant. She was more pharisaic than any Pharisee he had to deal with. The ways of Jews were certainly strange. He had seen women unveiled in the presence of Jesus of Nazareth. Some of his women followers had laughed openly when Jesus had called Saul and his Pharisees "hypocrites." Saul wondered if Esther could laugh.

Kezia studied Saul's report thoroughly, but his real information came from the face of Saul. "You did not like this Jesus of Nazareth very much?" The expression of the Ab-Bet-Din let Saul know that the question was rhetorical. "Of course not! Who could relish a man who calls him a hypocrite?" Saul understood, again, that the Ab-Bet-Din was not expecting a reply. He felt his face flush with anger and shame at what he had reported to one of the highest authorities in Israel. "I have been told before that he uses the expression 'hypocrites' in reference to Scribes, Pharisees, Priests and other Jews in rulership. This Jesus never speaks spitefully of the Romans. Would to God he did! There is nothing in this report by which we can bring him to trial." Kezia threw Saul's report on the table.

"When he comes to Jerusalem for the feast, perhaps we can set a trap and catch him in blasphemy or in violating the Law," Saul suggested.

"I cannot be a part of such a thing. After all, I must lead the Sanhedrin to judge him." Kezia, deep in thought, stroked his beard. A smile betrayed the fact that he liked Saul's plan. "If you, however, should happen upon the Nazarene while he was violating the Law or speaking blasphemy, you could arrest him. If not you personally, then other trustworthy witnesses who can testify to the fact. I then would be forced to call the Sanhedrin into court."

"I can promise the Ab-Bet-Din that it will be done," Saul replied.

"I will inform the High Priest, Caiaphas, of your words," Kezia said, thinking out loud.

Caiaphas! Saul thought as he left the Ab-Bet-Din. He had not realized that interest in the Nazarene went so high. If he could arrange to have Jesus brought to trial, it would certainly boost his position in the Sanhedrin.

When he returned to the house of Jacob after his meeting with the Ab-Bet-Din, Esther hung on to his every word. She was much more interested in his association to the Sanhedrin than in his relationship with her.

"The Ab-Bet-Din told you Caiaphas had an interest in your report. Saul, this trip of yours was of greater importance than we thought. If we succeed in trapping this Jesus for the Ab-Bet-Din, not only will the Sanhedrin be indebted but the High Priest himself!" Esther was ecstatic with the idea.

"You have a wedding to prepare for," Saul reminded her. "I will worry about the Sanhedrin and Jesus. He could be a genuine prophet who will not break the Law or blaspheme."

"Nonsense," Esther replied. "No man can keep all of the Law. I know how to catch him!" Her eyes sparkled with delight.

I wish her eyes twinkled like that when she thinks of me and our wedding night, Saul thought. "And how do you propose to trap the Prophet?" Saul asked.

"One of my father's customers has a wife, Danielle. It is all the talk among the women. Danielle has a lover by the name of Amaris. Well, Danielle's husband goes to bargain in the market on a set day and time every week. While he is gone, Amaris slips into his house. When this Jesus is in Jerusalem, we will have two of your Pharisee friends — that Johanan who is so eager and the one who is not so bright, Solomons — catch Danielle in the very act of adultery and publicly present her to Jesus for judgement. Under our law, she must be stoned.

"But if he stones her, or orders it done, he has violated Roman law and the Romans will crucify him. If he does not order her stoned, he has violated our law and the Sanhedrin has him. Only, you must tell Johanan and Solomons not to capture Amaris. He is a good customer of father's. We do not wish father to lose business because of us!"

Saul was amazed at Esther's craftiness and the relish with which she approached the plot. That she knew of such things as affairs and adultery astonished him. Esther was a virgin, of that he was sure. But she had more knowledge of sexual things than he had thought she did.

Esther's lack of passion did not change as the time for their wedding approached. While Saul was not counting on any real familiarity, he did expect a genuine friendship to develop between them. As the autumn nights grew cooler and the wedding date drew closer, Esther remained proper and detached from all personal involvement with or interest in Saul. Saul knew that personal contact was forbidden by Jewish culture, but he had seen Jewish maidens romance young men in a flirtatious manner. Try as he might to solicit a love affair, she accepted their relationship only as a matter of law and duty. Esther seemed more concerned that Saul was a proper Pharisee than that he was a loving bridegroom.

Jewish bridegrooms usually dressed in brilliantly-colored silk garments scented with frankincense and myrrh. Saul of Tarsus could afford to dress in the very richest garments, but Esther insisted that he array himself in the normal blue and white of the Pharisee. She wanted everyone to know Saul's religious status. She also arranged for him to wear a gold crown on his head and a gold chain around his neck from which hung a very costly jewel. While she wanted to impress everyone that Esther Bar Kochba was marrying a holy man, she also wanted them to know that he was a very rich holy man!

Esther was resplendent. Her skin had been prepared to make her complexion shine with a luster like marble. The locks of her hair were heavily braided with gold and pearls. Tier upon tier of jewels cascaded from her neck, and the silk of her robe was kept from flowing in the breeze by the weight of the pearls sewed into it. The daughter of a merchant king was being wed, and Jacob Bar Kochba wanted everyone of importance in Jerusalem to know it.

The procession from Jacob's home to that of the bridegroom did not take long due to the proximities of the homes, but Jacob made sure that there were demonstrations along the entire road.

Men played on drums and musical instruments while girls danced along the way. Gifts were scattered to those who stood watching.

A canopy had been erected in the courtyard of the house Jacob had procured for Saul. Esther stood beside Saul under the canopy, her face still hidden beneath a thick veil. Saul wished he could see Esther's expression. Did she have any love in her eyes? Did her lips tremble in anticipation for her bridegroom? Gamaliel gave the benediction on the marriage and the couple entered the house for the wedding feast.

Jacob presided as the ruler of the feast. Every small detail was taken care of by the servants under Jacob's watchful eyes. Jacob wanted everything to be done according to the Law, so Esther would know that all the ceremony was correct. All Saul's acquaintances from the school of Gamaliel attended the wedding. An array of Jacob's business associates were also present, still jesting and bickering about previous deals. Among them was a man Saul had not met before. He instantly liked this man called Joseph of Arimathaea. Joseph was a man of some age, wisdom and experience, who seemed very sure of himself. Even Jacob failed to intimidate this Joseph — a fact that greatly influenced Saul's impression of the man. Kezia, the Ab-Bet-Din, not only attended with his assistant, Nicodemus, but, to the astonishment of Saul's Pharisee companion, Reuben, he paid personal attention to Saul. Johanan, always impetuous, gave Saul some good-natured ribbing. Due to the mirthfulness of the feast and the wine and the fellowship of his friends, Saul did not notice that Esther had left the feast.

"Your bride awaits you." Jacob's voice was stern.

"Go ahead, dive into the well of delight," Johanan teased. Saul felt his face flush.

Jacob stood at Saul's side waiting to escort him to the apartment where Esther waited. "My daughter is ready to receive her bridegroom. May you have sons." Jacob's voice still had no joviality in it.

"May your wedding night be filled with enchantment and happiness" — Joseph of Arimathaea raised his wine cup. Saul appreciated the sincerity he felt in Joseph's salutation.

"Do not forget that the days of the marriage are thirty and then you must make atonement for your sins," the Ab-Bet-Din added. Saul felt like a lamb being judged for the slaughter. Jacob escorted Saul to the door of the apartment and opened it for him. Saul stepped into a stairway and the door closed behind him.

The place chosen was a rooftop apartment. Moonlight from a full moon lit the quarters with a soft, radiant light. Music and noise filtered from the court below. The sweet smell of roast lamb wafted up from the feast, but the smell of frankincense came from a couch in the shadow of an inside wall. There, in the folds of the lounge, lay Esther, her body shining like a marble statue in the light of the moon. Saul leaned over, placed his hand on her shoulder and tenderly kissed her. Her flesh was cold to his touch.

"Are you chilled?" he asked, concerned that the night air might be too chilly on her naked body.

"No," she whispered. "Hurry up! We must not keep my father waiting."

"What has your father to do with us now?" Saul asked in surprise.

"The sheet," she answered. "You must throw the sheet down from the roof so that he can examine it before his friends and prove, from the blood on it, that he gave a virgin daughter as a bride. If he has to wait long before his business friends, it will be awkward. Go ahead and take my virginity so that he will not be humiliated. I am ready for the sacrifice to be offered."

After the sheet was duly dropped by Esther, Saul heard Jacob's boasting and Johanan's jesting in the court below. He fell to sleep beside the unyielding, unloving body of his wife. As he slept, Saul dreamed of the warmth of a Roman girl's embraces and he heard her say, "Are you really a virgin? I have never met a virgin god before!" Esther had made a sacrifice of their wedding night, but Saul felt that he had been cheated.

22

The streets of Jerusalem were crowded with people arriving for the Feast of Passover. On every corner and in every passageway the subject was the Prophet from Galilee. His disciples caused a stir wherever they went. Their clothing, long strides and unique accent marked the twelve men as being his followers.

"Where is the Prophet?" someone in the crowd cried.

"Prophet?" another echoed the first. "Charlatan is more like it!"

"He is a compassionate man," another said.

"Compassionate? He fabricates miracles and preaches falsehoods," another replied.

The twelve men from Galilee continued to push through the crowd , acting as though they had not heard the jeers.

Saul was at the exchange with Jacob when the Ab-Bet-Din sent for him. The scene reminded Saul of his first encounter with Kezia, only this time it was the Ab-Bet-Din who was angry.

"The disciples of Jesus openly walk the streets of this city. The people gossip about him. Some have even gone so far as to say that he is the Messiah." Kezia's face was filled with fury and at the word "Messiah" he slammed his fist on the table. "The priests are afraid that he might diminish the feast. If the populace turns to him and the Temple offering drops, Caiaphas will have my head. The major income of the priesthood comes in during this feast. The attention of the people must not be swayed from their religious duties onto this Prophet of Galilee." Kezia spat out the words as if they gave him a bad taste in his mouth. "Find him and have him brought to the Sanhedrin for a hearing. We do not have evidence to convict him, but at least we can get him off the streets during Passover!"

Saul bowed his head respectfully and left the presence of the Ab-Bet-Din. There was no need to remind the man that there could be no hearing during Passover. That was Kezia's problem. Saul had a bigger problem. How does one find a prophet who has not made an appearance or prophesied even once in a city teeming with religious characters?

Saul brought the problem to Jacob, who in turn had the word passed through the system of street vendors and beggars. "Do not be concerned, Saul," Jacob assured him, "they will find anything or anyone on the streets of Jerusalem." The twelve disciples of Jesus were watched most closely. If the Prophet was in Jerusalem, it would be his disciples who would lead Saul's spies to him.

The disciples seemed to be enjoying the holiday in the city. They purchased sweetmeats, baskets, bread and wine from the very vendors Saul had looking for Jesus. One of the followers of Jesus, Judas Iscariot, did all the bargaining for the group and carried the purse. Saul's agents reported that this Jesus was not a poor man but received support from a number of wealthy persons. *Would to God that he was poor,* Saul thought. *The Sanhedrin would not be interested in his activities if he was.*

The Ab-Bet-Din was even more furious than the last time Saul had seen him. "Why have you not brought this Jesus to me?"

"He is nowhere in the city to be found," Saul assured Kezia.

"Nowhere to be found!" Kezia exploded in outrage. "He has been teaching in the Temple itself! He knows that we have been looking for him and he believes we intend to kill him."

"Do you?" Saul asked, noting that Kezia's veins were throbbing in the intensity of his rage.

"I told you we only intend to remove him from the streets so he is not detrimental to the feast," Kezia shouted at Saul. "He told an assembly at the Temple that Moses gave us the Law and we, the religious leaders, do not keep the Law. Then he told them that we are looking for him to kill him."

But, Saul thought, *since he has committed no crime, you are breaking the Law in trying to have him arrested.* Saul kept his tongue, knowing that it was not a time to argue with the Ab-Bet-Din.

"He told the Pharisees in the Temple not to judge according to appearance but to judge righteous judgement!"

Saul knew that the statement had a sting in it, but that it was true. Again he knew that it would not be wise to tell the Ab-Bet-Din his feelings.

"We were watching his disciples and the streets. He must have entered the city after they arrived and eluded us by going to the one place no one would think to look. Give me officers from the Temple Guard and I can arrest him in the Temple for disturbing the worship," Saul stated.

When Saul entered the Temple grounds with the guards, the Prophet was nowhere to be found. Noticing a group in heated debate, Saul approached them. "Where is the Galilean Prophet?" Saul demanded.

"Can you not find him?" came the sarcastic reply.

"He was here, openly healing the sick and preaching the kingdom," another answered.

"He said, 'You will look for me and will not find me; and where I am, you cannot come,'" another replied.

"Perhaps he has gone among the Gentiles and is teaching them," one said mockingly. "That is what he meant, 'Where I am, you cannot come.' If you find him, you might become unclean!" The entire group laughed at the jest.

Saul noted that things were getting out of hand. Two of the Chief Priests, several high-ranking Pharisees, and other Temple guards approached the group. Saul turned his bewilderment onto the Temple guards. "You knew that the Ab-Bet-Din was seeking this Prophet from Galilee. Why didn't you detain him?"

"I have never heard a man speak like this Prophet," one of the guards replied. "What he said was truth."

"Is even the Temple Guard deceived?" Saul questioned the guard. "Do any of the Temple leaders or the Pharisees believe that he is the Messiah?" Saul asked rhetorically. As he spoke, Saul recognized one of the ranking Pharisees. Nicodemus had been at his wedding feast. Nicodemus, sure that Saul had recognized him, looked squarely into the young Pharisee's eyes and said, "Does the Law judge any man before it hears him directly and knows that a crime has been committed?"

One of the priests who stood nearby broke into the argument. "Search the Scriptures. No prophet comes from Galilee!" Then, looking at Nicodemus, he asked: "Are you from Galilee?"

As Nicodemus turned away from the insult, Saul surveyed the faces around him. He decided that it would be best if he led the guards away before things got out of hand.

Kezia was even more hot-tempered when Saul returned with the guards and no prisoner. "Do not agitate yourself," Saul assured the Ab-Bet-Din. "I have a plan. Tomorrow is the correct day to use it. Now that we know he is in Jerusalem and speaking at the Temple, I will catch him. And I will give you evidence that you can try him with!"

When he returned home, Saul told Esther that it was time to execute her plan for trapping the Galilean. Johanan and Solomons were chosen to be the agents to catch Danielle and Amaris in adultery, and a watch was placed on Danielle's house. Tomorrow, in the Temple, Jesus would have to decide either to break the Law of Moses in front of witnesses or to condemn an adulteress to death!

The next day Saul made sure that he was as far from the incident as possible. Although it was true that Saul did not want to be directly involved so that at the hearing of the Sanhedrin the plot would not be revealed, he also felt guilt at being a party to the scheme. He truly believed that Jesus was building himself up to be a false Messiah. Nevertheless, there was a certain sickening feeling that what he and Esther were doing was unfair.

As the morning dragged on, Saul attempted everything he could think of to distract his mind from the plot. A little after noon, Solomons and Johanan came into the court. Their expressions were gloomy. Immediately, Saul knew that something bad had happened. Even though she did not speak, Esther listened intently for the report of how her scheme had worked.

"It was as you said it would be," Johanan began. "Amaris slipped into the house shortly after the husband left for the exchange. We waited a bit to give Aramis and Danielle time to get things started, then we broke into the house."

Solomons, his face slipping into a smile, interrupted: "They were both undressed."

"We allowed Amaris to escape, as instructed, and caught Danielle," Johanan continued.

"She stopped running and tried to wrap herself in a sheet," Solomons stated. Then he added, "I caught her by the hair and she scratched me!" He showed them long ugly scratches on the side of his face.

"It took everything we could do to restrain her," Johanan continued. "We pulled her out into the street and she fell to the pavement several times trying to cover herself. Her knees and legs got quite bloody."

"She had a difficult time trying to cover herself with the sheet while being dragged down the street," Solomons reported with the first sign of joviality that had crossed his face during the report.

"The Galilean Prophet was right where we had been told he would be," Johanan stated. "Numerous men were following us. By the time we reached him, it had become a throng."

Solomons muttered, "It's not every day you see a naked woman dragged down the street!"

"We literally threw the woman at his feet," Johanan continued. "By this time she was quite a mess. We were all wet with perspiration and it was difficult holding onto her. Her hair was wet and stringing around her shoulders, and her eyes were wild. She had cuts and bruises all over. As she lay on the ground, she was still trying to cover herself with what was left of the sheet. I told Jesus, loudly, so that all could hear, that we had caught the woman in the very act of adultery. Then I asked him the question you told me to ask: 'The Law of Moses commands that such a one as this should be stoned to death. What are your instructions?'"

"And what did he answer?" Saul demanded.

"He didn't answer," Johanan replied.

Saul smiled for the first time. He had caught the Galilean Prophet!

"He didn't answer," Johanan repeated. "He just wrote on the ground with his finger."

"Wrote on the ground with his finger?" Saul echoed. "What did he write?"

"Beulah," Johanan said, his face turning crimson.

"Beulah?" questioned Saul.

"The name of the Pharisee's wife I slept with last night," Johanan confessed. "Saul, I do not know how it happened. I went by his house to visit and he was away at the Temple, working on some things for the feast. Beulah was unveiled and lonely, and, well ... it never happened before and it will never happen again! This Jesus must have some spy system. He looked me straight in the face and said, 'The one among you who has no sin, he can cast the first stone.' What was I to do? If I so much as picked up a stone, he would tell them about Beulah and me. And Beulah's husband was in the crowd! He, or the crowd, would have killed me."

"And what did you do, Solomons?" Saul asked.

"Nothing," replied Solomons. "If Johanan did not want to hurt her, why should I?"

"Didn't anyone pick up a stone?" Saul cried.

"No," said Johanan. "Jesus wrote other names on the ground until, one by one, all the men had slipped away. I guess his spies had reports on all the men in the crowd! I am told that after all the Pharisees had left, Jesus asked Danielle, 'Where are your accusers?' She told him that we had all gone. Then he told her that without an accuser he could not condemn her."

"Fools!" Esther's voice shattered the conversation, which had softened to just above a whisper. Johanan and Solomons were shocked that Saul's righteous wife would speak that way to men and include her husband in her remark.

"You fools!" — she emphasized her opinion. Looking at Saul, she remarked scathingly, "You send an adulterer to catch an adulteress. You are a fool!" Then, turning her gaze on Johanan and Solomons, she exploded: "Do you know what you have done to Saul? It is doubtful, now, that he will ever be a full member of the Sanhedrin!" Esther stormed out of the room.

23

The winter had passed in Jerusalem. Julius had spent most of it behind the damp walls of Antonia. The days were uneventful, except for the changing of the guard and, at times, a game of chance played on the markings in the Lithostrotos (Pavement of Judgement). Julius felt bloated from the lack of activity. Popygos continually reminded him how well off both of them would be with Pilate at Caesarea where the waters of the great sea keep the winters mild.

Pilate was due in Jerusalem before Passover. Julius waited with anticipation for his arrival. The prisoner Barabbas had not yet been crucified because Pilate had not signed the order before he returned to Caesarea. Thus, Julius had to wait on him. Julius had promised Barabbas a crucifixion and he intended to keep his word in behalf of the members of his command that Barabbas had killed.

The Chief Priests and the Pharisees had passed the word that should the Prophet from Galilee attend the Feast of Passover, he was to be turned over to them. The populace was of the opinion that the Pharisees meant to kill Jesus. After his experience at Herod's birthday party, Julius hoped that the rumors were not true. Herod was the law in Galilee, but Pilate was the law in Jerusalem. Should even the Sanhedrin attempt to put a man to death, Pilate would be forced to judge them under Roman law.

Julius had seen Saul and his veiled bride on the street. He hoped that Saul had nothing to do with the plot against Jesus. While Saul's Roman citizenship and the ring of Augustus, if Saul still had it, would save him from Pilate, they would destroy him as Saul of Tarsus.

On the first day of April, Pilate returned to Jerusalem and Julius' duties increased considerably.

"Julius, wake up!" Popygos' voice penetrated his mind.

"By the gods, Popygos! What time is it?" Julius inquired.

"Very early," Popygos replied.

"What are you doing here at this time in the morning?" Julius asked.

"Caiaphas, the High Priest of the Jews, and his Temple Guard are just outside the Judgement Hall. Pilate has been awakened and is preparing to go to them. I thought you would want to know." Popygos spoke in almost a whisper.

"What are you whispering about?" Julius demanded. "There is no one else in my quarters."

"Sorry, sir!" Popygos replied in proper military fashion. "There is a mob gathering and I thought that you might wish to increase the guard lest trouble be stirring."

"Do it, Popygos! You are more in command here than I am."

"I did not wish to sound impertinent, sir!"

"Oh, go on, Popygos. You and I have been friends much too long for you to be impertinent. It is just too early in the morning!"

It was a strange sight that greeted Julius. Pilate was seated on a large cobalt-blue chair wearing nothing but a nightshirt and sandals. Soldiers held the eagle standard of Rome over the judgement chair, which was located on a platform three steps above a paved courtyard. In the arches of the courtyard stood the High Priest, dressed in a jeweled robe. Behind him was a crowd of worked-up Jews. Standing bound in the middle of the pavement was a rabbi dressed in a white robe tasseled in blue. It was the Passover, so Caiaphas and the mob could not enter the Judgement Hall for fear that they would become unclean. They had no concern for the poor Jewish Prophet who had been cast out onto the pavement.

Pilate noted the entrance of Julius and the guards along the Judgement Hall wall and nodded approval. He had to leave the judgement seat and cross the pavement to the gate in order to speak to Caiaphas and the Jews. The soldiers, under Julius' command, followed the Procurator with swords drawn.

"Of what crime do you accuse this man?" Pilate asked the group.

"If he was not a criminal, I would not have brought him to judgement," Caiaphas answered.

"Then you judge him according to your own law!" Pilate stated firmly.

"But it is your law that will not allow us to execute a transgressor," Caiaphas argued.

"A transgressor," Pilate murmured, as he recrossed the pavement and sat on the chair. He studied the prisoner intently, with his right arm resting upright on the arm of the chair, his left arm on his thigh, and his legs straight forward so that his back pushed into the chair. Everything in the morning air was silent as the two men gazed at each other. Pilate bit on his lip before he spoke. "Are you the King of the Jews?"

"Since no one has made that statement or accused me of it, are you making the statement or simply repeating what you have heard?" Jesus' eyes did not flinch from those of Pilate.

Julius watched in fascination. The Jew was right. No one had brought that charge or any accusation yet!

Pilate sat upright and leaned forward, trying to reestablish the fact that it was he who sat on the judgement seat, not Jesus. Due to Pilate's lack of deportment, the Jewish Prophet had turned the judgement back onto him — and Pilate knew it.

"Am I a Jew?" Pilate spit out the word with disgust. "Your own people and your Chief Priests have brought you to this place of judgement. What is your crime?"

Jesus never flinched, nor did he show any sign that Pilate's position intimidated him. "My kingdom is not of this world. If my kingdom were of this world, you would be fighting for your life. My servants would keep me from being delivered to the Jews. Know that my kingdom does not exist in this realm."

"Are you saying that you are a king?" Pilate asked. If this fool of a prophet would just say that he was a king, Pilate could find him guilty and they could all go back to bed.

"You are the one who asked about a kingdom and called me a king," Jesus pointed out.

Julius found himself nodding his head in agreement with the Prophet. Were Julius the judge, Pilate would have lost this case!

The Galilean continued, "You have said that I was a king and you sit on the seat of judgement. I was born and came into the world that I should bear witness to the truth. Everyone who judges truly and knows what truth is hears me."

Pilate left the judgement chair and walked past the Prophet in order to speak to the Jews. He stopped in the middle of the court only feet from the prisoner. His eyes glared at Jesus and his lips curled with disdain as he growled: "What is truth?" Then to Caiaphas and the Jews he pronounced, "I cannot find anything for which to judge this man."

There was total silence, then a murmur arose from the crowd. Julius signaled his soldiers and they turned again to face the rabble. The High Priest struck his forehead repeatedly and the people, seeing the gesture, increased their protest.

"He inflames the people!" Caiaphas declared. "He fabricates miracles and teaches against our religion. He started in Galilee and has ended up in the very Temple itself!"

Pilate had returned to the judgement chair. Suddenly he stood upright. "Galilee? Is the prisoner from Galilee?"

"Without doubt he is a Galilean," Caiaphas stated. "He is the son of Joseph, the carpenter of Nazareth. That is one reason we know that he a false Messiah!"

"Then this is none of my business," said Pilate, pleased with the turn of events. "He is under the authority of Herod, Tetrarch of Galilee. Take him to Herod and let me finish dressing."

Caiaphas was distraught. Pilate knew that Jesus was from Galilee. The High Priest had told him so at their secret meeting the night before. The Sabbath was approaching. If Jesus was not executed soon, his death would have to be delayed until after the Passover — a full eight days. During those eight days the followers of Jesus could assemble thousands against the religious authorities.

Julius was as distressed as Caiaphas. He still remembered the head of the Baptist on a platter. The last thing Julius wanted to do was to deliver another religious prisoner to that butcher. But he was under orders, so he had his soldiers surround the Jewish Prophet and lead him through the gates, west through the Tyropoeon Valley to the wall, and on to the Hasmonean Palace near the Xystus Gate of the Temple.

If Julius had been impressed with Herod's palace in Tiberias, the Hasmonean Palace made it look like a peasant's home. Once inside the porter's gate, the party had to ascend a steep incline. The Palace had a great hall and two wings of snowy marble. In front of the building and around the grounds tall colonnades glimmered in the rising sun. The great hall to which they were escorted held one hundred dining couches. Herod, who liked to amuse his guests with the spectacular, had invited them to come and see the famous Prophet from Galilee. Only the prisoner, the priests and Pilate's Guard were allowed into the Palace.

"Won't you be seated," Herod said patiently, as he sat down. He was wearing a cape and a crown and he held a scepter. Julius wondered how the man had prepared so quickly to sit in a kingly role. Julius accepted Herod's gesture, but he indicated that Popygos was to remain standing and on alert. The soldiers looked at Julius and he indicated that they could sit near the doors. Herod motioned for Jesus to sit, but the Prophet remained standing and looked steadfastly into Herod's eyes. Then he shifted his eyes to a wall and fixed his gaze.

"If you are God's son," Herod began, "you will not mind doing a little miracle for your king." Julius could hear the same sarcasm in Herod's voice that he had used on Salome just before the Baptist lost his head. "A simple demonstration of your power will do," Herod continued. "We will bring you a cup of water to turn into wine — I do not need a barrelful!!" Jesus remained unmoved, his eyes fixed on the wall. "A little magic trick will do" — Herod's voice seemed to be pleading. "I promised my friends that they would see something they have not seen before," he added. "I know — everyone has his price. I will give you your freedom and make you the official Prophet of Galilee. Just make the sun dark, as Moses did, or make it thunder on this cloudless morning."

Jesus answered the Tetrarch with silence.

"Speak to your king!" Herod raved. He stood and walked around Jesus, trying to unfix the gaze of the Nazarene. "Your cousin John had a voice. I had to cut his head off to stop it. You look as shabby as he did! Look at you, Prophet; your feet are unwashed in my house! What kind of holy man are you with unwashed feet? You claim to be a king. Look at me! This ... is how a king dresses! What kind of king are you?"

Herod suddenly smiled and whispered to an aide. He gestured to the priests with hilarity. Everyone waited in silence. Soon the aide returned with a cloak. It was a gaudy, red mantle like those worn by desert tribesmen. Herod placed it on Jesus, thus making him the funniest, most preposterous king they could imagine.

"Well, this sight is all the amusement our king can give you," Herod told his guests. Turning to Julius he said, "Tell Pilate that the only evidence for this case comes from Jerusalem, so I send him his King of the Jews as a present — a thank you for the splendid pair of lions he gave me."

Julius felt relieved when they left Herod's presence. Surely Pilate could now free the man and get on with crucifying Barabbas. Popygos and the soldiers led the Jewish Prophet back to the Lithostrotos and to Pilate. As they waited for Pilate to reappear in the Judgement Hall, Popygos gambled with the soldiers on a game of kings. He and Julius had played the game many times on the long winter evenings. It was played with two dice, on stones that had been chiseled with the symbols of the game. The symbols were of a bird, a triangle, a rooster and a monarch with a crown. Each player had a symbol and he moved according to the numbers on the dice. When one reached the mock king, he was the winner of the bet.

When Pilate returned to the Lithostrotos, he saw the men casting dice and noted that Herod had made Jesus into a mock king. *So Herod wants to play a game,* Pilate thought. *And he's using Jesus as the pawn.*

Turning to the crowd, Pilate rendered his decision: "You brought this man to me to be judged. He is from Galilee, so I sent him to Herod. Herod could find no guilt in this man and sent him back to me." The Procurator raised his voice. "This is my verdict" — everything was still and motionless. "He has done nothing worthy of the death penalty. I will scourge him and set him free!"

The crowd broke into a shouting, surging mass. Julius and his men pulled their swords and reenforcements from Antonia rushed onto the pavement. Pilate lost his composure and moved to the protection of Julius' sword. The Procurator was frightened. Only

Julius' unflinching sword kept the Governor from running for his life.

Pilate decided on a desperate gamble. He would offer them Barabbas or Jesus. Barabbas was a murderer. Jesus was a man of religion. Surely they would chose to crucify Barabbas and let Jesus live.

"It is the Roman custom to free one prisoner for Passover. Would you have me free Barabbas or Jesus?" Pilate asked.

The response from the crowd caught the Procurator by surprise. They cried, "Give us Barabbas!"

"No!" Julius heard himself shout at the crowd. Barabbas had killed men under his command. Pilate could not let that animal go free in order to kill the gentle Galilean. Hearing the resounding no that Julius had shouted, Pilate glanced at the man beside him who held the sword that protected him. He was almost afraid of his own guard. Pilate raised both hands in the air. "Which one do you want me to release to you? Barabbas or Jesus called the Messiah?"

"Barabbas!" came the shout.

Pilate was astonished. "What am I to do with Jesus called the Messiah?" he asked.

"Crucify him!" they thundered.

"Why? What wrong has he done?" Pilate asked.

The people simply shouted louder, "Let him be crucified!"

Pilate ordered Julius to release Barabbas at once and to proceed with the scourging of the Prophet of Galilee. Before going to handle the release of Barabbas, Julius ordered Popygos to oversee the scourging of Jesus. He knew that if Popygos was assigned the duty of freeing the murderer, Barabbas was a dead man. Julius was tempted to kill the man himself.

Jesus was led into a courtyard where three small, thick stone pillars had been positioned. Each of the pillars had two iron rings embedded in it about three feet from the ground. The Galilean was tied to the nearest post by his wrists. His feet were spread and leather straps were used to bind his ankles to the other posts. The binding of his hands and feet required Jesus to bend over at his waist. The lictor, a man trained in scourging, bent down to see the face of the man he was going to beat. Then he moved about six feet behind Jesus and brought the flagellum — an instrument made from a short, circular piece of oak to which strips of leather had been attached, with bits of bone and iron fastened to their extremities — across the back of the Jew. The leather straps whacked the back of Jesus and the bits of bone and chain curled around his body, making hemorrhages in his chest. The soldiers in the courtyard laughed about the spinelessness of the Jews, while Popygos forced himself to watch the torture. It was his job to see that the lictor did not kill the prisoner.

A sob came from Jesus and he almost passed out. With each blow the lictor aimed the flagellum lower so that it crashed against the prisoner's flesh, tearing pieces from his stomach covering. Popygos examined Jesus. His breathing was swift and shallow, so Popygos ordered the lictor to stop. Jesus was cut loose from the stones. Because he was unconscious, Popygos ordered that water be thrown on him. When Jesus regained consciousness, a laughing soldier dropped the scarlet cloak on Jesus' back and dragged him to his feet so that it could be draped appropriately. Another soldier, enjoying the jest, placed a crown of thorns on Jesus' head. One of the men, filled with hate for the Jews, took a heavy reed and struck him with it. Another spat in his face and shouted, "The King of the Jews!"

When Popygos led Jesus back to the judgement seat, Julius knew that he had given Popygos the toughest assignment. Two soldiers held Jesus erect to keep him from falling. Even the crowd cringed when they saw the Nazarene. His hair, under the thorns, was damp and streaked with blood. His face had been so marked by the reed that his features were indistinguishable. Blood, in strips, was beginning to show even through the cloak.

Looking at what was left of the man, Julius felt sick at his stomach. He felt the same shock and revulsion that he had known when the head of the Baptist had been presented to Herod. But this man was still alive. Pity filled the heart of the Centurion. For a brief moment, the eyes of Jesus and of Julius met. In that moment, all the sorrow and loneliness in Julius' life tried to surface. Julius did not know why, but he felt as if Jesus could see into the emptiness of his soul.

"Behold the man!" Pilate cried, hoping to elicit some sympathy from the Jews. No one but Julius recognized the declaration of honor Pilate had given to Jesus. Julius had heard the expression at the Triumph of Markus Paul Gabinius. Julius turned his back on the spectacle to wipe water from his eyes. It would not do to have Pilate see his centurion crying!

The crowd answered the Procurator's declaration with "Crucify him!" and "To the cross with him!"

Pilate could not believe that even the priests and the Pharisees could be so calloused to the man's suffering. "Take him and crucify him yourselves. I find no guilt in him!" Pilate stated as forcefully as he could.

"We have a law," one of the Sanhedrin said. "According to our law he must die, for he has declared himself to be the Son of God!"

Pilate walked back into the Praetorium and ordered Julius to bring the prisoner to him. "What is the source of your origin?" Pilate asked Jesus. Jesus looked at Pilate, but he did not answer. "Don't you know that I have the power to set you free or to crucify you?" Pilate asked.

"You have no power to harm me," Jesus said through stammering lips. "He who surrendered me over to you is guilty of the graver offense." Julius did not understand what Jesus meant by the words.

The Procurator seated himself on the judgement seat once more. "If you release this man, you are not a friend of Caesar!" the Jews cried.

Pilate looked in Julius' direction. The Procurator had never forgotten that Centurion Laco had been appointed directly by Tiberius. The name of Tiberius frightened him more than the results of any judgement he might give now.

Pilate ordered that a basin of water be brought to him. Then, looking directly at Caiaphas, he washed his hands and said, "I am innocent of the blood of this just man!"

Pilate walked across the Praetorium slowly and called Julius to him. "Make a sign of wood to nail to the top of his cross. It shall say in Hebrew, Latin and Aramaic, 'Jesus of Nazareth, King of the Jews!'"

Julius could not believe what he was hearing. *Has not this man, who Pilate has already declared to be innocent, suffered enough? Have not Popygos and I obeyed Rome in this matter even beyond our personal feelings? Now Rome, through Pilate, is commanding us to crucify a man who already is as much as dead. How inhumane can Rome be? How far beyond the leading of his conscience can duty call a man to go? Where is the line between being a soldier and becoming a murderer?* Julius Laco was a competent officer. He barked the commands that set the Procurator's judgement toward completion. His legion scurried to get the equipment together. Every detail would be taken care of to make the crucifixion efficient!

24

Enos and Ethan were twin brothers. Enos was the firstborn of a family of Samarian peasants. Ethan was an echo of his brother. It was as if Ethan had no mind or will of his own apart from the domination of his brother. So, when Enos decided to kill and rob a Roman merchant who had already passed through Samaria and was just across the border in Judaea headed for Jerusalem, Ethan took part in the crime. Had it not been for Enos, Ethan would never have turned to crime. Had it not been for Ethan, Enos would not have been caught. Both were now scheduled, with Barabbas, to be crucified. Pilate had released Barabbas in order to placate the crowd. Rome had only Enos, Ethan and Jesus of Nazareth upon which to vent its fury.

The twins were placed, single file, behind Jesus. Ethan, shadowing Enos as he had done all his life, was scheduled to become a pale replica of his death. As they crossed the pavement, the brothers were separated by a guard. In front of each of the three men a legionnaire positioned himself with a sign that announced the prisoner's crime. Even with the guards and the signs, Enos and Ethan were alike. A platoon of soldiers armed with spears formed on each side of the prisoners. Julius mounted his stallion, which had been saddled for his morning ride, and took his position at the head of the procession. The crossbeams were placed on the shoulders of the prisoners and their wrists were tied together with a rope that was tied to the beam to keep it from slipping and falling in front of the soldier who followed.

Enos kept assuring Ethan that they were not going to be crucified. Barabbas had done much worse things then they had done. Had not Barabbas boasted that he had killed Roman soldiers? Where was Barabbas? Pilate had let him go free! They were only being used to help crucify this blasphemer! Ethan, however, was not convinced. He wanted to know why they were carrying three crosses!

Julius started the line moving. The Jewish priests moved aside to watch the first halting steps of the Nazarene. Julius cared little for the brothers, but the Jewish Prophet still bothered him. The thieves were strong and could carry their crosses all the way to Golgotha, but the Prophet was weak from the loss of blood. Fortunately, the major section of the route was downhill and the weight of the cross pushed Jesus forward. At the bottom of the hill they turned left at the market, but the Jewish Prophet lost his balance and fell forward on the pavement. Julius saw fresh blood where the beam and the thorns were tearing into the side of the Nazarene's face. He turned his horse, moved to the prisoner's side and ordered him to rise. Jesus lay in a stupor on the pavement.

"You!" Julius commanded, pointing to a large, brawny black merchant who had been caught in the crowd. "Yes, you!" The Centurion gestured toward the man. "Pick up his cross and help him."

The eyes of the big black looked for a way out, but he could not find any. A Roman spear pointed his way. The Cyrenian easily lifted the cross to his shoulder. Blood stained his brightly-colored cloak. With his free hand, he reached down and helped Jesus to his feet. Julius appreciated the black for caring for the Jew. He had been told only to lift the cross, but compassion had compelled him to go farther than he had been commanded. The Jew was close to total collapse. Even without the weight of the cross, he could not have continued without the help of the Cyrenian as he half carried him.

The road to the place of crucifixion turned up a hill and through the Gennath Gate. The procession stopped at a rocky knoll about fifteen feet above the road on which some with a good imagination said that they could see the form of a skull. Julius ordered that Jesus be crucified first, just to get the man out of his torment.

"I am not a thief, but a Zealot for Judaea! Rise up and save me from the Roman dogs!" Enos cried. The gathering below the hill looked from Julius, to the Roman guards with their swords and weapons, to their own empty hands. Then they laughed. "He is not Barabbas!" someone jested. "If he was a great Zealot for Israel, he would be free with Barabbas!" another taunted. Julius felt perspiration in the palm of his sword hand. It was not from fear but from anger. In his concern for Jesus, he had almost forgotten about Barabbas. Ethan started murmuring a prayer. The crowd ridiculed him worse than they had his brother.

The fragrance of spring flowers wafted across the rock in the spring breeze. Julius was grateful for the gust. The sun was at high noon and bright. Without some wind, one could have smelled death on the rock.

Popygos tied an apron with pockets around his waist. From one of the pockets he drew a five-inch square-cut nail. A soldier pressed the forearm of Jesus flat to the board. Popygos found the spot he wanted, raised a hammer and brought it down as hard as he could. The reverberation of the sound of the hammer caused a flock of birds that had been feeding in the rock crevices to take flight. Popygos stepped over Jesus and nailed the other arm to the tree. Two soldiers lifted Jesus and the crossbar off the ground. The pull of the weight of his body on the nails through his wrists brought a scream from the Jew. As the soldiers, with the assistance of two more soldiers, lifted the cross high enough to set it, Jesus' feet dangled in the air and his body jerked with pain. Popygos asked one of the soldiers to help him nail the feet. The soldier lifted the right leg by the calf and placed it over the left. Popygos had to beat the nail repeatedly to drive it through the feet. Julius could not look.

Enos swore at God, the Romans and everything in general, but Popygos still drove the nails through his wrists and feet. Ethan passed out when the hammer fell, but he responded when his breath was cut off by the weight of his hanging torso.

As the crowd watched, the condemned began a strange dance. They would hang by their wrists until they ran out of breath. Then, finding that they could not exhale from that position, they forced themselves to stand on the nail until they could bear the pain no longer. Slowly they would allow themselves to sink until, once more, it was impossible to breathe. Thus the dance continued.

Julius only glanced at the tortuous movements before turning his eyes to the crowd in the pretense that he was protecting the prisoners. He could not suffer to look at the Nazarene. He was afraid that Jesus could look into his eyes and see his shame. Julius knew that he was killing an innocent man — and in the most cruel manner imaginable!

One of the priests, noting Julius' stance, could not help attacking the prisoner verbally. "You are the one who can tear down the Temple and bring it back in three days!" Another sarcasm followed, "Help yourself if you are the Son of God. Come down from the cross!"

There was no response from the Jew.

"He helped others, but he cannot help himself!"cried another of the priests. "If you are the King of the Jews, come down from the cross. Then we will believe you!" challenged yet another religious leader.

Julius looked at the prisoners in spite of himself. Enos and Ethan were moaning and cursing with every breath they could get. Their bodies were jumping in spasms and their heads were being thrown back and forth from one shoulder to the other. Jesus was also slowly doing the dance to get breath, but his head was laid back and his gaze was directed toward the sky, as if he was looking into the heavens. No sound came from him.

"He trusts in God; let God deliver him!" a voice cried from the priesthood. "Did he not say, 'I am the Son of God'?" another added.

Julius watched now, transfixed. There was a royal dignity in the deportment of the man on the cross. Even in the agony of crucifixion, he seemed to be in control. The priests knew it; that was the reason for their sarcastic remarks. Had any one of them been on the cross, he would have been blaspheming the God of Heaven. But the Nazarene simply looked tenderly toward Him.

One of the soldiers left his post and walked to a position in front of the cross. Perhaps he had seen Julius watching and had decided that he could get some release from the task. "If you are the King of the Jews, then save yourself," he added, after which he looked at the Centurion. Noting the scowl of disapproval on Julius' face, the soldier returned to his position.

Julius noticed that although the face of the Prophet was still turned upward, it was in shadow. He looked at the sky. The heavens were deepening from the bright light of noon to a deeper blue. Julius studied the sky intently. He saw no clouds and he heard no sounds of thunder. Julius looked to the horizon. He saw no flashes of lightning. Yet the sky continued to darken. Julius could now look directly at the sun at noon! It was not a storm. Perhaps it was an eclipse that would be over in a few minutes. The crowd, nevertheless, began to disperse. Women began to fling shawls around their children and run for shelter, lest a storm break. The eclipse did not pass. The heavens continued to darken into an evening sky.

When the crowd had thinned to only a few priests and some people Julius thought were either friends or relatives of the men on the cross, he released the soldiers from guard duty. But he told them not to leave Golgotha until he ordered them to go. The soldiers found a flat place and began to play knucklebones for the clothing of the dying men. Julius left them alone. The duty was hard and he knew it. Why not let them have a diversion?

"Father, forgive them, for they do not know what they are doing!" The shout from the Jew was so strong and sure and unexpected that everyone froze, including the soldiers.

By the gods, Julius thought, *he prays for our forgiveness even while we do this to him*. He was glad for the darkness so his men could not see the tears that streamed down his cheeks. At the scourging Julius had thought he felt empathy for the prisoner. Now he knew that he was weeping for himself. The man he was crucifying was the greatest man he had ever seen. Popygos had once paid the man the highest compliment he knew when he had told Julius that the Nazarene was one man who spoke the truth. Pilate had asked Jesus sarcastically, "What is truth?" Now Julius knew the meaning of the truth. Truth was what he had nailed to the cross!

Enos had vented his anger and blasphemy on God, the Romans and the crowd. Now he turned his venom on the Jew who was dying with him. Why not? No Jew would voluntarily enter Samaria. Now one was hanging on a cross beside him! "Are you the Messiah of the Jews?" he mocked. "Save yourself and two Samaritans!"

Jesus did not answer.

"Brother, do you not respect even God and a man's death," Ethan reproved Enos. "We did what we are accused of, but this man has broken no law." Enos was at the bottom of his cross dance and could not reply. Ethan took one more breath before he began to slump and cried in desperation, "Jesus! Remember me when you come into your glory."

Jesus painfully raised himself to answer, "Today you shall be with me in Paradise."

Julius thought, *Even to a thief who is dying with him, he gives hope*, and the remorse he had been feeling increased. Julius noticed a frail Jewish woman who was being supported by a tall young man dressed in the manner of a Galilean fisherman. They were attempting to come nearer to the cross. Julius nodded to the guard to let her pass. He saw the look of compassion toward the woman on the face of the Jew.

"Mother!" His voice carried his concern for her. "Mother, behold your son!" As his eyes focused on the young man beside the woman, Julius realized that the dying man was not calling her attention to himself but to the young man. "Son, behold your mother!"

My god! Julius thought. *He is giving his mother away before he dies!* Julius' mind raced to Rome and his own parents, whom he had not seen since that fateful day when the soldiers had appeared at their door. His thoughts and emotions tore at him until he began to lose all semblance of self-control. Julius realized that the death of the Jew was imminent.

Jesus pushed his body as high as possible on the nail in his feet and cried strongly in a tongue Julius did not recognize.

A priest said, "The man is crying for Elias." Then he added, with sarcasm, "Let's see if Elias comes to help him."

Jesus sank to the bottom of the cross and lost consciousness for a moment. Then slowly he came to and pushed his body upright. "I thirst," he said.

Julius nodded to a soldier, who thrust his spear into a sponge and offered the condemned man a drink of posca, a drink made from sour wine, water and eggs. The mixture wet his beard, but Jesus did not drink. Julius noted that the sky was so dark he could now see stars above the head of the Nazarene.

Again Jesus pushed his body upward to its full height. "Father," he said softly, almost lovingly, "into Your hands I commit my spirit!"

Julius looked at the man on the cross. Some of the man's tenderness and compassion penetrated his heart. Julius had experienced the man's devotion for his mother. Now, strangely enough, he was partaking of the Jew's relationship to a Father-God the Roman did not even believe existed.

"It is finished!"

Julius jumped at the strength of the declaration that came from the Prophet's mouth. He saw the body fall without life. Only the nails kept it from dropping onto the rock.

A sound went through the air as if a mighty wind was passing through, and a fresh breeze passed over the rock, bringing the perfume of wildflowers. Then the ground began to shake. The shaking became so violent that the soldiers had a difficult time standing. Popygos fell. A crack split the rock and ran through the gate toward Jerusalem. Popygos stood and fell again. Just as he regained his footing, he saw that Julius had fallen. Popygos ran across the rock to Julius, who he thought had been injured. He found the Centurion on his knees, his eyes transfixed on the Jew.

The empathy Julius felt for Jesus during the trial and the scourging was now turned inward. He realized that the Nazarene had been no normal man — he was convinced that the Jew, not the Centurion, had been in charge of the crucifixion. Although Julius did not understand how or why, he knew that his perception was a fact. Rome had not determined the events of the day. The Prophet had been in complete control. Julius felt unclean as he knelt on the hill. He experienced a profound sense of unworthiness in the presence of this man on the cross.

The passion and pathos of the crucifixion, and the events leading up to it, touched Julius deeply in the very essence of his soul. Popygos found him sobbing hysterically as he said over and over again, "Surely we have crucified the Son of God!"

25

Esther was furious. "Saul, there are two Gentiles at our gate," she announced. "I spoke to them through the door and told them that this is the house of a Pharisee. I warned them that their presence would make us unclean. One, who called himself Popygos, said that he was the man who brought your belongings from Caesarea. He told me that I was to tell you that he wears the sword of Paul Gabinius!" Esther was so indignant at the presence of the Gentiles that she forgot to be curious.

"I will speak to the Romans outside the house," Saul answered.

"Remember that if you are in contact with Gentiles you are unclean to me as a husband for thirty days," Esther spat out.

What difference will it make? Saul thought. His relationship with Esther had not improved since their wedding night. But he kept his thoughts to himself.

Saul recognized Popygos, but the officer with him was not immediately identifiable. That man was the most unkempt Roman legionnaire Saul had ever seen. His uniform was wrinkled as if he had been sleeping in it, and his hair and beard were uncombed. The man's posture was not that of a proud soldier but was bent and loose, as if he had no life in him at all. His face was swollen and his eyes were puffed and red. Saul's first impression was that the man had been drunk for a long time.

"He has been like this for two days" — Popygos' expression and voice showed his anxiety. "I have not been able to get him to eat or drink. He could not even assign guard duty over the grave. I had to do it for him. The only coherent thing he has said is that he wanted to speak to you."

Saul looked more closely at the Roman. Only then did he recognize the features of his former friend, Julius Laco. Saul indicated that the pair could come into the courtyard, though he knew that Esther would probably never forgive him.

"Julius, what is wrong?" Saul asked.

The first words he heard from his Roman friend after all the years since they had been comrades in Rome were, "I have murdered the Messiah!"

"Messiah?" Saul almost choked repeating the word from a Gentile. Surely Julius had not become a proselyte to Judaism! "What makes you think you could kill the Messiah of Israel?" Saul asked.

In a torrent of words and emotion, Julius told the Pharisee Saul of Tarsus about the crucifixion of Jesus. Saul had some twinges of guilt when Julius described the trial of Jesus. He did not tell Julius that much of the supposed evidence used against Jesus in the trial by Caiaphas had come to the Sanhedrin from Saul himself. Saul had some regret when he thought of the trap he and Esther had set in their attempt to discredit the Nazarene.

"Guard duty over the grave?" The question was directed toward Popygos. He had almost missed the remark about the guards while listening to Julius. "Why would Rome want you to guard a grave?"

"Well, Joseph of Arimathaea," Popygos began, but was interrupted by Saul.

"What has Joseph of Arimathaea to do with this?" Saul demanded. "He blessed me at my wedding," he added before Popygos could answer.

"Well, Joseph of Arimathaea," Popygos continued, "gave his own sepulcher for the burial of Jesus."

"Why would he want to do a foolish thing like that?" Saul inquired.

"I do not know, unless he is one of the followers of Jesus," Popygos replied. "Joseph of Arimathaea and Nicodemus ..."

Once more Saul interrupted Popygos. "Nicodemus! How is he involved?" Saul remembered with a flash of guilt how Nicodemus had corrected him at the Temple for judging Jesus without evidence.

"He's another of Jesus' followers," Popygos answered.

Wait till I report this to the Ab-Bet-Din, Saul thought.

Popygos was getting tired of the interruptions, but he pressed on with his story. "They had hastily prepared the body for burial — as the Passover was coming on the Jews — and placed the body in Joseph's new tomb. Some said that the man, Jesus, had prophesied that he would rise on the third day, so the High Priest asked Pilate to post a guard. Even now, my men are guarding the sepulcher!"

"How long has it been since he died?" Saul asked.

"This is the morning of the third day," Popygos answered.

The words Jesus had spoken to Saul in Galilee suddenly came rushing into his mind. *There shall no sign be given except the sign of Jonah. Jonah was in the belly of the fish three days.* "No!" Saul shouted so loud that it startled Julius, who had been listening like someone in a trance who understood but could not respond to the conversation. "No!" Saul stated again. "That's pure nonsense! The Messiah cannot die, and no man can come back from the dead on his own!"

Saul looked at his one-time friend. There was no more compassion for Julius from Saul of Tarsus than there would have been from Esther. "You, a heathen, talk to me, a Pharisee of Israel, born of the tribe of Benjamin, about the Messiah? When the Messiah comes, all Rome will know Him. He will break your iron yoke off His people. Crucify the Messiah?" Saul laughed at his own remark. "The sun will refuse to shine at noon before that will happen!"

The words of his friend stung deep into Julius' tender heart. This was not the Paul Gabinius whom Julius had laughed with in Rome. This man reminded Julius of the priests who had mocked while the Galilean had suffered.

"That's what happened," Julius remarked from the depths of his despair. "Were you not afraid, Saul of Tarsus, when the sun refused to shine and the stars came out at midday?"

Saul remembered how he and Esther had hid themselves and had worried that the end of the world had come, but he turned a defiant face to the Roman. "You are a pitiful man, Julius Laco. You are convicted of your sins, but you have no Day of Atonement. Rome will not allow Jewish Temple law to bring final judgement on a blasphemer, so the God of Israel used Rome to remove the sacrilege from us. You crucify a Jewish heretic and expect me to appease your guilt. No, I salute you for killing him! There is no forgiveness for you with the God of Israel. Go find appeasement with your own gods, if you can!"

Julius' guilt became unbearable. He seemed to choke as the intensity of his misery settled upon him. Every word his former friend spoke added to his despair. What hope did he have if Jehovah had no mercy? Could the gods of Rome forgive him for killing the son of the God of the Jews? Saul of Tarsus did not understand. Jesus was the Son of God! Deep sorrow tore at Julius' soul. The sun was shining on the street, but the mind of the Centurion was as dark as Golgotha had been when Jesus died.

The Pharisee turned through the doorway as Popygos led his suffering Centurion down the street. As they left, Saul could hear Julius saying over and over again, "Surely I have crucified the Son of God! Surely I have crucified the Son of God!"

Saul tried to explain to Esther how he had defended God against the infidels, but she would not hear him. She was consumed by the thought that two pagans had entered into their courtyard. Saul had not talked to them in the street as he had assured her he would. Now, not only was her husband unclean but her entire house. When the Ab-Bet-Din called Saul to the Temple, Esther knew that the wrath of God was about to fall.

"We, the Sanhedrin and the Jewish people have a grave problem." Kezia looked tired and anxious. "Although it is not really a new problem, it is one that you are uniquely qualified to help us with. Being a citizen of Rome has certain advantages" — the Ab-Bet-Din said his words slowly so that Saul would understand their gravity. "This again has to do with the supposed prophet, Jesus of Nazareth!"

"But I received an eyewitness account that Jesus was crucified by Pilate!" Saul exclaimed.

"That is true," said Kezia. "And he was buried with a Roman guard placed at his tomb. But this morning, early, the body was reported to be missing."

"Impossible!" Saul's expression indicated his doubt of the Ab-Bet-Din's words. His face only reflected what his mind refused to believe.

"Exactly!" Kezia shook his fist to emphasize the point. "Rome will not prosecute the soldiers. They say that all the men tell the same story. All were handpicked by the Centurion of the Antonia. His aide, a soldier named Popygos, swears that they are telling the truth."

At Popygos' name, the thoughts of Saul raced. *The guard was the one Popygos discussed with me. He must have received the report from the guard just after he left my house.* "The Centurion is not of his right mind," Saul stated. "But you can trust the word of Popygos," he added.

"How can you trust the word of a man who states, under oath, that a person of brilliant whiteness came and rolled away the stone of the grave, but that the sepulcher was already empty?" the Ab-Bet-Din asked angrily.

Saul knew that Popygos was not a man to make false statements or to imagine fantasy. There had to be a logical explanation!

"The guard reported that the grave clothing in which the body of Jesus had been wrapped looked like a cocoon from which the corpse had passed."

How could they stage that well enough to deceive Popygos? Saul thought.

The Ab-Bet-Din continued. "We must find and imprison his disciples before they spread this doctrine among the people. I am going to send you and your friends back to Galilee to find his disciples and stop them."

Saul's four Pharisee friends were eager to begin the adventure. Saul was not excited. The Ab-Bet-Din had commissioned him to find twelve men who might be scattered throughout all of Galilee. He knew the name of only one of the men, a fisherman named Peter from Capernaum. Even if the twelve were not scattered, how were five Pharisees supposed to handle them? Rome would not help. They had committed no crime against Rome and, as far as Saul could determine, they had not yet broken Jewish law.

The trip would be a long, dusty one. Thousands of pilgrims would be headed for Jerusalem on the same roads. The day of the Feast of Pentecost was approaching — Penetecost was one of Saul's favorite celebrations. Esther, of course, had sanctified herself for the feast by sexually separating herself from Saul, so her threats of abstinence because of his contamination from the Gentiles were ludicrous. Now, with Saul's absence, she would not have to pretend that her lack of passion was based on religion.

Saul was well aware that his relationship with his wife was based on pretense and formality, not on love and fervor. Saul had almost accepted that as a fact of life. His relationship with God and his relationship with Esther were similar. Although he had immersed himself in pharisaism and the Law, Saul still had not found the God of Moses. He was lonely. The only friends he had were based on economic needs or religious associations. In the night he often longed for the fellowship he had known with Julius and the desire he had experienced for the Roman girl; but in the light of day he denied those needs and presented the image of the self-sufficient Pharisee.

"We should not wait until we reach Galilee to start inquiries into the whereabouts of the disciples of Jesus," Saul told his companions. "During the time approaching the Feast of Pentecost, anyone traveling away from Jerusalem will attract attention."

"But how will we know which road they have taken?" Johanan inquired.

"It would be unlikely that his disciples would travel through Samaria without their leader" — Saul remembered the first time he had heard of the Prophet. "Since it is close to Pentecost, robbers will be looking for rich proselytes on the roads of Samaria. The Nazarene's disciples may all be Galileans, but that does not mean they are foolish. They will in all probability take the road to Bethany, from which they will go to Jericho. They will cross the Jordan to Bethabara so they can travel on the east side of the Jordan through Gilead. We will start our inquiries at Bethany."

"The people of Bethany will be afraid to speak to Pharisees," Hyman remarked, as much to himself as to the group.

"We could hide our identity," Solomons suggested.

Saul chuckled. They were so obviously Pharisees that if they were to take off their sacred garments and dress as peasants, or even as Romans, they would still be recognized as Pharisees.

"No!" — Saul spoke with authority. "It is best that we present the truth. We are men of the Temple searching for the truth concerning this Jesus."

"When we ask for his disciples, they will know that we are aware of his death," Reuben said with concern written on his face.

"That is a truth. Should we attempt to hide the fact that we know that truth, it will be recognized. Then they will believe that Jesus spoke the truth when he called Pharisees hypocrites!" The word "hypocrite" described how Saul of Tarsus felt about himself.

"The disciples of the Nazarene?" The beggar smiled at the ignorance of the Pharisees. "The first house you passed when you came to Bethany was the home of Lazarus. Jesus raised him from the dead, you know. It was the funniest thing you ever saw. There we were at the grave when the Prophet said, 'Take away the stone.' Lazarus' sister Martha told him, 'He has been dead four days; by this time he stinks!' Again the Prophet said, 'Take away the stone!' So they did it, and I held my nose." The beggar held his nose so Saul and his companions could see how he did it. " 'Lazarus, come forth!' the Prophet shouted. And sure enough, there he came, hopping like a rabbit! Just like a rabbit! He was all tied up in grave clothes, so he had to hop like a rabbit!" The beggar broke into a roaring laugh. Saul stared at the man as if the beggar had lost his mind.

"Lazarus will know where the disciples are." — The beggar continued where he had interrupted himself. "The whole crowd of them are always popping in for dinner. Lazarus' sister Martha sets a good table. Not that I have ever been a guest for dinner but I have stopped by begging, and she has always been generous. I really cannot blame the Prophet for stopping there. The man who gets that Martha for his wife will be one fortunate man!" Saul gave the man a coin and the five Pharisees turned back, looking for a house where a beggar always received a blessing.

Lazarus was a lanky man of middle age. His hands were knotted from days of hard work. His home was spacious for such a small village as Bethany. It had a special area for receiving guests. Lazarus welcomed the Pharisees into his home with all the hospitality and tradition Saul would have received in a religious home in Jerusalem. Lazarus' sister Martha was exactly as Saul expected — a short, slightly plump woman of great warmth and charity. Lazarus had another sister, Mary, who caught him completely off guard. She was vivacious — a radiant beauty with flowing black hair, black eyes, and an olive complexion. She seemed to have none of the intimidation of the normal Jewish woman. She wore no veil, yet there was no lack of humility. Saul could not help but compare her with pale, listless Esther. Here, by God, was a Jewish woman of passion and excitement that could stir any man! What Saul found to be her greatest attraction was her total lack of hypocrisy. Saul wished that he was not a married man and a Pharisee. When he said the name "Jesus," he noted that her eyes danced and sparkled.

The hospitalities taken care of, Saul asked his question. "Do you know where I can find the disciples of Jesus?"

"In Jerusalem with Jesus," Lazarus answered matter-of-factly. "They are waiting for the power of the Holy Spirit, as Jesus told them. We will be joining them before Pentecost."

"I am sorry to be the messenger of bad news," Saul replied. "They cannot be with Jesus, because he is dead."

"No, He's not!" interrupted Mary.

"I know the Roman Centurion who crucified him," Saul replied.

"Oh, that!" Mary exclaimed, tossing her hair, with the sparkle still in her eyes. "He is resurrected as He said He would be!"

"Resurrected?" Saul questioned.

"Of course! On the third day, just like He said! The disciples and some of our companions have all seen Him."

"Impossible!" Saul declared. "When a Roman Centurion crucifies a man, he is dead and remains dead!"

"Yes, normally," Lazarus replied. "And when the men of Bethany appointed to the task wrap a body in spices and enclose the body in grave clothes, it usually stays in the tomb. But with God, nothing is impossible. I fell into a terrible sickness and died. My body was prepared and buried. Four days after I had been placed in the tomb, Jesus called me back to life. Go to Jerusalem. You will find His disciples. But do not be surprised, Pharisee, should you meet Jesus of Nazareth somewhere on the way!"

Saul and his companions rushed back to Jerusalem. Saul decided not to tell the Ab-Bet-Din about his conversation with Lazarus or the location of Jesus' disciples until after Pentecost. Such a preposterous story could wait till after the holiday.

"You dim-witted jackass! You slow ox!" — the voice of Kezia bounced off the stone walls of the Temple. The Ab-Bet-Din was so angry he was hysterical. Saul had not been able to give his report for Kezia's outburst. "Saul, you are like a runaway jackass, always in the wrong place at the wrong time, and of no value at any time! Do you want me to tell you where the disciples of Jesus are? They are on the Temple steps. They are in the city streets. Do you want me to tell you what they are doing? They are preaching that Jesus was taken by the determinate counsel and foreknowledge of God and given over to an unholy priesthood. They dare to call the High Priest of Israel and the Sanhedrin *unholy*! And they accuse the priesthood of having evil hands that crucified Jesus, whom they proclaim to be the Messiah." Kezia looked as if he might have a stroke at any moment. "They quote the writings of David as if they were learned men, interpreting David as having predicted the death of Jesus. They claim to be witness to his being raised from the dead. They boldly proclaim that Jehovah has made Jesus both Lord and Messiah!"

"They are superstitious, ignorant fisherman," replied Saul.

"Superstitious, yes! Ignorant, no!" the Ab-Bet-Din fumed. "How many languages do you speak? Greek? Aramaic? Hebrew? Could you preach to the masses at Pentecost in their own tongues? These Galilean fishermen do! Parthians, Medes and Elamites; men from Mesopotamia and Cappadocia, Pontus and Asia, Phrygia and Pamphylia, Egypt and the region of Libya around Cyrene all declare that these fishermen spoke to them in their own tongues. And what did they preach? That Jesus of Nazareth was approved by God through signs and wonders, yet the priesthood had him crucified — but God has raised him from the dead! We cannot find the body to prove that they are wrong, and Pilate will not aid us in this. He has been in a depressed state of mind since the trial. His wife, we are told, believes on this Nazarene. The Centurion in charge of the crucifixion has had a complete mental breakdown, and Popygos and his guards stick by their story."

"Why haven't you done something?" Saul asked.

"Nothing but stoning the blasphemers will stop their mouths now," Kezia answered. "Jews cannot put a man to death in Jerusalem, and the only Roman citizen I have was vacationing in Bethany. You jackass!"

The words of the Ab-Bet-Din tore at Saul like coals of fire. So that was why he had been invited to be attached to the Sanhedrin! His Roman citizenship was what they needed. They wanted him to be their Roman assassin! Did Jacob Bar Kochba know? Did Esther? She did not want one drop of blood from her virginity to prove that she was the proper wife of a Pharisee; she wanted the blood of the Nazarene and his followers. Well, by God she would have it! She would bathe in it! And when it was over, the Ab-Bet-Din would no longer call him a jackass. He would call him a lord! Saul of Tarsus would no longer be the personal Roman of the Ab-Bet-Din. Now when they needed a Roman citizen, the whole council would be involved!

Saul waited and watched for his perfect opportunity. When the Ab-Bet-Din sent for him because Kezia had received a report that two of the disciples of Jesus, Peter and John, had healed a lame man at the gate of the Temple, Saul did not go. Esther was furious that her husband would insult the Ab-Bet-Din by refusing his commands, but Saul did not want another incident on the Temple steps. He had to have the involvement of the entire Sanhedrin. When the High Priests, Annas and Caiaphas, called a council to try Peter and John, Saul kept his distance. He did not want to be used. Esther was irate. When the council could not keep the disciples locked up, the High Priests and the Sadducees ordered them to be beaten. Saul the Pharisee made sure that he was not involved. Esther again fumed.

When Gamaliel told the leadership of the Sanhedrin to let the disciples of Jesus alone, Saul used it for justification of his lack of involvement. Esther was still cross. But when Saul received news that the synagogue of the Libertines and the Cyrenians had arrested a single disciple of Jesus by the name of Stephen and was bringing him before the Sanhedrin, Saul knew his time had come.

The council room of the Sanhedrin reminded Saul of the Senate chamber in Rome. Caiaphas was seated on an elevated platform, dressed in a garment covered with jewels. Tiberius would have been envious. Grouped to his left sat the Sadducees, resplendent in costumes trimmed with gold and jewels. They were the rich upper class of Jerusalem — though Saul knew that either Jacob Bar Kochba or Saul, himself, had more wealth than any of the members of the council. In fact, a number of Sadducees owed Bar Kochba money. To Caiaphas' right sat the Pharisees, all dressed alike in their dark blue costumes. Saul noted that Joseph of Arimathaea and Nicodemus were absent. Saul, a guest of the Ab-Bet-Din, stood near the Pharisees. He was not yet a voting member of the council.

The prisoner was a youth with curly hair and the beginnings of a beard. His face had a soft radiance that puzzled Saul. Witnesses accused Stephen of speaking blasphemy against the Temple and against the Law. They said he had stated that Jesus of Nazareth would destroy the Temple and change the Law of Moses. Saul studied the prisoner intently.

Stephen began his defense: "Men, brethren and fathers, hearken; the God of glory appeared unto our father Abraham." Saul was amazed. *This youth has never stood before the council, nor is he a learned man, yet he uses the formal address that is proper in such cases. He began his argument with a reminder of Abraham, thus establishing his racial and spiritual ties and proceeded to the witnesses' accusations concerning Moses.* Stephen continued to recite the history of Israel's religion better than either Saul or Caiaphas could have. *It must be tough to be a spiritual leader and try a man who is more spiritual than you are*, Saul thought. Stephen moved from Abraham to Moses, and from the Tabernacle in the Wilderness to David, to Solomon, to a history of the Temple.

When he had finished giving the Sanhedrin a history lesson, Stephen said, "The Most High does not live in temples made with hands. As the prophet said of Him, 'Heaven is my throne and earth is my footstool.' " Suddenly Stephen's lesson got very personal. "You pigheaded, uncircumcised in heart and ears, Jews! You resist the Holy Ghost as your fathers did! Which one of the prophets did your fathers not kill before they obeyed their words?" The man was signing his own death warrant and Saul knew it. "You who have received the Law and know it, have not kept it. You are betrayers and murderers!" Stephen shouted.

The council stood to their feet in anger as one man. Even the dignified Sadducees began to shout at the youth.

"Behold!" Stephen shouted above their protests. "I see the heavens opened, and Jesus, the Son of Man, standing at the right hand of God!"

The council ran from their seats, beating and tearing at the young man. Only three of the men in the room remained calm. Caiaphas sat smiling at the noise and the flagrant lack of order before him. The Ab-Bet-Din stood cold and emotionless until he nodded his head toward Saul, who led the excited throng out of the Temple, through an eastern gate, into the Valley of Kidron. Once outside the Temple wall, the Ab-Bet-Din told the witnesses to place their cloaks at Saul's feet, thus indicating that Saul was in charge of the execution. Stephen was thrown next to the wall. Stones flew!

The first stone was larger than a man's fist. It struck the youth on the forehead, leaving a trickle of blood running down his face. Saul expected the man to protect himself with his arms, but Stephen raised both hands as a sign of praise and cried, "Lord Jesus, receive my spirit."

Saul could hardly see the man for the hail of stones that followed. Then, in the midst of the falling stones, with his face and his upper body smashed to a bloody pulp, Stephen calmly got on his knees. "Lord, do not hold them responsible for this sin." The youth toppled dead under the mound of stones.

Saul was sick on the inside. He was disgusted with himself and what he had become. Anger raged within. As he stood there with the cloaks of Stephen's murderers at his feet, Saul of Tarsus was important. He was a man to be feared. He was the vengeance of the Sanhedrin. He liked the feeling of power, but he hated himself for liking it. The bloody mass that had been a young, good-looking youth enraged him. *Is it my fault that the man was a religious idiot?*

Saul thought of Lazarus' sister Mary, and the way her eyes had been filled with passion for this man's leader, the crucified Nazarene. *What a simpleton she is to waste all that love on a crazy Jewish prophet!* Saul hated her for her wasted devotion. Saul's scorn against Mary was fed by his desire for any woman who would willingly love and give herself. His resentment of his passionless marriage fueled the hate that raged within him.

"Give me official sanction from the Sanhedrin, and I will wipe this plague of the Nazarene from the face of Israel," he told Kezia. The sanction was given!

Esther was so pleased with Saul's political power that she actually showed some enthusiasm for their marriage. The Centurion, Laco, took no action against Saul, the citizen of Rome. Thus Saul of Tarsus began a systematic persecution and annihilation of the followers of the Nazarene. Each evening Esther wanted Saul to rehearse the anguish of the men and the cries of the women that Saul had pulled out of their houses by the hair of their heads and dragged to prison. The more brutal his treatment of the followers of Jesus, the more loving his pharisaical wife became.

"Caiaphas" — Saul no longer reported to the Ab-Bet-Din but to the High Priest himself — "many of the followers of Jesus have fled to Damascus. They feel safe there. King Aretas of the Nabateans has allowed the city to be a safe haven for slaves running away from Israel. The followers of the Nazarene have mingled among the slaves. Damascus is a Roman Decapolis city; the authorities will give me no trouble! If I have orders from the High Priest, the religious community will supply me with all the aid I need. Order some of your own Temple Guard to accompany me, and I will bring a quick end to the blasphemers!"

For the first time, Esther acted as if she did not want Saul to leave her. She knew that the trip to Damascus would be a long one. But Esther consented to his journey because she reveled in the righteousness of the cause.

On the journey north along the Jordan, Saul could not help but reflect on his journey with Johanan, Reuben, Solomons and Hyman. They had walked the dusty road. Now Saul rode with six members of the High Priest's Guard. When he passed peasants along the side of the road, they prostrated themselves before him and the High Priest's banner. Saul was finally a man of importance. Now he did not sleep on the ground but moved people out of inns and their private homes. He could stay wherever he wished and have whatever he wanted. The best food was served to him. Travelers opened the road to let him through.

At Beth-yerah, on the southern tip of the Sea of Galilee, the troop turned right and took the shorter but more mountainous access to the Yarmuk River and through the eastern valley. Saul enjoyed the trip, though he had to get reoriented to riding. (He was sore for the first few days in the saddle.) The hills and the high mountains were filled with multicolored wildflowers. The mountain river was clear, with cascading waterfalls. The river valley was green with high grass. Periodically Saul ordered a halt and allowed the horses to graze. He especially enjoyed those rest stops with the cool breeze, the warm kiss of the sun and the beauty of the meadows. He drank deeply from the cool water of the stream. The road upon which Saul was traveling and the road upon which Jesus had left Magdala, joined south of Damascus just north of the Pharpar River.

Damascus was a large city — one of the oldest in the world. When Saul and his traveling guard could just see the dust from the major highway, suddenly everything turned brilliant. It was as if the sun had suddenly flashed fully into their eyes.

Saul tried to control his horse, but he was soon thrown onto the hard surface of the road. A million flashes of light were striking him at the same time. Saul checked himself, but he could feel no pain. Still his head was filled with the glory of the light. Then, in the middle of the light, he saw the shape of a person. Although he could not be certain of the person's features, Saul recognized from the cut of his clothing that it was a man — and a holy man, for he could see the shadow of the tassels hanging from his prayer cloth.

"Saul, Saul." The voice rang in his brain. He had heard that voice before. But where? "Why are you persecuting me, Saul?"

"Who are you?" he asked the apparition. The light intensified as a hand reached toward him. Suddenly Saul knew that he was in the very presence of deity. He had wanted to encounter the God of Moses; now he was surely in God's presence. Did not Moses glow from the light after his visitation with the Almighty?

"Are you the Lord?" he asked.

"I am Jesus, whom you are persecuting!" — the voice spoke to his mind. "I have been spurring you and guiding you, as you do your horse. But like a jackass, you have been kicking. Is it hard for you to kick against the spur?" Saul thought he heard the sound of humor in the voice.

Saul's voice trembled as he answered with wonder, "What do you want me to do, Lord?"

"Get up, go into Damascus and wait. You will be told what you must do when I am ready!"

When the light left, Saul found himself in total darkness. "Master Saul, are you all right?" Saul recognized the voice of one of the guards.

"What has happened?" Saul asked.

"I do not know," the guard replied. "First there was a light, then a voice; but I could see no one."

"Where are you?" Saul cried.

"Standing next to you," the guard answered. Then, "Oh, my God; he is blind!" Saul felt the guard take his hand.

"Lead me into Damascus," Saul demanded.

"But sir! If the followers of Jesus have heard that you are coming and they see you are blind, they might try to kill you."

"The followers of Jesus will not harm me," Saul replied. "Do as I say. Lead me to Damascus."

As Saul walked, stumbling because he was unaccustomed to the darkness in his eyes, his mind and soul raced. *I am a dead man.*

I have been in the light of God's awful holiness and I am dead; yet I am alive! he thought. *I must be dead! I have been talking to a dead man. Jesus of Nazareth was crucified by Julius. He has to be dead! That day when I told Lazarus that Jesus was dead, Lazarus said that some day I would be traveling down a road where I would meet Jesus, because He is alive. Jesus was crucified by Julius, but on the morning of the third day ... In three days I will live again! Yet, Saul of Tarsus will not live! The Messiah will live — in me!*
Saul could not see, but his eyes were sparkling!

26

The guard of the High Priest spoke to his companion, "I have a place where we can leave him. It is a house on the street the people of Damascus call Straight. The back of the house is part of the city wall. The proprietor, a man called Judas, has agreed to take care of him for the month."

"But what if we get in trouble for leaving him?" the second man answered.

"Who will give us any concern?" his companion replied. "Our orders were to guard him on the journey to Damascus. This we have done! We also were to take back any prisoners he might give us. But how many prisoners can a blind man capture?"

"You are right," the other agreed. "What can we do? He just sits there, staring. He will neither eat nor drink. He is as one dead. When the money is gone, they will only throw him out onto the road to beg. What good to the High Priest is another beggar in Jerusalem?"

Saul sat in the room and stared at a blank wall. The noises of Damascus from the cobbled streets below penetrated his solitude. The voices from the streets included strange sounds. Although he recognized the speech of the Greeks selling merchandise and the Jews arguing over prices, the tongue of the Syrians he couldn't understand. Once in a while the passing breeze sent the smell of baking bread or the sweet, pungent smell of a dried dung fire wafting into his room. But he had no desire to eat or to venture out of the room. He had not yet learned how to be a blind man!

What kind of God is Jehovah? I know now that Jesus Christ is the Lord God, but what kind of Lord is He? Is He a God of wrath? If so, I deserve this state of blindness, or worse, for the remaining days of my life. I most certainly am a sinner! Or is He a God of grace? If He is, why am I blind? How will my blindness bring glory to Him? Am I right in thinking that my experience on the road was a kind of death? Will I yet truly experience a resurrection? Thus Saul's mind raced between doubt and faith; but he noticed that in his spirit everything was calm and at peace. Deep within, Saul wanted to sing!

Saul could tell when night came by the coolness in the air and the changes in the sounds from the streets. Even though his world was dark all of the time, the darkness of night seemed to be darker and more lonely than that of the day. As Saul waited in darkness, his thoughts also turned to his life in Jerusalem. *It is evident that the guards have left me. I wonder what they will tell the Ab-Bet-Din? And what about Esther? She certainly will not want to be married to a blind man. Yet what can she do? I know my blindness will certainly bother her, but I expect my surrender to Jesus as Lord will upset her more. She will undoubtedly be angry. There is too much Pharisee in her to remain married to a heretic!* Saul realized that it would cost him everything to follow Jesus. But if Jesus was a God of grace, He was the one Saul had been looking for all his life. He could do nothing less than surrender everything to that kind of Lord!

Isolated from the world by his blindness, Saul waited for the instructions that had been promised on the road to Damascus. The living Messiah had assured him that he would be given a revelation that would make clear to him what he should do. For three days, lying on a bamboo mat in the upper room of the inn, Saul waited. He could not eat or drink — he was a dead man!

On the morning of the third day, Saul heard a voice calling his name. "Are you a man or an angel?" he asked.

"Are you Saul of Tarsus?" came the reply.

"You are a man, no angel" — Saul spoke to the darkness. "An angel would have known who I am!" Then he heard the man cross the room to his side and he felt two hands flowing with fire as they were placed on top of his head. Saul felt as if the very life of God was pouring from those hands into his soul.

"Brother Saul, the Lord Jesus who appeared to you on the road to Damascus sent me." The voice was warm, strong and filled with compassion. "Be healed!" the voice commanded. "Be filled with the Holy Ghost!" the voice declared.

The fire from the hands felt as if it was pouring liquid love completely over Saul. His fears began to melt. His strength began to be rejuvenated. First he saw shadows against the wall; then the kindly face of an old man came into focus.

"I am called Ananias," the stranger said, holding his arms wide, as if waiting for an embrace.

"Ananias?" Saul answered, still gazing at the wrinkled face and the whitening hair.

"Did you expect, perhaps, an angel with white wings?" Ananias teased. "Believe me, I did not wish to come to you. I told the Lord Jesus that I have heard how much evil you have done to His saints at Jerusalem. I told Him that you had authority to bind all of His disciples and bring them to Jerusalem. He told me, 'Go!' in no uncertain terms. He said that He had chosen you — God forbid! — to carry His name to the Gentiles and to kings!"

Saul stood and embraced Ananias. In one moment, the dam of resentment broke. All the emptiness Saul had harbored — the rejection he had suffered from Esther, the loss of his father, the extreme loneliness he had endured in Jerusalem — came flooding out as the persecutor found himself sobbing in the very arms of the man he had come so far to destroy.

Ananias waited patiently for the expression of grief to subside. He could feel the pain in Saul's soul. He understood why Saul had been so zealous in his rejection of the way of Jesus. "Come" — he told Saul when the grief had diminished — "there will be salt between us. You will take food at my house. Then we will baptize you in the name of Jesus and you will meet your family in the Lord."

For the first time since he had been led into the city three days before, Saul viewed Damascus. The city looked very much like others he had seen on his journeys in Israel. The house in which he had been staying fascinated him when he realized that all the houses were connected, so that their back walls actually formed the wall of the city. He identified, by sound, the vendors he had heard from his room. Now he could see them. As Saul looked at the sky and the bright colors of the fabrics, he wondered that he had never noticed their brilliance. Things he would never have observed before his blindness now stood out sharply. Was it because he had been blind or because he was seeing the world through new eyes, the eyes of Jesus? The smell of bread now made him hungry. He realized that he was famished.

The house of Ananias may have been in Damascus, but it was Jewish. All the traditional rituals of receiving a guest were observed. Indeed, Saul had a problem restraining his appetite until all of the amenities had been satisfied. A group of believers in the Nazarene had been persuaded to break bread with them, though they were cautious. Was this not Saul, who had the seal of the High Priest to place them under arrest?

Saul began to tell them of his encounter with Jesus, but Ananias interrupted him. "Saul, we are due at the synagogue for prayer. If I fail to attend, my absence will be noted. You must stay here to rest and regain your strength. We will return after the service to speak of these things."

"No!" Saul replied. "I am a Jew. My place also is in the synagogue."

"You cannot go to the synagogue," Ananias answered. "By now the guards of the High Priest will have reported the condition in which they left you. The officials expect you to arrest all followers of the Nazarene. If you do not, your own life will be in danger."

"Ananias," Saul responded, "did you not tell me that the Lord Jesus told you that I was to be a light to the Gentiles?"

"Yes," Ananias answered. "That is what I was told while I was in the Spirit."

"Then how can the Jews harm me?" Saul answered with self-composure. "How can anything happen to me before the words of the Messiah are fulfilled? If I am to be the instrument of the Lord, nothing can happen to me!"

Ananias was astonished by the young Pharisee. Just hours before he had been sitting on a bamboo mat, blind, weak and uncertain. Now he was ready to venture into the synagogue. Ananias and the followers of Jesus baptized Saul of Tarsus before they went to the synagogue for prayer.

The synagogue of Damascus was not a single building. Rather, it was a cluster of buildings that had been erected over a long period of time. The community had grown from the proselyting of Gentiles. Some of the Gentiles still worshiped the gods of the Greeks, but they also believed in the Torah and came on the Sabbath to the synagogue. The Word was read in Hebrew and translated into the vernacular languages.

That day the synagogue was jammed with worshipers. They overflowed from the main building into the adjoining spaces. After the reading and translation of the word, the head of the synagogue called out:

"It has been noted that a representative of the High Priest is with us today for worship. We had despaired for his life, having received a report that he had encountered an accident and lost his sight. We praise God that the agent of the High Priest is well. We will hear from him now."

Leaving his place near the door, Saul wrapped himself in a prayer shawl and stationed himself in the pulpit. "I am a Pharisee of the Pharisees," Saul began. The worshipers nodded their approval, seeing that Saul wore the costume of a rich Pharisee. "I was trained at the feet of the Rabbi Gamaliel" — sounds of awe came from the members of the synagogue. "I was a persecutor of those who follow Jesus of Nazareth." The members of the synagogue who were followers of Jesus moved nervously. "Jesus of Nazareth was crucified by Pilate, yet I have seen Him alive!" What Saul preached did not cause any excitement. The belief in the resurrection of Jesus was no new idea in Damascus. Saul continued: "If Jesus of Nazareth is resurrected from the dead by His own power, He is no mere prophet or even the Messiah. If Jesus of Nazareth is resurrected from the dead — as I say He is — then He is not only the Messiah, He is God Himself! He is the purpose of creation and the redemption of the world!"

The brows of the Jews were raised in discontent. Never had they heard such heresy. To call Jesus a prophet was one thing; to call him the Messiah another. But to call him Jehovah was still another matter. The head of the synagogue rose and called for silence. "I bid Saul of Tarsus to be silent. I withdraw from him the privilege of speaking in this synagogue." As the members of the synagogue left the service, they argued what should be done to the blasphemer.

"Saul of Tarsus! Saul of Tarsus!" Saul recognized the voice of Ananias, though he could not see him in the dark room of the inn. He had been in the darkness of blindness when he had first heard that voice, so now recognition was easy.

"What is it, Ananias?" Saul answered.

"You must get up immediately and leave Damascus" — Saul could hear Ananias as he felt his way across the room.

"Here, let me light a lamp" — Saul reached for the olive oil lamp and the flint lighter.

"No, it is best if we do not give any indication that someone is in the room," Ananias responded.

"Ananias," Saul stated, "I thought I had convinced you that I could not be killed until my mission for our Lord was over!"

"It is not only your safety I am concerned about," came the reply from the dark. "The Governor has been reminded of your commission from the High Priest. He plans to put you into prison so he can use your authority to destroy us. Your words at the synagogue have been like a tempest. Merchants in the market, buyers and sellers, Jews around the city — all are arguing concerning the Messiah. There are quarrels even among families. They did not mind when we said that a man had been raised from the dead, but your words yesterday that Jesus is God Himself have put the city into an uproar."

"I have a plan," the old man continued. "There is an olive mill just below your window. The Governor has placed guards at the gates, so I will use a rope and a basket used by the olive traders to lower you onto a soft heap of olive kernels that are heaped against the wall. My brother, Eliezer, is waiting below even now. He is strong. He will carry you in the basket past the guards."

"But" — Saul started to protest. Then he thought how selfish he would be if he risked the lives of all the followers of Jesus who had befriended him. The basket, which was first raised to Saul's room level and then lowered by Ananias, was greasy with olive oil. Saul felt the humiliation of one who was forced to run away because he was being hunted. All his pride said no to the basket. He was Paul Gabinius, son of the Proconsul of Rome! He was not a criminal to be hunted! Now Paul felt what he had made so many others feel. For the first time in his life he knew what it was to be persecuted for the sake of Jesus.

Two powerful arms lifted the basket, with Saul in it, onto the back of Eliezer. It was no more to him than another basket of olives. The basket was filthy with the thick ooze from the olive waste. Saul rode on the shoulders of Eliezer as he made his way, bent under the burden. When they reached a spot deep in the olive grove, Eliezer gave the Pharisee a pouch containing bread and water to sustain him for several days' journey.

Saul stepped out of the grove into the star-filled night. No one challenged him. Where should he go? Should he return now to Esther and Jacob Bar Kochba? How he needed a sign from Jesus! Saul felt only the certainty that he needed to know more about the God of Israel! But how? Where could he find Him? Moses had found Him in the desert. In the vast wilderness of the Sinai, Moses had seen His light — a bush that was not consumed. Saul, too, had seen the light of Jesus, but there was much he did not understand. Thus he turned to the desert, as so many prophets before him had done. Perhaps in the empty vastness of the Sinai he could find the answers to his many questions. There, in the crucible of the lonely wilderness, God forged His man as He had done so many times before!

27

The man's skin had been burned by the sun. His once blue cloak was black from oil and dirt stains. His hair fell in tangles over his face. The desert winds had torn his garments, making patches where his lean, bronzed body was visible. His sandal straps had been broken and tied so many times that they looked like laced knots. He stood outside of the farmhouse in Bethany, under the shade of a great tree, and waited. A full-figured woman spotted him. As she went into the kitchen she said to her sister, "There's another starving traveler. When they find out that we are friends of Jesus, they always show up."

"It's your famous cooking they come for," her sister replied.

"Nonsense," Martha replied, as she scooped out a pan of warm bread and added a little mutton to the dish. She hurried out to feed the stranger.

"Martha." The voice was cracked from days of walking in the dusty heat. "I've come to see Lazarus. Can you tell me where I can find him?"

Martha looked intently at the stranger. "Do we know you?" she asked.

"Once you were gracious enough to have me as your house guest," Saul replied.

"Were you with the Master?" came the quick question.

"No, I was looking for Him."

"Did you find Him?" she asked.

"He found me!" Saul replied.

"My brother and his friend Barnabas are digging a well on the other side of the house," Martha answered, as she went back into the house.

The man she called Barnabas was the first to spot Saul walking around the house with the bread in his hands. "If you are looking for water," Barnabas said, "you will have to go to the old well. We have not found any in this one yet."

"Had you asked me, I could have offered you living water" — Saul smiled. Barnabas stopped digging and looked at the road-worn stranger. This was a beggar who walked more like a Roman than a Jew. Even in his rags, Saul had a regal bearing.

"Lazarus!" Barnabas extended his hand down into the hole to help Lazarus up. As his head emerged from the new well, Lazarus watched Saul.

"I told you that a centurion had crucified Jesus of Nazareth. You informed me that He had been raised from the dead. I told you that was impossible. You warned me that some day as I was traveling I would meet the inconceivable. I met Jesus just outside the city of Damascus."

"Saul of Tarsus!" Lazarus exclaimed. "We heard from the brothers in Damascus about your conversion and escape, but no one knew what had happened to you. Welcome home, brother."

"Is Saul of Tarsus your brother, Lazarus, after what I did to the followers of Jesus in Jerusalem?"

"The man who did those things," interrupted Barnabas, "died on the road to Damascus."

"But my hands have been stained with the blood of the saints," Saul insisted.

"And they were cleansed in the blood of the Lamb," replied Barnabas.

"But all of you looks as if it could use a bath," Lazarus said, laughing. "Mary, Martha!" he yelled. "Heat some water and get some of my clean clothing ready. We have a guest to prepare for dinner, and a dinner to prepare for a guest!"

When Saul had washed and rubbed himself with oil, and after he had been clothed and fed, Barnabas suggested that he be taken to Simon Bar Jonah.

"Simon Bar Jonah?" Saul inquired.

"The big fisherman," Barnabas answered. "Jesus said that He gave to him the keys of the Kingdom, and that upon God's revelation to him that Jesus was the Messiah, the Lord would build His Church."

Simon Peter greeted Saul warmly. The man was indeed a big man. He was taller than Saul and much larger across the shoulders. His form reminded Saul of Eliezer of Damascus, in that they were both big, powerful men. Peter, as Saul chose to call him, had slightly graying hair. His face was strong, with a square jaw. Deep wrinkles caused by many days at sea and the hardships he had endured for sake of the Messiah made a map of his face.

"Saul of Tarsus, you give me great concern," said the fisherman. "I praise our Lord for His great mercy to us and the message of Ananias from Damascus concerning your relationship to our Lord. Your presence in Jerusalem, however, presents a great problem. Have you not yet attempted to make contact with your wife or your father-in-law?"

"Not yet," Saul replied. "I wanted to find out how things stood before I went to them."

"Neither have you made contact with your Pharisee friends or the Ab-Bet-Din?" Peter questioned, his look obviously filled with concern.

"The answer is the same," Saul replied. "I stopped first in Bethany, not wanting to cause any problems for the Church in Jerusalem. I knew that Lazarus would know the Church authorities to which I should present myself."

"I greatly appreciate that wisdom," Peter answered, searching Saul's eyes with his own. "I am afraid that I have some distressing news for you. When word came from the Governor of Damascus to the Ab-Bet-Din that you had deserted your duties to the Sanhedrin, the Ab-Bet-Din stated that you were dead to the Jewish religion."

"That is remarkable insight," Saul said.

Peter passed by the remark. "He officially annulled your marriage to Esther Bar Kochba and she, in turn, married your Pharisee friend, Reuben." Peter waited for the younger man's reaction. Saul smiled. "Jacob Bar Kochba impounded your dowry and sent the rest of your wealth to your family in Tarsus."

"That is only fair," Saul stated with relief. "Peter, the Lord has called me to be a messenger of His love to the Gentiles. A man with such a life and mission has no business with a wife. I count all things gain that free me for His service. I would like to tell Esther that I hold no ill feelings toward her and witness to her of the love of the Messiah. She is bound by tradition and the Law. I would like to see her free."

"Saul, it would be unwise for you to attempt to see her or to stay in Jerusalem. Bar Kochba has placed a substantial price on your head. Someone would collect it. I have a further problem with your teachings. Our ways are the ways of Moses and the Prophets. The Lord has not changed these ways, only given them new meaning. I can see that if the Gentiles become Jews, they might be saved. But it seems to me that you are saying Gentiles can be saved apart from the Law!"

"Abraham was before Moses," Saul heard himself saying. "Father Abraham was not saved by law but by grace. Neither did any of us deserve by law to be saved — me, least of all. Yet, in His goodness and grace, He chose to reveal Himself to me. By grace you are made righteous, not by works, lest a man be able to brag about his obedience."

"You are hard to understand, Saul. Give me time to think about what you have said. Do not go out into Jerusalem. Do not preach in the synagogues. It would be too dangerous for you and the Church."

That night on his bed, Saul no longer thought of the Roman girl or of Esther. Somehow he felt relieved by the knowledge that the law said he and Esther had never been married. He remembered how Reuben had always wanted to be in his position. Saul knew that the ambitious Pharisee would take full advantage of his new political position. Saul wondered how Esther had handled the sheet on her wedding night. He understood that his attraction to the girl in Rome had been sin and his relationship to Esther had been only law. Now he had experienced something better than either sin or law could offer — the love that comes through grace!

Saul obeyed Peter and did not speak in the Jewish synagogue, but he went to the synagogue of the Greek-speaking Jews and argued with them that salvation had never been under the Law but by God's love and forgiveness. "You know how, when Moses was leading the people of Israel," he told them, "serpents bit the people so that many died. Moses called on God and received instructions that he was to make a brass serpent and place it on a pole. When the children of Israel looked at the brass serpent, they were saved. By what law were they saved? What work did they do in order to be saved? They only believed! Their salvation came by believing in the sign. The brass came from the looking glasses of the women. The serpent was the sign of sin. Thus, the brass serpent was God's judgement on sin. When the children of Israel looked at God's judgement on sin, they were saved by God's grace! Jesus on the cross was God's judgement on sin. Salvation is in Him! He took away your sins! No other prophet has ever done that! Jesus is the Son of God!"

So long as Saul spoke of Moses and things of the past, those who heard him remained calm. Even some of those who believed in Jesus were no longer punished for their beliefs. They said, "He was a great prophet. He rose from the dead and someday will return as the Messiah." When Saul called Jesus the Son of God, the Jews in the synagogue who had not accepted Jesus were upset. Arguments broke out, tempers flared, and anger increased until some decided to kill Saul. "Is this not the man who sanctioned the stoning of Stephen?" they argued. "What he says is worse than what Stephen preached. Stephen only said that Jesus had been raised from the dead. Saul is saying that Jesus is God!"

Peter stood before a group of the leaders of the Church. "Brother Saul is in great danger. His very powerful and rich former father-in-law has placed a price upon his head. The Ab-Bet-Din would like to have him executed. Now he has stirred up the Greek synagogue so that some of them wish to put him to death. He has no way to provide his substance here in Jerusalem, and we cannot protect him. It is my judgement that we should send him back to Tarsus. There he can be reunited with his family and have the finances he needs. He will also be safe from those who wish to kill him."

Saul stood to his feet — "Peter, am I permitted to speak?"

"Certainly, my brother," Peter courteously replied.

"The Centurion at the Fortress Antonia is a great friend of mine, though I owe him an apology for the way I acted the last time we met. I am a Roman citizen, and I can prove it." Saul had not thought for a long time of the ring that hung around his neck. His father's ring had simply become a part of him. "The Centurion will give me all the protection I need in Jerusalem and all the funds I will want."

"Centurion Laco has been returned to Rome." Saul recognized his old friend Joseph of Arimathaea, minus the robes of the Pharisee.

"Joseph!" Saul responded, as he rushed to embrace the man.

Joseph responded to Saul's exuberance. "It has been a long time since your wedding night, Saul of Tarsus. A long time indeed! Your friend Centurion Laco was in such a mental state after the crucifixion of our Lord that he had to be transferred back to Rome. I am afraid that the only recourse is what Peter suggested: You must return to Tarsus."

"If you do not leave," stated Peter, "persecution of the Church by the Sanhedrin will increase. Many Jews are greatly offended by your relationship to the Gentiles and your declaration of Jesus as God."

"I will go," Saul answered, "but not because my life is in danger. Although I did that once in Damascus, I will not do it again. Nor will I go because the Church is at risk. I will go only because Jesus said, 'Ye shall be my witnesses to Jerusalem and to Judaea and to Samaria and to the ends of the world.' I will go because to go is to obey Him!" Saul looked at Peter, who dropped his head in shame.

28

Once more the blue waters of the sea poured beneath the bow of a ship. All the way to Tarsus Saul reflected on the changes of events that had brought him to this journey. He had written to his mother about these events, but she had no way of getting a letter to him. It would be good to be in the house of Salaman again.

Tarsus was not as Saul remembered it. While some traders and vendors still worked the streets, the people moved with a despondent, plaintive manner. The shops were half empty and merchants from the trade routes were nowhere to be seen. The sadness of the people could be felt by Saul as he walked the familiar street toward his uncle Simon's tailor shop. Saul stopped to give a beggar a coin.

"Thank you, kind sir. May the gods bless you" — the man was only a little worse off than Saul himself.

"What is the great depression in the city?" Saul asked.

"I knew that you were not rich, but I did not know that you were ignorant," the man said, offering to return the coin. "Tiberius is dead and the new Caesar, Gaius Caligula, has ordered that the citizens of Tarsus pay 1500 Roman talents in back taxes. The soldiers have been in every home and shop. They have taken from every merchant and still have not received their tax. Even the beggars, such as myself, have been stripped of what we had. If the Romans see you, they will take the coin and all that you have, unless you can prove that you are not a citizen of Tarsus."

"Keep what I have given you," replied Saul. "I only wish I had more to give. I am a citizen of Tarsus, but I am also a citizen of Rome."

"If you can prove your Roman citizenship, they will leave you alone," the beggar replied.

"I can prove it," Saul stated. The beggar hastily pulled back the coin.

The tailor shop was just as Saul remembered, except for the lack of buyers. He recalled how he had felt when he had first walked through the curtain. His father's funeral had been in process. He and his mother had been fleeing from the Romans. His mother, Saraphina, and Simon were more than brother and sister. The old tailor had loved his father and mother intensely. Saul stepped eagerly through the curtain.

"Uncle Simon," Saul called out.

Simon had not changed much since Saul had last seen him. He was as gaunt and tall as Saul remembered, though his hair was somewhat grayer. He was standing in a mountain of cloth, just as he had been when Saul had first seen him.

Simon turned and scrutinized the man who had called him uncle. No look of recognition came to his eyes.

"Saul, son of Markus and your sister Saraphina," Saul answered the unspoken question.

"I have no sister, Saraphina," came the reply. "She died grieving over a heretic son who denied Jehovah." Saul wanted to scream as he heard the words, but the shock was so great that his vocal chords were paralyzed. "Markus Paul Gabinius left his Roman son a fishing hut on the Cydnus. His son's belongings were placed in a cave nearby. I have no nephew named Saul!" The man turned wearily back to his sewing.

"Simon!" Saul half yelled the name. "Let me speak to you!"

"Go, Roman!" Simon replied. "Go, or I will call into the streets and tell them that I have caught a Roman tax collector's spy. Then your blood will be spilt on my material."

Saul walked into the street, dazed. *My mother died believing me to be a heretic? It cannot be! I knew that following Jesus would cost me, but this price is too much!* Saul wandered aimlessly through the streets and eventually found his way to the inn. *It must be a lie. I will find Saraphina at the inn as my father did so many years ago.*

The first stone hit him in the chest. Isaac Ben-Ami called, "A Roman tax collector's spy. All our gold and silver is not enough; now you come to take the clothing off our backs and the food from our children's mouths." Saul saw his uncle Elkin picking up another stone. The large frame of Athaliah came through the door. She carried a pot as if she intended to use it for a weapon.

"I am a Jew, Saul, born in this very city," Saul yelled at the gathering crowd.

"You know every Jew in this city," Isaac Ben-Ami called out to the people in the street. "Does anyone here recognize this man who calls himself a Jew of Tarsus? No? He is a spy for the Roman tax collector!" A missile thrown from the street struck Saul of Tarsus. He had to run for his life from the very spot where his father and mother had found each other's love.

The hut was as Simon had said it would be. Tall trees almost covered the spot. Even though he and Markus had spent many summer evenings fishing on the river bank, Saul found it difficult to locate the hut. The tile roof needed repair and the place badly needed cleaning. Rats and forest creatures had settled in the crevices of the walls, and vines threatened to smother the building, but it was still there. In the cave hidden by some bushes, Saul found his belongings, still packed in their shipping trunks. Jacob Bar Kochba had not taken many pains to put things in order, but it was all there. Since the Romans had not bothered this broken-down camp, Saul was still probably the richest man in Tarsus. He cut away the vines, burned out the animal nests with a torch and swept the house clean. That night the only sounds that were heard near the fishing camp were the sounds of the creatures, the splashing of the Cydnus and the sobbing of a lonely, broken-hearted follower of Jesus.

Saul spent his days weaving mantles and tent coverings of goat's hair, which he sold to the merchants. In order to further prepare himself for his mission in life, Saul enrolled in the Academy of Tarsus, where a collection of both Jewish and gentile religious and philosophical works was available for study. He disregarded the edict of the Rabbis that no Jew could study where gentile writings were kept. At night, by the light of an oil lamp, he searched the scrolls for those things that could be used to prove that Jesus is the Son of God. His family and the Jewish community totally rejected him. Because they would not tolerate his presence, Saul spent his time isolated from his Jewish family. He told gentile merchants the story of Jesus, but he was considered an apostate by the Jews and thus was cut off from the synagogue.

Saul watched the seasons change on the Cydnus. Jerusalem, he was sure, had forgotten him, yet thoughts from the years past flooded his mind. *I wonder how Reuben and Esther are managing their marriage? Does Jacob have a grandson yet? Has Simon Peter ever learned who Jesus is? How, after living with Him for three years and experiencing His love and forgiveness after His resurrection, could Peter not know the truth? Will he ever know it? Is Mary as beautiful as she was the last time I saw her? Is Martha still feeding strangers? Is Ananias still obedient to the Lord? Where is the answer Jesus promised me?* At times Saul was so lonely that he wanted to scream or drown himself in the river. The seasons changed to years and still he had no word from the Lord.

The ships in the harbor of Tarsus were bright with decorations. The streets were full again with merchants and traders. It was festival time in Tarsus, the festival of their chief god, Sandan. Streams of color filled the streets. The sounds of music floated in the breeze. The Jews of the city hid behind closed doors and courtyards. The synagogue was filled with Jews who were fleeing from the abomination of the idol worship. But the Jew who had been ousted from the fellowship of the community did the unthinkable. He joined the pagans in their holiday.

Saul had not seen an athletic game since Rome, when he had watched Julius in the races. The celebration drew him to the Stadium of Tarsus where Sandan was to be worshiped in competitive games and sports. Saul found a seat in the crowd. The man who sat next to him, intently watching the athletes, was a young Greek. He looked as if he could have been a runner himself. Well-muscled arms and legs and a strong neck defined his body. His face looked as if he had been chiseled in marble. Long, black curls cascaded around his face and neck. The Greek cried, "Adonis! Adonis!" with the crowd. Saul thought, *This young man could be a Greek god himself.*

"I have seen you at the Academy" — Saul realized that the Greek was speaking to him. "I did not speak to you before because I thought you were a Jew and might be offended."

"I am a Jew," Saul replied, "but I am not offended."

"A Jew!" — the Greek's voice carried his surprise. "But this is a so-called pagan contest!"

"The gods I do not worship, but the games I can enjoy!" Saul replied.

"My name is Titus" — the Greek offered a Roman salute.

"And I am called Saul by the Jews, but Paul by the Romans," Saul replied, returning the salute.

"I will call you Paul," Titus replied with a smile. "I cannot have met a Jew called Saul at pagan games." Titus' smile broke into laughter.

After the games, Titus followed Saul to the house on the Cydnus. The waters of the river were sparkling with a slow flow of current in the evening sun.

"We have just seen a demonstration of the power of the flesh" — Titus spoke to his newly found friend. "Surely fulfillment of the flesh is the greatest force in life. Yet you live here without a woman and creature comforts. You puzzle me, Paul."

"The king and prophet of the Jews, David, said 'As for man, his days are as grass: as a flower of the field, so he flourished. For the wind passed over it, and it is gone; and the place thereof shall know it no more.' The flesh is temporary, Titus; the soul is eternal."

"How can you know that to be true, Paul?" Titus asked.

The sun had gone down and the stars were shining over the Cydnus when Saul finished answering the Greek's question. He told Titus of God's covenant with Abraham, and of Moses and Jesus. He told him of the cross, as Julius had described it to him. He told him of the resurrection of Jesus and his own encounter with Jesus as Lord at Damascus. When Saul had finished, they both sat in the moonlight in silence, listening to the flow of the Cydnus.

"My heart tells me that your story is the truth" — Titus finally spoke. "I do not need to see Him with my eyes. You have made me see Him with my spirit. Jesus is now my Lord and Saviour. I will serve Him with you."

"It has begun," Saul replied.

In the morning the sun rose bright on a cloudless day. Titus had spent the night with Saul, so the two friends decided to enjoy breakfast together. Saul baked bread from cornmeal and Titus enjoyed casting a net into the shallows of the river. They had just finished cooking the fish and were about to eat, when a man following the river path called out. "Saul! Saul!"

As the man pushed his way through some branches that were hanging over the path, the reflection from the river caught his face. Saul thought he was looking at a vision. It had been a full seven years since Saul had seen that face looking up from a dry well and offering him water. Now the man looked like a beggar who had been traveling. His clothes were worn, though not as tattered and threadbare as Saul's must have been when he returned from Sinai.

"Barnabas! Oh, Barnabas!" Saul's greeting was filled with joy.

The grizzled face of Barnabas broke into a grin. He flung out both arms, lifting his walking stick into the air, and shouted, "Shalom, Saul of Tarsus, favored of the Lord, mighty Apostle! I greet you in the name of our Lord Jesus and bring you great news!"

Titus prepared more cornbread and fish while Saul offered the amenities of not only ceremonial washing but a much-needed bath and change of clothing to Barnabas. When Barnabas was prepared, the trio thanked God together and shared the meal.

"What is the news you bring from Jerusalem?" Saul had held his curiosity as long as he could.

"It concerns a vision and Simon Peter," Barnabas replied. Saul interrupted long enough to explain to Titus who Simon Peter was. Barnabas continued. "Peter was in Joppa …"

"What was he doing in Joppa?" Saul asked, wanting to know every detail.

"He was in Joppa to raise Dorcas from the dead."

Now it was Titus who interrupted. "To raise who from what?"

"Dorcas from the dead!" Barnabas said emphatically, tired of the interruptions to his story. "Dorcas was, or is, a believer in Jesus who lives in Joppa. She made, or rather makes, garments for the widows and the orphans. She had died! Peter went to Joppa and prayed over her body. When he commanded her to live, she came back to life — she really did! Well, Simon the tanner asked Peter to stay with him."

"The home of a tanner, who deals with dead animals, would be unclean to a Jew, especially a Jew like Simon. What was he doing there?" Saul asked.

Barnabas did not bother anymore to answer Saul's questions. "At noon Peter went up to the housetop to pray …"

"Of course Peter would pray at noon, but why was he at the house of a tanner?"

"Because that is where he was!" Barnabas' voice began to rise in frustration. "While he was praying, he fell on the roof in a trance and saw a great sheet, knit at the four corners, let down to the earth. On the sheet were four-footed beasts of the earth and wild beasts and creeping things and unclean fowl. There came a voice that said, 'Rise, Peter; kill and eat!' Peter argued that he had never eaten anything that was unclean. The voice said, 'What God has made clean do not call unclean!'"

"Now may I ask you if Peter found out what the vision meant?" Saul asked.

"Three men came to the door," Barnabas continued. "They said they came from a Gentile by the name of Cornelius, who had been praying and fasting. Cornelius had been told by a voice to send men to Simon Peter who was in the house of Simon the tanner." Saul was silent, spellbound by the tale. "Peter interpreted the vision as meaning that he should go to the house of this Gentile." Saul placed his hand on Titus' shoulder, hoping that the story would not harm the Greek's feelings. "Peter preached to the Gentiles that Jesus is the Messiah, the Son of God. While he was preaching, the Holy Ghost fell on the Gentiles and they began to speak in tongues, even as the disciples had done on the Day of Pentecost after the resurrection of our Lord!"

Saul could not contain himself any longer. "And what did Peter do about that?" he asked.

"Why, he baptized them into the Kingdom," Barnabas answered.

"And what about the Church in Jerusalem?"

"They could not argue with the Holy Ghost," Barnabas declared. "Besides, reports came that some of the believers who were driven out of Jerusalem during your persecution of the Church went to Antioch and led a great number of Greeks to the Lord. And that is why I am here!"

"Why?" Saul asked.

"Because Peter and the Church in Jerusalem sent me to find you and take you to Antioch. Only you can teach these gentile converts the way of the Lord and bring other Gentiles into the Kingdom!"

Tears were streaming down Saul's face. After all these years, he had his answer. Jesus had said He would tell him what to do when He was ready. It was time. The visitation of God to the Gentiles had begun. In his exuberance, he placed his arms around Titus and hugged him tightly. "Will you go with me? Will you go with me to tell other Greeks about our Lord?"

Titus' dark eyes looked deep into Saul's. "I came to Tarsus to discover truth. I have found it. What is left but for me to follow Him wherever He leads us!"

29

Once more the waves passed under the prow of a ship. Saul was too excited about the future to reminisce about the past. The great adventure had begun. He knew what lay ahead. Antioch was famous for its idolatrous and sinful life-style. A Pharisee would rather be dead than to be forced to visit Antioch. If living in any gentile city was bad for a Jew, Antioch was hell. But somehow Saul believed that where sin abounded, grace could abound even more. The Pharisees in Jerusalem thought they were righteous. The Gentiles in Antioch knew that they were not. They would pay almost any price to become acceptable to their gods. Saul had the answer they were looking for, and he was excited about sharing it with them.

The boat trip to Seleucia was only a day's journey from Tarsus. From Seleucia, a short canal carried the boat to the Orontes River, which took them up to Antioch. The banks of the river were covered with groves of cypress and laurel, in which gardens committed to the worship of idols through sexual orgies blossomed with beds of violets, jasmine and poppies. Eunuch priests clashed cymbals at the passing boat, calling travelers to worship in the groves. The boat docked at the entrance of the colossal corso of Antioch, which extended from the river bank to the Golden Gate of the city. It was an avenue of pillars and images of gods. Seleucus had started the corso, but it had been finished by Herod the Great.

Clowns paraded down the avenue, hoping to collect a few coins. Stargazers sold their prophecies. Vendors of magic potions, swindlers, sellers of exotic goods and an incalculable number of sacred prostitutes plied their wares between the columns. A group of eunuchs were worshiping the goddess Apuleus as Saul and his companions left the boat and started up the corso. Apuleus was a half-woman, half-fish deity. Just as the group passed, the eunuchs castrated a young Greek boy. Titus took one look and ran to the river bank — sick. Saul looked at Barnabas, who had turned very pale. Saul's expression was livid.

"They do all this looking for salvation" — his arm arched in the air — "when it is here." Saul's hand stopped over his heart. "How wonderful of Jesus to send us here to set them free!"

Barnabas' mind moved from the circumstances swirling about him to the face of his companion. Saul's eyes had once flashed in hatred; now they burned with compassion.

"There will be no Jews among this crowd of heathens" — Saul addressed his companions when Titus had rejoined them. "The cargo ships seem to be docked further down the river. Where there are working men, we will find Jews. Where we find Jews, we will find believers from Jerusalem."

Saul was correct. Along the river banks were canopies where shopkeepers argued with their customers and money-changers jangled their trays. Rows of naked slaves carried bales of merchandise from the ships to the warehouses. Where the money was, Saul found the Jews.

"Where is the synagogue?" Saul asked a merchant. The man looked questioningly at Titus. "We are looking for those who follow Jesus of Nazareth as the Messiah," Saul stated, knowing that a Jew traveling with a Greek had already aroused the man's suspicions.

"Go to the fifth warehouse; it is the business of Manaen. He is a leader in our community who was brought up in the court of Herod, the Tetrarch of Galilee. He has become a Christian."

"A Christian?" Saul inquired.

"That is what we call those Jews who follow a Messiah who brings Gentiles into the Kingdom of God," the merchant replied. Saul recognized that the name was Greek for one who follows an anointed one. "Christians," Saul said, half thinking to himself. A smile came across his face, "Yes Christians!" he said strongly. "That is who we are looking for — the Christians!"

In the yard of Manaen, a crowd of workers was gathered around two men; one was a great black with rippling muscles, the other, a tall Gentile. They were both speaking to the group of men about Jesus, telling them that He had risen from the dead to bring salvation to all who would believe on Him. The black, recognizing Barnabas, brought his discussion to an end.

"Barnabas" — the greeting was filled with warmth and excitement. Saul could tell that there was a special closeness between the man and Barnabas. The Gentile studied Saul, but he remained aloof.

"My companion, Saul of Tarsus" — Barnabas introduced Saul to the black. The man stepped back instantly. A slight flash of fear crossed his face.

"Oh, I am sorry," Barnabas apologized to his friend. "I should have realized that you would have heard of Saul as the persecutor of the Church. He is a brother in the Lord, chosen by Jesus for a special mission."

The large man was still cautious, though the Gentile was warming toward Saul as if he was receiving some kind of inner witness. "My name is Lukus of Cyrene, and my now timid friend is Simon called Niger."

"Jesus is Lord, Lukus of Cyrene," Saul declared.

Lukus turned toward Simon Niger. "No Pharisee would make such a statement, not even a spy for the Sanhedrin!"

Simon Niger shrugged his shoulders and walked away.

"Please forgive Simon Niger," Lukus asked. "He was a God-fearing proselyte to Judaism when he went to celebrate the Passover in Jerusalem. The Romans made him carry the cross upon which our Saviour was crucified. He still has a problem trusting anyone connected with the death of Jesus. We have heard that the Roman centurion who crucified the Lord was your friend, and that you are the Roman-Jew who murdered Stephen."

"All of us crucified Jesus," Saul answered. "Tell Simon that Jesus forgave us all, even Saul of Tarsus, while He was on the cross."

Simon accepted that the forgiveness of Jesus was universal, but he was convinced that the Gentile had to become a Jew — as he had — before he could receive the Jewish Messiah. In Africa, Simon Niger had been indoctrinated in the rites of blood covenants. When the blood of two men was mingled, the men became part of the same tribe. When tribes sacrificed animals between them, they came into a mutual defense and protection covenant. Simon understood the circumcision he had endured when he became a Jew to be part of the blood covenant with Abraham, father of the Jews. How could a Jewish Messiah accept anyone apart from the covenant of circumcision? Saul argued that the blood covenant had been made on Calvary by Jesus. He believed it was the only covenant the Christian needed. He, like Simon, had been circumcised, but he believed that he was not saved by that circumcision. Saul contended that salvation was in Jesus, and Jesus alone.

Simon Niger recognized Barnabas as an authority in the Church because he had been sent by Simon Peter; *but Saul*, the giant black thought, *is an apprentice who needs a great amount of discipline.* Simon even recognized John Mark, a disciple who had confessed to running from the garden naked when Jesus was arrested, as being closer to Jesus than Saul. *Did not Mark know Jesus in the flesh?* he asked himself. *John Mark has not killed any Christians!* he further reasoned. *Perhaps Saul of Tarsus genuinely knows Jesus, but by whose authority does he say that a person does not have to be circumcised? John Mark says that circumcision is required!*

In the midst of all the suspicion and criticism, Saul continually preached that Jesus is the Christ. He preached to Jews and Gentiles, to slaves and freedmen. He preached in the synagogue, the workshops, the warehouse yards and the marketplace. He told all to whom he spoke that Jesus is the final sacrifice needed by man. "There need be no more sacrifice of animals," he said to the Jews. "You do not need to sacrifice the manhood of your sons," he told the followers of Apuleus. He challenged the gods of the Chaldaean stargazers, and the magic of the Aramaics and the snake charmers.

Saul preached from one end of the corso to the other. The idlers of Antioch were dissatisfied with lust and degeneracy. They were bored with naked bodies and sexual stimulation. The Christians did not use bright cosmetics and exciting perfumes to sell their God. They were absent from the sacrifices and the orgies. They preached a God of love and righteousness. Saul convinced them that they could be "born again."

Slowly the corso changed. Former temple prostitutes who had once lain naked in the square walked fully clothed with their eyes averted, refusing the attempted attention given to them. Men who had spent their days in wine and lust now walked soberly through the marketplace. The sight of the new converts to the Christ infuriated the priests and the remaining harlots. In rage they cried, "There are the anointed ones, the Christians." The more they mocked him, the stronger Saul's faith in Christ grew.

"Barnabas," Simon Niger said, "we have received word from Simon Peter that things are bad among the saints in Jerusalem. The taxation of Caesar Caligula has hit Jerusalem hard. The Romans stripped the city and the countryside of its wealth, taking it from the merchants both at their workplaces and their homes. Along with the taxation, there has been a severe drought. Many people are near starvation. Peter has asked us to send relief. I will collect food and goods, as well as gold. I want you and Saul to deliver it to Peter." Barnabas knew that Simon Niger was not only delivering the needed supplies but he was getting rid of Saul.

"I had hoped to visit my home in Cyprus before I returned to Jerusalem," Barnabas replied.

"Good!" Simon Niger responded. "Take Saul of Tarsus and John Mark with you. Saul seems to have a way with the Gentiles, and John Mark will see that they are properly circumcised. Even Saul will not rebuke a man who traveled with Jesus — though he is only a youth!" Manaen and Luke agreed with Simon Niger and so once more Saul saw blue water passing under the bow of a ship.

The sea tossed the small boat about as if it was a piece of cork on the open waves. John Mark was not only young, he was also prone to seasickness. Thus he was removed from being a problem to Saul. Whenever Saul saw the lad, Mark was hanging over a bucket or the side of the boat. The water at the harbor of Seleucia was trapped in a narrow sea corridor, which was enclosed by cliffs. The waves of white-crested green water seemed to hurl themselves at the granite cliff that sheltered the entrance to the harbor, only to be pushed back until they formed a mountain of water that tore again at the cliffs. White water flew over the prow of the ship as it slowly gained momentum against the waves. With every roll of the boat, John Mark became sicker. Saul knew that Mark would not recover until he had again stood safely on solid earth.

Saul watched the beauty of the Syrian coast pass to the east on the horizon. It was covered with green forests and the outline of the hills of Seleucia. Far in the distance he could see the glitter of the Orontes River as it wound its way seaward. Somewhere between Seleucia and Laodicea, the ship turned west toward Cyprus. Just as Saul had expected, John Mark remained sick until he was standing, white and pale, in Salamis, Cyprus.

"Barnabas," Saul said, "I have spent much time in prayer and thought during our journey. When we arrived in Antioch, you told the brothers that I was Saul of Tarsus. Simon Niger could never get that fact off his mind. If believers in Antioch know of me as the persecutor of the Church, it is likely that the Jews and the believers of Cyprus have also been warned to beware of me. I took my mother's name when I was being hunted by the Romans. Caesar Tiberius is dead and Claudius could not care if I am alive or dead. Would you mind if I used my Roman name again? I have never felt like a Saul of Tarsus. I never really got used to the sound of it. I would like to be known by the name of my birth. Could you introduce me to your friends as Paul Gabinius?"

"Gabinius is a powerful name in Rome," Barnabas answered. "I should think a simple 'Paul' would be enough!"

"Yes, you are right. The name Paul is all I need."

"Paul" — Barnabas tried it on to see if it fit. "Yes! Paul it is!" How good it felt for Paul to hear his childhood name again!

That Sabbath, Barnabas and Paul preached in the synagogue in Salamis. John Mark argued that the converts should be baptized. After services in the synagogue, Paul preached to the Gentiles. This time John Mark argued that the gentile converts should be circumcised.

Paul was getting tired of John Mark's legalism when word came that Sergius Paulus, the Roman Proconsul in the capital city of Paphos, had heard that Paul Gabinius was on the island. The Proconsul had ordered that Paul Gabinius should appear before him. John Mark was terrified at the prospect. The Roman Proconsul, however, provided an armed escort and three horses so that all three messengers could appear before him. Mark had no choice but to stay with Barnabas and Paul.

The trip to Paphos covered one hundred miles of the most beautiful scenery Paul had ever beheld. As they rode through a high mountain valley, the mountains soared to Paul's left. To his right spread a vista of the Cilician Gulf, reflecting sunlight on the tops of the waves as far as Paul could see. Sea birds circled above their heads and mountain goats scampered out of the way of the little caravan. Every so often they would pass a neat little farm. The walls of each house had been whitewashed and the gardens had been planted in neat rows. Red flowers lined the walks to the entrances and fat sheep grazed in the meadows. The mountain air was cool to Saul's face and the rays of the sun warmed his back. Everything would have been perfect, except for the complaining of John Mark. It seemed that although John Mark had traveled with Jesus for over a year, he had never been required to travel by boat or to ride a horse.

"Peter is a fisherman," Saul reminded Mark. "Did you never fish with him or sail in a boat with Jesus on the Sea of Galilee?" he asked.

"Once," John Mark replied. "We were in the middle of the sea when a storm arose. I got so sick — I thought we were going to perish. But Jesus woke up and rebuked the storm. And it left!"

"Woke up?" Paul smiled.

"Yes, He was sleeping on the fishing nets," Mark answered.

"Some storm," Paul remarked.

"Well, it was!" Mark's lip quivered as he defended his statement.

When the group turned south toward Paphos, the road came to the edge of the cliffs overlooking the sea. The water was green crystal, like looking into the essence of a precious gem. Paul could see great white chalk columns rising from the depths. He understood how the mythology of the goddess, Aphrodite, could have formed from this very spot. But it was impossible for Paul to understand how a high-born wife of a Roman could offer herself as a prostitute to a stranger at least once in her life and give that money to the priest in order to save her soul!

The Proconsul's residence was made from white marble. Great columns graced its entrance. The three guests of the Proconsul were allowed to bathe and rest from their journey. Tomorrow they would appear before Sergius Paulus to explain to him the word of God.

The Roman Proconsul was a man of keen intelligence. He had been educated in logic and wisdom in the best schools of Rome. While the Roman and pagan gods and goddesses may have pleased the uneducated populace, Sergius Paulus recognized that the priests were using religion to control the masses. He saw the sexual orgies of the temples only as an unrestrained attempt to satisfy that which brought no satisfaction. All the priests and the magicians could do was to offer the helplessness of a hopeless fatalism. The vendors in demonic powers could foretell the destiny of their patrons, but they could not change their evil fates. Yet, Sergius Paulus kept a staff of stargazers, including a Jew by the name of Bar-Jesus, who now called himself "Elymas the Sorcerer." It was Bar-Jesus who had told the Proconsul about the group of Christians.

Barnabas knew that as the head of the group sent from Antioch he should be the first to speak, but he could not find his voice. Sergius Paulus was seated on a throne. Seated on both sides of the Proconsul were his officers and counselors. Along the wall sat the sorcerers and the soothsayers. There were Chaldaean mathematicians, Syrian healers and black African witch doctors. In the center was Bar-Jesus. He was wearing the covering of a priest of the Jerusalem Temple. His clothing was dyed in many colors and adorned with the designs of constellations and mystic signs. Over his clothing he wore an apron. But inside all the tapestry, a little Jew with dark holes for eyes stared at the Christians. John Mark froze in fear at the sight of him.

"Paul Gabinius of Rome greets the Proconsul of Cyprus." Paul's arm went across his chest in the same salute he had once given to Tiberius Caesar.

Sergius Paulus was visibly startled. He had expected more swindlers and magicians. Here, in the apparel of Jewish scholars dressed in formal attire, stood men of high education and decorum. The leader had addressed him formally and correctly. He had stated that his name was Roman — Paul, the same name as that of the Proconsul. Sergius Paulus was sure that the name Gabinius was one of meaning in Rome.

"Your father?" — Sergius Paulus was looking intently at this man who bore his name.

"General Markus Paul Gabinius, former Proconsul of Tarsus, now deceased," Paul answered.

"He received a Triumph under Tiberius, did he not?" Paulus asked.

"Yes," Paul replied.

"And what is your business in Cyprus?" Sergius Paulus asked.

"We are ambassadors of the Most High God who carry the Good News of His Christ, who is the salvation of the world!"

The words of Paul merely startled Sergius Paulus, but they made Bar-Jesus turn white with fear. "Saul of Tarsus," called out the magician. "Do you not remember me from the school of Gamaliel in Jerusalem? Great master, Proconsul of Rome, this man and I were both trained in the arts of the Jews. But I have learned to foresee events and to read the stars. I have learned to see into the spirit world and to control the spirits. May I display a sign, great master?"

"Show us your sign, magician!" the Proconsul said wearily. He had expected more than a contest of magic and tricks.

"You claim the light, but present dark magic" — Saul's strong voice interrupted Bar-Jesus. "You desecrate the name of God and the teaching of Rabbi Gamaliel! You violate the word of God and call it light! You are filled with trickery and are a child of the devil!" Barnabas could not believe what he heard Paul saying. Was he trying to get them killed? John Mark was looking for a way out, but he could find none. "Bar-Jesus, you carry the name of light, but you are an enemy of all righteousness! Behold!" —Paul stopped in midstatement, his right hand in the air. Proconsul Sergius Paulus watched, transfixed. "Behold! The hand of the Lord is upon you!" The man who called himself Elymas the Sorcerer trembled. His helpers ran to him from the wall. "Son of darkness — be dark! You shall become a blind man that you might search for the light!" Bar-Jesus flung both hands over the dark holes from which his eyes had been watching Paul's face and screamed. The face of Paul was suddenly gone and his world had turned black. Bar-Jesus, called Elymas the Sorcerer, was blind!

The next day Bar-Jesus lost his position because Sergius Paulus, Proconsul of Rome, accepted Jesus Christ as his Lord. The Proconsul had a ship sailing for Pamphylia, to the port of Perga. He assured his brothers in Christ that he could send letters from there that would insure their transportation back to Antioch in Syria. Paul accepted for the group because Barnabas felt compelled by the events to recognize Paul as being the authority under Jesus. John Mark had been frightened so badly that now he was afraid of Paul.

"I walked with Jesus," Mark murmured. "Jesus gave men their sight; He never took it away. Jesus never converted heathen, nor did he break the Law by not making converts be circumcised. Jesus was baptized; Paul did not even baptize the Proconsul." Mark felt so insecure that he could not bring himself to call Sergius Paulus by his name, even after his conversion.

"Your problem, Mark, is that you saw too much of Jesus in the flesh. Did He not tell a Samaritan woman that He would give her living water? Did He baptize the Samaritan? Did he ever baptize anyone? Jesus made *me* blind. When Bar-Jesus sees again, as he will see tomorrow, he will be a changed man. I know! What you need, Mark, is to see Jesus the Christ. The carpenter from Nazareth has left you blind to the Christ of God!"

As the ship plowed the green waters of the Pamphylian Sea, Mark was separated again from Paul and Barnabas. He was not seasick as he had been on their last boat trip. The waters of the Pamphylian Sea were soft and smooth. A gentle breeze flowing from the Cilician Gulf funnelled between Cyprus and Cilicia and gradually pushed the boat toward Pamphylia. Mark was pouting and sulking because of the way Paul had taken charge — and the way Paul had spoken to him. *Did not I, John Mark, walk with the Lord? All the Christian Jews in Jerusalem treat me as special because I have been with Jesus. Now this gentile Roman — who is, after all, only a half Jew — demeans my place with Jesus. Just wait till I tell Peter what this Paul has done! The big fisherman will straighten out this Gentile.*

Barnabas pleaded with Paul to go to Mark and apologize. "Apologize!" Paul thundered. "Apologize! That young man needs someone to lift his skirt and paddle his bottom. He is a baby and needs to be treated like one!"

"Perhaps if you treated him like a man, he just might become one," Barnabas suggested.

"The salvation of the world is no task to give to a baby!" Paul declared.

When the trio arrived in Perga, Mark found a ship that was sailing for Caesarea and booked passage. As he was boarding the ship, Paul stood on the dock, his hands on his hips, and shouted at the young man. "What does your face look like, John Mark? All I have ever seen of you is your backside! Your backside leaning over a bucket! Your rear while you hung over a ship's rail! Now your backside again while you run to Jerusalem! All Jesus saw of you was your rear when you were running away, naked, from the garden in Gethsemane! When you get to Peter, turn your back to him so that he will recognize you!" Paul laughed at the thought.

"Come on, Paul," Barnabas begged, embarrassed. "Let the boy depart in peace."

"Boy is right!" declared Paul, as they turned toward Pisidian Antioch.

Behind the ship's rail, John Mark hid and sobbed uncontrollably. He was filled with shame and fear. He wanted to cry out. "Don't let me go! I want to be a man of God! I want to be a man of faith and power! I, oh God ... I want to be just like you, Paul! Do not let me go!" Instead, he trembled hysterically, his face in his hands, weeping for his lack of courage and faith. That is where the sailors found him when the ship was well at sea.

Paul tackled the five-day walking journey from Perga to Pisidian Antioch like a man who was compelled. Barnabas would have liked to remain in the coastal region of Perga because they had not preached the message of Jesus there and it was comfortable. But with an instinct like that of a bird, Paul was drawn toward Pisidian Antioch. To reach their destination, they had to cross the Taurus Mountain range by one of the most formidable roads in Asia Minor. At first the road upward was shaded by large forests of cypress. The white and red flowers of the oleander evergreen sent their aroma floating on the sea breeze. Paul picked a ripe pomegranate from a wild bush and enjoyed its sharp taste. The travelers had to cross over a stream that cascaded downward toward the sea. Along the road they passed houses made from dried clay, with roofs of straw and branches. But as they climbed, the houses disappeared and the thick woods turned into lone trees that had been shaped by the winds. They no longer had the use of overflowing streams but found their water in pools where it had been trapped by rocks. The air became thin and the men found the climb very tiring.

Antioch of Pisidia stood on a plateau 3,600 feet above sea level. Barnabas thought they had touched the roof of the world. Though weary, Paul pressed forward to the synagogue. When the

Law and the Prophets had been read, he took the Psalms of David and used them to prove that Jesus was the Christ. On the next Sabbath, the entire city assembled to hear Paul preach the word of God. Everything went well until Paul once more struck the spark that caused a conflagration. Once more Paul declared that righteousness was theirs without surrender to the Law. In Pisidia Antioch were some gentile women who had been proselyted from the gods to the God of the Jews. These women had been rejected by their own families. Now suddenly Paul was preaching that their sacrifice was meaningless. They could have become righteous without the Law and without their sacrifice. Jesus would save Gentiles without their becoming Jews. The women were scandalized!

Paul declared, "It was required that the word of God be preached first to the Jews. But since you reject it and do not consider yourself good enough to receive eternal life, we will take it to the Gentiles."

Barnabas thought, *Here we go again.* He was right! Once more the road was under their feet. Now Paul headed for the city of Iconium, which lay across the upland plain, about eighty miles from Antioch. The road wound among brown hills where wells were scarce. Those that could be found were some of the deepest in the land. *At least*, thought Barnabas, *he doesn't have us climbing mountains like goats.* Mountains loomed in the distance and volcanoes rose above the plain like great sentinels. The people who inhabited the land believed that their forefathers were the first people to inhabit the earth. Hittite gods had ruled this area before Israel had found her God or Greece had invented hers. Statues of the gods of the Hittites marked the road on which they traveled. These were the same erotic figures Abraham had rejected, and they had been old then.

Iconium stood in contrast to the brown-black hills through which Paul and Barnabas had traveled. The city was located on a vast, green, fertile plain. Water was abundant and the soil was fruitful. The people were different from those of the Roman colonies the two travelers had visited earlier. Iconium was a simple settlement of Phrygians, Greeks and Jews who labored as farmers, craftsmen and merchants.

When they had settled, Paul began to preach in the marketplace, then in the synagogue. He taught the rich and the poor, the freedman and the slave. At first the word was received with much gladness and many believers were added to Christ. Barnabas began to believe that they would settle here for awhile and build a church. But soon, Jew and Greek against Jew and Greek divided the city. Whenever Paul appeared to preach, a bitter dispute broke out. Paul decided that it was time to leave. Barnabas could not believe that Paul could start out with a spiritual revival and always leave with a physical riot.

Once more, Barnabas found himself on a mountain road. This time Paul was leading them to the region of Lycaonia, to the cities of Lystra and Derbe.

The people of Lystra told a story that once the gods Zeus and Hermes had come to this earth disguised as men. No one in Lystra would give them hospitality, except two old peasants, Philemon and his wife, Baucis. The result was that all the people were destroyed except Philemon and Baucis, who were made the guardians of the Temple of Zeus. The Greeks of Lystra believed in Zeus, and the high priest of the Temple of Zeus had stated that Zeus and Hermes were about to appear in Lystra again. Zeus was the god of the gods and Hermes was the messenger of the gods! Since Barnabas was a man of noble presence and Paul was his voice, the two strangers were scrutinized carefully as they entered the city.

"Paul," Barnabas remarked, "have you noticed how the people stare at us?"

"Perhaps they do not get many visitors," Paul answered. "Or perhaps they have never seen the dress of a Pharisee before. I am sure there must be Jews and a synagogue somewhere in the city."

"I don't know, Paul. We have come a long way from civilization. I have not seen even a sign of a Roman since we left Pisidia Antioch. I thought Rome had legions in every part of the world. I have not heard a word of Greek since we entered the city. The people I hear in the market are speaking in a language that is foreign to me."

Paul and Barnabas had come to a central square in the city. A public well was located in the middle of the plaza and the shops of merchants opened onto the road. "Let us see," Paul said, as he stepped onto a small rock wall that ran alongside of the well. He turned and spoke loudly so that everyone in the shops could hear him. "People of Lystra, gather to me, for I have great news. I bring you news of God's salvation for all men."

People began to leave the shops to see what the stranger had to say. They had never seen men dressed like Paul and Barnabas. They had never seen anyone who walked and looked so stately as did Barnabas. Soon there was a large crowd gathering.

"They know Greek," Paul said to Barnabas. Paul's face showed his pleasure at the prospect of preaching the gospel in the open air of the public plaza. Paul had just started to preach when there was a scraping noise and the people scurried aside to make room for someone. Barnabas could not see the object that had caused the confusion. At first Paul also missed it, for his gaze was centered too high. Then, at the feet of those standing around, there appeared a strange man riding a type of wooden sled. The man was full size from the thighs up. His legs were miniatures of what legs should be. Skinny, undeveloped and useless, they were strapped to the sled. The man moved the contraption by placing his fists, which had been covered with leather for protection, on the ground and lifting himself, and the apparatus to which he was bound, upward an inch and forward a few inches. It was the runners of the sled that had made the scraping sound.

The man's skin was covered with a thick coating of dust and dirt. His clothing was ragged and torn from being caught on rocks and brambles. Paul realized that the man had been born defective. For some unknown reason his legs had not grown with his body. Then Paul saw the man's eyes. They were not the eyes of hopelessness. The man had heard Paul say that he brought a message from God. Whatever it was, the man on the sled wanted to receive it. Faith blazed in those eyes! Paul remembered how Peter had, more than once, performed miracles with the power of the Holy Spirit. He remembered the heat that had come over him when Ananias had prayed that he, Paul, would receive his sight. He felt that same heat in his body now. The longer Paul gazed at the cripple, the more he knew that it was Christ's will to heal him. Doubt, however, gripped at his mind. Paul could not step down from his position, for the crowd might misinterpret his actions should he attempt to lay his hands on the man. What if he commanded the man to rise and he did not? Would their entire mission be wasted? Yet Jesus had instructed them to heal the sick as they went to preach the gospel!

Barnabas waited to see what Paul would do or say. The crowd saw that Barnabas was waiting for Paul to speak. They were getting anxious, not knowing what was transpiring. Then, while Paul's feet rested soundly on the wall, his spirit took a leap of faith. He suddenly looked squarely at the cripple and commanded the man to do what he could not do, had never done, and would never be able to do without a miracle. "Arise, stand on your feet and walk!"

Time seemed to stand still. The people looked from Paul to Barnabas, not believing that they had heard what the man had said to the cripple. The man on the sled continued to gaze intently into the eyes of the man who had commanded the impossible. Then, abruptly, there was a gasp from one of the crowd. A merchant stood transfixed as he pointed to the straps that held the emaciated legs to the board. Before their eyes, the legs were becoming filled with sinew and muscles. The calves of the legs grew in fullness and strength until the straps could no longer hold their captives. They were torn apart by the pulsating strength that flowed through the man's legs.

The man swung free from the sled, reached up to the edge of the wall and pulled himself upward. For the first time in his life, he felt the ground beneath his feet. He took one step forward and leapt into the air, shouting for sheer joy.

Bedlam broke out among the watching crowd. The people of Lystra recognized the man on the sled. All had seen him scraping along since he was a lad. They admired him because he was not carried like a beggar to sit by the gate and wait for a handout. No, this man sold woven goods his mother had made or trinkets he made with his hands. Everyone had bought something from him sometime. He always had a good word and he never complained, even when the village dogs worried him.

Now, he stood before them on brand-new feet and legs. He stood as tall as anyone else. Yes, his face was still dirty from the dust he had stirred up with his little sled, but streaks from tears ran down his cheeks from the sheer ecstasy of what he was feeling. He was showing everyone his legs. He leapt and jumped, proving to himself and the village that it was true. He had legs! He had feet upon which he could walk! He would never again have to scoot about in the dirt! Where his dirty, torn tunic ended, he had long, full, muscular, clean legs and feet! He grabbed Paul in his powerful arms and swung him up from the rock wall to his shoulders. Others lifted a protesting Barnabas upon their shoulders and began to carry him through the streets. Others cried to those who passed by, telling them what had happened. Paul and Barnabas, with the crowd, were swept down a street to the Temple of Zeus where the throng called out to the high priest. Someone had already carried the news that the gods had created new legs and feet on a cripple.

"How was it done?" the high priest asked.

"The dignified one just watched," he was told, "and the other one spoke the words."

"The one who spoke is Hermes," the high priest proclaimed, "and the one who watched is Zeus!"

Paul and Barnabas, not understanding what had been said, were not aware of the significance of the celebration. They were simply caught up in the jubilation of the crowd. The beat of a drum increased the intensity of the throng's celebration. Women danced in the streets around the two strangers. Merchants threw their goods to them and upon them in admiration. As they came to the gate of the city, Paul saw the priest with garlands of flowers and the oxen waiting for sacrifice. Suddenly he realized what had happened.

Paul slid from his perch on the shoulders of the men and raised both hands in the air as a sign that he was about to speak. A hush fell over the crowd.

"Do not do these things," Paul cried out. "We are men just like you. We have come to tell you that you should turn from this empty kind of worship to the God who made the heavens, the earth, the sea and everything in them. We have come to tell you that God has made provision for your worship through His Son, Jesus, whom God raised from the dead."

The next day the Jews of Lystra found Paul. They were not a throng but a mob. Jews from Antioch and Iconium had joined the local Jews to form a rabble controlled by emotion and impervious to reason.

"There he is," one cried, spotting Paul.

"He claims to be the god Hermes," one of the Jews from Lystra shouted.

"He brings uncircumcised Gentiles into the synagogue," a Jew from Antioch added.

"Stone him!" a fellow Jew from Iconium demanded.

Paul did not see the first stone coming. It struck him squarely in the middle of his forehead. Paul's knees turned to jelly and his head started spinning. He felt nauseous. As he started to fall, he felt as if all the heavens had turned into hurling missiles. He remembered the death of Stephen. He recalled the body that had been pelted and finally covered with stones. Paul knew that this was the end of his life. Unlike Stephen, he saw no visions from heaven. He really felt no pain after the first blow, only the sickness and weakness in his inner being and the darkness that grew as he faded from consciousness.

A sphere of light hovered above him. Within the light, Paul could see the radiant face of a Greek god. The god's hair was cut short to his neck, but it was filled with black, cascading curls. His features were those of a man slightly younger than John Mark. His expression showed compassion and concern. Paul could hear the sound of tumbling water. Then he realized what the god was doing. Paul felt a cool, moist cloth rubbing against his skin. The god was giving Paul a bath. Paul shifted his gaze from the face of the god to his surroundings. Paul was lying on soft grass beside a flowing brook. A pool of water trapped between rocks was red with blood. Hanging on a branch of a willow tree was Paul's clothing, freshly washed and drying in the sun. Paul turned his face back to the person he now realized was a young man.

"Good, you're awake" — the voice matched the vision. "Are you some kind of god?" the youth asked. "As soon as I wash a wound, it heals."

"I am not a god but a messenger of the Most High God, — the only God, the God of Abraham and of His Son, Jesus Christ," Paul replied weakly.

"Good" — the young man shook his head in agreement. "You had me worried, for I am a believer in the God of Abraham. My name is Timothy. My father was a Greek. My mother, Eunice, is a Jew. We live just across the meadow with my grandmother, Lois.

Your clothes are almost dry. When they are, you can dress and come to my house. Somebody beat you and cut you dreadfully, but as soon as I washed a wound clean, it healed."

"Perhaps I will visit with you, Timothy," Paul said, as he started to get up, "but first I must go back to Lystra and find my friend Barnabas. I do not know what has happened to him."

"Oh, let me help you," Timothy said, as he gave Paul a hand. "I will go to Lystra with you. You may not be fully well."

"No, I do not think that would be wise," Paul replied. "The men who stoned me might still be there."

"No one in Lystra will harm me," the youth said, laughing. "They are afraid of Grandmother Lois. She would take her cane and whip them with it. I know. She did it to me when, as a boy, I talked back to my mother. She would still do it!"

Paul and Timothy walked into the plaza of Lystra. Men stood in the doorways of the shops in abject fear. They thought Paul had been stoned to death. They had seen the rocks smash into his head and face. They had helped to drag his body out of the city. Yet, there he stood, his clothing clean, his face shining, and not a trace of the cuts or bruises from which had flowed much blood. This man was more than a mere human. Perhaps the priest of Zeus was correct. Maybe this was the Greek god Hermes. The Jews from Iconium and Antioch had persuaded them to strike out, but now they were gone. What if this god decided to pour out his fury on them?

"Barnabas" — Paul's shout broke the silence.

Barnabas came running, followed by a group of men. "Thank God!" he cried as he grabbed Paul, not able to restrain himself. "They told me you had been stoned to death and carried outside the city. These are new Christians who are protecting me until I can leave the city."

"Blessings on you," Paul told the assembled group. "The Holy Spirit will show you how to worship and live as believers in Jesus. Barnabas and I will leave the city. We will go with my young friend, Timothy." Paul placed his hand on Timothy's head. "And we will eat stew from the pot of his grandmother." Then, turning to Timothy, Paul asked, "Grandmother Lois can cook a good stew, can't she, Timothy?"

"Oh, yes!" Timothy replied, "and as quickly as she can wield her cane!" Timothy looked at the Jews who were still cowering in the corners of their market stalls. Paul caught the direction of Timothy's glare.

"Come, my young friend. Let us go to the protection of grandmother's cane!" Paul laughed as the trio left the plaza of Lystra.

Paul and Barnabas found Eunice and Lois to be women of great fortitude, faith and knowledge of God's Word. The little farm was the first suggestion of a home that Paul had known since leaving for Damascus as Saul of Tarsus. As Paul and Barnabas grew strong again, they helped to put the little place back in order. Paul replaced the thatch roofing and helped Eunice weave new wool blankets for the winter. His skills as a tentmaker came in handy as he made new coverings for the food storage. It was not until Paul knew that the little family was well supplied for the winter, and snow had started to form on the mountains, that he told them he had to leave. Paul and Barnabas would retrace their path back to Pisidian Antioch. Then they would take a boat back to Antioch in Syria to report to the church that had sent them on their journey.

On a crisp day when snow threatened to close the mountain passes, Paul and Barnabas returned to the believers and confirmed the churches that had been started. Then they departed the shore of Galatia on a boat sailing for Seleucia, agreeing that they would stop at the church in Antioch of Syria to receive the offerings and the goods Simon Niger had asked them to transport to the needy in Jerusalem.

30

Popygos hated duty in Jerusalem. He had always detested the atmosphere of the city. It was hot, dusty and noisy. Now it was hotter, dustier and noisier than he had ever remembered. Jews by the tens of thousands were pouring into the city for the Passover. Pilgrims came from Mauritania, Africa, Cyrenaica, Egypt, Cappadocia, Pamphylia, Macedonia and even Rome itself. And the Jews of Jerusalem were in an ugly mood.

Caesar Caligula had taxed the people unmercifully, but Caligula, his wife, Acetonic, and his daughter had all been killed under the direction of Tribune Cassius Chaerea of the Praetorian Guard. Now Caesar Claudius, elected by the Praetorian Guard, had increased the taxes to sustain his military supporters.

Wealthy Jews had lost their holdings of a lifetime. Poor Jews had been made poorer by the taxes and a drought. The fields were burning for lack of water. The Jews had nowhere to turn for help except to their God. Thus a record number of pilgrims had come to Jerusalem for the religious feast.

Pilate was replaced by Procurator Cumanus and Popygos, though he could never receive the rank of centurion, had to handle Julius' duties. No one had heard from the Centurion since he had been ordered back to Rome. It was rumored that Pilate's wife had become a Christian and Pilate himself had been banished because of the death of Jesus. Pilate had tried to blame Popygos for the empty tomb, but too many men had testified about the unusual nature of the event.

The messenger approached Popygos, "Sir! The Procurator Cumanus orders you to reenforce the guards on Antonia Tower. He fears lest there be an uprising."

"Tell the Procurator that it is done," Popygos replied. Then he murmured to himself, "What can a hundred soldiers do if the Jews decide to mount an insurrection?" Popygos had no experienced men to assign to the tower, but he decided that the soldiers just assigned from Rome could not get into much trouble from the summit.

Under the Tower of Antonia, the walls of ancient Zion came together. One wall ran south to the Middle Gate and the Lower City. The other wall ran east and south around the Temple. The Sheep Gate, used for bringing animal sacrifices to the Temple, was narrow, causing a kind of funnel that trapped people beneath the so-called tower. The tower was really a raised portion of the roof of the fort with a wall around it. Sentinels stood in the openings in the wall.

Below the new Roman soldiers who served as sentries, a mass of Jews waited to get through the gate. Trapped in the space between the walls were hot, tired pilgrims. The dark-skinned Jews of Cyrenaica and Africa appeared in costumes dyed in bright colors and trimmed with the feathers of exotic birds. Light-skinned Jews from Macedonia and Dalmatia stood covered from head to foot in garments as black as midnight. Some Jews from Italia wore Roman clothing. Peppered throughout the crowd were the blue and white of the Pharisees and the shimmering gold of the Sadducees and the priests. Near the tower side of the wall, beggars received a few coins and merchants tried to sell items to be used in the sacrifices. Opposite the tower, a pilgrim, trapped by the mass of the crowd, urinated on the wall.

"Where do we go when we need to do that?" a guard called to the man stationed in the next lookout.

"What?" his friend called. Then he laughed as he saw the man his fellow soldier was pointing to. "Popygos said that we could not leave our post. He did not say that we could not urinate while on duty."

"I really have to relieve myself," the first man answered.

"I'll wager that it would blow back into your face," another sentinel called out.

"How much will you wager that I cannot hit the other wall from here?" the first man called back.

"One of the new gold coins Claudius had made to celebrate his becoming Emperor," called another.

"The wager is taken," said the first man as he untied the belt that held his dagger and two swords, removed his leather skirt and leaned out to get the best possible advantage.

Below, a Jew wondered how water was falling on such a hot day. He looked up and saw the sentinel and what he was doing.

"Uncircumcised heathen," the man cried out as he picked up a rock and threw it with all of his might.

The sentinel, caught off balance due to his position, fell from the tower. The guard at the foot of the tower, seeing his fallen comrade, drew his sword. Another Jew pointed to the Roman and cried, "Desecration! They are desecrating the Temple of the Most High." The crowd surged and the guard stationed at the foot of the tower used his sword.

Popygos was climbing the stair from the Lithostrotos when he heard the trumpet call to battle from the tower. The cry "desecration" had been carried over all of the Temple grounds. Jews surged against the tower guards. From the walls of Antonia, the guardsmen fired crossbows with deadly arrows. Onager catapults stationed on the roof of the Antonia Fortress began to hurl javelins, spears and rocks indiscriminately at the crowd. Women and children fell with the men in a shower of arrows. As spearmen and bowmen exited the fortress, they aimed their weapons at the nearest target and pulled them out to aim them again. Popygos' sword dripped red with blood. Indeed he had trouble standing on the pavement because of the carnage at his feet.

The surge of pilgrims continued to come, armed only with rocks and sticks. Just as steadily, they fell beneath the onslaught of the trained Roman legions. Popygos and his men drove them through the gates onto Mount Moriah itself. The blood of sheep and goats was flowing on the altars of the Temple for the Passover; the blood of the Jews was flowing at its gates. When the last of the insurrection was over and the Jews had scattered, Popygos returned to his quarters to wash the blood from his face, arms and legs. He was so covered with blood that even the bright, jeweled hilt of his dress sword had lost its luster.

"Report, sir!" — the sentry addressed Popygos.

"Yes, what is your report?" Popygos replied wearily.

"Ten Roman legionnaires dead, twenty wounded, hundreds of Jews killed."

"Oh, the gods!" Popygos cried, thinking of the bodies of the women and the children. "All because he was uncircumcised!"

31

Paul had not placed his foot on Jewish soil in over fourteen years. Now he traveled from the port of Caesarea through Samaria as he had done on his first trip to Jerusalem. He had no fear that he would become unclean by passing through the land. Now Paul traveled with Barnabas and with Timothy and Titus, who had joined them in Antioch. They were greeted by Samarian Christians who helped them and prayed for them during their journey.

Although Paul was hurrying to deliver a large caravan of food and goods for the Christians in Jerusalem, there was another reason for his haste. Men who had come from Judaea to Antioch had told the gentile Christians that they could not be saved unless they were circumcised after the way of Moses. It seemed that John Mark had been spreading tales about Paul to the brothers in Jerusalem. Consequently, a great controversy had arisen concerning his work with uncircumcised Gentiles. Some of Paul's former Pharisee friends had united themselves to Christ and were spreading pharisaism throughout the Church. Paul was being led by the Holy Spirit, and he wanted Peter and the elders of Jerusalem to know it!

Where the land had once been green with fields and running with water, only brown stubble and dry clay remained. The results of the drought could be seen everywhere. The closer the group got to Jerusalem, the more parched the earth seemed to be. The Christians they met along the way spoke only of the soon coming of the Lord and His Kingdom and little about winning the heathen to

Christ. *I wonder*, thought Paul, *how this will effect the Church's response to world salvation?*

Paul noticed the fresh graves and the women dressed in mourning as he approached the city. *Surely*, he thought, *things must be much worse than we were told.* It seemed that every household was weeping and the entire nation was lamenting. When Paul and his caravan turned into the gate through the Wall of Herod toward the Tower of Antonia, they could smell death.

"Your food is needed, but it may not be accepted," Peter said as he looked at Titus and Timothy.

"Not accepted!" Paul cried out. "For heaven's sake, why not?"

"Because it comes from uncircumcised Gentiles," Peter answered.

"It is food — grain and flour, lentils and beans, goat's milk and wine, figs and dates! It was not sacrificed to strange gods. What difference does it make whose hands prepared it or who gave it? Gentile brothers in Christ have given what they did not have to give just to bless their brothers. Now do you tell me that they choose to starve rather than eat food provided by the hands of uncircumcised men? What does circumcision of the foreskin have to do with a man's hands?" Paul's voice was rising in anger.

"An uncircumcised man urinated on the holy pavement, desecrating the Temple. Hundreds of Jews died!" Peter's voice also rose.

"You are telling me," yelled Paul, "that the waste of an uncircumcised man is foul and the waste of a circumcised man is holy?"

Paul's argument brought a smile to Peter's face. "No, my brother" — Peter's voice was calm now. "I want neither spraying me. But I am telling you how the people feel. Jews are a proud people; they may choose hunger over eating with Gentiles or receiving food that came from Gentiles."

The food was taken to the courtyard of the home of John Mark's mother, from which it would be distributed to the Christians. While Barnabas was rejoicing at seeing family again, Paul was worried that Peter's concern might be legitimate. As the day began to pass, no one entered to receive the food.

Just before the evening prayers, a woman appeared at the door. "I have come to receive the food and money for myself, Mary, Martha and Lazarus," the woman said to John Mark's mother.

"Yes, of course" — came the reply. "You are most welcome." Paul could tell from her stooped shoulders and torn clothing that this was a woman of great burdens and desperate need. "Come, sister in the Lord. I want you to greet your benefactor. He is the Lord's great Apostle to the Gentiles. He has brought us this food and clothing from afar."

Paul was a bit embarrassed by the introduction, but he did want everyone who received the food to know that it had been given by gentile Christians. Tufts of graying hair peeked out from under the woman's shawl. Her face was deeply lined with the marks of suffering and toil, and her trembling hands had become rough from working in the fields.

"Rabbi Paul, I would like for you to meet ..."

"Esther!" Paul exclaimed.

Esther was visibly embarrassed to have been recognized by Paul. But the mother of John Mark arranged for them to have a private place to talk. *How can John Mark's mother be so thoughtful and kind, when Mark is such a Pharisee and a coward*, Paul wondered. Mark had avoided Paul's presence since Paul had come to Jerusalem.

Esther told Paul that after the Romans had taken all Jacob Bar Kochba's treasure for taxes, he had killed himself with a dagger. Her husband, Reuben, seeing that all the fortune was gone, had deserted her and left Jerusalem. She did not know where he was, but she still held that her marriage was binding. Martha, responding to Esther's desperation, had come to the home Esther had shared with Saul of Tarsus and had taken her to Bethany, to the home Martha shared with her sister, Mary, and her brother, Lazarus. Esther told Paul that she had never loved him or her second husband, but had married each for political and religious purposes. She had received Christ's forgiveness; now, crying, she asked for Paul's. Esther was still very much a Pharisee in that she accepted the Sanhedrin's ruling that she and Paul had never been married. Likewise, since the Sanhedrin said that she was still married to Reuben, she prayed regularly for his salvation and return.

Paul watched her go with sadness in his heart, but with the assurance that God was using all of this to carry His light to the Gentiles. After Esther left, she told the Christians about all the food. It was at John Mark's mother's home! She knew the man who had brought it! He was not, as it had been told, an uncircumcised Roman! He was a great Pharisee from the school of Gamaliel! The Christians and the Jews all respected Esther. Was she not perfected in the Law? They came to receive the bread of life given through the hands of uncircumcised Gentiles.

The church council met in an old dwelling place in the David Wall. It was here, on the Feast of Pentecost, that the early disciples had received a mighty baptism of the Holy Spirit accompanied with mighty signs. Paul had expected Peter to take the leadership of the council, but he found that the honor had been given to James. James, the brother of Jesus, was now the pastor of the church in Jerusalem. As pastor, he was the leader of the community.

James was a comparatively young man with a dark, shiny beard, a strong face, and coal-black eyes. He was a very pious Jew who went daily to pray in the Court of Israel. He also observed all the requirements of the Law. Paul felt that James could be a great threat to the concept of welcoming uncircumcised Gentiles into the Church. Peter was called an apostle and, as such, was the leader of all the Jewish Christians. But here in the Jerusalem church, he submitted to James, the pastor. Peter vacillated between the Law and grace, so Paul did not know where he would stand.

John of the Zebedees had lost his brother, James, whom Herod had executed by the sword. John was often deep into the Spirit, seeing visions and speaking in tongues. Paul wondered if he could be rational about the Gentiles.

John Mark was there, seated close to a group of older men with white beards and long earlocks. They were still dressed in the blue and white of the Pharisees, except that their fringes were larger than any Paul had seen in a purely Jewish community. These men, Paul recognized, were the greatest threat to the new gentile churches. These men were disputing among themselves the propriety of even being in a room with Titus and Paul.

One of the men seated with John Mark spoke first. "This assembly appointed Barnabas to be the leader of the mission to the Gentiles. It was his purpose to bring them to Moses and the Law, then to Jesus as the Christ, even as we came. Saul of Tarsus usurped the authority given to Barnabas and brought Gentiles into the Church without circumcision or baptism."

Barnabas stood to his feet. He was trying to be calm, lest Paul have one of his outbreaks. Barnabas' voice trembled with emotion. "How do you know what happened? Were you there? Were you there when Bar-Jesus was made blind by the Holy Spirit through Paul? Were you there when the Proconsul surrendered his life to Jesus or when Bar-Jesus received his sight and his Lord?" Barnabas looked strongly into the face of his nephew, John Mark. "Were you there when the cripple of Lystra grew legs? Were you there when they stoned Paul and the Holy Spirit brought him back to life and healed his wounds? Will you argue with the evidence of the Spirit of God?" Mark did not move, but he averted his eyes from Barnabas.

Paul had meant to be quiet, but his passion would not let him. The starting point of his argument startled even him. "Jesus said that if a man has broken the Law in his heart, he is guilty of all the Law. Which of us has never lusted, envied or been untruthful? Do we, who are under the sign of the Law, keep the Law? Jesus died so that the curse of the Law might be broken and we might be saved. If we make circumcision necessary for salvation, we say it has to do for the Gentiles what it could not do for us. We make the cross of Christ of no effect!"

Paul's remarks caused a demonstration against him. Indeed it seemed that all semblance of order would dissolve. Suddenly, there was silence. Peter had stood to his feet. "Brothers, you know that through me God spoke to the Gentiles. He baptized them in the same Spirit and in the same way as He did us, and without circumcision. Why would you put a yoke on them that you yourselves cannot carry?" The assembly froze in disbelief. Peter was backing the Roman, Paul! Peter walked over to Paul and placed both hands on his head. "This is the Apostle to the Gentiles. Will you fight the Holy Ghost?"

James stood next to Peter. "It is my decision," he said, "that we require no more of the Gentiles than that they refrain from eating meat offered to idols and from fornication; but that is all!"

The men rose to their feet, accepting the word of James as a command from Jesus. Each, except John Mark, came and welcomed Paul as the Apostle to the Gentiles. Mark slipped out of the assembly, too ashamed to face him.

As Barnabas and Paul walked into the cool of the evening, Barnabas, with a glowing face, looked at Paul and said, "The Holy Spirit had His way, Paul — we were right."

"The fact that every man there had a belly full of gentile bread helped," Paul replied, after which he repeated the words of Jacob Bar Kochba: " 'Religion is politics and politics always follows the wealth' — in this case, bread," he added. He returned Barnabas' smile, thinking of the part Esther had played in getting them to eat.

How wondrous are Your Ways, Lord! he prayed silently. *You take the most pharisaical of the Pharisees and sift her as flour. You fill the bellies of the self-righteous with physical food, enabling them to act with the spiritual strength of grace!*

James decided to send Judas Barsabas — whose brother, Joseph, had been suggested to take the place of Judas Iscariot, the apostle who had betrayed Jesus — with a letter from the council explaining the decision. Judas Barsabas was a large man, a Jew with long forelocks in his hair and a full, black beard. He had been an opponent of Paul's policy, but he would back the decision of James.

James also decided to send a man he called Silas, but who introduced himself to Paul with the Roman name, Silvanus. Silas was a man of medium build, delicate features, a closely trimmed beard and the air of a scholar. It took Paul only a moment to find out that Silas, like himself, was a Roman citizen who believed that salvation was for the Gentiles without the Law. He was a scribe conversant in Greek, Aramaic and Hebrew. He too had a call on his life to carry the message of Jesus to the ends of the earth. *This Silas*, Paul thought, *will do more than carry this message to Antioch*. Paul felt that he and Silas were kindred spirits.

"Paul" — Barnabas was trying to be careful with his strong-tempered partner — "I know that you have it in your heart to return to all the churches we established and see what the Holy Spirit is doing with them."

"I have expressed myself concerning that desire," Paul stated. "I know you too well, my old friend. What is on your mind?"

"I want you to give John Mark a second chance and take him with us!"

Paul's reaction was immediate and violent. "Have you lost your mind! That no-good, spoiled, pouting child almost thwarted God's purpose in getting the Kingdom of God to the Gentiles!"

"Paul," Barnabas replied gently, "your message is one of grace. Surely you can extend that mercy to a brother in Christ who has a strong anointing and calling on his life. John Mark has kindred on Cypress. He could be invaluable to us there."

"Absolutely not!" Paul's face was beginning to show the fervor of his passion, and his voice was trembling from the depth of his emotion. "I saw enough of his backside the last time he was with us. Suppose we encounter violent opposition. Will he stand or run when the going gets hard? We do not get a second chance when we are dealing with the unconverted. Why should I give him an opportunity to nullify the word of God?" Paul pounded his fist on his chest as a Jew in mourning would do. "No! Positively no! I want nothing to do with your John Mark!"

"Then I will take him with me," Barnabas replied, with as much composure as he could manage.

"I will not be with you!" Paul declared vehemently. "I will take Silas with me, and you take your John Mark. We will see who converts the Gentiles!"

Paul watched the ship that carried Barnabas and John Mark slip out of the harbor bound for Cyprus. He knew in his heart that Barnabas was right in the feeling that they needed to be training young men to preach the gospel and plant gentile churches. He also believed strongly that John Mark was the wrong young man. As much sorrow as he felt in Barnabas' departure, he still, somehow, could not release the anger that almost consumed him when he thought of John Mark. *Somewhere there is an anointed youth*, Paul thought. *When I find him, Barnabas, I will show you what a Christian prophet can be!*

Silas was an amicable traveling companion, so Paul enjoyed many evenings on the boat or camping by the bank of a stream. Their conversations concerned the Law and the Kingdom of God. The pair traveled the same route Paul and Barnabas had taken on their first mission. The churches had grown and flourished, making the trip like an uneventful vacation spent visiting old friends — until Paul returned to Lystra.

Paul stopped beside the flowing brook. He knelt, scooped the cool water into his hand and washed the perspiration from his face. "Silas, a great miracle happened to me the last time I was at this brook. I was healed through a Greek god!" Paul smiled at the memory as he told Silas of his encounter with Timothy and the way God had healed the wounds from his stoning. Silas, thinking how easy this trip had been, was amazed by the story. "There" — Paul pointed — "the house in the meadow with the thatch roof. I put that thatching on the last time I was here. Lois and Eunice are terrific people; you will enjoy their company."

"You, by the stream! Drink your water quickly and depart!"

Paul looked up to see where the challenge had come from. Silhouetted in the sunlight, with feet set apart and firmly planted on rocks in the stream, was the tall, muscular figure of a man. He was holding a shepherd's staff as if he knew how to use it. Because of the glaring light, Paul could not make out the features of the man. He quickly realized that his adversary had positioned himself in the best possible location to present his challenge. The head of the man moved sideways, revealing his features. His face was mature, with features that looked as if they had been chiseled in marble. His hair was black as a raven's wing. Paul thought, *This is what young David must have looked like when he challenged the giant*! Five years had greatly changed Timothy, but his hair still curled in locks around his face.

"I was telling my friend that these were magical healing waters," Paul said. "A Greek god once washed my wounds with this water and I was healed!"

"Paul!" came an exuberant shout.

Timothy ran across the slippery rocks, grabbed Paul by the waist and lifted him off his feet in a passionate greeting. "Paul, you came back, you came back!" Timothy did nothing to suppress his joy. "I did not recognize you without Barnabas," Timothy apologized to Paul while greeting Silas at the same time.

"Nor I you," Paul declared. "You have grown into quite a man, Timothy. You had me fearing for my very life," he kidded. "Are Lois and Eunice well?"

"They are well," Timothy replied. "Grandmother cannot use her cane as well as she once did, but I still would not want to come within reach of it if she was angry." Paul smiled at the thought of the little woman and her fearful cane.

As he had done before, Paul used the little cottage in the meadow to find refreshment and peace. Paul and Silas helped Timothy plant the crops and put the little farm into excellent condition. Lois and Eunice both agreed that it was the will of Jesus for Timothy to join Paul and Silas on their mission. Paul had his replacement for John Mark!

Now the mountains were covered with wildflowers instead of snow, so Paul led the trio across the mountains into Asia toward Mysia. But the message was not received. Paul then headed toward Bithynia, but the message was not received. When Paul would tell the people about Jesus and His resurrection, they would just shrug their shoulders without understanding or concern and walk on. It was as if the Spirit of God had left them and their message had no power to convert. Finally they came to Alexandrian Troas. By this time Paul was in despair, not knowing where to go or what to do.

Troas was the gateway to the Roman world. The port of Troas was crucial to the north-south trade to Macedonia. Troas was the gate through which the grain of Asia Minor poured into Macedonia and finally to Rome itself. Paul felt as if he was encountering

Rome for the first time since his youth. The city was filled with the red and gold uniforms of centurions and their legionnaires. The city did not have the nefarious aura of Antioch of Syria. True, statues of the Roman gods were everywhere, but the sorcerers and the soothsayers and the idlers of Asia Minor were missing. This city had been connected to Macedonia by Alexander the Great, whose influence remained.

The Aegean Sea shimmered in the sun and sparkling waves rolled gently onto the beach. Above the hills, Paul could see the sacred mountain, Ida, where the Greeks believed their god Zeus lived. The Greeks believed that Olympus and all its gods stood on the other side of the Aegean. Troas was indeed the gate to the world!

Paul was excited about his visit to the city, but he became ill before the trio could locate the synagogue. Silas and Timothy brought him to an inn. He was burning with fever and his forehead was covered with perspiration. From time to time his body trembled with chills.

Paul was delirious. In his mind he saw the faces of laughing demons. Glaring eyes leapt at him from the dark recesses of his affliction. It seemed as if hell was laughing at his failure to preach the gospel of Christ. Within the frenzied hallucination, a man dressed in unfamiliar clothing appeared. Swirling around the man were the gods and goddesses worshiped by the Greeks. The goddess Diana approached the man with her nymphs, who turned into gruesome demons. A multitude of fiends tore at the man with their teeth. Evil spirits saturated the air, looking like locusts with faces of Greek gods. They filled the skies and attempted to carry the man away. "In the name of the Lord, come and help me," the man cried. "Come! Come!"

Paul's bed covering was drenched with perspiration. It felt cool to his body. A wet rag washed his face. His eyes focused on the strange room and, though he was conscious, he waited for a demon to attack from the edge of his blurred vision. A face came into focus and Paul's heart jumped. Was the nightmare over or was what he had experienced real? He looked into the face of the man. The man's features were as if they had been formed from a bronzed statue. All fear left Paul when he saw the man's eyes. They were clear eyes, holy eyes, in which Paul saw concern and compassion. The man was athletic in stature, though he was no longer a youth. His gray-streaked black beard was trimmed short, like the man in Paul's fantasy.

"My name is Luke," the man said. "I am a physician from Macedonia. Your friend Silas brought me from the synagogue where he had come to pray for you. I became a follower of Jesus when I heard you speak of God's grace in Antioch. You have been sick for three days. Sometimes it happens when one comes down from the mountains to the sea. It may be a change in the air or in the water, but I gave you an herb that helped the fever pass. Timothy will bring you some hot broth made from herbs and leaves that will help you cast off the rest of the fever. When you feel better, we will talk. While you were in the fever, you kept saying, 'I must go to Macedonia.' If you decide to go, I would like to go with you. I believe a healer could be useful to you."

32

This time it was the blue-green water of the Aegean Sea that passed under the bow of the ship. Luke had already proven to be more than a healer. The man was an experienced seafarer who was skilled in dealing with both Greeks and Romans. Silas was pleased with the new company. He found Luke to be not only pleasant fellowship but also an astute thinker. Young Timothy had never even seen the sea before, much less sailed on it, but he proved to be an able man at sea as well as in the mountains. Timothy was excited and curious about each new encounter that expanded his knowledge. He was as excited about learning the word of God as he was about exploring his new world.

Timothy did not lose his interest when they reached the port of Samothrace, nor did his enthusiasm lessen when their journey led them to the port of Neapolis and by land to Philippi. Timothy found adventure in every field, vineyard and grove.

Everything in Philippi was Roman. The houses and the streets looked as if they had been exported from Rome. The men and the women were draped in togas. Not only did Paul encounter Roman soldiers as he had done in Troas but the merchants and the shopkeepers were all Roman. Timothy was especially attracted to the women of Macedonia. Unlike the women of his village and the women in Judaea, the Macedonians were tall and statuesque. They walked unveiled with free-flowing dresses and fragrance.

While watching Timothy watch the ladies, Paul could not help but have a little envy. He remembered for the first time in years the goddess in the Roman baths. Gone was the lust he had once held in his heart and the guilt he had felt about that experience. But with the passing of the lust had also vanished all desire for a relationship with the opposite sex. Something had happened deep inside, and Paul knew that it had nothing to do with Jesus or the Holy Spirit. His marriage to Esther had destroyed his desire for women. Paul knew that he had never really found the love of a woman — wholesome, true love — and he wondered if he could still love that way. For the present, however, the love of Christ was enough. It was Paul's love for Christ and the world that did not know Him that drove him onward.

The city was filled with the temples of Greek gods, but Paul looked in vain for a Jewish synagogue. It was Luke who led Paul out of the city on the Sabbath to the river bank. There, in the shadow of willow trees, the Jews sat. The women were seated apart from the men, their faces hidden by their veils. They sat in silence, having no rabbi and no synagogue. They dreamed of Jerusalem and the Temple, which most of them had never seen. They sat in a land filled with idols in the only place they could find that had not been desecrated. They sat without the scrolls of the Law and without a teacher. They simply thought about the stories they knew of their people. Some gentile converts sat among them, attracted to the moral life of the Jews, but they understood little of the Jewish religion.

Luke was recognized, but the Pharisees and the Greek that were with him caused a stir. Luke introduced Paul as one who had been taught by the Rabbi Gamaliel and had sat on the great Sanhedrin. Paul, with fire in his voice, told them that the long-awaited Messiah had already come. The Messiah had become the Passover Lamb for all who could not come to the Temple. He had given His life so that their sins might be forgiven and they might be freed from the Law. This salvation was not only for the Jews but also for the Gentiles! Timothy, quoting from the Prophets, told them that all Paul's news of the Messiah had been proclaimed long ago.

Then Silas unrolled the scrolls and read to them that the holy ones in Jerusalem had declared that all Gentiles who accepted the Messiah were released from the disciplines of the Law.

The first to receive the message was Lydia, a widow and a dealer in dyestuffs. She was not a Jewess but a Gentile who believed in the God of Israel. Lydia and all the members of her family were baptized in the name of Jesus, the Messiah. She requested that Paul and his companions make her house their home. Her request was not simply one of hospitality; she wanted proof that they considered her equal to those who were born Jews — that they would not call her unworthy because she was not a Jewess.

Paul found Lydia attractive because he had never before encountered a woman like her. This slightly-stout, slightly-graying woman was the manager of a far-flung enterprise. She saw to both the manufacture and the sale of her dyestuffs, and she directed slaves, workers and shop managers with equal ease. She was a gentile, female counterpart to the entire Salaman family. On the Sabbath, she was the discreet veiled woman. In the shop and the office, she was the unveiled director and power behind a merchant empire. Soon, with the help of Lydia, a little synagogue was built in which the worshipers of the God of Israel could meet together, and where Paul and others could preach the good news of Jesus, the Messiah.

The household of Lydia, including Paul and his associates, were on their way to the new synagogue when they passed a demented girl who was possessed by a demon. She was a slave who was led about on a leash like an animal by the servant of her owner. It was common in the slave market to find a slave who was possessed. Slaves were sold for every use imaginable. Women were sold as concubines and whores. Boys were trained and sold to be used by those who had unnatural lusts. Slaves were sold to be the educators and trainers of their master's children. Snake charmers, sorcerers and Asiatic stargazers were kept as fortunetellers. Slaves like the girl were owned by associations of men who leased the slave to rich people to forecast their futures. They were dragged from house to house, where they were tormented until a lunatic frenzy would come over them and a demon would speak through their lips.

The slave girl had no awareness of who Paul and his companions were, but the demon within her immediately recognized, by the presence of the Holy Spirit, that they were messengers of God. "These men are servants of the Most High God. They can show you the path of salvation," the demon, speaking through the girl, said in mocking sarcasm.

The steward of her owner dragged her away from the Christians, angry because she was prophesying without his receiving any pay. As she was being forced down the road, she turned toward Paul and cried again with a high, screeching voice, "There is the servant of the Most High God!" The wail of the deranged creature caused the people to look from her toward the Christians.

As Paul and his associates were returning from their Sabbath prayers, the possessed girl again caught sight of them. Fervently she began to drag on her leash. Her eyes became dilated and unfocused, and foam formed on her lips. Her face became twisted in a hideous manner and a deep guttural voice declared with mockery that Paul was the servant of Christ. People were beginning to associate the Christians with the possession of the demon spirit!

Paul whirled to face the girl and her guardian. As he began to approach them, the girl drew back to the full length of her leash. A whining, pleading voice began to beg before the steady gaze of the Apostle. The Christian congregation and the onlookers stood transfixed, watching the ongoing battle. Repeatedly the girl writhed like a snake, trying to get away. A hiss came from her inner being. Paul continued to advance. Luke became concerned when Paul walked within the reach of the chain.

"In the name of Jesus Christ, I command you to loose her!" Paul's command shattered the air.

Luke watched the struggle that was ravaging the girl. He could almost see the serpent writhing within her. It seemed as if the thing was struggling against a force mightier than himself, and the girl's body was the battlefield. A nonhuman sound of wailing and gurgling begged Paul to allow it to stay within the girl. Paul stood tensely, waiting to be obeyed. He repeated the command. "You heard me. I said that you must loose her and leave her. In the name of Jesus Christ you must go! And you will obey that name!" There was a scream as if something had ripped her body, and the girl fell, unconscious, to the ground.

Her keeper lifted her up. "Prophesy!" he thundered. The girl was limp in his grasp, looking around with a look that asked, "Where am I? What has happened to me?" The keeper slapped her, trying to bring her back to her former self. "I said, prophesy!" the steward repeated as he struck her with the leash. "Why are you doing this to me?" she asked. The keeper led her away now, fearful because the crowd had seen what he had done to her and anxious to find out what the owners of the slave girl were going to do.

Later that evening a large group of men rushed into the shop of Lydia. Luke had taken Timothy on an excursion, so the mob found only Paul and Silas. They grabbed the two men and dragged them out into the street shouting, "These are Jews who are troubling our city!" The mob brought Paul and Silas before the magistrates of the city and accused them: "These Jews teach customs that are not lawful for Romans to receive or observe."

There was no trial. Paul's clothing was ripped from his back. His arms were pulled around one of the columns of the building. He could see Silas being tied to a column next to him. Paul thought of the ring of Augustus hanging on the strap around his neck. *All I would have to do is call out to the magistrates "I am a Roman!" and produce the ring, and they would be forced to stop. But what about the Jews? What about the new Christian church? I led them to Christ as a Jew. Will they feel betrayed if I use my Roman authority now? If I escape the wrath of the mob, they may unleash it on the new believers.* Paul bit his teeth and waited for the lash.

The thongs whistled through the air. Then Paul felt the burning, tearing pain in his neck. Again he heard the sound of the leather and felt the pain stinging through his shoulders. Paul felt faint, but he forced himself not to surrender to the weakness. Again there was the sound of the whip. He braced himself. The hot, agonizing sting of the lash tore at his flesh. Blood glistened on his cheek. He looked at Silas. His friend was hanging limp next to him, his body crisscrossed with stripes of blood. The watching Romans called out vulgar, obscene jests. The scourge came again and a moan attempted to pass through his teeth, but he swallowed it. The Romans would not receive the satisfaction of even a whisper, much less a scream, from these victims. Deep inside, where the Romans could not hear, Paul said, *O Lord, give me the strength to sustain as You did, to be mute before the shearers.*

The Roman soldiers dragged Silas and Paul through the corridors of a building and shoved them into a cell. A chain was fastened to their legs, then it was secured to a block of marble. The door clanged shut. They were left in the dark. Paul's body was throbbing all over. His arms and legs refused to function, as if they were not a part of his body.

"Silas," he called into the blackness. No reply. Had they killed his friend? "Silas," he repeated. Still no reply. The marble stone was cold to his body. He was too weak to stand up, but he could not lie down because of the chain. He extended himself as far as possible toward where he knew Silas was, but he could not reach him. "Silas," he called to the dark. The only sound he heard was the dripping of water, or was it his blood? The hours went by and his body shook involuntarily from the cold and the spasms of pain. "Silas" — his voice was trembling, begging, hoping.

Then the sound came. It was a deep, resounding sound that echoed against the hard, marble walls of the prison. It was a melodious sound, strong with faith.

"Praise ye the Lord. Praise, O ye servants of the Lord, praise the name of the Lord. Blessed be the name of the Lord from this time forth and for evermore. From the rising of the sun unto the going down of the same, the Lord's name is to be praised."

Silas was singing the psalms of David!

"The Lord is high above all nations ... "

Paul joined with Silas in praise. At first his voice was weak, but soon it soared, seeming to gain supernatural strength.

"... and His glory above the heavens."

Two voices carried through the prison darkness. Paul felt an indescribable ecstasy in his soul. Light seemed to flow over his body, which was still chained in the dark cell. With strength and power, the voices of Paul and Silas blended and swelled. The sound of their song reverberated through the prison.

"Who is like unto the Lord our God?"

The prisoners in the other cells listened with wonder. Word had spread about the Jews. Had they not just endured scourging? Were they not chained as all others to the blocks? Yet they were singing! They sang praises to the God who had allowed them to be scourged! Their song was filled with exultation!

The jailer heard the song. He knew that the Jews had endured the scourging in silence. Now, in the dark pit, they were singing with joy! *Is it possible that they, indeed, are the servants of God? Were the words of the slave prophetess true? Have not these men told of a Saviour who was scourged and crucified, but three days later came back from the dead?* The jailer felt fear grip his soul.

Suddenly the jail floor trembled beneath the jailer's feet. A rumbling noise mingled with the sound of the Jews' song. The rumbling increased and the building began to shake until the jailer could not stay on his feet. His children began to cry and his wife called in terror from the dark, but he could not move. Another sound, the sound of iron doors being burst asunder, came to him, and a greater fear clawed at his heart. All of the prisoners were loose! He could feel it rather than see it, but he knew that the doors of the prison were open wide. The prisoners were escaping. *Perhaps they will come to kill me and my family! But is that really all that bad, for I am doomed. If the prisoners don't get me, the magistrates will sentence me to scourging and imprisonment because I let the prisoners escape.* The jailer could not endure that thought.

The building shook, prisoners screamed, iron broke, stones fell, the rumbling continued and still he heard,

"Plead my cause against an ungodly nation, O deliver me from the deceitful and unjust man. For thou are the God of my strength ... "

The song of the Jews now contained the sound of laughter. All was hopeless! All was lost! The jailer seized his sword and drew it from the scabbard. Just as he tried to find a place where he could impale himself on the sword, the song ended.

"Hold! Don't harm yourself!" Paul and Silas had found their way through the dark corridors, singing all the while. Coming from the darkness of the cell, Paul could easily distinguish the jailer and the sword in the lighter room. "We are all here!" Paul added, to comfort the man and give him assurance. The jailer threw his sword to the floor of the room and fell at Paul's feet, stammering, "My lords, tell me the way of God! What must I do to be saved?"

After Paul and Silas had helped the jailer restore order to the prison, the jailer took them into his house. By oil light, the jailer and his wife washed the blood from Paul and Silas. Then they listened eagerly as the two missionaries taught about Jesus and His salvation. The jailer of the prison of Philippi was received into the faith of the Christ and baptized.

When morning came, a message came from the magistrates that the jailer should allow the Jews to go free. The messenger was surprised to find Paul and Silas as the house guests of the jailer, but he was even more surprised when Paul said, "Yesterday they beat us openly without a trial and cast us into prison. Today they wish to take us out of prison privately. No way! Tell them that I am a Roman citizen. If they wish to take me out of prison, they will have to come and do it themselves."

There was alarm in the houses of the magistrates of Philippi when they heard the news. They had scourged Romans! Although the council came to beg their forgiveness, the magistrates asked Paul and Silas to leave Philippi.

Leaving Luke with the church at the house of Lydia, Paul, Silas and Timothy departed down the mountains, along the Roman Road toward Thessalonica. Paul's torn back reminded him of the humiliation of being beaten and imprisoned, yet he wondered at the grace of his Lord. Jesus had told the other disciples to be as wise as the serpent, but as harmless as doves. Paul thought that he was beginning to understand.

33

Caesar Tiberius Claudius Nero Germanicus was having a new port built for Rome at Ostia. A section of the Praetorian Guard had been moved to Ostia to protect the Emperor. Marches Furius Camillus Scribgonianus, Governor of Dalmatia, had led an aborted rebellion against Claudius scarcely more than a year after his accession. Since that time, the Caesar lived in fear for his life. Therefore, Claudius was always looking for centurions he could trust. Now he particularly needed a trustworthy officer to serve as the Praetorian Prefect of Ostia. Claudius considered Julius Laco to be the likely candidate.

The warm west wind softly caressed Julius' cheek as he slumbered. The seaside villa, with its rooftop terrace, had greatly aided in his recovery. Gone were the haunting memories of the dark day on Calvary with its smell of death. Julius had never settled in his mind who the Prophet Jesus of Nazareth had been. Perhaps Paul had been correct in his assessment that the Son of God could not have been crucified. What, then, had caused the terrible depression Julius had gone through? Crucifying a god could certainly bring on such a condition. But, on the other hand, maybe Julius had been cursed by a sorcerer. Whatever the cause, getting away from Judaea had lifted the plague, and now the clean winds of the Etruscan Sea were blowing it away. Should Claudius assign him as the Praetorian Prefect of Ostia, Julius would ask Diana to marry him. They would make the villa their home.

Julius touched his face to remove an annoying insect. Again, the sensation of his face being lightly touched brought a hand to swat the culprit away. Laughter penetrated his consciousness.

"Some praetorian prefect you would make! Why, Caesar could be assassinated and Ostia pillaged by barbarians, and you would be on your veranda snoring!"

The soft light of the sun made her hair glow as it waved in the breeze. The blue of the sky above her head enhanced the blue of her eyes. She was wearing a flowing white gown that seemed to give her wings.

"Venus?" Julius asked, teasing. He reached up and grabbed her, pulling her down to him. He was barechested and she felt warm and silky to his flesh. He positioned himself for a kiss and received a mouthful of fig.

"Goddess of love? I know what you have on your mind!" she mocked him.

Julius pulled the stem of the fig out of his mouth and reached for her again. "Diana, virgin goddess of the moon" — he continued to charm her.

She yielded to him with a quick kiss. "Diana, the hunter who spies on her victim in the moonlight" — she attempted to make her voice low and menacing. "I have ordered your servant to bring your breakfast to the veranda and to give you your morning bath," she told him, as her voice returned to its normal soft tone. Then she left the veranda, but Julius heard her say as she disappeared, "I'll be watching you. When you are naked and defenseless, I will have Cupid shoot you in the proper place!"

Had it not been for Diana, Julius might never have gotten well. He had visited her at her family's home when he returned to Rome, just to make sure that she had received his letters. He also wanted to tell her about Saul the Pharisee and Esther. When Julius had left for Judaea, Diana had been a moonstruck child in love with the first man who had rejected her. When he returned, he found a mature, confident woman who was capable of entering into a loving relationship. The light of her love and understanding had washed his soul of whatever curse had been placed upon it at Calvary. It was not that she had placated his guilt. No, she had dealt with his problem in a most mature way.

"If this Jesus was the Son of God," she told him, "then His Father must have allowed His crucifixion for some redemptive reason. If Jesus was just a good man, then the priests of Israel are responsible for his death. For if they had been righteous men, they would have recognized that He was a virtuous man. You obeyed Rome," she reminded him, "but Jesus forgave you from the cross." Although Diana knew that most men would have felt nothing, she assured Julius that she understood his deep remorse. Indeed, it was that very sensitivity that first awakened her love for him. Diana did not see his depressed spirit as failure, as did Rome and Julius himself. She saw beyond the consuming depression to a tender, caring spirit, and it touched her. Soon they were both very much in love.

Julius had persuaded Diana's parents to bring her to Ostia. They were very interested in the new port, but they were more interested in the fact that their future son-in-law might become the praetorian prefect.

"I had better not be wounded tonight, huntress of the moon," he called after her. "Tonight we dine with Caesar!"

Diana immediately reappeared in the doorway. "Did you say that we are dining with Caesar tonight?"

"Ah, I was not dreaming" — Julius continued to tease her. "I did see a goddess, but she has not yet seduced me!"

"Don't lay there grinning at me, you half-naked baboon. You have only one thing on your mind, and that will have to wait for the honeymoon. Why didn't you tell me before now that we are meeting Caesar tonight? I have to get my dress ready and my jewels picked out!"

Diana ran down the stairway. As she exited the villa on the beach side, Julius stood and almost called out, "I knew you one time when you would not have waited!" but he held his tongue and called instead, "Tell your parents that they are also invited. Claudius is anxious to meet them!" Diana paused just a moment to look up and make a face at him. Then she turned and ran across the beach. The sand, caught by the breeze, flowed with every movement of her feet. The reflection of the sea and the sun made her hair shine in the wind like polished gold. *A goddess*, he said to himself. "Your cupid already hit the mark," he yelled. But she could not hear him.

The first thing Claudius had built in Ostia was a magnificent villa from which he could oversee the work on the port. It was situated high on a bluff where the Tiber River met the Etruscan Sea. Great marble blocks had been floated down the Tiber to make the villa equal to those on the Palatine Hill in Rome. Great columns had been erected, and a large, covered portico that overlooked the sea had been built. There Caesar entertained his guests and watched construction on the port. Gilded couches and tables laden with fresh fish, stuffed quail, roast suckling and all manner of vegetables and fruits graced the piazza.

"Julius, you must race for me in the games," Claudius said, when introduced again to the man he was considering for the post of Praetorian Prefect of Ostia. "I remember well seeing you race in the Circus under the banner of Tiberius. You must carry the colors of Claudius!"

"It would be an honor, Caesar!" Julius replied. "Please meet my soon-to-be bride, Diana, and her parents." He brought Diana to his side.

Diana felt as if Claudius' eyes had undressed her in public. He took her hand and pressed it between his fingers with a massaging movement. "A gorgeous creature, Centurion. You are to be congratulated. You have the prize and have not yet won the race." Diana feared that she was a prize Claudius would take if she did not watch out. Caesar did not so much as recognize her parents.

"I do not like our Caesar," Diana whispered to Julius as they sat at their table.

"He's a lecherous man you have a right to be afraid of," Julius whispered back. "His wife, Messalina, is worse. No wonder he is a lewd bastard. She attempts to seduce every man she meets. I am told she even goes into the brothels of Rome and gives herself away for the pleasure of it. I'll try to protect you from him, if you will protect me from her!"

"Like you need protection!" Diana replied.

"I do," answered Julius. "That oversexed whore is going to get someone killed!"

"Where is the lady?" Diana whispered back. "This woman I have to see."

"The word is, Gaius Silius is her latest conquest," Julius replied. "Silius is a very rich, noble, reasonably young and extremely good-looking man. Messalina is supposed to be with him at his villa. But who knows, she may be down on the docks selling herself to the slaves." Julius smiled at the joke he had made. Julius and Diana may as well have been alone as far as Caesar or any of his guests were concerned. Julius realized that everyone in the crowded party was really alone.

Claudius was constantly approached by Romans who tried to use their relationship to the Caesar to further their careers. This fact isolated the Caesar from his fellow Romans and caused him to make Greeks or Hellenized Orientals — who had formerly been slaves, but were now freedmen in rank — his confidential advisors. The most important of his aides was Lucius Vitellius. Vitellius was a short, stocky man who kept nervously eyeing Julius and Diana, trying to decide on Julius' qualifications for the job of Praetorian Prefect. At the same time, his voice was heard above the noise of the party, shamelessly flattering the Emperor. Another that never seemed to be detached from Claudius was Narcissus, the Minister of Letters. Narcissus seemed to be a strong character. It was whispered that he, and he alone, shared all of Claudius' secrets. Of the women present, Diana was most impressed by a lady wearing a flowing gown. Her name was Agrippina. She was aloof, dignified and in control. Her very detachment seemed to fascinate Claudius. Diana was happy for Agrippina to have the Emperor's eye, for she had a feeling that any interest Claudius had in a woman could be dangerous.

Julius and Diana sipped their wine, enjoyed the music and the food, and got a little romantic in the moonlight of the patio. Diana was the first to notice the disturbance at Caesar's table. A messenger had spoken to Vitellius, who, in turn, spoke privately into Caesar's ear. When Narciscus joined the conversation, there soon developed what looked like a debate between Vitellius and Narcissus, with Claudius caught in the middle. Narcissus left the room and Vitellius approached Julius' table.

"Centurion Laco!" Lucius Vitellius, Knight of Lucera in Apulia and Governor of Syria, addressed Julius.

"Sir!" Julius had stood as Vitellius approached their table. Fear came into the heart of Diana.

"I ask your pardon for interrupting your evening with the charming lady."

"My betrothed," Julius replied.

"We have a most urgent matter," Vitellius continued. "A plot has just been discovered against Caesar's throne. Gaius Silius is even now attempting to marry Empress Messalina in an attempt to enthrone her son, Britannicus, with Silius and Messalina as his regents. Caesar has ordered the Praetorian Guard to catch the conspirators and end their attempt to seize the throne. Now is the time for you to show your loyalty to your Caesar. Narcissus will be in command, but should you show your loyalty, you will be appointed the new Prefect of Ostia."

Julius assured Vitellius of his loyalty and slipped out of the party with Diana. After sending her back to the villa with her parents, Julius rushed to get the Guard marching. Then he arranged for the fastest riders he could find to go to Rome with him.

Messalina had arranged to have a mimic grape harvest on the grounds of her estate. The winepresses were working and the vats were overflowing. Women were prancing in the vats and worshiping the goddess Maenads in wild rites. Messalina, her black hair streaming with wine, stood in the midst of them, her arms raised. Brandishing a Bacchic wand, she posed as the goddess waiting to be seduced by the god Dionysus. Beside her, splattered with the blood of the grape, stood her consort, Gaius Silius.

This is the way Julius found them when his Praetorians tore through the gates. Messalina managed to get out of the vat and run into an adjoining garden. Silius, drunk, climbed over the vat and attempted to defend himself with the Bacchic wand. "Behold the god of wine," one of the Praetorian Guard cried. "Shall we see if he can drink all of it?" another asked. Julius nodded his head and went to look for the Empress.

Members of the Guard grabbed the wine-covered Silius and tied his feet to a lift used to raise the grapes into the vats. Silius writhed and attempted to right himself as he was lifted feet first above the wine vat. "A drink, oh god of wine," a guardsman mocked. Silius was dropped head first into the flowing vat of wine. Wine splashed over the edge as Silius attempted to rise from the brew. The guardsman drew him out. Silius gasped for breath, only to have his mouth and nose filled with wine. Coughing in spasms, he was dipped again into the vat. Again the wine splashed and his body wriggled. Once more he was pulled out to hear the jesting of the guard. He tried to get his breath, but could not because of the choking smell of the wine. Again he was dropped, head first, into the vat. Again the struggle. Then the body relaxed and a guard cut the rope. Silius lay with his head under the brew, drowned in the wine.

Narcissus entered the gate and saw the body of Silius. He nodded his approval and went to the garden toward which a Praetorian guardsman pointed. Messalina was sitting in the flowers, moaning. This was the wife of Claudius. Thus Julius had not allowed his men to put their hands on her. He saluted Narcissus when he entered the garden.

"It would be best," said Narcissus, "if the Empress took her own life." He took a sword and placed its hilt between two large rocks in the garden so that the blade pointed outward. "If the Empress will please end this matter," Narcissus continued, and pointed to the sword. Messalina only continued to sob. He nodded to two guards who lifted Messalina to her feet. The two Praetorians thrust her onto the sword. Her scream was cut off. Her body jerked on the iron. "I will tell Caesar that the Empress' lover drowned in a wine vat and she impaled herself on a sword in grief." Narcissus looked at Julius as he spoke.

"It is as you have said, sir!" Julius replied.

"Thank you, Praetorian Prefect," Narcissus answered.

The cool breeze of the Etruscan Sea brought the sound of crashing waves and the smell of the sea into the terrace. The moon was full and Julius held Diana snugly in his arms. "Promise me that we will not have a religious wedding," he pleaded.

"Why?" she asked.

"I have seen what a Jewish wedding did to a good friend of mine. All that religion turned a sane man into a sanctimonious despot. I just attended a wedding celebrated in the rituals of Bacchus that I considered lewd. I have no faith in any god or goddess, so why should I pretend. Let's just sign the letters of marriage for Rome and let that be that!"

"I would like for our parents and our friends to witness the signing," she replied.

"That will be fine," he agreed, "only no big party!"

"Just a little wine," she suggested, thinking of what she had heard about Silius and Messalina.

"Only the wine of your lips," he replied, also thinking about what he had experienced. "I don't believe I will ever want to drink wine again!"

Diana laughed.

"We will have to sign the vows quickly," Julius continued.

"What's the big hurry?" she teased him.

"Narcissus is sending his new Praetorian Prefect to Caesarea to bring back prisoners to work on the harbor and man the oars for the ships," he replied. "I will not be gone long, but I want to taste your wine before I go. Besides, Claudius is marrying that woman, Agrippina. I want to make sure he is a happily married man before I go. I did not like the way Caesar looked at you!"

Diana smiled. "Is next month in Rome soon enough?"

"Let's seal that with a kiss," he said.

"Or some wine!" she chuckled.

A lone sea bird crossed the moon, headed down the coast toward Messina and the open sea toward Judaea.

34

As the ship approached the port of Athens-Phalerum, Paul could see the sparkling white marble buildings and the statues gracing the hill of the Acropolis. On the very peak of the Acropolis, standing in stark relief against a dark blue sky, was the gigantic form of the goddess Athena. Paul knew that Athena was supposed to be the daughter of Zeus. According to their myth, Athena had leapt, fully developed, from the head of Zeus. She was the goddess of all wisdom. She blessed only the strong and the victorious.

Paul did not feel very strong or victorious. His recovery from the scourging at Philippi had been slow and painful. Unlike when Timothy had found him and he had been supernaturally healed from the cuts and the bruises from the stones, the stripes of the whip had left permanent scars. In Thessalonica he had known modest success in leading Greeks and women to Christ, but once again the Jews had driven him out before his work was really started. After he, with Silas and Timothy, left Thessalonica, they had gone to Berea. The same thing had happened there. The Jews from Thessalonica had followed them to Berea and caused another riot. Silas and Timothy had remained in Berea, but they had persuaded Paul to leave for his own safety.

Strong! Victorious! Paul felt weak, humiliated and alone! The road from Phalerum to Athens was bordered by two high walls that had been built during the Trojan Wars. It was paved with blocks of stone for carriages, and the walking was easy. Had Paul Gabinius, son of the Proconsul, entered Athens, he would have ridden on the marble pavement in a carriage gilded with gold. Had Saul Salaman, Rabbi from Jerusalem and the house of Gamaliel, entered the city, the Jews would have sent out a delegation to welcome him and he would have ridden on a donkey.

But Paul, Apostle of Jesus Christ, came to Athens and walked beneath the empty and deserted temples. It was like walking through a cemetery in which only gods were buried. Paul felt so lonely and deserted that he wondered for a fleeting moment where the tomb of Jesus was. In the crossroad was the figure of Hermes. *His tomb*, Paul thought. He also saw the statues to Aphrodite, Hera and Zeus. All of the statues and the temples were magnificent, except one. Something inside Paul caused him to look more closely at that temple as he passed. He stopped and went to the altar. No image or likeness of a god stood over it. The inscription at the base of the altar read: "To the unknown god."

"Praise You, Lord!" Paul shouted uncontrollably. Passers-by stared at the traveler standing at the foot of the desolate and unadorned altar. Someone seriously worshiping in this garden of gods and temples was a rare sight.

Tears streamed down Paul's face. "You are not dead like their gods, oh Lord! Forgive your servant for not understanding. They once trusted in these gods, but their trust is gone. The real tomb is within the heart. You are not gone, but simply 'unknown.' Athena is not wisdom, for wisdom cannot be known without words, and she cannot speak. But You, oh Lord, have spoken through Your Word, Jesus! I will introduce You to them, Father. You will never be 'unknown' again!"

Paul found the market of Athens, located at the base of the Hill of Agora. An immense statue of Mercury dominated the market square. A throng of people from all over the world filled the market streets and alleys. In the stalls, merchants sold gold, silver and jewels. Weavers, sellers of cloth, and a tailor shop that reminded Paul of his uncle Simon were intermingled with the shops of the goldsmiths. Paul could smell the sweet scents of perfumes that came from the East. Slavers called out for buyers of their human merchandise. Mingled with the naked bodies of Ethiopian women and Greek boys, their bodies perfumed and oiled to attract customers, were unadorned statues of the gods. Both the slaves and the gods were being offered for sale. They would be used as well as worshiped.

Paul saw immediately that there was a great difference between the market of Athens and that of Jerusalem. In Jerusalem, the shop of Jacob Bar Kochba would have been filled with old men of wealth. In Athens, the shops were filled with youths. The nobility of Rome sent their children to study with the scholars of Athens. True, they were wealthy children of wealthy fathers, but the fathers had deserted Athens and had turned it over to their sons. The sons spent their time learning how to wear their robes so that the folds of the cloth would be the most graceful. They bought perfumes and oils that they were told would awaken a woman to passion. They gambled with dice on tables provided by those who swindled them. The youth bought generously of flowers, perfumes and gold to give as love gifts.

A Greek boy was sold to a youth little older than himself, who could not keep his hands from fondling his new acquisition. The Ethiopian mother on the slave block was of little interest to the youthful shoppers. Paul knew that any city or society that had been abandoned to its youth was in its decline. Athens was already wrapped in its death shroud.

As Paul watched the youth of Athens, anger burned in his soul. These lost children did not even know that they were lost. They were so caught up in lust and striving to fill their that emptiness they did not know they were empty and hollow. They attempted to fill the void in their lives with music, poetry and empty philosophy. When that did not satisfy, they turned to lust and unnatural affection. They stood in the shadow of gods who did not care and could not have helped if they had wanted to. For the gods were more immoral and empty than the children. Paul was not enraged at the children but at the waste. He was watching the living dead, yet he knew that the Lord of life had already given them eternal life through the cross. Somehow he had to get through the maze of stone gods and awaken the youths' stone hearts to their true condition. He felt compelled to show them the God of love.

Not everyone in the market was young or foolish. The older populace, and by far the richest members of the market scene, were the merchants. As Paul had suspected, most were Jews. These, though no different in physical appearance from the merchants of Jerusalem and Tarsus, were different from any Jews Paul had ever known. Never in Jerusalem would Paul have seen Jews standing brazenly with their heads uncovered and their eyes raised in the presence of idols. The merchants of Jerusalem would never have called out to passing youths, encouraging them to buy images that give wisdom and goddesses that bring love. The Pharisee of Paul's past rose up within him.

"You men of Israel!" he cried at the top of his voice. "You who have sacrificed to Jehovah in His Temple. Have you forgotten that the Lord our God is one! Did He not say upon His burning mountain, 'Thou shalt have no other gods before Me. Thou shalt not make unto thee any graven image, or any likeness of any thing that is in heaven above, or that is in the earth beneath, or that is in the water under the earth. Thou shalt not bow down thyself to them, nor serve them, for I am a jealous God'?"

One of the old men, his bald head red with embarrassment and his hand shaking with agitation, spat out at Paul, "We do not worship these gods; we only sell to those who do."

"Do you not proclaim the powers and the wisdom of these idols to these youths? Did I not hear you, just a moment ago, call out that the image of Aphrodite could give love and satisfaction?

Are these statues real gods and goddesses, or do you lie and cheat in order to profit from them?"

A crowd of youths gathered around Paul. One pale youth who was little more than a boy called out, "He sold me an image of Apollo and said it would turn me into a man. I had to sell my body to men in order to pay for the image. All I got for my effort was this!" The boy tore open his tunic to reveal part of his body that had been eaten away by disease.

"He is no man now!" declared another youth.

"He is not even a virgin girl," another mocked.

Paul saw no humor in the plight of the youth.

"You sell demons that pursue men in the form of sickness! You corrupt youth and sell them into idolatry. You, being a Jew, know better!" Paul declared forcefully.

A tall Greek dressed in the long white robe of a Stoic teacher had been attracted to Paul's declaration. "The Jewish scholar is partly correct," the teacher began, recognizing Paul's position as a rabbi. "Zeno taught that there is but one god, who is the beginning and the end of all things. God delegated the management of the world to demons. These demons are the gods of the Greeks. But," the Greek scholar continued, "the demons are of a kindly disposition toward men."

"You call this boy's sickness a 'kindly disposition'?" Paul questioned. "You call those gods who, according to your myth, rape the most beautiful of human women to produce bastard-god sons, who in turn go whoring after the daughters of men, of kindly disposition? The idols are nothing! You are correct. Their attraction is from the demons! This boy's disease is centered in demons. It is from hell!"

Paul felt in his spirit that he ought to lay hands on the diseased boy and proclaim his healing in Jesus' name, but something inside prevented him.

"My name is Dionysius" — the Stoic scholar interrupted Paul's thoughts. "We have a place at the beginning of the Sacred Way where, since the days of Socrates, scholars have had the right to speak on any subject of their choosing. Called the Areopagus, it is located in the Painted Portico near the statues to Solon, the founder of the Athenian constitution, and the god Mars. May I invite you to accompany me to the Areopagus? There we will hear what you have to say about your God and any new revelation you might have of Him."

Paul could not resist Dionysius' invitation. *What an opportunity!* he thought. To be able to present Jesus to the most developed minds in the world and argue His case before them was something Paul had never dreamed possible. *The only thing that could be greater*, he thought, *would be to present Christ before the Sanhedrin in Jerusalem*!

One of the teachers lecturing in the Areopagus taught that the immortality of the soul was achieved through education. Another, an Epicurean professor, was proclaiming that death did not exist but was only a state of the mind. The two teachers were trying to prove the keenness of their rationality and their resourcefulness in argument. Neither was concerned with seeking truth. Paul realized that most of the students had come for the same purpose. The Areopagus was little more than a circus in which mental gymnasts demonstrated their tricks. Paul was introduced by Dionysius as a visiting scholar from Jerusalem. While they had climbed the hill, Dionysius had learned from their conversation that Paul had studied under the great Rabbi Gamaliel. He was quick to make mention of that fact to the audience.

Paul began: "Men of Athens, I notice that you are a very religious people. As I passed the statues of your gods, I found an altar dedicated to the unknown God. You worship Him without understanding, but I have come to present Him to you!"

The Athenians nodded their approval of Paul's introduction. It was good rhetoric to start with a known and to proceed to an unknown. Paul's introduction had merit.

"God, Who made the world," Paul continued, "and all things therein, seeing that He is Lord of heaven and earth, dwells not in temples made with hands."

The Athenians again nodded in agreement. Zeno the Stoic had taught the same thing. It was good when arguing to start with a familiar theme.

Paul quoted a Greek poet, "In God we live and move and have our being."

Ah, thought one of the Athenian listeners, *the Jew has prepared well*!

"Since we are the children of God," Paul continued, "we should not think of the Godhead as being made from silver, gold or stone art made by men."

"The same old Jewish thinking," one said as he turned to seek a more exciting speaker.

"God has allowed your devotion to idols because of your ignorance," Paul declared. "But now God will judge you because He has given all men assurance of His power by raising Jesus from the dead!"

A scholar who had been listening intently called out, "You give us more than the Stoics. They only promise the continuation of the soul. Tell me, great man of learning, how will the body, which corrupts away in the earth, be brought back to life? With what elements will it be raised? Its own or someone else's?" the scholar laughed.

Another followed suit, "Give us a demonstration, Jew! Please die and be raised so that we can see the evidence of what you say!"

Paul turned from the ridicule. Another called after him, "Come back when your head is well, Jew, and we will let you try again!"

Dionysius, a woman called Damaris, and some others turned to leave with him. Paul was flushed from embarrassment. The mocking calls of the philosophers were not bringing the shame that showed in his face; it was the inward thought.

Oh, my God, Paul said in his mind. *Your word says that it is not by might or power but by Your Spirit that we attain new life. Lord, they wanted a miracle as evidence. Had I obeyed You and healed the sick boy in the market, I would have had evidence. Instead, I chose to listen to the voice of the philosophers rather than You, Lord. The Jews require a sign and the Greeks seek after wisdom. Christ crucified is a stumbling block to the Jews and foolishness to the Greeks. But Your power will set aside the wisdom of the wise and the understanding of philosophers!*

As Athens disappeared behind the stern of the ship, Paul felt, once again, the humiliation he had experienced on the Hill of Mars. He had not failed completely. Dionysius, Damaris and others had come to know the Messiah. He had, however, missed a great opportunity. He should never have attempted to minister on the same level as the philosophers of Athens. To stoop to rhetoric was to lower God's wisdom. Christ crucified and resurrected was a miracle, and only a miracle could explain a miracle! The message of Jesus must be confirmed in Corinth by Jesus Himself or there would be no message!

Where Athens was a city of culture, Corinth was rough, uncivil and crude. The ancient city had been completely destroyed by Pompey. Now it was a place without either tradition or quality. The great Greek architecture seemed to have passed by Corinth. The Temple of Venus was the only dominating structure in the city. The temple was, however, little more than a brothel where more than a thousand prostitutes carried out their trade as a sacred service. In the narrow alleyways lay drunken sailors and whores. As usual, Paul sought out the marketplace of the city. Paul was not looking for Jews to criticize. He was seeking a miracle door to help him present the news of the Messiah.

In the city square, Paul found many stalls and booths. He surveyed the setting. There were the customary sellers of jewels and gold, the money-changers and the food merchants. Jews were sprinkled among Phoenician and Egyptian merchants. Men argued their prices while women waited patiently for the bargain to be sealed. Olives and bread were being sold. Paul continued to observe the people, but he did not move. He was waiting for something — something inside that he had not waited for in Athens. Somehow the Holy Spirit would have to direct his steps. Paul would no longer trust in his own intelligence or experience. He needed a sign, a miracle sign from God.

One of the booths had an awning of goats' hair cloth. Women were washing goats' hair at the foot of weaving looms. The products of the looms were being sold next to the very looms that produced them. Paul saw cloth for mantles. Near the looms were stacked materials for tents. Paul's attention was centered on the booth. Perhaps it was the sight of tent material like he had made in Tarsus, perhaps something else, but Paul's attention was riveted on the activity at the booth. Two Jews seemed to be in charge. A middle-aged Jewish man was selling the products, and a woman of similar age was overseeing the weaving. Paul thought of Lydia as he studied the graceful form of the woman moving amongst the workers. Paul approached the booth. The woman was the first to glance at him. She stopped what she was doing and stared at him with a friendly, curious look.

"You are the anointed one the Holy Spirit said would come" — she directed her remarks to Paul. The Jewish man looked around, turning away from the customer he was attempting to serve. Paul was startled by the woman's remarks and the frankness of her gaze.

"I am a weaver from Tarsus. I was interested in your skill. You make tent cloth very much like what I made when I was in your trade" — Paul addressed the woman.

"And what is your trade now?" the woman asked.

"I am a rabbi," Paul answered. "I teach concerning the Messiah of Israel."

"You are referring to Jesus Christ, Who was crucified in Jerusalem and rose from the dead, are you not?" the woman inquired.

"What do you know of Him?" Paul replied.

"I am Priscilla, and my husband is named Aquila," the woman answered with a warm smile. "We are Christians who were recently driven out of Rome by an edict of Emperor Claudius. The Holy Spirit directed us to Corinth where we were told to wait for a great one, an apostle of our Lord."

Paul recognized that Priscilla was a Roman and her husband a Jew, so he replied, "I am called Paul by the Gentiles and Saul by the Jews. Jesus appointed me to be the Apostle to the Gentiles."

Priscilla poured water from a pitcher into a basin. "Wash and refresh yourself from your journey. Aquila and I will close our booth and take you to our home. A room, a bamboo mattress, a table and a bench have been provided for you."

Paul stood in stunned silence. He could not believe how simple everything was. Everywhere he had gone on his journey, he had paid for his lodging and struggled to find someone to whom he could relate. There stood Priscilla holding the basin of water, and Aquila had already started closing up the booth! They were both Jews, both tent makers, both open to work with Gentiles, and both believers in Jesus! Paul had trusted for a miracle, but he had not counted on receiving one for himself. His eyes filled with water, but it was not the water from the basin from which he washed. He was filled with gratitude to the Holy Spirit. "Oh, Lord," he prayed, "You are our wonderful provider!"

"Yes, He is," said Priscilla, amazed that the man of God was surprised by the provision of the Spirit.

That evening Priscilla and Aquila's home was illuminated with the light of many lamps. Believers in Christ came, each bringing a contribution for a common meal. They crowded into the small house. There was an atmosphere of festivity. Each greeted Paul with a hug and a kiss. Instruments of music were produced and the group began to sing from the Psalms. They all joined hands and danced a Jewish folk dance as a part of their worship. Paul's heart soared with joy as he worshiped and danced with his brothers in Christ. Someone in the group spoke in an unknown tongue and everyone stood still with heads bowed. From another person came an interpretation, telling the group of God's love and His pleasure in their fellowship. Another stood and told of Jesus' sayings when He taught in Magdala and Capernaum.

"What the brother has reported is true!" Paul declared. "He has told you Jesus' very words. I was there when the Lord said them!" Every eye turned to Paul.

"Brother Paul," said Priscilla, "is the one testified to by the Spirit in our last Sabbath worship. You will remember how it was prophesied that an apostle of our Lord would come and labor among us. Paul has stood with Peter in Jerusalem and was sent forth by the elders under James, the brother of our Lord."

Excitement swept through the group. "Let us hear our brother's testimony and his word from the Spirit!" one of the men requested with enthusiasm. The night was well spent and the dawn approached before the last of the congregation said good night. Paul fell into blissful rest, knowing that he was fully in God's will and at home for awhile.

The next morning, Priscilla and Aquila protested in vain as Paul sat himself at a loom. "If a man will not work," he told them, "he should not eat." The mounted spools whirled across the frame of the loom. Paul's hands moved swiftly on the threads before him, while his feet drove the treadles. Threads of many colors seemed to move into place on their own as he brought the wooden beam against the frame of the loom. A highly developed skill was needed to bring the teeth of the board to the exact place against the framework. The viewers in the marketplace had never before seen anyone work the loom with such speed and skill. The hands and the feet of Paul seemed to work by themselves without thought from the Apostle. Men and women gathered to watch the loom, and Paul seemed to carry on a nonending dialogue with them.

"He was crucified," Paul said of Jesus. "I knew the Centurion who was in charge. He is very efficient with his work." Paul slammed the board home. "But on the third day He rose from the dead." The loom seemed like an instrument of music highlighting his remarks. "I met Him in the Temple court and He told me to carry the news of His coming to the ends of the world." The shuttle paused to set a bright thread. "This is why I came to Corinth — that you might hear of Him and be redeemed!" The teeth of the board brought the threads into place. Those watching nodded their heads in agreement. Paul did not know whether they were approving his skill on the loom or the message he was sharing. Did it matter now? They were hearing the word. The Holy Spirit would have to do the convincing!

"Your skill has not departed from you" — the voice came from the midst of the very large group that had gathered around Paul. The loom seemed to stop in midstroke, but neither the thread nor the pattern was broken.

"Silas," Paul exclaimed joyfully, "and Timothy!" The crowd watched dumbfounded as the three men embraced and danced in each other's arms, there in the marketplace. When Paul caught his breath from the excitement and the emotion, he asked, "And Luke?"

"He's in Philippi," Timothy replied, "getting fat on Lydia's cooking."

"Has something happened between them?" Paul asked.

"No!" exclaimed Silas, laughing. "Luke is too ugly and poor! Lydia has sent a good sum of money to help you in your work. I believe that if Lydia was looking for a man, you would be in trouble, my friend." Timothy enjoyed Paul's embarrassment.

"And the churches?" Paul asked.

"They are all strong and growing!" Timothy replied. "The word produces in good soil even on its own. It is like Jesus said, 'Good seed that is sown ...'"

"God's mercies are everlasting," Paul replied. "See, He has given me work with Priscilla and Aquila, and they have provided a place for me. But now I will need somewhere else, for we need to spend much time together in fellowship and prayer. You will sleep in the booth tonight. After the Sabbath tomorrow we will find more suitable lodgings."

Aquila was delighted that Paul's brothers in the Lord had arrived. While he prepared sleeping places for them, Priscilla prepared wooden bowls of hot water for the disciples to wash in. At the Sabbath service in the synagogue, Paul spoke like a man whose authority and faith had been restored. After the service, the head of the synagogue, a man named Crispus, invited Paul and the disciples to his home. Crispus, though a man of little learning, was a committed Jew who kept all the laws of hospitality. After the Sabbath meal, he listened to the stories of Jesus and was filled with faith. Silas and Timothy baptized him, with his family. Crispus provided the place that Paul had prayed for, and once more the friends were together.

One day seemed to flow into another at Corinth. Daylight would find Paul setting up the loom and helping Aquila open the booth. Priscilla fussed over him like a hen over her chicks. She worried that he did not eat enough. She tried to persuade him that he did not need to spend the days on the loom. She brought basins of hot water in which he could rest his tired feet. Each day, however, would find Paul at the loom. The wooden beam made a cracking noise as it slammed into the framework of the loom, and the spools whirled across the frame as Paul told the watching crowd about Jesus. When the sun no longer allowed Paul to see the threads, he would stand in Priscilla's overflowing house and talk about Jesus to the crowds that gathered there. On Saturdays he preached in the Jewish synagogue. On Sundays he started another day of worship at a new synagogue in the house of Justus, which was located next door to the Jewish synagogue.

It happened on a Sabbath day that the two congregations, the Jews and the Christians, met at the same time on the street. Paul and Crispus, the former leader of the Jewish synagogue, appeared at the door of the new synagogue. A member of the Jewish synagogue cried out, "Crispus, you have made your circumcision unclean, as filthy as the uncircumcised dogs you run with!"

The Gentiles among Paul's congregation shouted back, "You have a circumcision of the flesh, but you need a circumcision of the heart!"

"Let no unclean dog of a Gentile call me uncircumcised!" a Jew called back, as he started angrily toward the Christians. The two groups surged toward each other.

Sosthenes, the head of the Jewish synagogue, called out to his people, "Children of Abraham, do not act so!" Sosthenes was old. His head and beard of white hair gave him a special look of dignity. The congregation momentarily constrained itself. Crispus took advantage of the pause and told the followers of Jesus to return to their homes. The crowd surged again. Paul felt a blow to the side of his face, and then he was lifted by the crowd and carried through the streets. The tumult ceased in front of the portico and the judgement of Junius Aeneus Gallio, brother of Seneca the philosopher, Procurator of Corinth.

Paul watched the Proconsul and remembered when his own father had been in such a position. Gallio's face was as marble. No hint of his judgement or concern was seen. His military bearing was evident in the way he held his body at attention. His eyes were cold. Not once could Paul see any hint of interest in the crowd or the argument.

"Were this a matter of law or justice," Gallio stated, "I would listen to your arguments. But this is only concerning words — the words of Jews. Rome has no interest in such things. You Jews will have to judge this among yourselves."

Paul thought of his father's ring. *Is this the time to use it? Gallio is a great man in Rome. He would honor the ring and I would have the opportunity to witness to him about Jesus. But what of the Jews? I would probably lose the Jews of both congregations.* Paul clutched the ring beneath his tunic, but Gallio gave the signal to his officers to drive the Jews from his judgement seat.

Once back on the street, the Greek Christians, excited by their supposed victory, tore the clothes from old Sosthenes and beat him before the very judgement seat of Rome.

Paul was sick when he saw what the followers of Jesus had done to Sosthenes. In spite of the ridicule of the Jewish crowd, Paul followed when Sosthenes was taken home. Paul and Aquila helped to wash and bind the wounds of the old man. All evening Paul sat next to his bed. Because Paul had taken a Nazarite vow not to cut his hair, long, gray locks fell upon his heaving shoulders. Paul wept and prayed for Sosthenes throughout the night. Followers of the Crucified One had done this to Sosthenes, and Paul mourned their loss of His compassion. It was as if Jesus had been crucified all over again, and this time it was gentile believers who had nailed Him, in the form of Sosthenes, to the cross.

On the next Sabbath, Paul addressed the congregation of Christians with a voice filled with anguish. His listeners would not look at his eyes. They began to weep and seek God's forgiveness. Suddenly, Sosthenes, covered with bandages, entered the Christian synagogue. In a weak, trembling voice he began to speak: "I forgive you, even as Christ has forgiven me. I do not hold this thing against you. I only ask you to forgive each other as He has forgiven each of us."

That evening Paul told his companions that he had to visit Syrian Antioch by way of Jerusalem. "I must return to the Temple and complete my vow to God," he said. "I must return to my roots and to Calvary where my Lord was crucified."

"It will be dangerous for you in Jerusalem," Silas warned.

"Yes," Paul agreed. "But I must go back to Jerusalem and to Rome. For I must testify of Him in the places of my origin." Paul became very quiet as the thought came to him: *The road back to Rome leads me through Jerusalem!*

35

As the ship approached the port of Ephesus in the first light of day, the Temple of Diana of Ephesus seemed animated. The sun as it caught the reds, blues and gold of the temple, created the illusion that the temple was moving and glowing with its own power. The one hundred and twenty-seven jasper pillars set in Pirian marble and mortared with pure gold reflected every light from the sun, sand and sea. Statues of pure silver graced the walk that led from the docks to the temple.

Paul had not wished to visit Ephesus, but the ship had to unload cargo before continuing on to Israel. Paul had always avoided Ephesus on his previous journeys because of the inner voice that warned him against attempting to carry his mission to the center of the idolatry of Asiatic Hellenism. Ephesus was the western conclusion of the great trade route that ran through the valley of the Maeander and the Lycus Rivers into southern Galatia. Therefore it was filled with peoples from all over the world. They came from Babylonia and Mesopotamia. The rich came to offer homage to the image of Diana, the poor to sell their goods and their souls. The sick were everywhere. The wealthy were carried on litters while the poor, maimed and blind were led through the crowds.

Paul and his companions, Aquila, Priscilla, Silas and Timothy, had to force their way through the throng of people. Along the road leading upward from the docks were clusters of men, women and children that surrounded stargazers, magicians, snake charmers, herb sellers and Chaldaean doctors.

"Luke" — volunteered Timothy — "could have made a fortune here!"

Paul did not appreciate the jest. "Luke is an honest physician. We need dedicated men of science and skill. These are charlatans who make merchandise of human misery."

A stargazer grabbed Paul by the arm. "I will tell your fortune, visitor to Ephesus. It is all in the stars and in your hand."

"May your abomination of idolatry be a curse to you!" Paul shouted as he pulled his arm away like any Pharisee who had been contaminated would do.

"Here's a Jew who does not give honor to Diana," another stargazer called out. Paul and his Christian friends disappeared into the crowd.

In the streets and the market there seemed to be no end to the merchants who sold gold, silver and copper replicas of the goddess Diana. One merchant was selling water that he said came from a lake in which the goddess had bathed. He declared that it would heal all sickness. Another was selling roots and leaves as medicine. Yet another sold compounds that he swore would awaken love. He claimed that Diana had given them to him. It was the Sabbath, and Paul was pleased that he did not see a single Jew in the market. That some could have been found doing business at any other time, he knew, but at least they still kept the Sabbath holy.

When the travelers entered the court of the synagogue, they were greeted warmly by the elders who invited Paul to speak. As Paul shared the Good News of the Messiah, he told them that Moses, himself, was a witness to the message that he brought. He told them briefly of the teachings of Jesus and of His death and resurrection. After the message, they broke bread in the house of the head of the synagogue. The Jews had asked him to stay there and tell them more about the Messiah.

"I must celebrate Passover in Jerusalem," Paul said, "but Aquila and Priscilla will remain. I know they will have a thriving business here making cloth. They can tell you about the Messiah until I return. Timothy, I want you to go by land to Lystra and visit your mother and your grandmother while I attend to Jewish things in Jerusalem. You can meet with me again at Syrian Antioch and give me a report on the Galatian churches!"

Some of the Jews from Ephesus were taking a pilgrimage to Jerusalem for the Passover on the same boat on which Paul was sailing. Thus the entire synagogue went to the harbor to see them off. The stargazers gave way to the white-headed elders with their prayer shawls and staffs. The crowd murmured, but the elders kept their eyes focused straight ahead. Thus the conglomerate parted, pushing into a mass on each side of the road. Paul could not help but smile as he passed the place where the stargazer had detained him on his way up. *Moses parting the sea!* he said to himself.

Paul reflected on the first time he had sailed into the port of Caesarea. He had been so young, so afraid and so excited about the adventure. As he watched the fortress come into view, it seemed as if time had stood still. He was no longer the dashing, romantic Roman soldier, nor was he pretending to be a rich Jewish merchant. His head was covered with silver hair, his face was scarred from whippings and his body ached from his travels. Still his eyes burned with fire and zeal. He was a messenger of eternal hope, a royal ambassador of the King of Kings.

As he stepped off the gangway onto the dock, he could see the decline of Rome. No longer did the legionnaires line the dock to welcome and inspect the passengers. Now only one soldier and an aging customs officer came on board to inspect the ship's records. Still the officer tried to present some appearance of dress and decorum. His red and gold uniform was correct, and he wore a breastplate in spite of the perspiration that had stained his tunic. Paul would have paid little attention to the officer had not his sword hilt flashed red and gold in the sunlight. Paul would have recognized that sword with its large ruby and a hilt shaped like an eagle anywhere.

"Popygos!" Paul exclaimed.

"Are you speaking to me, Jew?" came the caustic reply.

"Popygos," Paul called again. "It's me, Paul Gabinius!"

"Gabinius? I know no Gabinius, only a Pharisee who goes by the name Saul of Tarsus." The rancor in Popygos' tone was evident.

"Yes," replied Paul, "and you have a right to hate him. But he died one day near Damascus. I am truly sorry for how he treated you and Julius the last time we met. Julius was right; Jesus is the Son of God!"

"I do not know about your Jewish Messiah," Popygos answered. "I only know what you did to the best man I ever knew."

Popygos turned back toward the fort, but Paul continued to walk beside him. "Tell me about Julius?" he asked.

"The thing, whatever it was, that happened with your Jesus almost destroyed him. He would wake up in the middle of the night, covered with perspiration, calling out, 'No! Do not crucify Him!' It got so bad that the commandant had him sent back to Rome."

"Have you heard anything since?" Paul inquired.

"He got better. Now he's the Praetorian Prefect of the fort at Ostia. He had me transferred from Jerusalem back to Caesarea. He married a Roman woman by the name of Diana. It has done me a great deal of good to know the two of you. When we first met I was doing customs in Caesarea and that's what I am doing now!" Paul lost the last bit of Popygos' sarcasm. He was remembering a golden goddess of his youth. *Diana! I wonder if ...?*

That night the two drank wine into the small hours of the morning as Paul shared with his old comrade his belief in Jesus and his adventures serving Him. Paul explained that Jesus was not the Messiah of the Jews only but that he had also died to pay for Popygos' sin. Popygos shared with the Apostle his experiences at the crucifixion. The next morning, after Paul left, Popygos asked Jesus to be his Lord.

Paul had hoped to spend time with Peter in Jerusalem, but the elders of the church there informed him that Peter had gone to Cappadocia. John Mark was in Libya, John was in Sardis and Thomas had sent word from a place called India. The news of the resurrection was covering the world. Paul decided then and there that he would not rest until he had ministered in Rome and Spain. But before he left Jerusalem again, he had to visit the Temple. He also had to see Esther.

They met in the shelter created by the church in Jerusalem. Esther studied his face, marked with the tell-tale sign of the whip, and with the scars of sorrow and hardships. Silently she allowed her fingers to trace a dark scar running across his cheek. Her eyes were filled with tears.

"It is nothing," he said.

"It is our Lord's signature on your faithfulness," she replied. Her face, though now touched with wrinkles around the eyes and the lips, was soft with love and compassion. When she was young, her face had looked as hard as that of one of the goddesses in Athens; now her countenance carried a warm gentleness. Her hair was lightly streaked with gray and her form had achieved a rounded, motherly look.

"You look wonderful," he remarked.

"For an old woman?" she questioned.

"Let's just say for a beautiful, mature lady," he replied.

She placed her hand in his and they walked toward the patio where they could have privacy. "Reports have filtered to Jerusalem about your work with the Gentiles," she said. "Many are disturbed because they say you preach against Moses and the Prophets. I know better than that, but they have never been Pharisees and do not understand the full terror of the Law. Do not let your experience in our marriage harden you against your people."

"Our relationship has nothing to do with it," he replied. "They try to force the Gentiles to carry a weight that even they cannot carry. If only by becoming a Jew and being circumcised one can become a son of Abraham, then all I preach is in vain."

"Do you remember when the Jerusalem church, through James, declared that the Gentiles did not have to be circumcised?" she asked.

"They said it, but they did not keep their word," he answered.

"I believe the door the Holy Spirit used was the gift from the gentile churches" — he nodded his agreement to her statement. "Well, we do not have a famine now," she continued, "but many are hungry, nevertheless. When a Jew accepts Jesus as his Messiah, he can no longer find work. Many are cast out of their families. That is what I do here at the center, Paul, I feed them. I could use that gentile help now, and I believe it would once more soften the hearts of those Christians still under the Law."

"I will see what the gentile churches will do," he assured her, "but not because of the legalistic Christians! I will do it because you have asked me."

"I wish we had known when we were young what we know now" — she smiled as she said it. "Not that I would have married you like you are. Being married to an apostle would have been as bad as being married to a Pharisee — or worse!" She again put her finger on his scars.

"Worse!" he called out as he left the room. "Pharisees stay with the Temple. Apostles always have somewhere else to go!"

Because of that "somewhere else," Paul was soon trudging again across the slopes of the Tarsus range. On the other trips Paul had made into the area, his companion had been Barnabas, a Jew. On this trip, the half-Jew, half-Greek Timothy and the fully-Greek, uncircumcised Titus traveled with him. Paul remembered well his first trip through the Syrian Gate, as the mountain pass was called. While Timothy and Titus enjoyed the soft moss on the ground and the good walking under the cypress trees, Paul remembered the lone trees, gnarled by the winds, and the sharp rocks that lay ahead. While Titus enjoyed the fragrance in the air from the oleanders, Paul remembered the thin, cold air of the plateau that Barnabas had called the roof of the world. But when they reached the heights, Timothy and Titus helped him climb. Thus, by the old formidable path, they came to Galatia.

Once more he came to the cottage by the stream, and once more Eunice welcomed him and prepared warm bread. There he found Gaius helping Eunice run the little farm. And once more when Paul started to leave, Eunice gave up her help and Gaius, like Timothy before him, followed Paul.

Paul and the little band passed quickly through Pisidia and Colossae, where Paul saw those he had first led to the Messiah. He now preached their continuance in grace. He attempted to stop the storm of law coming from Jerusalem, and he persuaded the gentile believers to take a collection for the Jewish Christians in Jerusalem. Paul would not stop long, for now there burned in his heart a desire to return to Ephesus and take on the demonic forces associated with the goddess Diana. This Diana, the oak image of the great goddess Artemis, was a hideous creature with a dozen breasts. It was as grotesque as the temptress Diana of Rome had been beautiful. Paul now saw in the goddess all the grim reality of sin. Perhaps it was the thought that Julius may have married that same Diana, transferred over to Diana of Ephesus, that provoked Paul into a passionate attempt to lay the whore goddess beneath the feet of Jesus.

Paul had learned well the lesson of Athens. Argument and rationality would not persuade the superstitious followers of Diana. Talismans, sacred books, magic charms, herbs, roots, spices and sacred waters were all sold in the name of Diana to the sick and the ill, with the promise of healing. Some of the Jews of Ephesus were becoming rich from the trade in mystery books, amulets and sacred medicines. The sick came. The blind, the lame, the weak and the infirm came to be healed by Diana. What Paul needed was a demonstration of real power, the power of the Holy Spirit!

The demonstration began in a manner little imagined by the Apostle. There was a Jew by the name of Sceva who, with his seven sons, was making a great profit selling talismans and acting as a priest. A man possessed of an evil spirit came to Sceva to be delivered. In the market, in front of a multitude of people, Sceva decided to mock Paul. He spoke to the demon-possessed man and said, "In the name of this Jesus whom Paul preaches about, come out of him!" Sceva expected no reply and no reaction. Suddenly, the possessed man's countenance changed. His face twisted out of shape and he acquired a beastly, nonhuman look. Out of the man came a deep, guttural voice that said, "Jesus I know and Paul I know; but who are you?"

Sceva reached for the demon-possessed one to quiet him. It was if a lion and a bear had been turned loose. Sceva found himself being lifted above the man's head. Fanglike teeth ripped into his shoulders and his back. Sceva's seven sons attacked the beast that held their father only to find that when the beast released Sceva, he ripped their clothes from their bodies, dug into their flesh with his hands and teeth, and tossed them like straw bales against the walls of the market stalls. The onlookers began to run from the market, screaming. The guttural sounds of the raving maniac followed them. Paul calmly commanded the demon to leave the possessed man, who became quiet and sound in his mind. The next day when

Paul entered the market to attend to the booth of Priscilla and Aquila, he was greeted with awe and respect. Many came to Paul for healing and for information about Jesus.

Paul continued the ministry in the same way he had prospered in Corinth. Once more his feet made the treadles whirl. Once more the spools shot across the frame of the loom. Paul's hands and feet seemed to have a mind of their own. He talked passionately about Jesus as the loom carried on its own life. When Paul had to replace a thread or a spool, he would stand, shake the dust from his head, hands and feet, and lay hands on the sick. So many were healed that people began to take articles from his clothing to the sick. They placed cripples where his shadow would fall on them. The anointing of Christ was so strong on Paul that even those who received the cloth or came under the shadow were healed.

At midday, when the sun was hottest, the people of Ephesus stopped working. Paul found a cool, shaded porch where Timothy and Titus joined Priscilla, Aquila and himself for lunch. Priscilla provided salad, olives, bread and honey for the group. After Paul had finished eating and had washed, he would begin preaching about Jesus. The merchants of Ephesus reclined in cool places and listened. Joining them were merchants and visitors from Colossae, Sardis, Philadelphia, Thyatira and Laodicea. They heard Paul speak of the Messiah who had risen from the dead. They carried the message along with their merchandise when they left.

Gentile converts to Christ stopped buying statues of the goddess Diana. Jews converted to Christ stopped selling images and horoscopes. Even some who did not convert to Paul's Jesus lost their belief in the sacred relics of Diana. Then one night, without Paul's direction, the believers assembled with their artifacts of Diana worship, lit a fire in the square and began to burn them. The fire was fed with scrolls from soothsayers. Interpreters of dreams and those who used mysterious invocations of the goddess added their wares to the conflagration. They burned sacred roots and herbs and wooden statues. When the fire was hot enough, they threw in idols of silver and gold. These were very costly artifacts, but the new converts to Christ willingly sacrificed them to the flames. As Paul watched them burn he exclaimed, "Accursed be the abomination!" Inside the fire, it seemed to the Apostle that he could see demons and evil spirits writhing like serpents. "Accursed be the abomination!" he cried again. Within the sheets of fire and the upward soaring sparks, Paul saw the world of paganism being consumed.

"Great is Diana of the Ephesians!" The cry started with Demetrius, astrologer of Diana and head of the guild that produced the silver idols of their goddess. Behind him came a mob of fanatic worshipers of Diana. Like the rhythm of a marching drum, the cry was picked up by the throng, "Great is Diana of the Ephesians!" Others cried, "The Jews burn the image of Diana!" Still others, misunderstanding the first group, carried the word, "The Jews are burning the Temple of Diana!" "Throw them to the beasts," someone shouted. "To the beasts! To the beasts!" came an echo.

The court was a confusion of bodies and cries. Jostled men struck out at the person nearest them, all the while shouting, "Great is Diana of the Ephesians!" The mob seemed to take on a mind of its own. It was like a great beast pulling its prey into its lair, as it wrapped its tentacles around the entire company and dragged them into the amphitheater. Several of the disciples, including Aquila and Priscilla, drew Paul into the tent booth and covered him with the goat's hair cloth. In the darkness of the folds, Paul tried to protest, but he could feel Priscilla next to him shaking with fear. So he put his arms around her for protection.

Gaius and Aristarchus, along with a large number of Jews — most of whom were not Christians — were dragged into the amphitheater. "Great is Diana of the Ephesians!" the crowd shouted, though they did not know why. The sight of a cohort of legionnaires in full armor brought a deathly silence.

The Roman Chancellor of Ephesus raised his hand. "Men of Ephesus! Who does not know that the people of Ephesus are worshipers of the goddess Diana? Since that has not changed, you ought not to act in an irrational manner. No one has burned your temple or desecrated your goddess. If there is a violation of the law, it will be settled before the assembly. I cannot allow this disturbance. Go to your homes lest I have to order the legion to act!"

The mob looked at the legion with their swords and spears and began to disperse. After that night, Paul began to make preparations to leave Ephesus. He would return to Jerusalem once more.

36

Jerusalem! As usual, Paul took the longest way possible. First he visited again the churches in Macedonia and Greece. Then he sailed to Troas and Philippi, where Luke joined him. (Luke had gained some weight through Lydia's cooking.) The two then sailed to Assos, Miletus, Rhodes, Phoenicia, Tyre and Ptolemais. Everywhere they went, Paul was warned by the disciples not to go to Jerusalem, but he would not listen. He was like a man driven. Neither he nor Luke understood why.

Jerusalem was ageless. The walls of the city still had a pinkish golden hue about them in the morning sunlight. Shepherds were bringing their choice flocks for the Temple sacrifice. The smell of freshly baked bread hung over the city. The streets were already busy with merchants setting up their stores. Some pious Jews were still at their morning prayers. Paul could hear, like a murmuring song, their weeping and petitions before God as he passed by open windows. The sounds of metal striking stone came from the sentry posts on the top of Fortress Antonia as the Romans changed the morning guard. Paul passed two elderly Pharisees on their way to the Temple. He smiled within, thinking, *There I go, except for the grace of God. Esther and I would still be married and still be miserable as we tried to find salvation through the Law!* Paul turned and followed the road that came from Samaria into the Upper City. He would go to the house of John Mark's mother and inquire about the apostles. Perhaps some of them had returned for the feast.

"Paul!" The greeting was warm and loving. "Oh, it's good to see you!" Paul did not recognize at first the man who greeted him and hugged him so strongly. A close-cut beard accented a face covered with lines of character and strength. The body was thin and angular, with muscle tone like that of a runner in the games. This was a mature man in his prime. Paul felt confidence and anointing coming from him. "Barnabas!" the man called. "It's Paul!" Paul immediately recognized Barnabas. His hair had gotten a little whiter and the character lines in his face were stronger, but Barnabas had not changed much.

"Well, don't make him stand in the door all day, Mark. Bring him in."

Mark? Paul thought. He looked again at the man who had hugged him so vigorously. *Mark? Could this strongly anointed man be John Mark?*

"Forgive me, brother Paul" — Mark apologized and bowed before his elder. "In my excitement at seeing you, I forgot to be a good host." Mark kissed Paul on the cheek. "Please allow me to wash your feet and rest you from your journey." Mark turned and placed a basin next to a low stool. Paul sat down and watched Mark intently. Mark took a towel, tied it around his middle, knelt before Paul, poured water into the basin and began to wash the dust from Paul's feet. Paul knew that this was just a matter of custom and courtesy to a guest, but somehow it meant more than that. As Mark washed his feet, long-forgotten resentment was being washed from Paul's heart.

"Saul of Tarsus!" Barnabas had reached Paul. "Do not rise. Allow Mark to finish his greeting," Barnabas said as he bent down to hug Paul. "Be sure to anoint his head with oil, Mark. I realize that it is just a custom, but when old men have lost their hair it soothes the burn of the sun." Barnabas patted Paul on the thinning hair at the back of his head. "You are dusty and road-worn as usual," he said to Paul. "Have you discovered the ends of the earth yet, brother?"

"I do not believe that the task the Lord has given us has any end," Paul replied.

"Nor do I," Barnabas agreed. "Now that Mark has made you presentable, come and join us."

"I came in search of James," Paul stated.

"Your search is successful," Barnabas replied. "Both James and Peter are in Jerusalem, and both are expected here for the evening meal. Where are your things? We have extra sleeping places on the roof. You will share with us!"

"I have a brother with me," Paul replied. "He is even now camped just outside the gate by the Fortress Antonia. We traveled by the way of Tarsus where I recovered the final part of my possessions. I also have brought a collection from the gentile churches for the poor of the church in Jerusalem. My friend is watching over our supplies." Paul looked intently at Mark. "His name is Luke. He is a gentile believer from Macedonia!"

Mark replied, "I will go and fetch him. A Macedonian in Jerusalem should not be hard to recognize." As Mark rushed out of the room, Barnabas answered Paul's unspoken question.

"Mark and I have been ministering to Gentiles on Cypress for the past three years. He has a strong anointing and gift among them. Paul, the young man you once knew has grown to be a courageous witness for our Lord."

"Thank you, Barnabas," Paul said.

"What for?" Barnabas replied.

"For being a better judge of character than I am — for receiving both of us with love when no one else trusted us. Your faith in John Mark has prevailed."

"It is not in John Mark that I trusted," Barnabas stated. "It is in the Lord of John Mark and Paul that I always trust!"

When Luke joined Paul, he was treated with the same respect that had been given to Paul. That evening, Paul recited to James all the workings of God among the Gentiles.

"Paul" — James answered his report — "there are thousands of Jews who now believe in Jesus. These Jews are still ardent believers in the Law of Moses. They have been told that you are teaching other Jews to forsake Moses. They have heard reports that you are saying Jews should not circumcise their children or walk in the customs of their fathers. I know that this is not so, but I ask you to do me a favor. Go to the Temple with some Jewish brothers and show the others that you still walk in the customs of Israel."

"So long as you do not require Gentiles to first become Jews in order to be saved, I do not mind going into the Temple," Paul replied.

"It is agreed" — James smiled and closed the conversation with a holy kiss.

The Temple retained all of its beauty and mystery for Paul, although he believed that Jesus had made the sacrifices unnecessary. He and his companions entered through the Coponius Gate in the Mount of the House. This area was not considered to be holy ground and non-Jews had access. Standing in the shade of the roofed colonnades that ran around the quadrangle of the Mount, Paul viewed the sacred enclosure of the House. As he approached the sacred precincts, he noted the peribolos, tablets on which was written, "Let no Gentile enter within the peribolos around the sanctuary. Whoever is caught shall have himself to blame for his consequent death."

The wall Jesus tore down, Paul thought. *There can be no Jew or Greek to God!* Paul passed through the peribolos and ascended the twelve steps that directed him through the gold-overlayed doors into the Court of the Women.

The mother of my Lord came here, he said to himself. Beside the lower east gate he found the curtained-off area known as the Court of the Nazarites.

"I bring an offering for my Nazarite brothers," Paul told the priest. "I receive purification for myself." Inside Paul said, *I am purified by the blood of the Lamb, Jesus on the Cross!*

"Have you been in contact with Gentiles?" the priest asked.

"I have," Paul replied, proud of the fact.

"Then," said the priest, "you will have to receive the sprinkling of holy water twice. You will receive now and on the seventh day!" The priest dipped his fingers in a bowl and proceeded to sprinkle Paul.

What a waste, Paul thought. *As if any amount of water or any number of sprinklings could cleanse a soul from sin.* He said nothing and passed from the ritual chamber with bowed head with the rest of the Nazarites.

"Men of Israel!" Paul looked up and recognized one of the Jews from Ephesus whom Paul had rebuked for selling silver idols. "Men of Israel, help me," the silversmith cried. "See, there is Paul who discourages Jews from being faithful to the Law of Moses!"

"He brings Gentiles into the Temple! Just a moment ago I saw Trophimus of Ephesus who declares that baptism in the name of Jesus has made him a true son of Israel!"

"The man who teaches this dares to show his face in the court of God's House?"

"See! There he is among the Nazarites!"

It was as if the Temple had broken into a sea of angry waves. Men came running from everywhere. The cry went up, "Gentiles have desecrated the Temple!"

The tone of the voices and the action of the mob reminded Paul of another cry, "Great is Diana of the Ephesians!" Was there any difference between the Temple worshipers and the idol worshipers?

"He has brought Gentiles into the Court of the Nazarites!" came the cry.

"Kill him!" came the answer.

"To the wall of stoning!" someone in the mass cried.

In a moment, Paul was carried out of the court by the throng. In Paul's mind, he saw Stephen being carried out of this very court to the wall of stoning. He saw himself holding the cloaks of those who had stoned him. Was this the way it was going to end? Had Jesus brought him back to the place of his sin to die? What of Spain? What of Rome?

From the balcony of the Fortress Antonia, the Roman sentinel saw the riot. He knew that it had to be stopped quickly. He struck his sword against his bronze shield.

Tribune Claudius Lysias and a guard of Roman legionnaires were situated just outside the Temple gate for the purpose of keeping order on this festival day. The Romans well remembered the blood spilled in the Temple court. In an instant, the guard was set into motion. Bronze shields locked together and smashed into the Jews carrying Paul. Like a cork being snatched from a wave of the sea by another, stronger wave, Paul was snatched from the Jews. A wall of brass carried him toward the Antonia.

"Tribune, may I speak to you?" Paul said in Greek.

Claudius Lysias stared at the Jew in amazement.

"I am a Jew of Tarsus in Cilicia. May I speak to the crowd?"

"Speak!" commanded the Tribune, still bewildered.

"My brothers," Paul cried out in Hebrew.

"He is not a Gentile! He speaks in Hebrew! Silence!" someone shouted.

"I am Jewish, born in Tarsus, a disciple of Gamaliel!"

The name of Gamaliel was like magic. The mob became silent. It was as if they were suddenly sitting under the feet of a great rabbi. Paul told them about his life and how he had come to know the Messiah. The crowd listened, transfixed by the story until he told them that the Messiah had told him to carry the message to the Gentiles.

"The Messiah never told you to go to the Gentiles," they shouted, and the frenzy broke out again.

"Carry him into the fortress," commanded the Tribune. Chains were placed on Paul and he was dragged behind the doors of Antonia. Once they were inside, Paul's hands were chained to rings in heavy, wooden blocks. Over him stood a soldier with a long whip.

"Will you dare scourge a Roman citizen without a trial?" Paul yelled at the Tribune.

"A Roman citizen?" the Tribune replied in shock. "I paid a great sum of money to purchase my citizenship," the Tribune continued.

"I was born a Roman citizen," Paul answered.

"We will see about that," the Tribune stated. "I will send you to the Procurator of Judaea, Felix. If you cannot prove that you are a Roman, you will be put to death for impersonation."

"I can prove it!" Paul declared.

"Before I send you to Felix, I will know what the charges of the Jews are against you. You will be examined by the Jewish Sanhedrin!"

The Roman guards stopped at the door. Paul entered. Memories flooded his mind. He remembered how the Ab-Bet-Din had sent him to spy on Jesus. He remembered the intrigue and the politics that had occurred in this chamber. He remembered the false accusations against Jesus spoken in this place, and the plot he and Esther had devised. The assembly was now predominantly made up of members of the Sadducean party. But the Pharisees were well represented. Paul devised a plan. He would make them fight each other instead of him.

"Men and brothers," he called out. "I am a Pharisee from a family of Pharisees. I am accused of having preached the hope of the resurrection."

"He confesses it with his own mouth," a Sadducee called out. "He preaches that one has been raised from the dead."

A Pharisee responded, "This man has not done anything evil. If a spirit or an angel has spoken to him, it is well."

A Sadducee called out, "To believe in a resurrected god is blasphemy!"

A scholar of the Pharisees answered, "God is the God of Abraham, Isaac and Jacob. Have you not read, 'The dead do not praise God'? Therefore, Abraham, Isaac and Jacob are not dead! All our rabbis have taught the resurrection!"

The voices grew louder and the Tribune, fearing for Paul's safety and the consequences of an attack on a Roman, broke into the room with his legionnaires and took Paul back to the Fortress Antonia.

"Saul!"

The Apostle had to concentrate to see the man whose voice spoke to him through the window.

"Aaron Salaman!" came the identification. Paul had not seen Aaron since the two of them had been in the house of Jacob Bar Kochba.

"Do not talk now, Uncle, for I have great information I must give you" — Aaron spoke softly. "The High Priest has men called sicarikoi who carry daggers under their robes. He is going to request a new trial and have you murdered before you leave the Sanhedrin. I do not believe in what you are doing, but I cannot let a member of the house of Salaman be murdered. Enough evil has come on our great house!"

"Tell the Tribune what you have told me," Paul whispered back to Aaron. "He is a just man. He will prevent the plot. And, Aaron, may the Lord bless you for what you have risked for my sake this night."

When the Tribune heard what Aaron had to report, he ordered two hundred soldiers and eighty cavalry to escort Paul to Caesarea.

The cell door opened and the soldier stated firmly, "You are to come with me." The prison in Caesarea reminded Paul of his imprisonment in Philippi. He kept waiting for the sound of shaking earth, but it did not come. The guard led him through long, damp, dark, underground passageways. From the outside, the fort did not look as large as it evidently was underground. Paul had to close his eyes as he came to the surface. The guard waited for a moment, then he led Paul through a door in the garrison's wall defenses. Once they were inside the room, the guard saluted and dismissed himself.

"Brother Paul! I am so sorry about your plight. But I could do nothing about it until you were released into my custody!"

"My dear Popygos!" Paul responded. "How are you in the Lord?"

"My faith grows daily," Popygos answered. "But I am concerned about my brother." He placed a hand on Paul's shoulder, a look of concern on his face. "I cannot tolerate the fact that you are a prisoner — a prisoner in my keeping, thank God! I have assured my superiors that you will not attempt to leave Caesarea. Therefore you are free to leave the dungeon and stay with Christian friends. Philip the evangelist and his daughters even now wait to take you with them. You will have to return when your trial comes before Procurator Felix."

Paul found Luke waiting with Philip and his daughters. The girls had prepared a proper Jewish feast in honor of Paul. Five days after Paul had been brought to Caesarea, the High Priest, himself, arrived. He was so threatened by Paul and his witness to Christ that he personally had come to destroy them! What he had not counted on was Felix.

The Procurator, an obese man of unrestrained lust, had been the slave of the Emperor Claudius. He had served Claudius as the executor of every sinister, underhanded and ruthless incident the Emperor had instigated. Felix had only contempt for the High Priesthood of Israel. Only one criteria governed his judgement. What could he get out of it?

The High Priest offered him no bribes, only the Law of Israel. Felix had been informed, on the other hand, that Paul had come to Jerusalem twice carrying a great donation of funds for the poor of Jerusalem. It was obvious that Paul was a man of importance in the Christian world.

His customs official, Popygos, reported that when this man, Paul, came to Jerusalem, he was known as Saul of Tarsus, a member of the rich merchant family of Salaman. Felix's spies in Jerusalem had already informed him that the man had, at one time, worked for the Sanhedrin. He also knew that Paul's father-in-law had been the merchant prince Jacob Bar Kochba. Felix could smell money. Jewish money!

But there was more! Popygos said that there was proof that this man, Saul the Jew, was also Paul the Roman! Popygos had reported that Tribune Julius Laco, Praetorian Prefect of Ostia, had once told him that this Paul had political influence. Indeed, Paul's political influence in Rome was so great that he had been the guest of Tiberius for the games.

Felix could receive no personal gain from the Jewish High Priest. Perhaps he could command a ransom for Paul from the

Christians or from the house of Salaman. Perhaps he could gain some more political influence with Claudius.

Felix told the High Priest that the trial of Paul would be delayed until he could receive further information. He needed details from the Tribune. Because information indicated that Paul, indeed, was a Roman citizen, the Procurator felt it best to move with caution.

The Messianic Jews of Caesarea did all they could to see that Paul's needs were met. The church gathered in Philip's home and gave great encouragement to the Apostle. Paul counseled them on the business of the Church and sent out messengers to the different assemblies in response to their appeals for guidance. From time to time he was invited to the great marble home of Felix, where the Procurator played a game trying to get information from Paul so he could decide what move was to his best advantage. Paul was one of the greatest puzzles that Felix had ever faced. It was a puzzle Felix tried to unravel until he was recalled to Rome for questioning about his stealing of Roman taxes.

The new Procurator, Festus, was very different from Felix. A lean, bronzed soldier, he wore the armor of Rome as if it was a part of him. His silver breastplate was polished to perfection. For Festus, everything was duty. He had no opinions or feelings, only duty. He would do whatever the law declared had to be done. Nothing would prevent him from obeying. His first official act was to visit the Jewish capital of Jerusalem where he quickly encountered the demand of the High Priest that Paul be released to him to be judged by Jewish law. Festus informed the High Priest that he could only release Paul after there had been an open trial. He also ordered the High Priest to report to him in Caesarea.

Festus took his place on the cobalt judgement seat as Pilate once had at the trial of Jesus Christ. Paul was brought before him. The High Priest made his charge.

"I have broken no law of the Jews. Nor have I acted against the Temple or Caesar!" Paul declared.

Festus soon learned that the charges were strictly Jewish, having to do with the Jewish court. As the representative of Rome, it was his duty only to see that the decree of the court was fulfilled, unless it required the death sentence. He learned that Paul, himself, had once carried out the instructions of the Sanhedrin, bringing others to Jewish judgement. While there was slight evidence that Paul was a Roman citizen, Festus decided that could be faced later, should the Sanhedrin demand the death penalty. He turned to Paul: "Will you agree to be judged in Jerusalem if I sit on the chair of judgement?"

Silence filled the room. Rome waited for the reply. Paul knew that a trial in Jerusalem would be messy. There was no way that the Pharisees would agree to having one of their own sentenced by Rome or a Sadducee High Priest! He knew the feelings of the Jews in Jerusalem. They might take out their hate on Christians if he was released.

"I stand at Caesar's judgement seat, where I ought to be judged. I appeal to Caesar!"

"Appeal to Caesar!" Festus almost exploded.

"I am Caesar in Judaea! If you are a Roman, your right to Caesar is to be heard by me! Do you think that a Jew accused of disturbing the Temple will be tried by the Senate of Rome, or perhaps by Caesar himself?" By then Festus was on his feet and his face was flushed with anger. "You stand before me for judgement and dare to demand a trial before Caesar?"

Festus was so angry that he paid scant attention as Paul reached up and untied the leather thong that had been around his neck for so many years. He placed the ring on his finger and turned his hand into a fist. He raised the closed fist into the Procurator's face and made his demand again: "I appeal to Caesar!" It came as an order — a command, not a request!

Festus saw the raised fist and was about to teach the upstart Jew a lesson when his eyes fixed on the face of the ring. The Procurator felt his knees turn to water and fear gripped his being. He was staring at the personal signet of Caesar Augustus. He knew what it meant. The one who wore the ring had supreme authority from Caesar and the Senate of Rome. There was no rank in the Roman Legion or no appointment that came above the man who wore the ring. If Paul had a right to wear Caesar's signet, it was Festus' duty not only to have him transported to Rome but to do it with dignity. Festus asked only one question. "How did you come by the ring?"

"I am Paul Gabinius, son of General Markus Paul Gabinius, Proconsul of Tarsus, who was appointed to the Triumph by Augustus and honored by Tiberius! My father gave me the ring as his heir. As his heir, I have the word of Rome and Caesar! Will you honor Caesar's word?"

The judgement hall was silent. Festus looked stunned. He struggled to regain his composure. His voice was low, steady and deliberate: "I will honor the promise of Caesar. You have appealed to Caesar, and to Caesar you will go."

The Christians in Caesarea understood Paul's decision, but they were as surprised as Festus had been to learn of Paul's background. The next morning Luke had himself branded with the earring of a slave.

"Luke, why?" Paul asked.

"A Roman of great importance is entitled to a personal servant," he answered. "The Tribune will not refuse you the right to take your personal physician with you. Do you think Rome would give me passage to Rome with you any other way?"

"But a slave, Luke?" Paul's voice disclosed his humilation for Luke.

"Are we all not bond servants of Jesus?" Luke inquired. "Do you not even now carry the marks of your service to Him in your body? What matters a slave ring in the ear if I have already given my soul?" Paul knew that Luke was right, but it galled him to treat Luke as a servant in front of the Romans. The test of Luke's plan came more quickly than they had imagined. Festus ordered that Paul appear before King Agrippa of Galilee and his sister, Bernice, who were state visitors.

The judgement chamber had been decorated overnight with great banners representing the provinces of Galilee, Cherea, Caesarea and Philippi over which Agrippa ruled. Two thrones had been installed to the left of the chair of judgement. Paul and Luke, as his servant, awaited the arrival of the royal pair. The sound of a trumpet fanfare split the morning air. The king, wearing a gold tiara on his head and cloaked with a royal purple robe, entered with Bernice.

Bernice wore a diamond tiara. She was the former queen of Chalcis and the reigning queen of Cilicia. Bernice reminded Paul of one of the goddesses of Athens. Beneath the tiara, a golden cascade of wavy hair swung to the movement of her body. Her beauty was so famed that a statue of Bernice stood in the Agora in Athens. The whiteness of her skin was even more noticeable, for the queen was wearing thin veils of black to represent that she had made a Nazarite vow. Bernice was not yet thirty years old and she had already put away two husbands. The first — her uncle, King Herod of Chalcis — had died. Bernice had left King Palema of Cilicia — her second husband, a Gentile — and returned to her brother. Rumors concerning her relationship with her brother were scandalous.

Luke held Paul's cape and staff as Paul was ordered forward to present himself before the king. Paul's hands were in chains. Luke wished he could have removed them. No one paid the slightest attention to the slave.

Paul addressed the king in the Hebrew language: "King Agrippa, because you are an expert in the problems and the customs of the Jews, I ask you to hear me with patience. I am a Pharisee trained under Rabbi Gamaliel. As a Pharisee, I was taught the promise of the Messiah and the resurrection of the dead. It is because of this promise that I am accused by Jews. As a member of the Sanhedrin, I taught against and persecuted the followers of Jesus of Nazareth. One day I was on my way to Damascus under the authority of the Sanhedrin to punish those who were followers of Jesus. As I approached the city, a bright light like the sun shone all around me. A voice spoke to me in Hebrew saying, 'Saul, Saul, why do you persecute me?' I said, 'Who are you?' The voice replied, 'I am Jesus, whom you are persecuting! I have appeared to you for the purpose of making you a minister and a witness. Open the eyes of men so that they will turn from darkness to light, and from satan to God. Through me they can receive forgiveness of sins and inheritance among those who are cleansed by faith!' King Agrippa, I have been faithful!"

Agrippa was sitting on the edge of his throne, looking intently at Paul. "King Agrippa," Paul continued, "Moses said the day would come when Christ would suffer and be raised from the dead. Moses also foretold that He would become a light to the Gentiles!"

Paul's last statement was fantastic, even ludicrous, to Festus. "A saviour of Israel," he called out, forgetting who he was with, "who is a light to both Jew and Gentile? Paul! You are mad! Too much study on these things has made you insane!"

"No, sir! I am not crazy! The king knows what I am speaking about! King Agrippa, do you believe in the Prophets? I know you do! They spoke of Jesus!"

Agrippa was sitting on the very edge of the throne. He would not allow himself to show any response to the suggestion that the Jews might be freed from Rome, but he was not indifferent to the Messianic hope. He had to come out on the side of Rome, so he said to Paul, "You almost persuade me to become a Christian!"

Bernice spent a great deal of time in the Temple. She had a deeper insight into the spiritual than her brother or Festus. What Paul said stirred her deeply. Her breathing was intense and her blue eyes stared at Paul. Paul remembered another time, many years in the past, when he had looked into eyes that blue and heard breathing that passionate. Diana had been saying yes to something much less spiritual. Paul hoped the woman in Bernice was saying yes to the right thing.

"I would to God that you and everyone who is listening," he said, looking at the queen, "might be as I am — except for these chains." He lifted up his chained hands.

Agrippa and Bernice turned to Festus. "This man," Agrippa said, looking again at Paul, "has done nothing that calls for death or even for the use of the chains. I could set Saul of Tarsus free, but Paul Gabinius is another matter! If we did not know about the ring, and if he had not appealed to Caesar, he could be a free man. But he is Paul Gabinius and Claudius will want that ring! His servant can go with him and he must be treated with respect, but to Rome he must go!"

37

𝒜 long line of prisoners dragged their chains toward the waiting ship. Paul and Luke watched as the men were taken below to the hold and the oars. Had it not been for the ring of Augustus, Paul and Luke would have been placed with those poor wretches who had no hope except to die chained to a oar or working on Caesar's new port at Ostia. The ring of Augustus ensured that Paul was treated with dignity, as a ward of Caesar, until his hearing in Rome. Popygos had been assigned as his guard to Rome. Paul, Luke and Popygos would share a cabin together. Paul had to remain chained to Popygos until they were at sea. The other prisoners would live in their chains and, should the boat sink, die in their chains!

The port of Caesarea was hot even for the time of the year. The rigging of the ship hung limp. The sea was like glass. Paul knew that the captain would use the prisoners at the oars to get them to sea if necessary, but not even the oars would count if the wind did not come. The ship was low in the water. Paul surmised that it was carrying a cargo of wheat, for the smell of it filled the air. Paul counted over two hundred prisoners being packed below the decks. Some of them were women and children destined for slavery in Rome if they survived the trip. Some of them, no doubt, were being punished for stealing a wheat cake because they were hungry. Now they would be sailing with more food than they could have imagined, but they would still be hungry!

At long last, the prisoners were all on board and Popygos led Paul and Luke up the gangway. A tribune was directing the placement of the last of the prisoners. He turned to see who else was coming on board. Popygos snapped to attention, his right arm across his chest in salute. The Tribune acknowledged the salute and turned back to his supervision, but not before a cry escaped Paul's lips: "Julius!"

Tribune Laco turned back toward the sound of his name. He stepped from the platform on which he had been standing. "Popygos!" he said, as he tapped the legionnaire on the shoulders in a friendly gesture.

"Sir!" Popygos replied, remembering that they were still in public and Julius was now a tribune. "I am charged with the care of prisoner Paul Gabinius under special edict of the Procurator for a special hearing by Caesar!"

Julius looked at Paul with disdain. "Centurion, I see no Roman called Paul Gabinius, only Saul of Tarsus — a Jew." The contempt in the voice of the Tribune was evident! Paul wanted to reach out and hold Julius, telling him how sorry he was for the way Paul had treated him and for all the things Julius had been through. Popygos' look froze Paul in position. For the prisoner to touch the Tribune would have meant instant death.

"I will see my charge and his slave to their quarters, sir!" Popygos snapped back.

"Do that, Popygos. As soon as we have cleared port, you have an invitation to my quarters for wine."

"Thank you, sir!" Popygos replied, still keeping his military formality.

That evening, over wine, Julius hugged Popygos and let him know how good it was to see him. He assured Popygos that he had not forgotten him. Julius told Popygos that he had requested Popygos' transfer as his aide in Ostia. Popygos did not tell Julius that he had become a Christian but he told him all he knew about Paul and that Paul wanted forgiveness and restoration. Julius agreed that he would examine his heart about Paul, but in the meantime Paul would be Popygos' responsibility. Paul would be granted the privilege to go ashore at each port and visit his friends, so long as Popygos was present. While they were aboard ship and in front of the ship's officers, strict military decorum would be expected. Popygos knew not to push the issue further.

It was late the next morning that the ship, reeking with the smell of the hot, sweating prisoners at the oars, caught the wind. Paul wondered if the captain thought the little, overcrowded boat could ever make it to Rome. The ship made port in Sidon of Syria, where the Christians gave Paul a warm cloak to be used as a cover on cool nights. They also gave him medical supplies for Luke. From Sidon they sailed to Myra, in Lycia. There they found a large ship waiting for them. The prisoners were used to transfer the wheat from the first ship to the second. In addition, they loaded linens, flax and pottery. Paul, watching the loading with Popygos, wondered if he had woven some of the tents and the tenting materials that were being loaded on board. The ship took on passengers, a group of Jewish merchants whom Paul saw as prospects for evangelism.

The new ship was an Alexandrian built merchant schooner that had no need of oarsmen. The prisoners were chained in tiny cages in the lowest holds of the ship. Those who were condemned to die in the arena could hear the roaring of the tigers and the lions that were being shipped to Rome to fight them. Paul moved between their cages and told them of the Messiah, who had conquered death. Many of them believed. Paul helped the sailors work the ship, telling them the story of Jesus as he labored. Many of the Jewish merchants had heard of Saul of the house of Salaman. They too listened to him talk about the Messiah of Israel. Paul found that among the passengers there were also Christians. When they gathered for meals and said their prayers, the others studied them. The ship traveled slowly through a rolling blue sea. At first they hugged the shore; then, rounding Rhodes on the west side, they sailed for Crete. The captain put on all the sail the vessel could carry, but still the sails were hungry for wind. They moved east of Crete, between the island and the Strait of Salmone, then hugged Crete's southern shoreline until they dropped anchor at a port called Fair Haven, which was near the city of Lasea.

The Jewish Day of Atonement came while the ship was anchored at Fair Haven. No Jew would set foot on a ship after the Day of Atonement — if he could help it — for it was considered dangerous to travel by sea after that date. Paul had no direct contact with Julius, but he begged Popygos to try and persuade Julius and the captain to remain in Fair Haven for the winter.

"We have two hundred and seventy-six people on this ship to feed and to provide with fresh water!" the captain stated in no uncertain terms. "But, Tribune, they are your responsibility," he told Julius. "Fair Haven has no places for my men to entertain themselves. At least the port of Phoenix has some place to drink and some whores!" the captain explained.

"Whores and drinking houses are not the issue here," Julius answered. "These prisoners are needed in Ostia. If we stay here, we will be delayed several months. Besides, my wife is expecting a child. I would like to be with her before my son arrives."

At high tide a moderate south wind began to blow and the captain turned the ship westward. The large brown sails filled for the first time in their journey, and the ship that had moved like a camel of the sea became a chariot horse. White spray flared over the ship's bow as it raced from one wave to another. The captain told Julius that their journey to Phoenix would be a short one; he wished that he dare cross the Sea of Adria, but he knew that would be too risky.

Wind usually diminishes during the night, but that night it increased. When dawn came, it was hard to distinguish the day from the preceding night. Darkness still covered the sky and the sails began to flap violently as the wind tore at them. The captain shortened the sails and finally ordered the crew to climb the masts and furl all the sails, but to place a storm jib on the forward mast for steerage. Even with the reduced sail, spume, instead of spray, began to roll down the bow of the ship. Whipping, lashing rain began to hit the deck. Two men at the helm tried to keep the ship from turning sideways and capsizing. One of the helmsman yelled at the captain above the noise of the wind and sea as he pointed his finger forward and upward. The dark mass of water appeared even darker than the storm cloud above it. "The seas of the Euroclydon!" the captain cried.

The massive mountain of water seemed to tower above the bow of the ship. In vain the vessel tried to raise itself high enough on the surface of the sea to meet the oncoming wave. A wall of water smashed down, carrying rigging, rails and blocks away. The ship's forward movement stopped and it trembled like some live thing caught in a trap. Timbers made cracking sounds. Water poured from the decks onto the screaming prisoners below. The ship shook itself free, rising on the crest of the wave, only to plunge into the trough of the following wave. The sailors clung to every piece of the ship and the rigging they could grasp. The passengers in the hold were hurled from side to side among the sacks and the bundles of rope. The cages of the prisoners were slung about, crashing into the keel of the ship and the animal cages. Their cries were mingled with the roaring of the caged beasts. Rolling waves of water in the bilge keel of the ship now washed the hold, carrying with it the bodies of drowned rats and the smell of salt, rot and vomit.

Paul, Luke and Popygos were faring better than the poor souls in the hold. Though the waves sounded like they would cave in the retaining wall of the cabin at any moment, they were safe — at least for the present time — from the water. They received air through a vent facing aft through which they could also see the waves as they passed over and the helmsmen who were holding on to the tied wheel. At times, when the ship was plunging into the trough of a wave, they could see the lighter area of the sky. The furnishings in the cabin had been secured to the wall. All three men stood, holding onto the hammock hooks and swinging with the movement of the ship. Luke was seasick, but he dared not attempt to lie down or go out to relieve himself for fear of being thrown into the bulkhead of the sea. All he could do was to attempt not to foul himself or his companions.

While its bow was into the waves, the ship was actually being driven before the wind. At times it sat suspended on the crest of a wave, after which it dropped to crash with a bone-wrenching jolt between two walls of water. At other times, the stern was so high above the sea that the rudder hung in midair, making it useless for steering the vessel. Although the captain was afraid that the ship would break in two at any moment, the timbers held. Ice-cold waves relentlessly hammered the deck. The vessel ascended the walls of water, then plunged into the depths as it was driven across the sea.

After two days in the storm, the captain ordered the sailors and the passengers to lighten the ship by throwing the cargo overboard. Those working the deck had to tie themselves to the rigging. Over the side went sacks of wet grain, cloth, pottery, bronze vases and even spare ship's tackle. Paul could not see that it helped. No one could tell how low the ship sat in the water because of the height of the waves. Day after day the ship was driven by the wind and the waves until everyone on board was too exhausted and sick to care about living.

Then suddenly, the wind died and the sea flattened. The ship was becalmed. The sun shone brightly on a placid blue-green ocean. Paul and the other passengers walked out onto the deck. Bits of driftwood and seaweed floated near the boat on the surface of the sea. The stillness was eerie. They took buckets of sea water and began to rinse themselves and their cabins. Sailors and passengers alike were repulsed by their own foul flesh. They felt revulsion at the sight of each other. The captain had the soldiers tend to those in the hold. Miraculously, no one had been killed; nor had anyone died. Luke tended to the wounds of those who had been injured. The captain walked nervously on deck, watching the sky.

"This is the eye of the beast," he told Julius. Then he called to the sailors. "Put up a new storm jib," he ordered. "Run lines under her bow and work them aft. Take block and tackle and tighten the lines together. Bring three tight lines all around her keel. This ship has taken a lot of pounding. I don't know if she can continue to hold together. Secure anything that has come loose. And do it in a hurry!"

The passengers and the crew seemed tied to the deck, as if they could not believe what they were hearing. Paul passed through those assembled and approached Julius. To the others he said: "Do as the captain has ordered, but you do not need to fear. Not one person will be lost." To Julius he said: "Had you listened to me when I warned you against leaving Crete, this would not have come upon you. Julius, when you knelt beneath the cross of Jesus you called Him the Son of God. Well, He is! He sent His angel to me last night to assure me that I would stand before Caesar for His name. He also told me that no one on this ship would be lost!"

Julius and the captain stared at Paul in shock. This man was a prisoner going to Rome for trial. Yet he dared to speak to a tribune of Rome and the captain of the ship in this manner. Popygos moved to Paul's side, hoping that Julius would not have Paul killed or beaten but would hold Popygos responsible for Paul's actions. The ship turned slightly as the new storm jib caught some wind. The sound of block and tackle tightening the rope bands the captain had ordered was heard on the deck. Below deck, word was being passed that the man who had spoken to them about salvation had received word from an angel that no lives would be lost. Some thought that it was a good time to say such a thing, since the storm was now over. As Julius pondered what to do or say to Paul, a cry pierced the air: "Look!"

Everyone turned at once. The ship seemed to be sinking lower and lower on a flat sea as it was sucked toward a large jade-green wall with white froth that was rushing toward them. The helmsmen quickly turned the wheel to put the bow of the ship at right angles to the wall. As the bow rose to encounter the wave, the stern of the ship began to take on water as it was pushed beneath the surface of the sea. Sea grasses and debris sucked up by the surface water rushed past the boat. As the bow rose another two degrees and cut into the wall of water, the ship shot upward to the summit. Suddenly a torrent poured onto the decks. The ship's timbers groaned and the rope bands tightened, but they held. The moment the ship cleared the mammoth wave, the storm broke on them again with all its fury. The wind blew from the opposite quarter, but its effect on the ship did not change. Because the captain had not been able to plot their course by the stars since the storm began, he did not know where they were. He believed, however, that they were being driven constantly westward and feared greatly that the vessel might go aground on some unknown island or sand bar.

Day after day the tempest drove the ship. The sailors watched the sea and the horizon — when they could see it — for signs of land. They had decided that they would throw themselves into the sea should the opportunity come to attempt a landing. The soldiers had agreed that they would kill all the prisoners rather than risk their getting free should it look like the ship was coming apart. The prisoners also watched, looking for an opportunity to escape or die in the attempt, rather than drown. The captain had lost control of both ship and crew. Only one man remained in control of himself and the situation — Paul.

On the fifteenth day after the storm hit, the sea began to calm and the ship rode the waves more normally. Rain continued to pelt them out of dark gray clouds, but the swell had changed to the surface flow that comes near land. The lead line was dropped from the bow and marked. Twenty fathoms! As lighter clouds signaled the approaching day, the lead line was dropped again. Fifteen fathoms! They were near land and moving toward it! But what land? No one knew, not even the captain. Was it rock or sand? No one could tell.

"Drop anchor!" came the command.

The sailors disobeyed. As they started to unloosen the rescue boat and lower it into the sea, Paul found Julius. "Don't allow them to leave the ship," Paul told him. "If they do, they will die! We need them to get the ship to shore!"

"Legionnaires! Stop those men!" came Julius' command.

Roman broadswords cut through the mist. The boat rope was severed and the boat fell into the sea. The sailors found themselves surrounded by a ring of steel.

Paul broke the tension. "Do not worry, we will be saved. Here, take some food. It may not be as available on shore." Paul took a piece of bread and prayed loudly, "You have saved us from the rage of the sea. We give You thanks in the name of Jesus!"

As the rain slacked, they could see land. They were not far from the entrance of a cove. The captain commanded the sailors to unfurl the mainsails. The rudder was broken, but perhaps the wind would blow them into the harbor. The sails were set before the anchors were released so that the ship would be under tension. Then, when the captain indicated that the wind was right in the sails, Julius ordered his soldiers to cut the lines. The ship seemed to leap for the entrance to the cove. Salt spray once more crossed her bow. Then, without the rudder, a swell turned the schooner's bow. They felt the keel scrape on a sandy bottom. The bow stuck fast and the stern, driven by the waves, gyrated back and forth. Then they heard a cracking noise as the beams of the ship broke, the masts snapped and the ship began to disintegrate. A dreadful cry came from the holds. The soldiers pulled their broadswords, waiting for the order from the Tribune to kill the prisoners.

Julius looked at Paul. If he gave the order, Paul would have to die with the rest. "Open the cages!" he ordered. "Let the prisoners out! Let them take to the water. Those who cannot swim, hold on to a plank!" There was a wild scrambling from the cages. In seconds the water was filled with bobbing figures. Each in turn passed safely into the cove and on to the sandy beach of the island of Melita.

Some sat up; others lay on their backs, the cold rain pelting their faces. All were too exhausted to move, much less run. Miraculously, all were alive. Likewise, all had been stripped of dignity. The distinctions of position no longer mattered. On the sand rested an apostle, a tribune, prisoners, merchants, slaves, sailors, soldiers — two hundred and seventy-six souls. Each was equally filled with the wonder of being alive!

Debris from the wreck was scattered up and down the beach. No one made an effort to pick it up or search through it for valuables. What did those things matter now? No longer were they in cages, slamming against the bulkhead. No longer were they holding on to ropes and railings, trying to keep from being cast into the sea. They were covered with clean sea water. Most of the foul-smelling clothing had been torn from their bodies. They held handfuls of sand and wondered at the world that did not move beneath their feet. Someone cried! Someone laughed! A lion freed from his cage growled contemptuously, shook the water from his mane, and ambled across the beach, looking for shelter from the rain. Slowly they got up and followed the direction the lion had taken.

On the edge of the beach, they found rock cliffs with large caves that could shelter them from the storm. They also discovered natives of the island who had been watching from the safety of the caves.

Someone found dry kindling in the back of the cave — dried sea grasses and driftwood that had been washed up in some other storm. One of the native men used a flint to start a fire. All just stood by the fire, saying nothing. They were too bewildered by the experience to speak. Each tried to warm himself.

Paul, without looking to see what he was doing, reached into a pile of driftwood to get some more fuel for the fire. With a hissing noise and a flash of movement, a serpent uncoiled from his hiding place and struck. Pain shot into Paul's arm. The wet, slimy coils of the snake tried to wrap around his hand, but Paul shook the serpent into the fire. A soldier standing near the fire struck it with a stick as it tried to escape the flames. Luke rushed to Paul and grabbed the arm. There was nothing he could do. The puncture wounds were deep. Already the poison was spreading through Paul's body.

"In the name of Jesus!" Paul laid his other hand over the wound. His response was as natural as getting rid of the serpent. "Lord, You said, 'They shall take up serpents; and if they drink any deadly thing, it shall not hurt them; they shall lay hands on the sick, and they shall recover.' I stand on Your word!" When Paul removed his hand, the puncture wounds were gone! The natives watching the bedraggled group had cried out when Paul was struck, "He has an evil spirit! He is a murderer!" Now they cried out, "No, he is a god! He has a good spirit!" The islanders crowded about Paul. They begged him and the other survivors to come to their village. With the jubilation of children at a parade, they led Paul and the others to their homes. When they arrived at the village, the head man, Publius, took Paul to his father's hut.

In the dark of the hut, Paul found an old man, ashen in color and spitting blood. Luke entered with Paul, not knowing what he could do. All of his medicines had been lost in the shipwreck. Paul did not notice that Julius had entered the hut as well.

"Well," Paul said in Greek to the old man, "the Lord God must love you very much. He went to a lot of trouble to get me to visit you. He wants you healed so that you can tell everyone in the village that Jesus died so they might have life eternal." Paul placed his hand on the sick man's head. "In the name of Jesus, I command this spirit of infirmity to leave so the healing grace of Jesus may be revealed."

The man coughed blood. Paul, seeing a water dipper near the door, went out of the hut, filled the dipper from a cistern and brought it back to the old man. "Wash out your mouth with this! Spit it out! Wash it again!"

The man did as Paul had told him. The second time there was no blood. The man touched his chest. "I felt the healing," he told Paul and coughed again. "Yes! See, it is all gone!"

"Paul" — the voice of Julius came from the back of the hut — "I crucified Him. How can I ever receive His forgiveness?"

"Why, Julius! Don't you remember? He forgave you from the cross!" Julius wrapped his arms around Paul and cried the bitterness of years away from his soul.

Julius changed as the winter passed on Melita. He wanted to know everything about Jesus. He venerated Paul for his knowledge of Christ and for his service to Him. His relationship to Popygos — always the best of friends — became the intimacy of brothers. He treated the soldiers with respect and the prisoners with kindness. He promised the prisoners, many of whom had become his Christian brothers, that he would ship them all to Ostia, where they would be treated humanely. By the time the early spring winds rustled through the coastal grasses and the wildflowers that covered the beaches, Julius had blossomed into a full disciple of Jesus Christ.

"Sail on the horizon!" Popygos was the first to spot the Roman galley. On its prow were carved the twin figures of Castor, the mortal, and Pollux, the immortal — sons of the Greek god Zeus.

"How fitting of Jesus," Paul remarked when he saw the ship. "He bids the sons of Zeus and they come to do His bidding."

The galley had a high, curved bow and a stern that curved upward like two elephant tusks. There was only one large cabin located near the stern. It was divided into several rooms. Julius told the captain that he could share the space with Paul and Popygos. In addition to the one central mast with a large square sail, the boat contained thirty rowing posts. Julius informed the captain that his prisoners would all take turns on the oars, but they were not to be whipped.

The sea was smooth with a gentle breeze. The boat, however, leaped forward with the constant thrust of the oars, as the prisoners enjoyed the activity after the winter of idleness on the island. With rapid speed, they reached the port of Syracuse in Sicily, where Julius had the captain stop for three days to rest his men. With the aid of the oars, the boat passed through the narrow straits between Rhegium and Messina and reached the southern end of the Etruscan Sea. Once they had passed through the straits, a steady sea breeze drove the galley to the port of Puteoli.

The docks of Puteoli were filled with merchants. The captain of the ship that had been stricken had to report the loss of the precious cargo of wheat to the Alexandrian grain dealers who had their warehouses in Puteoli. In Puteoli, there was a large Jewish community and, in the midst of the Jewish brothers, there was an assembly of Christians. Word spread quickly among them that the Apostle Paul was on board the Roman galley. Soon Julius found himself caught up in a celebration of joy. It hardly seemed fitting that the Christian brothers should treat him well, since he was Paul's captor. But they rejoiced with Paul and Julius as if there was no difference. It was a festive time of music and wine, as they fellowshipped and celebrated the saving power of Jesus. Julius loved every moment of the seven days they tarried with their brothers in Christ.

Julius sent mounted riders to Ostia. He instructed the garrison to send a relief guard to a place called Three Taverns, on the Via Appia Road. There he would divide his force and send his prisoners to Ostia as promised, while he and Popygos escorted Paul, with Luke, to Rome. Julius also sent a message to Diana, telling her that he was safe and asking her to meet him at Three Taverns. Strangely enough, both Tribune and prisoner were eager to reach Three Taverns — Julius to see and hold Diana, Paul to finish his journey and stand before Caesar.

Julius did not like having to chain Paul to him on the journey to Three Taverns. He knew there was no danger that Paul would try to escape. The chains were protection for the Tribune rather than a deterrent to Paul. Paul was an important political prisoner. For Julius' reputation, proper military order had to appear to be maintained. As the two walked side by side into the court of the taverns that graced this junction between Puteoli, Ostia and Rome, two women were waiting — the one, a blue-eyed blond dressed in silks and heavy with child, the other a dark-eyed brunette veiled and dressed in homespun. Both women came forward to greet them — Diana, to lavish a homecoming on Julius; Priscilla, to greet the Apostle of her Lord!

Luke kept a wary eye on Diana. "The lady is too far with child for a journey," he said to Popygos.

Paul hugged Priscilla properly and blushed when Julius presented his wife. Paul was grateful that neither knew of the lust he had once held in his heart for this lady or the nights of fantasy in which he had dreamed of her. All that had passed after his encounter with Jesus.

That night, Julius and Diana talked long of their love and of the events during their absence from each other. Julius spoke about Jesus and the meaning He had brought to His life. Diana talked of her decision just the day before — through the witness of Priscilla

— to give her life, as well, to Jesus. Finally toward dawn, Julius fell asleep with her head on his arm.

"Julius!" her cry brought him suddenly awake. "Julius! I'm giving birth!" she said through clenched teeth. "I cannot take the pain! You must get me a midwife!"

By the time Julius lit a torch and tried to find the innkeeper's wife, everyone in the inn was awake. "There is no midwife in the place," the innkeeper reported to Julius. "This is only a crossroad where travelers stay. We do not get women travelers who are going to have babies!" he added, as he looked at the Tribune in fear.

"My wife needs help!" Julius yelled at the man, picking him off the ground with one hand.

"It is all right," Luke said warmly, confidently. "I am a physician."

"But you are a man!" Julius exclaimed.

"Yes!" Luke stated emphatically. "I am also a physician. I have delivered children before!"

"You —" he directed the innkeeper's wife, "get me some soft cloth and put water on the fire to boil!"

"You —" he directed the innkeeper, "go down the road from which we entered the courtyard. You will see a little bush with red berries. Pick the leaves of the bush, not the berries; then have your wife make a tea from the leaves. The broth will help kill Diana's pain and break her fever."

"Julius —" he ordered, "sharpen your dagger and place it on the hot coals of the fire. Then you and Paul go outside and pray!"

Julius was apprehensive about Luke taking care of Diana, but Paul kept trying to reassure him. Paul told Julius how Luke had helped him when he was burning with fever; but Julius reminded Paul that he was not a woman. Julius was fearful that Diana's traveling to meet him had caused her to have the baby at this time. Julius sobbed as he told Paul of his love for Diana, of the sea villa and of all their plans. The sun was fully risen when Luke came out of the inn with a big grin on his face.

"Well, Tribune, you have won the battle. You have a fine son!"

"And Diana?"

"She needs rest, but she will be fine. Go to her! The innkeeper's wife will show you your son!"

Turning to Paul, he said, "Let's get some rest. You look worse than you looked after going through the storm!"

It was two days later, when a delegation of Christians from Rome arrived to greet Paul, that Julius came into the main room of the inn carrying the infant. Each of the men respectfully looked at the child and nodded their approval.

"And what name have you given him?" Popygos asked.

"We have named him after the man who has had the greatest influence on our lives," Julius stated. "We call him — Paulus!"

Later that evening, Julius revealed that he and Diana had agreed that Diana and little Paul would remain at Three Taverns, with Priscilla and Luke as attendants. Julius and Popygos would go to Rome with Paul to present him to the Praetorian Prefect of Rome, Afranius Burrus.

"Praetorian Burrus," Julius told them, "is a man distinguished for his virtues as a Roman. He is a very cultured man, with an irreproachable character. I have no doubt that when the Praetorian of Ostia informs the Praetorian of Rome that Paul has the ring of Augustus and that the charges against Paul are Jewish and of a religious nature, the Praetorian will place Paul under military guard. Under military guard, Paul, you will be allowed to move about freely and live where you choose. Only Popygos or some other guard will have to be with you."

"I am most anxious to be presented to Caesar," Paul replied to Julius' plan. "The Lord Jesus directed that I should witness before rulers and kings. I would like to tell Caesar about Jesus!"

"Which Caesar?" one of the delegation from Rome asked. Then he explained that Claudius had turned the rule of the Empire over to his wife, Agrippina. Claudius' son, Britannicus — by his first wife, Messalina — had been effectively set aside by Agrippina and her son, Nero, whom Claudius had adopted. "Nero is not yet seventeen years old, but he could be Caesar by the time we reach Rome in the morning!"

"Who, then, is the power of Rome now?" Julius asked.

"The Praetorian Prefect Burrus, to whom you plan to present Paul!" came the reply.

"The Lord is even now controlling Rome," Julius told Paul. "Now I know that I can keep you out of the Castra Peregrinorum Prison and set you free to witness!"

The three groups parted early in the morning. Julius' soldiers led the prisoners to work on the port at Ostia. Luke, Priscilla and some of the brothers and sisters from Rome stayed with Diana and the baby. Julius, Popygos and Paul traveled toward Rome.

The situation in Rome was even more confused than the delegation from Rome had reported. It was very favorable to Paul's situation. Afranius Burrus, Praetorian Prefect, received Julius at the Castra Praetoria. Paul showed the Praetorian Prefect his father's ring, and with no further questions the order was given that Paul was to be treated with all the clemency possible under the law. Since the Gabinius residence, which was located in the northwestern district of the city, not far from the Via Nomentana, was available to the Castra Praetoria, Burrus ordered that the property was to be cleared of any who were using the estates so it could be prepared for Paul.

Memories: *"Take me back to the apartment, Saul." "Do you not wish to see the excitement of the Triumph, Mother?" "If you strut like a Roman peacock and I meekly follow, we will draw no attention to ourselves." "What is another fool peacock in a flock?"*

Memories: *"Rome is a lover, a concubine and a whore. Never trust her. The cold steel of your sword slapping on your buttocks may be uncomfortable, but never take it off to make love to Rome!"*

Memories: *"I will not need the ring any more in Rome. There are many here who would like to have it on their finger."*

"Rome has not changed, General," Paul said, speaking to the empty room. "She is still a whore with many lovers who are still trying to wear her ring."

Julius turned to see to whom Paul was speaking. Then he nodded his head in understanding.

The whore was Agrippina — wife of Claudius, mother of Nero, mistress of Nero's tutor, Seneca, and, at the same time, mistress of Burrus, commander of the Praetorian Guard. She had become too powerful for Rome. Everyone wanted either to possess the beautiful Agrippina or destroy her.

Her son, Nero, was short, even for his age, and covered with freckles from head to foot. The color of his hair was not blond, but somewhat yellow; it was cut with bangs that fell over his forehead. His eyes were gray and he was short-sighted, which made him blink or squint constantly. His face was full and fat, with a large neck. His belly stuck out. This toad of a boy hated his beautiful mother and admired her lovers. Above all other men, he admired Seneca.

Seneca was the son of a Roman knight who had settled in Cordoba, Spain. He had become a convert to the occult during his youth in Spain. Using occult practices, he had risen to power under Caesar Caligula. Because Seneca had seduced Julia Livilla, the young sister of Caligula, he had been exiled to Spain by Claudius, until Agrippina had called him back to court as Nero's teacher.

Burrus and Seneca were good friends and loyal collaborators in the government of the Empire. Each knew of the other's relationship with Agrippina, but accepted it as a part of Rome!

Burrus had been only too glad to assign Paul to his own home to await trial. Nero would rule Rome, of that he was sure. But the political situation being what it was, a man wearing the ring of Augustus could further complicate things. For the time being, it would be best if Paul Gabinius was forgotten by Rome.

Forgotten he was, in the turmoil that surrounded Proconsul Burrus and the power of Rome! Nero visited his mother in the Baiae Villa, came to her bed, tore her gown, and said in all love, "These are the breasts that suckled me." Then, with eyes filled with tears, he handed her over to the executioner. Seneca wrote his acceptance speech, and Burrus' Praetorian Guard guaranteed its acceptance by the Senate.

Julius, Diana and little Paul were at Ostia, safely removed from the turmoil of Rome. Popygos again served as Julius' aide. In Rome, Burrus had assigned various guards to watch over the political prisoner. He wanted to make sure that Gabinius did not attempt to get involved in Rome's political upheaval.

Thus the Roman guards came to Paul's house. Paul first asked each man about his original home. "Ah!" he would exclaim, "the hills of Phrygia. How well I know them!" Or, "Yes! Philippi in Macedonia! Do you know my sister Lydia, the dealer in purples?" Then he would compliment the guard on being in the Legion. "My father was a general," he would say, "and I was a candidate! Do you know my friend Julius, the Praetorian Prefect at Ostia, or his aide, Popygos?" "It is good to serve Caesar," he would add, "but Caesar is no god! Look at the turmoil in Rome! The statues are not gods, for they do nothing." Then he would tell them about Jesus! "Jesus forgave all men," he taught them. "Come, let us break bread together, for there is neither Jew nor Greek, free nor bound, in Jesus!" Frequently Paul talked to his guards about the cross. He told them that Jesus had died for them and rose from the dead so they could have eternal life. A great number believed.

Although Paul could not visit the synagogue on the Sabbath — for the gentile guards could not go with him — the Jews would come to his home to visit him. They felt sorry for a rabbi chained to a Gentile. In those visits they too heard of Jesus, the Messiah of the Jews!

Julius visited Paul and brought little Paul with him as often as he could. With Nero as Caesar, it became more and more dangerous to be a Roman officer. By this time, all Rome knew that Nero had arranged for Claudius to be poisoned. He had also ordered the murder of his own mother, the daughter of General Germanicus. The whole Praetorian Guard was shaken by that news. Octavia, the daughter of Augustus, was rejected by Nero and died mysteriously. Nero made a slave woman his wife, then a known harlot. At night Nero would disguise himself like a robber and, using his guard as protection, he would lead a band of thugs into the streets of Rome to rob his own citizens. Nero made a black list of those he thought were his enemies and planned their deaths. No leader of Rome could be sure that he was not on Nero's list! Meanwhile, a Roman/Jew witnessed day and night, and wrote letters that became the seeds of a spiritual revolution that would topple the Roman Empire!

Praetorian Prefect Burrus had unknowingly become the instrument God used to assure that Paul could witness and write unhindered. By his order, members of the Legion not only guarded the Apostle but protected him. Agents of the Sanhedrin could not get near Paul to assassinate him for fear of the guards. Christian friends visited with the Apostle at will. Members of the Praetorian Guard became loyal followers of Jesus.

Julius and Diana often brought their son to see his "uncle." The child enjoyed climbing on Paul's lap and playing with his beard. These were happy, complete days for the Apostle. Nearly two years after Julius had escorted Paul to Rome, Burrus — the great soldier of Rome, the commander of the Praetorian Guard — died of throat cancer. When the armed escort arrived for Paul, it reminded him of the time when the Guard had been looking for his father's ring.

"Am I to appear before Caesar?" he asked.

"Before Seneca," came the reply.

Paul was not displeased. He knew that Nero was only a buffoon behind whom Seneca, the real power and intelligence of the throne, ruled Rome.

Once more Paul ascended the stairs that led to the Senate building. Once more he passed the place where his father had been assassinated. This time the boxes of the Senate were empty. Only when and if he was tried by Caesar would he appear before the Senate. Paul faced the platform of judgement. Now there was only one seat. The only member of the Praetorian Guard to enter the chamber was the one to whom Paul was chained. Seneca was not dressed in the robes of the royal but wore a simple toga. The last time Paul Gabinius had stood in this place he had worn the armor of Rome. Today he wore the scholar's robe of a rabbi. Seneca was a stoic scholar. Two great minds from two different points of view stood and admired each other.

"Are you standing before me," asked Seneca, "because you plan an insurrection against Rome?"

"I am standing before you because I believe in the Kingdom of God!" Paul replied.

"What kind of kingdom does your God have?" Seneca asked.

"A kingdom of the heart," Paul answered. "A kingdom that removes man from the tyranny of his sin through Christ and brings him into a relationship of love."

"Then you are not plotting to overthrow the Roman government?" Seneca leaned forward to study the prisoner.

"The kingdoms of the world will become the Kingdom of my God," Paul stated. "Righteousness will overcome sin and good will overcome evil. Since Rome is filled with greed, lust and all sorts of evil, it will fall! But it will not be earthly armies that cause its fall. Rome will fall by its own corruption." Paul watched to see Seneca's reaction. "You know of its corruption, Your Excellency!"

"Why will it fall to the kingdom of your God? Why not to the kingdom of the Greek gods? I have heard that the Jews believe there is only one God, Who chose them. What insolence!"

"Not insolence, Your Excellency!" Paul stated boldly. "God chose the Jews because our fathers alone recognized that there is only one God and worshiped Him!"

"Insolence, I say!" Seneca's voice trembled. "An audacious statement. All of us recognize that there can be but one living God. We are very aware that the gods of the Greeks and the Romans are only intermediaries between ourselves and the true God!"

"Seneca! How near to the truth you are!" Paul declared. "You recognize that man needs an intermediary between him and God. Would to God the Jews recognized that fact! God has sent His Christ as His intermediary. Only one who partakes of both natures, the nature of man and the nature of God, could be such an intermediary. Jesus proved he was God's intermediary through His resurrection from the dead!" Paul told Seneca the story of Jesus.

"Paul," Seneca replied, "your God is a God of goodness. Goodness is for the weak and the oppressed. Your God is a God of suffering and slaves, for only a slave dies on a cross! Your God will never conquer Rome, for Rome exists, breathes and lives on evil. Her gods are the mysteries of demons, the occult and spiritualism. I am going to let you fight her gods just to prove which is the greatest — the demons of Rome or the God of slaves. I was raised in the occult, even as you were reared in the God of Israel. Jerusalem is your source and Spain is mine. I banish you to Spain! Let us see how your God sets up kingdoms there!"

As the Praetorian guardsman led Paul from the chamber, Paul's heart was singing: *From Jerusalem, Judaea and Samaria to the ends of the earth — Lord!*

38

Servius Sulpicius Galba, Procurator of Hispania Tarraconensis, had just celebrated his sixty-fifth birthday. His body was lean and bronzed, like that of a thirty-year-old warrior. The breastplate of his armor was embellished with the face of a woman made from silver. Her hair was of solid gold. The Procurator's own hair was full, wavy and snow-white. His nose was large and turned downward to a strong cleft jaw. His eyes were gray and showed a gentle strength. Galba had served with distinction under Caesar Augustus. He also had known both General Laco and General Gabinius when he had served under them as a young legionnaire. He had watched General Gabinius receive his Triumph under Tiberius.

"You have been exiled from Rome and sent to me by Caesar Nero." It was not so much a question as a statement. He continued to read Paul's documents, which had been supplied by the ship's captain.

"I was requested to leave Rome by Seneca," Paul replied. Galba nodded.

"You are a political threat to the Empire?" This time the Procurator voiced a question.

"If preaching love and salvation is a threat," Paul answered.

"To Nero, it would be," the Proconsul answered with sarcasm. Then he asked, "Do you wear the ring of Augustus?"

"Yes!" Paul responded, raising his hand for the Proconsul to see the ring.

"If you were not preaching a kingdom of love but the overthrow of the Roman Empire, do you think that this would be the proper time?"

Paul was puzzled by the Proconsul's question. "Rome is invincible so long as the Legion backs Seneca," he responded. The Proconsul, deep in thought, nodded his agreement.

"I have been asked by Gaius Julius Vindex, commander of Gaul, to put my legions at his disposal to overthrow Nero." Paul was shocked at Galba's lack of discretion before a political prisoner. "I agree with your analysis, Paul Gabinius. The time is not right. Seneca has to be dealt with first!" Paul did not know how to respond. He relaxed as Galba smiled.

"Forgive me for making you uneasy," the Proconsul stated. "I know more about you than is contained in this message I received from Lucius Pedanius Secundus, the new Praetorian Prefect of Rome. Secundus is Spanish. We in Spain know him well as an unscrupulous thief. Nero picks his men from his own demented spirit! I knew and respected Markus Paul Gabinius as my senior officer. I met your mother, a stunning woman of Judaea. I know that you are Jewish as well as Roman — a Hebrew scholar of the merchant house of Salaman. I know that you are a leader of the Christians!" Galba had placed the letter on his desk and was watching Paul intently.

"Your religious preference is of no importance to me. There are many Jews in Tarraconensis and a good number of Christians. They worship freely, as do those who worship the Greek gods or participate in the occult. I have found that the best way for me to keep the peace is to allow freedom. The Jews will keep an educated rabbi busy." Paul was spellbound. He had never met a man like Servius Sulpicius Galba before.

"I believe that you will find the Jews of Spain less legalistic and more tolerant than those of either Rome or Jerusalem," Galba continued. "Most of the Christians come from poor backgrounds.

Many do not speak Greek. You will have to learn to speak Spanish." He wrote a note and handed it to an attendant. "Let me provide you with some help. I will give you my best translator. She can also teach you the language, if you are not so Jewish that you refuse to be helped by a woman!"

"Not at all," Paul replied, remembering Lydia and Priscilla.

"You will be free to go as you wish with no guard, but I must warn you: Do not attempt to return to Rome. Nero's edict is certain death if you attempt to return."

Just as Galba finished speaking, the most beautiful creature Paul had ever seen entered the room. Her form was refined, her complexion olive, and her lips pink like a flower. Her hair fell to her back, shining and black like a raven's wing, but with just a touch of gray at the side of her face, which accented dark sparkling eyes. The Proconsul spoke to her in a language Paul did not understand but had heard around the docks when the boat landed.

"His Excellency has asked me to inform you" — she spoke to Paul in Greek, in a voice that matched the warmth of her presence — "that I am Victoria Dio Cuevas. His Excellency wishes for me to interpret for you and teach you the native language. This I would gladly do without his request, because I am a Christian and have read your wonderful letter to the Christians in Rome. But since you are also a Jewish rabbi, I do not wish that you would be offended by having a woman interpreter."

This stunning creature was also a Christian! Never had Paul been so affected by the simple appearance of a woman or so captivated by a woman's presence. "My only concern is for your reputation, not my own," Paul replied.

"I am a widow," Victoria Dio Cuevas replied. "It is perfectly permissible for me to attend to you in public or in the synagogue, so long as I am veiled and do not enter the Court of the Men."

"It is done, then," interrupted Galba. He did not notice Victoria's slight blush when she addressed Paul.

Priscilla and Aquila had accompanied Paul to Spain, planning to set up a weaving business so they could witness as they had done in Corinth. The ship that carried them to Spain had arrived at the port of Carthago Nova on the Mediterranean Sea. Paul's exile papers required that he report to the Procurator in Cordoba, the capital of Spain. The trio had traveled to the city of Murcia, then westward along the valley of the Guadalquivir River to the capital. Paul had been amazed at the grandeur of the land. He had never seen such contrasts. The river valley was lush and green with thick forest running up to its very banks. Yet whenever he looked up, he saw a continual line of snow-covered rock that made up the Alpujarras region of southeastern Spain. Cordoba rose from the very banks of the river and covered a large plain. There were no broad avenues, such as those of Rome, but narrow, rock streets that ascended like stairs between adobe houses that blended one into the other so that no space was left between them. Paul recognized dark-skinned peoples from Mauritania, Numidia and Cyrenaica, only nine miles across the straits from Spain. Light-skinned Gauls from Gallia Lugduensis were scattered throughout the population.

"I do not see many Jews," Paul remarked to Victoria, as he took her to meet Aquila and Priscilla.

"There are some, but not many," she replied. "Most of the Jews in this area have mixed with other peoples. My mother was Spanish and Jewish. My father was Roman. There is a very large Jewish community in Toletum, my mother's home. We can go there, if you like, after you have mastered enough of the language and the customs."

"I would like very much to see where your mother came from," Paul answered.

Priscilla liked Victoria from their first meeting. It was as if both had been looking for female Christian companionship.

"Victoria says that there is a large Jewish community in Toletum," Paul informed Priscilla and Aquila. "Perhaps that is where we can set up a weaving business."

"How long have Jews been in Spain?" Priscilla asked Victoria.

"According to our legends," Victoria began, "it was Jews who fled from Israel six hundred years ago who founded Toletum. They called it 'Toledoth' which I am told means 'City of Generations.' "

"That would be correct," Paul stated. "I mean the meaning of the word Toledoth." Paul's voice shook as he realized that he had presumed to coach Victoria.

Priscilla noted Paul's dilemma and smiled. "How long have you known our Lord, Victoria?" Priscilla asked.

"Three years ago, merchants from Cyprus brought us word of the Messiah," Victoria answered.

Paul was visibly distressed by her answer. "Is something wrong, Master Paul?" asked Victoria.

Paul cleared his throat. "Nothing" — he coughed. Paul was thinking of the argument he and Barnabas had had concerning John Mark and their going to Cyprus. It must have been one of Barnabas and Mark's converts who had brought the word to Victoria.

Priscilla knew something was going on and she thought she knew what it was. Paul was usually abrupt and brash when it came to relationships with women, but this Victoria had the Apostle uncertain and sensitive. In all the years she had known Paul, a woman had never affected him as a woman. Priscilla thought it had something to do with his marriage to the Pharisee, Esther. Lydia had always been, to Paul, a comrade in supporting the gospel. Priscilla and her husband had always been like a brother and a sister to Paul. But Priscilla could tell that Paul was seeing Victoria as a woman, and she was shaking his all-masculine world!

Victoria informed Procurator Servius Sulpicius Galba of Paul's desire to seek the Jews in Toletum. Galba graciously granted Victoria permission to attend to the trip and supplied Paul with all that the group would need for the journey. They traveled east along the south bank of the Guadalquivir River until they intersected with a road leading northward from Granada to Toletum. At the intersection, they joined a caravan of Jewish merchants who were transporting goods from the port of Almeria to their homes in Toletum. Oxen were used to pull the laden carts ever higher into the mountains. Always on both sides and ahead they could still see higher snow-laden peaks. Paul thought, *I believed that the mountains of Tarsus were the roof of the world, but surely these must be higher!*

At the end of the day they would set up two tents. Priscilla and Victoria would sleep in one, Paul and Aquila in the other. Priscilla and Victoria shared in preparing the evening meal while the men tended to the stock and recited the evening prayers. All along the route, Victoria would point to objects and say their name in Spanish so that Paul would learn the language. After the evening meal, Paul and Victoria would have their lessons. He would instruct her about Jesus and the gospel; she would practice Spanish with him. Often they would climb onto a ledge or sit under a tree together, giving Aquila and Priscilla time to be with each other. Victoria listened intently as Paul recounted the life of Jesus or his own adventures in serving Him. One day as they returned to the camp by way of a rocky path, she lost her footing. Paul grabbed her by the hand to keep her from falling. When they returned to the fire, Paul was still holding her hand!

The Anas River, flowing through a gorge, blocked their path. The white water rushing to meet the Atlantic Ocean at Pax Julia, in the section of Spain called Lusitania by the Romans, gave off a spraying mist as it passed through sheer rock with evergreen trees clinging precariously to its banks. Every vista in Spain seemed more beautiful to Paul than anything he had ever seen. The most beautiful sight, however, was Victoria. They turned eastward again and came to a fiord in the Anas, then continued north.

Toletum was located in a bend of the Tagus River, which circumvented the city on its eastern, western and southern sides. Two great hills rose from the river to its east and west, with a valley running to the south toward the river. There was no place to cross the river at this low point, so the caravan had to move along the river bank until they came to a place across from the eastern hill. Red dirt and rock formed the hill, which was topped with a stone wall. A river flatboat ferried them across the river at a place called Alcantara. Paul realized why the first Jews had chosen this place to build a city. The location made it easy to defend, it had plenty of fresh water and the river gave it access to trade with Lusitania, Gallia and Britannia on the ocean side, and Mauritania and Africa through the Port of Tingers in the strait. The caravan crossed the river and followed the northern wall on a road called the Calle de Gerardo Lobo until they came to the western bank of the Tagus and the section of the city called Juderia. The streets and the houses with their courtyards reminded Paul of Jerusalem.

Victoria stopped at the door of a courtyard. "My parents' home," she said, looking to see what Paul's reaction would be.

Paul jangled the bell. "Salam alakum (Peace be on you)," he greeted the servant who opened the door. "My name is Saul, and I come from Jerusalem. I bring with me two weary travelers who ask hospitality in the name of the God of Abraham and the daughter of the master of the house." The servant hesitated and looked bewildered. Few men had treated him in such a correct manner. The knowledge of a visitor from Jerusalem overwhelmed him.

"Rafa, where are your manners?" scolded Victoria. She was enjoying Rafa's confusion.

The servant bowed, "Wa alakum es-salam (And on you, peace)." Paul and the others took off their sandals and entered the courtyard.

"Rafa, what is going on?" came the voice of an elderly woman. When she came into the courtyard, Paul could see her resemblance to Victoria. Though bent from age, her form still carried with it a dignity. Victoria's mother spotted her daughter. She wanted to greet her daughter as fast as she could, but she eyed the strangers.

"I am Saul, of the tribe of Benjamin, Rabbi of the school of Gamaliel, and officer of the Sanhedrin of Jerusalem. I have traveled a long way and you have not offered water that I may wash my feet, nor have you properly greeted your daughter!" Paul was doing all that he could to keep from laughing at the look on the face of Victoria's mother.

"From Jerusalem!" she said, placing her hands on each side of her face. "A rabbi!" — she stood transfixed.

"It's true, Mother!" came Victoria's voice, filled with pleasure and yet sympathy for the old woman. "Rafa will get water and a basin for the Rabbi and his associates. You may greet the Rabbi and kiss him for father."

"A rabbi! From Jerusalem!" The old woman was overwhelmed with awe.

"An apostle of the Messiah!" Victoria added.

The gentlewoman put her hands on Paul's shoulders and looked into his eyes. "Did you see Him?" she asked. "Did you see Jesus?"

"Yes!" Paul replied.

She kissed him on both cheeks!

Victoria remained at her parents' home while Paul, Aquila and Priscilla found residence just east of Juderia bordering a plaza called Paseo del Transito. The house was located next to the El Transito synagogue. Priscilla found equipment and opened a weaving shop on the plaza, while Paul taught in the synagogue. There were several hundred Jews in Toletum who were, as Galba had said, less legalistic and more tolerant than those in Jerusalem. They were hungry for the word of God and received the message of the Messiah with joy. The Gentiles listened as Paul spoke about Jesus at the weaving looms and in the Paseo del Transito. The occultists neither paid him attention nor attempted to stop him from witnessing about Jesus. They had no real following except with those who had accepted their practices in Africa.

Paul was also welcome in the Roman section just outside the northern wall of the city. The centurion in charge had received word that Paul Gabinius was the son of a famous general, and that Procurator Galba had served under General Gabinius. Paul wandered freely among the Romans, telling them about the Christ. Soon the majority of the citizens of Toletum were Christians.

Victoria frequently joined Paul in the Paseo del Transito and translated for him to the Spanish-speaking population. Thus, by Jewish merchants and Spanish laborers, the story of Jesus was carried by river and by overland trails throughout Spain.

Paul found a place, called El Calvario, where the southeast hill of the city jutted out sixty feet above the Tagus. In this section, not far from the Paseo del Transito, the cliff was covered with tall grass and wildflowers. One old, massive tree graced the summit, producing a large, shaded area beneath it. Below the cliff, the river came to a spillway, producing a deep, reflective surface on one side and white, shimmering water on the other. Beneath the protective limbs of the tree, Paul and Victoria often shared their lunch. When the evening sun was low, they would build a fire and sit by it. She taught Spanish there, and he talked about Jesus. Sometimes they would just sit, watch the reflections of the sunset on the Tagus and hold hands — two slightly graying people feeling young and in love.

Paul knew for the first time in his life that he was really in love. He could have wished that he had met Victoria in Rome — before Esther, before he had hardened his heart to women. In youthful Diana he had known lust, and in Esther he had known duty, but with Victoria he knew peace. *The difference between law and grace*, he thought.

Inside his mind, a discussion concerning law and grace claimed his attention. Should he, could he, ask Victoria to marry him? The law in him said that he was condemned to live without her forever because he had married Esther. His heart said that he and Esther had never been married because there had been no love and Saul of Tarsus had died on the road to Damascus. Why should he pay for Saul when Jesus already had? His mind said that he was too old to marry, and his heart said he was now wise enough to really love. His heart said that he wanted to spend the rest of his days under the tree in El Calvario holding her. His mind told him both that his mission was not yet completed and that it would not be fair to Victoria to ask her to marry a man condemned by Rome! So he held her, not asking the question; but she drew his robe around her for warmth and fell asleep in his arms, having already given an answer.

The soldier found him the next morning in the Paseo del Transito. "Paul Gabinius!" he saluted, bringing his arm across his breastplate. "Greetings from Tribune Julius Laco and Legionnaire Popygos! Greetings from Procurator of Hispania Tarraconensis, Servius Sulpicius Galba!"

There was something familiar about the legionnaire, but Paul could not put it in place.

"Some cool water, sir!" Victoria handed him a dipper from the well, not forgetting her manners. The legionnaire drank deeply and thanked her; then, smiling, he turned to Paul. "I am Eprius Metellus, one of the guards of the Castra Peregrinorum. I accepted Jesus as my Lord through your witness!" Astonished Jews watched Paul and the legionnaire embrace each other in the plaza. It was not often one saw a Jew put his arms around a Roman, even in Toletum. Paul led Eprius into the privacy of Priscilla's booth.

"To come this far, you must bring new of great importance," Paul said to the legionnaire.

"I was delayed by Procurator Galba, who thought the same," Eprius replied. "The Procurator sends you this message, 'It is time!' "

"I do not understand," answered Paul.

"Galba said you would understand after I told you the news from Rome!"

"Which is?" Paul asked, anxious to find out why Julius had sent the legionnaire so far.

"Lucius Pedanius Secundus..." began Eprius.

"Yes, I know the name" — Paul interrupted — "the Spanish security chief of Rome and a compatriot of Seneca!"

"Lucius Pedanius Secundus," Eprius began again, "was assassinated by one of his male slaves, who resented Lucius' favors given to another male member of the household. Caesar Nero, to reprimand the death, put out an edict that all the slaves in Rome were to be put to death. This produced a revolt by many Roman nobles who did not wish to part with their properties and endangered many Christian brothers who are slaves."

"The man is mad!" Paul declared.

"Two Praetorian Prefects were appointed by Nero, Faenius Rufus and Gaius Ofonius Tigellinus," Eprius continued. "Seneca could not deal with Tigellinus and offered the Emperor his resignation, which was refused. Nero then discovered a plot against his life. He was to be murdered in the Circus Maximus during the games, and Seneca was to be placed on the throne. Nineteen senators, seven knights, eleven officers and four women were charged with the plot. Faenius Rufus was executed and Seneca killed himself by opening his veins with a knife."

"Seneca dead!" — the news struck Paul like a blow. "I understand Procurator Galba's message. If he is joining Gaius Julius Vindex of Gaul, all the Roman world, including Spain, could soon be inflamed by war."

"There is more," said Eprius. "A section of Rome caught on fire and many think Nero, himself, started the fire to clear out a section of the city for a massive building project. Nero has placed the blame on the Christians and widespread persecution has begun. Some brothers are defecting from the faith, saying, 'The apostles are in Jerusalem and Paul is safe in Spain. Why should we die for this faith?' "

Paul was terribly hurt by the implied accusation. "I must return to Rome!" he exclaimed.

39

Paul decided to return to Rome by the fastest route. Accompanied by Legionnaire Eprius, Aquila, Priscilla and Victoria, he crossed the mountains to the port of Valencia. There he left Aquila and Priscilla, who had decided that they wanted to remain in Toletum with the church. Leaving Victoria was the hardest thing Paul believed he had ever endured for the sake of the gospel. He watched her waving from a hill as the ship took on sail, and for the first time in his life he felt lonely. He had not told her of his wishes to marry, thinking that it would not be fair to her.

Ananias had told him that day in Damascus that he would suffer many things for his Lord's sake. Five times Paul had been beaten. He had been imprisoned, stoned and ridiculed. But leaving Victoria was the greatest sacrifice he had been called to make for Jesus. How he wished he could have told her of his love for her. He knew, now, on the inside, that he would never again hold her in his arms.

In his mind, Paul could see the cliffs of El Calvario. The Tagus was shimmering in the sunlight. A soft breeze was flowing through their tree. She was standing beneath it, with her black hair shining in the light and her veil blowing in the wind. "I love you, Victoria," he whispered. The breeze filled the sails taking him back to Rome. The empty sea mocked him.

Julius, Diana, little Paul and Popygos were all standing on the wharf. "Popygos has met every ship arriving from Spain since the day Legionnaire Eprius left to find you!" Julius declared.

Julius had turned decidedly bald since Paul had last seen him. Diana had put on some weight, but she still looked lovely. Popygos was moving slowly, the result of too many days on the damp breakwaters, guarding the workers who were still building the port. Little Paul, dressed in a copy of his father's uniform, was tall enough to reach Paul's waist. Paul bent down and told the boy that he had been there when he was just born. Paulus hugged his "uncle's" neck.

Julius and Paul spent that night in conversation. "Paul, I fear for your life," Julius told him with obvious concern, "but I fear more for the life of the Church. Even since Eprius left for Spain, the entire Empire has been in turmoil. Nero is terrified and suspicious of everyone. The extremely conservative senator, Thrasea Paetus of Patavium, was absent from the Senate. Nero took his absence as a plot and had him executed. Annius Vinicanus was accused of a nefarious plot in Beneventum and was executed. Vinicanus was the son-in-law of General Corbulo, who was in charge of the eastern Legion. Corbulo was ordered by Nero to take his own life! Scribonius Rufus and Scribonius Proculus, commanders of Upper and Lower Germany, where the greatest part of the Legion is stationed, were ordered to kill themselves — and they did! Now rumors have come to the Legion that Gaius Julius Vindex in Gallia Lugdunensis and Servius Sulpicius Galba of Spain have joined forces and plan to march on Rome itself!"

"It is no rumor!" Paul replied. "I know Galba. He will not obey an order to kill himself. I have little doubt that if he gets to Rome, Nero will fall!"

"But in the meantime," Julius continued, "Nero is trying to get the citizens' minds off the national problems by giving them a sport — killing Christians in the arena. Paul, as the children of Israel looked to see Moses when they crossed the sea, or when Joshua and Hur held up the hands of Moses when Israel defeated Amalek, the Church of Christ needs to see you now!"

"I go to Rome in the morning," Paul said. "I know that you want to go with me, but it would be best for you to stay here and watch over Diana and Paulus."

Paul had a lot on his mind, but when he finally slept, he dreamed of running in a high meadow, hand and hand with Victoria. The next day Eprius led him to the Church in hiding. Under the Caelian Hill and along the Appian Way, Christians had discovered the damp, musty, underground burial places called catacombs. Here, in the place of the dead, the followers of "The Life" met to receive encouragement from His apostle. Lamps were hung along the underground passages where they came to stand and listen. A sea of faces, partly hidden by the shadows, stood silently as he greeted them and encouraged them by recounting the sufferings of Jesus and the salvation He came to bring. Paul moved to another location and found the same scene.

"Are they following us from place to place?" Paul asked Eprius.

"No!" Eprius replied. "They are all different groups."

"How many souls in Rome are Christian?" Paul asked.

"More than you can count!" came the reply.

Among the followers, Paul saw people of every cultural, racial and economic class. The wealthy of Rome stood next to their slaves and listened to the message.

"The more Christians Nero feeds to the lions or crucifies, the more Christians there seem to be!" Eprius exclaimed.

"Unless a seed falls into the ground and dies," Paul said softly.

"What is that you said?" Eprius asked.

"Just something I heard someone say about seed!" Paul replied.

Paul found that the city of Rome had changed greatly during his absence. Due to the fire, many streets had been widened and straightened. Construction workers were rebuilding the Circus Maximus. As Paul watched them, he could hear the crowds cheering for Julius in his mind. Nero was having his new palace, which he called the Domus Aurea, or the "Golden House," built in the center of the city. Everything Paul saw, he wished Victoria was there to see it with him. Eprius and Paul had just turned to enter the estate of a wealthy Christian, when some legionnaires approached.

"Are you Paul Gabinius?" the captain of the guard asked.

"I am!" Paul replied.

"I have an order for your arrest," the captain stated. Then, looking at Eprius' uniform, he said, "I will relieve you of your prisoner!"

Paul warned Eprius with his eyes. "Tell Julius!" was all that he said.

Paul was led to the foot of the Capitoline Hill where he was placed in a subterranean chamber, called the Tullianum, beneath the Mamertine Prison. The chamber was a hole barely twenty-one feet in diameter, with twelve-foot-high walls that dripped with noxious fluids. Except for the light of a single oil lamp, the hole was dark.

Day and night passed equally for the Apostle as time lost its meaning. He would have lost his sanity had it not been for the flights of fantasy that played through his mind. In his imagination he swam with Victoria in the Tagus and climbed their special high hill. He stood with her on the snow-capped mountains that nearly touched the sky, after which they danced a Jewish folk dance on the clouds. He walked with Luke on the top of the earth and told the world about Jesus! He stood in the Temple of Jerusalem and saw Jesus proclaimed as its King!

Paul's beard was ragged, his hair unkept, and his clothes filthy when the guard at last opened the door and dragged him out into the blinding light of the sun. His mind was disoriented and his limbs unsure as he climbed the steps of the Basilica.

The massive doors between the Basilica Julia and the piazza opened, then closed behind him, cutting off the light again. Two legionnaires dragged him by his chains across a marble floor and cast him down on the marble pavement before a judgement chair. The toad-like form of Nero looked down on him. Caesar was wearing a purple robe, which he pulled across his shoulders.

"Paul Gabinius, you have no right to a trial!" Nero declared with force. "You were exiled from Rome by Claudius. If you were not wearing that accursed ring of Augustus, you would not be here at all!"

"Take the ring from him!" he shouted at a legionnaire. The ring was wrenched from Paul's finger. The legionnaire handed it to Nero. Caesar put it under his foot and crushed it.

"This Christian" — Nero spat out the word — "has caused me enough problems. Take him from my sight! Cut off his head!" The toad-like man swung from the side of the chair and disappeared through a curtain.

The guards turned Paul around and started back toward the massive doors. Nero did not see the slightly bald Tribune raise his sword in salute, nor the responding salute as the Praetorian Guard lowered their spears. He did not hear the Praetorian Prefect of Ostia declare the Triumph, "Behold the Man!" or hear what Julius heard as the massive doors were closing — the sound of a horse's hoof on the pavement.

Paul stepped out onto the piazza. The light blinded his eyes. It seemed every bit as intense as the light he had experienced on the road to Damascus. He remembered again the words, "I am Jesus!" The light seemed to be intensifying. He heard the sword of steel being pulled from its scabbard.

Suddenly, light flooded his being with glory. Before him stood a glimmering white stallion prepared for a rider. A command came: "Mount him!" Paul's body felt as agile as it had when he was a young man. He placed his foot in the stirrup and swung lightly into the saddle. The steed sprang through an arch of pure light, carrying Paul — son of a Roman general, Rabbi of Jerusalem, Apostle of Jesus Christ — to his long-delayed Triumph in the Kingdom of God!

******

Now thanks be unto God, which always causeth us to TRIUMPH in Christ ...
                                                    Paul

Bells and Pomegranates
by
C. Paul Willis

The Holy Spirit gives Christians both bells to ring (gifts) and fruit to develop (character). Taking an analogy from the bells and the pomegranates on the hem of the High Priest's robe, this devotional teaching book will challenge you and tell you how to ring your bell and develop your character.

Order your copy of *Bells and Pomegranates* from:

Christian Word Books
4501 Lake Jeanette Road
Greensboro, NC 27408.

Also available from your local book store.